AF243951

The Beginning's End

Nikki Martin

Thorncraft Publishing
Clarksville, Tennessee

ISBN-13: 978-0-9979687-8-1
ISBN-10: 0-9979687-8-8

Cover Design by etcetera...
Cover photo by Tobi Martin-Flemming.

Library of Congress Control Number: 2021936960

Thorncraft Publishing
Clarksville, TN
http://www.thorncraftpublishing.com
thorncraftpublishing@gmail.com

10 9 8 7 6 5 4 3 2 1

For Jody, whose friendship has been a light in the dark
and a deep breath before every plunge.
For Shana, champion of all this story stands for.
For those of you brave enough to live ordinary lives, full
of love, and honor, and grace.

CONTENTS

	Acknowledgments	ix
1	Prologue: Froste	1
2	Part One: Sleeping	3
3	Part Two: Dreaming	35
4	Part Three: Awake	221
5	Epilogue	255
	Author's Biography	267

ACKNOWLEDGMENTS

I'M NOT SURE I've written anything before this novel so affected by the climate in the world and the upheaval in my own life. I sat down to write the first draft of this book in the winter of 2019, not even eight months after a split from my partner of ten years and only four after selling our dream home; a place that was my sanctuary and had inspired me to chase my dreams. I moved into a basement apartment and began rebuilding my life while letting go of a great, big, beautiful story that would no longer be. It's no surprise that in amongst the hardship and triumphs of that time, I should want to escape to one of my favorite places with some of my favorite characters, and so a story I had known was coming for many years finally began to arrive. For the second time in my life, the very same characters who had in many ways saved me in my twenties found me once again; and when I needed them most. For months, I lost myself in that world that I loved so much and, once again, I could dream of being the hero, of saving the day while the real world screamed and shouted that it needed such things. Yet, despite my best efforts the story led me somewhere else—to a quieter kind of truth and a more honest kind of unfolding. Then, the world changed. As I wondered about the kind of people who could rule with cruelty and indifference, who could delight in harm and vitriol and still inspire legions to follow, the story continued to evolve, and though it was maybe less hopeful than I thought it would be, it was ever more real and so much more *me*. And the world shouted now not about needing heroes but about needing everyday people to do something. While the world raged, and while I met myself over and over again in what I saw outside of myself and within, this story unfolded, and I truly learned something.

So, in many ways, this story is a kind of love letter to the best of us, humanity, and how my deepest wish is that we will get there collectively one day. Even if I don't believe it quite as forcefully as I did a year or two ago, I still believe it's possible all the same. This story is a love letter to the everyday hero: People showing up when things are hard, and yet quietly carrying their load, people finding ways to bring joy and peace and laughter into the world, people fighting for what's good and right even when the path ahead seems hopeless or just too damn long sometimes, people who take the time to know and do better, and don't settle for the easiest choice. This story is a love letter to

Love, friendship, and fighting for the people who matter, even when they are on the other side of a great divide. This story is a love letter to Hope, which lives inside us, always, even when we don't know it.

To the people who have been with me in the darkest and brightest years of my life and who have celebrated with me the birth of this story, thank you. To my sister, Tobi, and my best friend, Pete, her husband—I am so lucky to have you both and am endlessly inspired by how you show up for each other and the people you love. To Jody, who I could exhaust a list of clichés for, thanks for reminding me that my *too much* is actually *just enough* for the right people, and the right cause. To my friends, Livia, Elly, Sandra, Em, Ashton, Janna, Les, Lauren, Wanda, and so many more, and to everyone who asked month after month when this story was coming, I can't thank you enough for believing in me and loving this story and these characters as much as I do. To my mother, Valerie, and my nana, Helen, gone this past year, thank you for showing me what it means to be strong and resilient; to be everyday heroes by showing up for the people you love. To my family, growing up you were the first to teach me about fighting for what's right and for never judging people by anything but their merits, I thought of you so many times along this path. My brother, Travis, my Uncle George and Aunt Donna, cousins Kelly and Jennifer, my Aunt Lynne, my Aunt Margaret—my sense of who I am has, in some way, been shaped by all of you. To Paula who is always overjoyed for every success in my life and to my dad, now gone almost ten years, thank you both for continuing to show up to help me along the way. And lastly, but never least, to Shana, who said *yes* to this book without having read a single word of it, thank you for always knowing what I'm capable of even before I do. You are a champion for women and those who need to be seen and heard, and I am so very grateful we found each other along this wild and wonderful journey of ours.

To all of you, like me, who need a place to escape to once in awhile, who need a place where you can dream and believe anything is possible, I hope Alpha Iridium and my Earth of a far off future, can be that for you like they were for me.

Deep love and gratitude to you all.

Nikki

xx

The Beginning's End
Book Two of *Awake While Dreaming*

Prologue

FROSTE

WHEN SHE DOVE into the darkness, the whole universe took one long, deep breath in and one long, slow, easy breath out, before it started moving again. In that pause, there was an eternity and yet it passed in only a moment. One in which I was carried back, back, to the memory of what I'd been before I was a servant...back to a love that had anchored me, so that everything that has come after it has been like drifting, drifting.

For the longest time, so long, there has been only this: Crossing the vast ocean of the universe, traveling where I'm told I must, coaxing one last hope out of species who have run their course and long run out of time and chances. One step ahead of a Darkness that cannot be satiated nor stopped, I have done it willingly, because it matters— beating back that dark—and because there has been no other choice.

Until her.

Until now.

Somehow this is both the end and the beginning of a story that whispers to me of memory and eternity, of what once was and what will be again.

Her heart is a whisper in the deep, a single drop in an infinite sea, and yet I hear it loud and clear as it crosses the darkness, calling, calling, calling to me. She is a kind of home I thought could only be a memory. In that pause, that quiet deep in eternity, I do what I thought I never would, what I have sworn not to do: I take something ready for forever and I make it small again.

I give her what I cannot have. What she finally deserves. For a moment, just a moment, it feels like it is mine again, too.

I will not stop searching the deep for what was, and what will be again; if only I can wait and remember, and believe.

Part One

Sleeping

ONE

GRAVITY WAS A WHISPER. Just memory, both faint and fading, so that she felt at once buoyant and set adrift.

It had to be a dream.

There was the familiar widening at the periphery of her vision making it seem like she was looking through a panoramic lens. There was a deep stillness around her where there should have been movement and sound. She felt unsettled and had the strange sense that she was outside of herself, outside of time as well. For a moment she wasn't sure who or where she was. The truth had become a deep pause. It was like the world flexed and then relaxed around her before everything stilled and became clear and calm; familiar again. The cougar took her in, finally meeting her gaze, and then froze. She realized she was holding her breath and let it out in one long, slow silent sigh. Still the big cat watched her—all pent-up strength and possibility. She'd never seen an animal so large in real life before. Not a dream she realized as she took a slow and shaky breath in. Not a dream, a sign. Something was coming.

The cougar seemed willing to let the moment stretch out around them. So much power and all of it put on pause. It looked deep into her and she knew there wasn't a secret within her left unknown in that long, drawn out moment where the animal met her captivated gaze. She'd never seen anything so elegant and terrifying all at once and yet she knew the animal had no intention of harming her. No, most animals these days, even the predators, understood humans were a sad and sorry memory of the once threatening and all-consuming monsters they'd become at the end.

The cougar looked at her a moment longer, almost as if acknowledging a truth that could never be escaped nor forgotten, and then stalked off into the woods, all muscle and sinew and strength, and was gone. Not a sound followed it through the trees to mark its passage. She wasn't sure it had even been real except there was that moment when their hearts had whispered to each other and she'd heard that truth again.

Something was coming.

Of course that wasn't entirely the truth now, was it? No, something had already arrived.

She shook her head and sighed, trying to shake off both the strange encounter and the reminder it offered up. Who knew strange days could get even stranger. Yet somehow over the past few weeks it seemed that's exactly what they'd done.

Above her, the sun was a golden reminder hanging in the sky. It remembered a world that could pause and rejoice in something as simple as a warm summer day. Even if Rogan could not. She'd been five when the world had ended. When there'd been a different kind of stepping into every single day. When the people who'd lived their lives thinking their destruction was an impossibility were the ones laying the very groundwork for it to come about. It had been a different time, so long ago, and they had been a very different people, and yet in the tragedy of it all there was still a sense that they'd somehow gotten away with something. Like maybe it had all been meant to end and yet, at the last moment, in the midst of the Earth being torn to shreds, there was some kind of pause, a deep breath, and the course of it all had been altered.

It was a foolish kind of thinking, Rogan knew, getting lost in the past. What did any of it matter when you were living in the aftermath? When you were fighting to find your way through every day, did it really matter if once, long ago, the world had known a moment or two of magic, of dreams coming true? No, she was living in what mattered, which was the dark and dismal truth. A world wandering back from the brink of destruction, one they'd all chased down whether they were willing to admit it or not.

The wind dipped and danced around her playfully, pulling at her wild mane of golden hair to join it, and she lost herself again in the remembering of a world where anything was possible. It was of course absurd to think she really remembered it. The world before the breaking was one she'd been far too young to remember. But there was something inside her that spoke of that time. A kind of collective memory that lived somewhere deeper than the mind and that she knew she shared with the pitiful few who'd survived.

That's the place that pulled at her. One that belonged to a greater whole and yet also was hers alone to hold and cradle and carry, for a short while at least.

It had been happening more and more lately, this losing of herself to something out of reach and somewhat out of her control. If she was being honest she knew exactly when it had begun. It was three weeks ago now. Like most days she'd woken early before the sun and made her way down to the shore. The waves that morning had been shy. Still rolling and powerful and yet they seemed hesitant, like they were waiting for a reaction and she couldn't help wondering if it was hers they were waiting for...*but why?*

A silver sliver of moon had hung overhead in the last dark of night, and it, too, with that smile seemed to know something she did not. Her bare feet sunk into the soft, damp sand, and as always she felt connected to the earth in a way that soothed her. The salt wind was warm, as if it was hurrying from the place where the sun had already risen and she knew later her skin would taste like salt and sun and stardust even if she never met the day to come. On the horizon a golden thread began to warm the night sky and somewhere deep in the canopy of trees behind her a bird cried out, announcing the first moments of day. That's when she felt it. For just a moment, when the tide turned, there was a shifting. She felt somehow connected to the entire universe, and in that tethering to the vastness of it all, felt a deep and pregnant pause. It was as if the ground dropped out from under her, and she gasped and stumbled, and for the briefest of moments thought she might even be brought to her knees as time stood still. Then just as quickly as it had come upon her, the moment passed. The waves crashed once again. More birds leapt into the day and cried out to one another. The wind began quietly singing again—songs whispered of a different time. The sky brightened, as did the day. That's when she saw it there on the sand in front of her.

And, then, she screamed.

TWO

THE DREAM SHOOK him loose and tossed him into the waking world with so much force he gasped. His heart hurried to catch up with the moment. His mind disoriented as it tried to both settle into the present and understand what he'd just seen, and where he'd just been. Sweat beaded on his forehead so that the cool morning air sent a chill down and through him and he shuddered, unable to shake off both the strangeness and this sense that something big and important had happened. He took a few calming breaths to steady his heart and mind and finally, finally, the world around him came into focus and the dream began to fall away and out of reach. He longed to grab hold of it again, to hold on tight to a world and a truth that were easier to sit in than his own, but then he let it tumble away and out of reach. That kind of dreaming was for another time and another place, and he wasn't sure he was the man who deserved that kind of escape any longer.

"We won't make it home in time for the celebration if we don't get going soon. You know that, right?" Derin's tone was hopeful but Alex wasn't entirely sure if his brother hoped they'd make it back or hoped they wouldn't.

Home was a place that had become too many things to be comfortable for either of them. That's why they were here: Camped out on the northern beaches of Samnar, one of the six continents on Alpha Iridium. Building a house by hand, log by log, mud brick by mud brick. Neither talking about a truth that haunted them both in different ways. Neither willing to face a future just yet that kept demanding they step into it.

Alex nodded and dropped his iridescent blue eyes from his brother's, the same light shade, while a wave of gentle shame washed through him though he couldn't quite figure out why. He grunted his acknowledgment as he got up and began to gather his things while Derin disappeared out of sight, the tent flap closing quietly behind him. Suddenly, the dream slammed into Alex again and his breath caught in his chest as his heart gave one big knock, and then another.

Then, it was gone. So quickly it seemed as if it had never really been there. The moment hurried past him, too swift to grab hold of, and he let it pass. It was time to face the present, and in some ways, the past. He steadied himself with a deep breath and then rose and began to gather his things.

Two hours later, the brothers were well on their way home. They kept a quick pace, making good time, rarely uttering more than a word or two, and only when necessary. Long legs and muscular bodies carried them like agile forest dwellers through narrow paths, over rocky terrain, and amongst dense brush with little trouble. They were at home in those wild places, and the forest around them rarely startled into action because it knew two of its own were passing by.

Even with five years between them, they were so similar that from some angles you couldn't tell them apart; except that Alex's mane of ice blue hair was a stark contrast to Derin's dark blue-black. There were, however, subtle distinctions between them, though not always easily glimpsed. The heavy burden of the past was carried by them differently, in ways that could, at times, make them unrecognizable as brothers. Both fought for their place in the present, but neither had found his way fully there and in that they were identical.

Alex couldn't help himself; he let his mind wander back, years into the past, to a time after tragedy and before the world had changed again for the better. They were lost years, the ones while Caine had ruled Alpha Iridium. Alex couldn't help but see them from the outside looking in because during that time he'd had to be someone else, someone who'd died that same night Kale had.

"Another hour and we'll be there." Derin shook his brother loose of his memories. "You wanna talk about it or are we going to make this whole trip in silence?"

Alex's first instinct was to ignore his brother and just keep going but he knew Derin well enough to know there were times when it was easier to relent. He decided to offer him a truth, one his brother would grab hold of in a second, even if it wasn't the one that was really bothering him.

"I guess, knowing everyone will be here, well, it's just been such a long time. It draws me back, to that night..." Alex paused, took a deep breath, and then went on. "I'm sorry. It's selfish of me to even say it aloud." Alex cringed and cursed himself for casually throwing out something that always had the potential to wound them both. He saw it again. Almost as if he was actually there. Transported back five years to a mountain shelf cloaked in the deepest darkness he'd ever seen. He'd been helpless to do anything. Bound and restrained by Caine's soldiers. He'd had to watch as Kale fought for them and then lost; tumbling over the mountain's edge and out of sight. He'd had to watch as Caine killed his brother so casually it had been both surreal and unbelievable. He'd struggled and screamed but had been too weak. That's what haunted him. He'd promised to kill Caine but in the end he'd failed and because of that Kale had died and his brother had lost the chance at eternity with the woman he loved.

He could still hear the echo of her words as she'd looked deep into his eyes. He'd believed her then. He wasn't sure if he believed her anymore. "This is the beginning of a different kind of life." Kale had said. "Trust that. Trust your heart." *Bullshit,* he thought. What kind of life had he lived since, realizing his only purpose in life had been a lie and there was nothing to hope for past surviving, past being left alone by the greater powers in the universe that seemed to enjoy making a chess match out of them all.

"She's gone because I wasn't strong enough," Alex finally said aloud. A truth he admitted because it wounded him deeply and he felt like he deserved it.

"She's gone because of me," Derin had said it so many times it had almost begun to lose its meaning. Almost. "And if I can live with it, so can you," he said with a kind of matter-of-fact-ness that told them both this was a statement practiced and yet not quite believed

"Says the guy building a house as far away from his mother as possible," Alex said, the first hint of a smile showing up in his voice. "Among other things."

"You really want to do this now? Today?" Derin stopped and turned around forcing his brother to stop and meet his gaze.

This was the real problem. Five years had gone by and yet neither of them had fully moved on or quite figured out how to get past what their mother, Cyan, had done. What she'd allowed both Caine and Kale to do, all to get both of them back. They could say they forgave her, that they'd gotten over the shock and hurt and betrayal, and yet the thought of facing her every day, of facing their disappointment and distrust, was more than either of them could bear. Because of that they'd spent more and more time away from their home, avoiding what inevitably had to be faced, until it became apparent it might just make sense to build a new one. Their father, Dellerim, hadn't entirely understood their inability to let go of the past, and yet he'd supported them completely despite how it wounded the woman he loved.

Her choices would haunt them all for a long time. They all believed that Cyan would have an eternity to try and unmake her mistakes to get her sons' forgiveness. Yet, eternity is a thing not easily tamed.

"Sorry, I don't know what's gotten into me." Alex shook his head and smiled.

"You are a sucker for punishment, my dear brother," Derin said with a shake of his head before adding, "What else is new?" He turned and started off again at an even quicker pace. His words, filled with fondness and finality, beckoned his brother to follow and for now to leave their worries behind.

Alex let go of the desire to keep picking at a wound that just wouldn't heal and took a step to follow his brother through the trees. The truth was they'd had this conversation so many times before, in so many different ways, it was foolish to think it was going to end differently, especially on this particular day. Alex wondered if what kept him from moving on was simply that he hadn't told his brother the whole truth. But he couldn't. He hadn't entirely faced it yet himself. Nor had the truth entirely faced him. Yet they were drawing ever nearer to one another and soon he would have no choice but to see what had been true for a long time now. As he poked at it, that secret thing that he wasn't yet ready to know, the dream came rushing up and out of his memory. As suddenly as it had left him earlier, it wrapped itself around Alex again and squeezed. He saw it clearly, the place that hadn't stopped calling to him all day. The place that had shaken loose the past and left him spinning.

A bird cried out in the woods. The spell the dream had cast over him was once again broken. Alex shook himself, unsettled, and then took off, hurrying to catch up with his brother, in more ways than one. *When will I forgive myself, and her,* he wondered, but no answer arose inside him. His breath came in short, ragged gasps, a mixture of worry and trepidation tightening his chest as the brothers kept an aggressive pace through the uneven terrain.

The dream stayed out of reach for the rest of their trip home and yet this time some of its truth remained. Even though he wasn't sure where it was or why it was haunting him, Alex knew one thing for sure: he wasn't dreaming of any place on Alpha Iridium.

THREE

SALT WIND, SUN warmed, hurrying from some far off place, kissed her cheeks and tossed her long brown hair towards the horizon. Her dark brown skin was radiant and hid well the story of recent nights devoid of sleep and dreams. There was both a kind of memory and a kind of beginning locked in the gentle greeting of the salty breeze. It was like the wind and the sea were whispering to her, telling a story of other lives and the possibility that not all that is gone has leapt into oblivion. Medea reached with that remembering, felt the familiar sense of having her best friend close, and closed her eyes, believing, believing, anything was possible.

When the boat hit land she was thrown out of her musings and into the truth. Her eyes flew open and she saw it just as clearly as she saw the day around her. If her life had taught her anything, it was that all kinds of wonders and unimaginable things were possible... and yet some things still were not.

It was while lost in thoughts of the one impossible thing she wanted but that she could never have that Medea's gaze landed on a site that still took her breath away. She'd been to

Samnar more than once in the past five years, and yet each time was like the first. She was in awe. It felt like she was about to step into a living painting, one in which only the most vibrant colors had been used. Standing on the shore, tall, beautiful, striking and kissed with that sheen of magic and mystery that never dulled, the Founders and most of their children, adults now, stood on the sand waiting to welcome their party. It was a reunion five years in the making and yet in that moment, to Medea, it felt like no time at all had passed; not since that first time she'd arrived here on the continent the Founders and their children called home, not since the last when she'd left and promised herself she'd never return.

Yet here she was.

She scanned the faces on the beach and in a split second she knew that both Derin and Alex were missing and that something was wrong. She felt a pang of guilt shoot straight to her center. How long had it been since they'd been here and what had they missed while they'd been gone? Her eyes were drawn immediately to that magnetic center, the one among them who was forever different, in more ways than one, and she gave Cyan a gentle and sad smile. After acknowledging her with a nod, Cyan dropped her gaze and burrowed a little closer into Dellerim's side, as if trying to protect herself from some unseen force.

They were a striking couple: Dellerim, almost six feet tall with those strange, iridescent, crystal, blue eyes that both his sons bore, and a mane of ice blue hair almost the same shade. His skin was creamy pale next to Cyan's amber glow and her black hair and brown eyes were exotic even next to the vibrancy of his. Cyan was half a foot shorter and yet her stature took nothing away from the strength and quiet power she radiated. Together they were an imposing pair and yet there was a calm that flowed between them, a gentle kind of peace that was maybe the most striking thing of all. But beneath the current on their surface, something else was churning. Medea wasn't sure what it was but she suspected she'd know soon enough why the woman who had crossed the ocean of space and time for love, who had already faced and overcome so much, looked so worn and worried.

"We can do it a million times but sea travel just ain't for me," Corin said with a rueful smile, his blue eyes twinkling playfully as he wrapped an arm around Medea's waist and stared out towards the small crowd waiting for them on the beach. "Something about it all is a little too uncertain." He ran a hand through his short dirty blond mane and left not a hair out of place when he dropped it back to his side.

Medea smiled and sank into his side, savoring what she suspected were the last moments of peace she'd get for the next few weeks while they remained on Samnar.

"I can't disagree with you there, Corin," Jaren said stepping up to Medea's other side. They could be brothers, he and Corin, even as they were opposites in many ways. Jaren had matured in the last few years and at twenty-seven looked every bit a man, while Corin, at twenty-five, still had that boyish look about him that made it seem at times like he was still the teenager she'd first met. Jaren's grey eyes were deep wells that mirrored his compassionate heart and he'd somehow managed, despite his already good looks, to get even better with age.

"I mean the adventure of it is just fine but I'm never disappointed to get my feet back on solid ground again, that's for sure." Jaren scanned the group on the beach and Medea knew he too was looking to see who had come out to meet them and more importantly who had not.

"Look at them," Medea whispered with a hint of reverence in her voice. "It looks like not a moment has passed." It became more striking the older they got. The Founders had barely aged since time had found them and though their children were now all in their mid to late twenties, in another decade or two, it was possible you wouldn't be able tell who the parents were anymore.

"Don't be fooled," Cyan cautioned them, her voice a quiet melody inside of their heads. "A lot has changed." The three friends startled and then each one let out a surprised laugh. Cyan approached the boat, stepping away from Dellerim and the safety he'd seemed to impose upon her, and this time when she spoke she did so out loud. "Come, my old friends. We're so happy to have you back. We've much to catch up on before this evening's celebrations."

Later, when Medea looked back on this moment, she would realize Cyan hadn't just seemed sad she'd seemed scared as well. It had been a long time since she'd been reminded that they were all prisoners of fate, pawns in a game of Light and Dark that had raged since the beginning of time. There was no escape. No getting passed over or forgotten along the way. The game played on and they were forever trapped in the struggle. Cyan knew it. She always had. Though she wasn't sure what awaited them next, she knew something was coming for them all, once again.

FOUR

CYAN TOOK ONE last, long look over her shoulder and then hurried out into the night to be alone. Above her the night sky told the story of eons, of broken worlds and shattered stars, of ends and beginnings, of mysteries that would go untold and some that would be told for lifetimes. All of this painted like simple glitter on a stark black board and yet she knew better. The universe could be both more gruesome and more beautiful than it seemed; and was vastly more complex. She'd learned that long ago, when she'd met Dellerim in a dream and discovered that love could coax you across the ocean of space and time to find a life that could fill you to bursting with joy, bliss, and purpose. She'd learned it every single day for fourteen years while Caine had ruled their tiny world and held her hostage, and she'd done awful things to keep herself and her son alive. She'd learned it in the five years since they'd stopped the coming of the Darkness and destroyed Caine, and since he'd been destroyed by love, forgiveness, and destiny; and a brave young woman named Kale who had in the end been what Cyan was not—willing to sacrifice herself.

Cyan often wondered if she'd known what it would be like to survive, to live with what she'd done once Caine was gone, would she have done anything differently? She imagined that she would have. That she'd have been braver, less selfish and consumed with saving herself and Derin. That she would have refused Caine and paid the price then for her strength instead of paying the price these past five years for her cowardice and uncertainty.

It hadn't started with betrayal. At first, it was little bits of information handed over—what seemed like harmless facts and stories. Every single one paid the price for Derin's safety while he grew up as Caine's son. But somewhere along the way, Caine had begun to take from her carefully guarded facts and secrets. Stories of the Founders, how they'd come to create Alpha Iridium and later its people, and what kind of powers their children possessed. She'd not given everything but any of it was too much when looking back. Every time she'd tried to resist, he'd threatened Derin's life and safety and over and over again, she'd cracked. It didn't matter that she'd held back the most important things. That she had done it all to protect her son and her family and, yes, even the people of Alpha Iridium and Kale. In the end, Derin and Alex remembered what she'd given away, the last of which they both believed was Kale's life.

Cyan looked out across the vast stretch of ocean before her, as if it would wash answers up upon the shore at her feet. The waves were inky and secretive tonight. They seemed to sneak up onto the sand and then just as warily sneak back down again. They unsettled her a little which was a strange thing, as they most often brought her comfort. It wasn't surprising she jumped when the voice spoke behind her.

"My love?" A question half-formed and yet wholly understood. Cyan took a deep breath, steadying herself, and then turned to meet Dellerim's ice blue gaze. He looked right into her, searching, trying to find the hurts he could heal and the heartache he could soften with his own love, but some pains, even between them, were out of reach. She moved towards him, he towards her, and in a moment they were pressed into each other, heartbeats taking only a moment to find a rhythm that was a steady conversation they'd had a thousand times over what was much like a thousand years.

"I'm fine," she offered into the warmth of his chest, though of course she was not. He heard the truth in her voice and still he let her have the lie. They shared almost everything and yet some things were allowed to remain secret; safely kept from the other. For now. Didn't he have things he'd kept from her. Secrets that were also born in the time of Caine that he still worried the consequences of would find him again. Hadn't they all found ways, small and large, to learn that their humanity made them capable of both wondrous, beautiful things and awful, terrible missteps and mistakes.

"I'm fine," Cyan repeated, this time more so for herself than for him. She drew her face up towards his and paused. When he kissed her she got lost in the eternity that was being loved and cherished by him, and she let it take her breath away. It still amazed her how much you could love someone after so long a time, and so far a journey, and she lingered in that awe as long as she could.

It was the ocean that coaxed them apart a few moments later—a swift salt breeze sent up onto the shore and startling them back into the present. They stayed just an inch apart to let the crackling energy around them settle, as the dissipating static began to lay their hair back in place. They breathed into the last moment they would steal together like this for awhile and then Dellerim finally spoke.

"Shall we go back to this party of ours?" He met her gaze letting her know he was with her, now and always.

"Just give me another minute or so and then I'll join you." She smiled but it didn't reach her eyes. He knew her well enough not to argue or even say anything more. With a smile of his own, he turned and left the love of his life on the beach alone.

It was not a thing she delighted in, the way she had growing up on Earth: being alone. As a child, a teen, even a young widow, she'd found solace and comfort in being on her own. Long, long ago, before Alpha Iridium, before birthing a whole society and then watching the Dark and Light in the universe fight to save or destroy it, before all of this, when she'd been an ordinary human back on Earth, she'd been an artist and had relished time alone to imagine and dream and create.

Even all the years she'd spent with the five other Founders, the creators of this world and the four others that circled the giant star, Polaris Mu, there'd been hours of solitude and time to herself that she'd relished alongside feeling grateful every single day that this was her family. That the five of them were her home. They'd spent years filled with joy, wrapped up in the possibility that the dark and true nature of time would never find them. Lost in a dream of utopia. It all seemed so long ago now, and so far out of reach; and so damn foolish to think they had escaped their humanity.

Being alone now was a thing Cyan had to brace herself for. Fourteen years lonely and afraid, imprisoned in a cell in Caine's castle, could do that to you. Truly it wasn't the being alone that was the worst. It was being alone with the person Caine had made her into. Or maybe it was being alone with the worst of herself, someone she never would have imagined she could be or become. What she'd wondered at least once a day for the past five years was whether Caine had made that monster or if she'd always been in there. *Maybe I'll never know* she admitted to herself for the thousandth time.

It was then she realized that she could hear the party wafting out of the tent and down the beach. She'd been so consumed with her thoughts and her misery she hadn't even noticed. Somewhere in that cacophony of laughter mixed with music, mixed with conversations, were the voices of her two sons, who she'd still managed to lose despite saving all those years ago.

She sighed and dropped down to her knees on the sand, still warm from a sun long set, and dipped both hands deep into it before drawing up two big scoops. She turned her palms to the sky as she opened them and watched the sand begin to trickle and pour free until both her hands were empty. She could feel the universe watching, winking at her, letting her know the war was long from finished and there would still be a price to pay yet. Who would she become if faced with more hard choices? She closed her eyes and breathed deep. *Not again*, she shook her head once, twice, *I won't lose myself again, not for any price.*

She rose, dusted her palms off on her legs, sending the last grains of sand into the salt breeze. One last, long look upward. One last, long deep breath in. One last moment to herself, alone, to be reminded that it had once been something she'd delighted in and maybe could again. Then she turned and walked back toward the festivities. It was time to face her sons and the truth they carried around like scars.

FIVE

MEDEA LEANED INTO the comfort of Joah's muscular side and craned her neck to look up lovingly into his emerald eyes, flashing with mischief and intent. He was tall and lean, but also strong, and he could hide none of it with his slouching, casual stance. His skin was smooth and deeply tanned, a mixture of genetics and long hours spent in the sun. His shocking mane of white hair was worn short enough to be manageable but long enough to be a bit wild; enticing women to want to run their fingers through it. He was gorgeous when he smiled, dazzling really, and he knew it, but not obnoxiously so. When he looked down at Medea, her dark skin radiant, brown eyes warm and welcoming, anyone around them would be a fool to miss that he loved her, too.

It was a relationship born of common ground and understanding, of mutual respect and of being able to see the much better, bigger person the other was both capable of being and becoming. It had begun with a friendship born during one of the darkest nights Berdune had ever seen, when the Darkness that crept across the universe devouring worlds and species had almost swallowed them all whole as well. They'd survived, beat the Darkness back, and stepped into a brighter world, in some ways, broken but also new. One of the things born in that darkness was this, a friendship that had grown nameless but that had sustained them both.

Beside her, Joah stiffened without taking his eyes from hers but they flashed annoyance and something a little darker and more sinister for just a moment or two.

"What is it?" Medea asked though she knew only one cause for a reaction like that and she fought the urge to look around.

"Your boyfriend's back," Joah said without taking his eyes from hers. "And, he's headed this way. Shall we make a run for it?" When she didn't move or answer, he simply sighed and rolled his eyes. She didn't bother being annoyed with him. She didn't have time. A moment later they were no longer alone, and when Medea finally tore her eyes from the comfort of Joah's, she was carried back, back, to another time in almost the same place, when she'd lost herself for a little while in more ways than one.

It had happened three years after Caine was destroyed. Sometimes, Medea liked to think of it like that. Three years since the Darkness had been stopped and they'd all been given a second chance at living lives filled with hope and love, and free of destinies decided by unseen forces. She had to think of it like that because otherwise she fell back into thinking of it as three years since Kale had given herself to save them; to save Derin.

She could still see it all unfolding if she closed her eyes and recalled the memory. Kale tumbled over the edge of the mountain shelf and out of sight. The certainty she was gone forever and yet, minutes later, there she was again, but different, bigger somehow, more whole. They'd found out that Kale was a piece in a bigger puzzle, a part of a story she'd been destined to tell with both her life and her death. Medea didn't really understand it all. Honestly, she didn't want to. No matter how big or how small, the truth was that all she knew was that she'd lost everything in the years Caine ruled Alpha Iridium. Her parents were gone, murdered by Caine. Her best friend was dead, sacrificed to beat the Darkness back. Ryan, her love, had been murdered. Now, like some perverse joke the universe had decided to play on her, she'd done the unthinkable. What could any of it mean?

Of course, it was bigger than all that. Bigger than single lives and solitary stories. There were forces in the universe fighting to keep balance, and there were forces struggling to unravel it. Somewhere in the midst of this battle that was always being fought but never quite won, wandered the many civilizations of this universe, across countless planets, in an unlimited number of galaxies, including their own. There was a Darkness, a force beyond anything you could imagine that crept across the universe challenging species to survive it, and long ago, when humanity failed that test, six beings were chosen from the wreckage to cross the universe and start afresh on Alpha Iridium. They were the Founders. The first people on Samnar: Dellerim, Ariana, Joachim, Kiernan, Kendra and, of course, Cyan, the only one of them who had truly lived a life on Earth before their journey. They had children and lived joyful, happy lives, and yet, still unsatisfied, they dreamed a civilization into existence on Berdune, another of Alpha Iridium's continents. They slept for a thousand years, and when they woke, they left the people of Berdune and returned to their lives and their solitude. Until the Darkness, led by its puppet Randall Caine, found them once again. Their children, young adults by then, and a group of rebels led by Kale and her friends beat it back and the Light triumphed.

But Kale, Medea's best friend, her sister in many ways, never got to see the world she'd fought and died for. It still made her ache, knowing her best friend had given up so much, everything, really, including the chance at a life filled with love and happiness. Every year on the anniversary of that last battle, Medea, Corin, and Jaren, the trio that had led the rebels with Kale, traveled to Samnar to honor what they'd lost and what they'd won with the people who could truly understand it all, the Founders and their children.

Medea had begun to feel more at home on Samnar than she did in Braedon Ridge where she'd grown up and eventually shared a home with Kale, Jaren, and Corin. The first year after Caine had been destroyed they'd spent months with the Founders and their children, nursing both the joy and the heartache of that time. There was comfort in helping others rebuild when you felt your own heart in ruins. She'd lost the love of her life in the fight against Caine and then days later had lost her best friend. Being at home, all she could feel were the holes in her life and her heart that they both had filled so fully and easily.

Her heartache had a mirror on Samnar, too. Derin had loved Kale, and losing her had torn him to pieces. Even though she believed it was his fault that Kale was gone, she also knew it tortured and wounded him in ways not many could understand. Despite herself, Medea found comfort in his company and they'd formed a tentative friendship in that first year that had grown and blossomed as time had gone on.

There was also Joah. Each time she returned to Samnar, they were drawn together—two magnets in a quiet storm of heartbreak and healing. She didn't know why but he was easy to be around. He acted tough and sure of himself, but, with her, he was raw, humble, honest, and authentic. There was often no pretence or boasting; he simply settled down and got real about everything, including himself. Medea wasn't sure why but there was something between them, unspoken and deep—timeless. In that friendship, an easy intimacy was reborn and they both found a kind of home in it that took care of them both. In the past two years when she'd stopped traveling to Samnar, Joah had spent months with her in Braedon Ridge and yet, despite what it looked like, he'd pressed her a thousand times to face her heart and what it was trying to tell her. Face what she'd figured out the last time she'd visited Samnar and made the mistake that haunted her still.

She couldn't do it because the truth was that if she faced her heart, she was admitting something she didn't want to— that her best friend, Kale, was better off dead.

Medea stumbled back into the present, shocked as always by that single truth, one that had somehow come to control much of her life.

"I didn't think you'd come." Crystal blue eyes, wounded, full of longing and hope, pleaded with hers. *For what?* She didn't even know anymore.

"It felt," she began, but paused, searching for the words to describe that inescapable feeling that had drawn her to Samnar once more. "Important this year," she finally finished, no closer to describing the truth which was stranger and more eerie than she could put into words. She'd felt pulled by a force she couldn't quite understand. Night after night, her dreams were filled with stories that led her here, to this place, now, and so she'd listened because she'd learned that what was possible in the universe was far more profound than you could imagine or dream. When those possibilities whispered to you in the dark, you listened, or you got left behind.

The truth was that she was hoping it was Kale who was calling out to her from some far off place. If that were true, what did it mean for her heart? It was already put back together so many times.

"I'll leave you two to it," Joah said, giving Medea a squeeze and then sauntering off without another word to either of them. He knew her too well to hope she'd give in quickly, but he knew her well enough not to give up so soon.

Joah did love her, with all of his heart, but he also knew he wasn't the one who was going to make her happy or give her the life she deserved. Just like she knew the same about what she could offer him. In this time, in this place, they were simply meant to be friends, and yet he loved her so deeply, so infinitely, that he was sure their love had known lifetimes, and would again. He felt a deep sense of needing her to be happy and fulfilled, and so he held out hope she would find a way to move past what had been lost and grab hold of what remained.

"I didn't think you'd come," he offered again, and she couldn't tell if he was happy or not that she was here.

And do I care? She wondered but realized almost immediately that she did.

He stepped towards her until there was just a breath of space between them. He couldn't understand it and didn't want to. There was so much pain, suffering, and sadness already. All he understood was that the thought of this made him wonder if happiness was possible, even as he understood it was wrong somehow. He brought a hand to her cheek, her dark skin smooth and silky soft, and delighted in the fact that she leaned into his touch for a moment, eyes fluttering shut. He'd looked into her radiant brown eyes so many times he could picture them behind her closed lids, pained but beautiful. He traced her bottom lip with his thumb. One single stroke, feather-light. She sighed. Then her eyes flew open and she pulled away from him and his hand dropped back down to his side.

"I can't," was all she was willing to offer.

"Please, Medea, I know..." He was desperate and determined.

"You don't." Her tone made it clear there was nothing to discuss. "You should know better." Cold. A bit cruel. She couldn't help the tone. She hated him and herself for their weakness. "I need some air. Don't follow me. Please." She offered it gently, soft and pleading. It almost hurt him more than if she'd been harsh. She turned away from him and disappeared into the small crowd. As she wove her way through it, being jostled, bumped and sometimes spoken to, her mind whirled and she cursed herself for thinking she could come back and not feel anything at all. The hurt, the heartache, the guilt, it all came rushing back threatening to crush her under its weight. She was an awful person. She had to be. What kind of person fell in love with the only man their best friend had ever loved? A man Kale had given her life for. The last gift of a life too damn short and filled with mostly war and vengeance and not nearly enough love.

Derin stood there sadly, watching her go. He knew their exchange had been seen but who were they hiding from anyway. The only person who mattered, the only person whose opinion they really cared about, was gone. She'd died five years ago and sacrificed her life for his. He felt the weight of it every single day. A bright light, snuffed out, so that he could have a life. *And what have I done with it?*

He ran his fingers through his dark blue hair, black in the dim light, and sighed, not once but twice. There'd been a time when he couldn't bear to imagine his life without Kale, when he'd convinced himself she'd be back, that some kind of magic or twist of fate would return her to him. Yet, he had to face the truth, eventually. She was gone and she wasn't coming back. The only thing left to do was live a life that made her sacrifice worth it. It didn't have to be love, or a family, or any great, big endeavor, but it did have to be something worthy. It mattered that Kale had given her life for his; and he knew her, she wouldn't be okay with what he'd built so far, wasting away in isolation and hiding from the truth and himself. It was time to begin building a life, a real life. One that had room for joy and for love as well. He owed it to her, and to himself.

It began, of course, where he didn't want it to—with Cyan, his mother, and the beginning of finding a way to forgive. He scanned the small crowd, looking, looking, and then he saw her. Their eyes met almost as if she'd been waiting for him. She smiled, shy and a bit unsure, and he nodded, a small acknowledgment that things might be changing, and then headed her way.

On the other side of the room, Alex caught the exchange and resentment shot through him. Unlike his brother, he wasn't ready yet.

SIX

ON A BEACH, under a sliver of moon and a cascade of twinkling stars, they gathered. They'd done it every year since one fateful night when the people of Alpha Iridium faced darkness and survived to step into the light. The group had changed and evolved, grown and at times shrunk, but always they came together to remember and, through it, in some ways, also, to forget. There were the Founders, the six beings who'd traveled from Earth long ago and who had birthed both the civilization that followed and in many ways the path that led to the coming of Caine.

There were their children, all in their twenties now with Alex being the oldest and Derin the youngest, all born here on Alpha Iridium's northernmost continent of Samnar. Of those eight, Dellerim and Cyan's youngest son had endured fourteen years raised by Caine. For most of that time, he was unaware of who he or his true family really was. He'd been raised to sow fear, to prey on weakness and ignorance, to dominate and control, and yet despite it all had still become who he had been meant to be. Kedall and Milar, the youngest of the other Founder's children, had spent fourteen years in Caine's castle as well, though in a much different way. They'd spent their time locked in isolation, starved of the outside world and any idea of what had happened to their parents, their siblings, or the rest of their family. Joah, Arin, Beran, Arwyn, and Alex had all lived on Samnar alone. With five of their parents trapped in an inescapable sleep and Cyan missing, they'd grown up fast and had to build the kind of life that prepared them to one day fight to take back the world into which they'd been born.

Medea, Corin, and Jaren were here as well, as was that ever-present space left by the missing member of their family, Kale. It was a hole that seemed as if it could never be filled and, so, in some ways, they still took her everywhere. James, Archer, and Jet had also journeyed from Berdune with them by sea. Once soldiers in Caine's army, they'd redeemed themselves on that darkest night and even more so since; and they were bonded to this band of survivors in ways that ran deeper than any of them could explain or needed to.

Now, it was time to tell a story: One of love and loss, of life and death, and, yes, of those two oldest of companions and foes, darkness and light. The story never changed because they'd all been there in one way or another. There was no need to soften the ugliness of what had happened and no need either to make the truth more exceptional than it was.

No one in particular told the story, and it was rarely told chronologically. Instead, they offered pieces, some handed over sadly, and some tossed into the space between them with a laugh or a smile. It took all of them to make it complete and it always unfolded differently than before. Only one practice went unchanged—the pieces kept secret and safe. There cannot be a night as dark as that one five years ago without the presence of the unseen.

Dellerim stared into the flames of the fire and watched as it both devoured and created. He hadn't always understood that balance—there could not be a taking without also a sacrifice. Even in his wisdom, in all he'd learned and been forced to face, he still hadn't seen the entirety of how things worked and how the universe maintained a delicate balance between all things.

They had upset it once, by dreaming a whole civilization into existence to cure their loneliness. That single act of self-service had allowed both time and the Darkness to find them. They'd upset it once again on the night Caine first arrived on Alpha Iridium when they'd dreamed together to try and stop his coming. Instead, five of them had been locked in a coma and Cyan had somehow been captured. They'd torn a hole in time and space that night and tore a young girl's life in two so that she had to live two half lives, one on Alpha Iridium and one on Earth. And Dellerim, unknown to the rest of his friends and family, had upset it one other time, not for himself but for another. It hadn't ended the way he'd planned and he knew his decision was still going to cost him; even though he couldn't yet fathom how.

"And then she kicked your ass, in front of everyone." Archer couldn't stop himself from laughing. "She was a whirlwind and I think most of us had no clue what to make of her when she waltzed into that training camp." Even though most of them hadn't been there, his words painted a picture of that long ago moment.

"Except, of course, that she was special somehow. Always had that aura about her." James shook his head and smiled fondly.

It was the same every year—nowhere else to go in the end but to settle on Kale, to talk about her ordinariness and her exceptionality, to remember she was flawed and imperfect, unrelenting and often unreasonable, unwilling to live a life until she fulfilled a destiny she didn't even realize was hers.

She'd been gone five years and yet still she could walk into a space and be the centre of attention, no matter who else was there. But, there was something a little different in the air this year. It all felt a little akin to *goodbye*, as if an ending had somehow come looking for them and, even though they didn't realize it, things were getting left behind that could not be picked up again.

Medea glanced across the fire and met Derin's eyes. It didn't matter what was ending, Kale would always be between them. It wasn't that she didn't know, didn't believe deep down to her core that Kale would want her to be happy and to move on. It was simply that she couldn't seem to make the choice that told the world her life was better because Kale was gone.

She was the first to look away and to let her thoughts wander back, reaching for another time and place. The present disappeared and it was just her and her best friend. *I don't know what to do,* she pleaded with the memory of Kale, that anchor that tethered her to the past and her unhappiness.

Sometimes, Kale answered. Tonight, there was only silence.

Alex only heard bits and pieces of the story offered up into the night. More and more lately, he'd found himself lost in the memory of that long ago night. "This is the beginning of a different kind of life. Trust it. Trust your heart." She'd spoken those words and they sank deep into him, rooted there, and had never shaken loose. Nor had they bloomed. Of course, he'd never really nurtured them, never done any of what it would take to bring them to life. Had he ever really taken that first step forwards and away from his suffering? Could he trust his heart? Trust what it whispered to him in the dark when he woke shaking and alone and certain he'd been far, far away and yet connected still to this place? His heart lurched once, twice, and then it found itself again. In that strong and certain beating, there was a whisper of another, a ghost or an echo. Then, it was gone, and he stumbled back into the present moment where his friends and family told a story, for what he suspected was the last time, though he didn't know why.

It was a story like any other, with heroes and villains, with loves and losses, with destinies fulfilled and others denied. Yet, this story was theirs and, somehow, as he looked around their group, this family that they'd built in love and loss and survival, Alex understood the story wasn't quite done yet.

SEVEN

ROGAN WALKED BACK toward their camp carrying the few small fish she'd caught that morning. To her left, the ocean was a mysterious blue expanse dotted with waves that looked like they were capped with gemstones, twinkling in the mid-morning sun. She felt unsettled. Nervous. As if something was hunting her down and, yet, of course, that seemed foolish to her. She told herself again it must just be sighting the cougar that had left her feeling on edge, but she didn't quite believe that. She'd been feeling this for weeks, a dark and ominous cloud rolling towards her. Toward them all. A reminder that life could change quickly and that the struggles they'd already faced could abruptly resurface.

Not all the years, since the Earth had tried to cast them off, had been difficult. It had been a reasonable balance of idyllic stretches and challenging months. At times, the struggles were welcome because they reminded them not to get too comfortable in the world after the breaking. They'd been so caught up in what they escaped and survived that they sometimes lost sight of what they still had to face. Holed up in their safe little corner of the world, they'd become both comfortable and lazy when it came to being afraid humanity was still capable of turning on itself.

The lean times reminded them to plan, prepare, and be ready for what might be coming. Of course, they needed to be able to imagine the worst to be ready for it; and no one could truly be prepared for all possibilities. Was that not always the way of humanity, to both underestimate its own potential and its own capacity to throw it all away?

Of course, those long ago humans had done it to themselves—finally created something they could neither control nor stop. When the destruction began, only a miracle paused that tearing apart of rock, earth, sky, and sea; and that miracle left some of them to survive, but not many. Certainly not enough to wage wars, inflict suffering and harm, or to walk sure-footedly along the same path as every generation that had come before in search of their own destruction in a feverish way through greed, might, hate, fear, and war.

Rogan didn't remember it but some among their small community did. It had been a Tuesday in spring, and in their part of the world, unseasonably cold. Most everyone had awoken with expectations of absolutely nothing being different than it had the previous day. They expected nothing, even with the news that the world government was testing a new device, one meant to sustain the whole planet energetically and eventually make space for them to undo the destruction they'd wrought upon the natural world and all the beings who shared it, many of them long ago extinct thanks to man.

The end had begun with a shaking, so soft and gentle at first that most people didn't even bother to register that something was happening. Within minutes, buildings toppled, roads were torn apart, and the earth was ripped open, plumes of gas, fire, and poison being thrown out. There was a tension in the air that kept building, and now the people who had survived the beginnings of the end could feel it, in their hearts and in their souls, that thin veil between the earth and the vast dark nothing of space was being pulled apart. There was also the feeling, just below that deep surface of terror, so intense it changed everyone it gripped irreversibly, that was somewhat like drowning yet also like being squeezed tight in a vice. There was an awareness that the end, if it was glimpsed, would be awful and painful, the kind of manmade unnatural force they had inflicted on countless species for millennia, and they'd only finally found for themselves.

In the midst of the final tearing apart, rock screaming, fire and magma spewing into thinning air as it spilled into space, oceans boiling and tossing steam so hot it incinerated anything that got in its way—in the midst of that last violent but sorry goodbye for humanity—there was suddenly a pause. Some outside force squeezed tight and all of it stopped and drew itself back to find its way to some semblance of whole.

As with all moments, it contained all moments. Eternity settled into one tiny and yet infinite space. There, in that now and forever, humanity was given one last chance. Not because humans earned it but because somewhere on the other side of the universe someone decided it should be so, even without realizing.

Rogan was a child when it had all happened, yet, somewhere deep within her, as with everyone else who had survived, there was a memory of both the horror and the hope that day offered. She couldn't remember any of it, yet it had come to her in dreams here and there over the years since. She was never really certain if they were fantasy or memory, but she always woke from them soaked in sweat and crying. It wasn't the fear or horror that broke her heart; it was that she wasn't sure people had changed. She wasn't sure they'd truly earned another chance. *Were they any different than the humans who had chased down their own destruction so whole-heartedly? Would they one day suck up every last resource and hope, obliterate entire ecosystems, and damage food chains irreparably once more? Would they take from others, even when they had enough? Would they ignore every single sign that time was running short and therefore running away with any chance they had at a future?* This is what haunted her, not the far off past, but the present and the possibility that everything was the same even though the world was not.

As she walked, Rogan poked at this worry. It hadn't always haunted her so fully, but all that had changed a few weeks ago when the ocean had washed up a mystery on the beach in front of her. She still wasn't sure what to make of it all, but she had a feeling brewing deep down inside, one she imagined was like that of many people on that last day when the earth was unmade. It was an inkling, a whisper in the dark, a tiny voice in the back of her mind. It could say a million phrases and yet all of them led to one place: you are not as in control of your destiny as you might think.

Be ready, it said to her. *Something is coming.*

As Rogan rounded a corner and stepped onto the path that would carry her away from the shore and back home, she saw it—a story of smoke and ash rising up into the morning sky. There was one last moment where she got to be this Rogan, the one who existed after the world had been torn apart and yet survived, and before this new horror truly woke her up into a world not even she recognized. Then, reality slammed into her and her breath caught in her throat. There was a deep and aching desire to reach for another truth, to turn away from what she already knew was unfolding in front of her, to run and hide and only come out when the world had gone back to normal again. It passed in the blink of an eye. So many difficult days had already been survived. What was another, even if it seemed possible it might be worse than all the ones that had come before? *Only one way to find out,* her heart whispered, *and maybe, maybe, some of them had survived.*

EIGHT

WHEN FIRTH WOKE that morning it was with the sense that something awful was looming. In a world where many days were a struggle, it was an oddly unsettling feeling to have. She turned over in bed, a mess of golden-brown hair following behind her, and placed a hand on the empty spot beside her and sighed. Cold. Another night she'd fallen asleep by herself. Another morning she'd awoken alone to start a new day. It was a troubling thing, to feel so alone when you were supposed to have a partner. It scared her in ways she didn't know were possible. Living on Earth after it had almost extinguished the plague of humanity that had swarmed across every possible acre consuming and destroying, she'd gotten used to being afraid so much so that often a lack of fear was a more uncomfortable state of being. Yet, these past few weeks something had really changed. It wasn't just the discovery Rogan had made on the beach and brought back with her. There was something in the air, some kind of poised and prowling energy that had them all on edge. Waiting, for what they did not know.

This morning, it felt closer. Something was hunting them down. She was sure of it. Then, she heard the scream.

Firth leapt out of bed, but before she could even reach for something to throw on over her underwear and t-shirt, the front wall of her cabin came crashing inside. She jumped back and out of the way of the flying debris, wood shards, and smoke. She couldn't even begin to imagine what kind of machine had broken down the wall but as the dust settled and the shadows began to move, shift, and then become people through the haze, she saw between them a large battering ram. Her thoughts took off, searching for reason and sense, trying to understand what kind of misunderstanding she'd landed in the midst of, hoping to find some kind of sanity in a world that had suddenly gone madder than she'd ever imagined it would again. Two of the strangers, men, charged her, wrapping rough and calloused hands around her throat and arms and lifting her off her feet before she even had a chance to react or resist.

"Burn the whole goddamn thing to the ground once we've got them all!" screamed Egan, the leader of the raiding party, and before Firth could make out which one he was, she was punched once, twice, in the face and then thrown to the ground. The world got darker, and then began to tumble out of reach and she hurried into that darkness, slipping away from what she didn't want to face.

"Goddamit, what did I say?" Egan shook his head, managing a combination of annoyance and fury. He was tall, over six feet, and barrel-chested. He was unusually strong, deeply arrogant, and infinitely cruel, and his men feared and respected him in equal measure. His eyes were so dark they seemed black as if there wasn't a barrier between the iris and that dark and seeping center of his eye.

"You gonna carry them all back?" he shouted, scowling. "Hurt another one like that before we get them back to Bex and you'll regret it, I promise you that."

The man who'd knocked Firth out wrapped his arms around her waist, hoisted her up onto his shoulder as if she weighed nothing more than a sack of fruit or flour, and hurried out of the ruined cabin to join the others of their group. He never paused to consider she might need clothes or even that it would be the decent thing to do. No, they were taking her somewhere where decency would be lost anyway, so why reach for it now?

From every building, large and small, came their prisoners, rounded up as easily as if they were children, and in many ways, they were. Naïve enough to have believed they were safe until morning tore away that veil and showed them the truth.

As Firth was carried out of her house, she began to rouse, and so saw the beginning of the end of the home they'd painstakingly built, together. In the center of their tiny village of Iri was a small square. On its outer edge sat a main building where they ate, met, celebrated, and mourned among so many other activities a community was meant to do together. From that center, roadways radiated outward and were lined with the tiny cabins which served as homes to their little band of survivors or were used as storage for food, supplies, and anything else they might need.

All of it was on fire. Houses and other buildings had been set alight. Flames licked at the morning sky as they sent first tendrils and then towers of smoke up towards the heavens. She saw her friends, her family, bound and gagged, prisoners, every single one. Some strange fate awaited them all and it was now, quietly, as the nagging feeling began that she realized she should have seen it coming. From that morning three weeks ago when she'd begun to hear whispers that the world was going to shift and change underfoot and she should be ready, and yet she'd pressed that voice aside, hoping to sit in her comfort for just a little while longer.

Mixed with her horror and heartache was a deep wave of relief. Rogan was still not at home and that meant she was safe. *But for how long? There's no way she won't see the smoke and hear the screams if she's headed back this way,* she thought wildly. *What will she do,* wondered Firth, *now that war had come looking for her, come looking for us all?*

Before she could pursue her fear and worry for her partner in love and life, Firth saw *her*. The stranger. She knew it was irrational but she wondered if the stranger in their midst was somehow the cause of all this. She was huddled next to a burning building, and yet neither the flames nor the heat seemed to touch her. Her eyes were wild, terrified, and yet there was so much more swimming in those depths, a kind of knowing that had been there since she'd first boldly met Firth's gaze a few weeks ago and that still sent shivers running down her spine when their eyes met. The woman was covering her ears, trying to block out the sound of lives being burned to the ground and heartache winding its way into the world through wailing and tears.

Fear lit up her face and boasted that she heard it all. She was rocking a little too which seemed at first as an act of terror but then Firth realized it was much different than that, yet she couldn't quite put her finger on it. Around the stranger, their captors and foes burned, raged, and never relented, and yet not one of them saw her crouched low next to the building that was really no longer a building at all; it was becoming just flames and smoke and endings.

Firth realized it was strange, her not being seen. She was not being touched by any of the awfulness around her, but Firth could tell she'd been touched by far worse, and much of it was still with her even if she couldn't remember any of it. The woman looked up then, startled into realizing where she was and met Firth's intense and curious gaze. For a moment, Firth saw an eternity there; the whole of existence was born and then died within those eyes.

Before Firth could stop herself, she looked away—afraid. *Why had the woman come here? Why had she stayed?* She looked around, avoiding the stranger's gaze and the questions inside herself. She was horrified, heartbroken as everything they'd painstakingly built was being undone by madmen—a rampage of fury and fire.

They passed by the woman without seeing she was there, and Firth couldn't help but wonder one thing more... *what was she really, the woman with the chocolate ruby eyes who had washed up on a beach three weeks ago? An omen they'd all ignored.*

On the other side of the universe, crystal blue eyes shot open in shock. He gasped and sat up in bed with the pounding of his heart echoing in his ears. He could still smell smoke and fire, could still hear the echo of screaming. He could feel the fear of sitting in all that chaos without being able to move. Yet, as his eyes adjusted to the dark and he began to understand what he'd seen, only one thing mattered.

"Kale," he whispered into the darkness, "she's alive."

Part Two

Dreaming

NINE

THE DREAM HAD been like falling. She'd tumbled through the vast, dark, cold with little light to guide her way and no chance to catch hold of a moment of calm or peace. It had seemed like an eternity, that long dive down into the ocean of space and time, and when she'd finally been pressed back up onto the surface of herself, there was nothing beneath it. No memory. No sense of self. No name. Just the deep black mystery of being which is what she felt she'd crossed to reach the waking world again.

She'd woken in a storm of sea, stars, and vicious rocking. The violence of it all was so shocking that for the first few moments all she could do was gasp, panicked, desperately searching for a sign of where she'd landed while the deep pulled her under again and again; begging her to surrender. For just a moment, a memory threatened and then it was gone. With its leaving, she burst up into the air again to draw a couple ragged, terrified breaths. There was no light, nothing to place her in the vast reach of sea and night, nothing to comfort or offer her a calm moment to catch her breath. She wanted to scream, terrified, frantic for peace, but she didn't want to give anything away to the darkness. Somehow, she knew that what it took could not be reclaimed. She knew also that whatever she gave it could either make it stronger or wound it, and she wasn't sure which it would be.

There, alone and exhausted, somewhere far from anywhere she'd been before, she dipped under the surface, once, twice, and then she was gone. A new dream found her as she sank. Surrendering to the deep below, this one was both familiar and yet not at all. She saw a beach, a bonfire burning tall, and a crowd of people seated around it, sharing, laughing, crying, and connected to one another by some secret she couldn't quite catch, even as the wind tried to pick it up and carry it her way.

A new dream came. Crystal blue eyes shot up and looked into hers. They were familiar and yet forgotten. The truth of them out of reach and not hers to grab hold of anymore. She had something to tell him, something she was meant to pass along. When she reached for the memory, she realized that both it and every other one she'd ever collected was gone. Before she could even be shocked by that betrayal of mind and memory, the scene before her began to fade and then wandered fully out of sight. As she let it go, the darkness wrapped itself around her again and that familiar embrace cradled her back and into herself once more.

She woke, hours, days, maybe weeks later; *how could she even know?* Coaxed out of a deep and fretful sleep by waves pressing her onto a sandy beach, the morning sun stung her eyes when she first opened them, and she had to squint to make out the faint outline of trees in the distance. The warm sand cradled her head, and she licked her chapped and sunburned lips before trying to lift herself. She failed. The trees disappeared and faded into the grey mystery of exhaustion and dehydration, and once again the world went dark.

It was Rogan's scream that woke her some unknown amount of time later. That was the beginning of the story that led her to living with the people of Iri in their little farming and fishing community. She'd been unable to tell Rogan anything. Not her name. Not where she'd come from or how she'd found herself in the sea. Not even how long she'd been wandering, lost and alone apparently. It was all a great big mystery. Except, there was a kind of memory below the surface of all that nothing, a kind of feeling that she couldn't find the words to express. It was sort of like having been done, finished with a task, and yet she was now settled into the aftermath of that completion. She couldn't explain it, especially since she had no reference of time, place, or of who she'd ever been to measure it all against. Still, she repeatedly had a nagging feeling that she *both* was *and* wasn't meant to be. Not here. Not anywhere, maybe.

Or, was it, *not anymore?*

The people of Iri welcomed her easily into their midst. For a tight knit community that lived simple and interdependent lives, it only made sense to take in the woman who was stranded alone in a world she could not remember. They took care of her as she healed and recovered, and when it became apparent her memory may not return, they worked to help her belong. Unlike Rogan, they had no sense that her arrival heralded the coming of something dark or ominous and so they delighted in the mystery of her. At night, when Rogan and Firth sat together under the stars sipping tea or on the rare occasion homemade wine, Rogan would wonder aloud about the possibilities of the stranger's origins and Firth would chase all that absurdity away, convinced her partner was being paranoid.

Still, the stranger had settled into life with them fairly easily. She was a kind of enigmatic fascination for most everyone, and they went out of their way to take their time with her. She learned how to fish, how to forage for berries and other fruit, and how to cook. She learned how to sew and repair worn and old clothes. She learned the rules of their tiny and gentle society, one that had grown anew out of the ruins of humanity. She'd even begun to feel at home. Yet, like Rogan and eventually Firth, and many others in their little community, she had the sneaking suspicion that she was very different than everyone around her, even if she couldn't figure out how. Much like Rogan, she had begun to sense a looming kind of dread that had finally chased her to act. Over the last week, everyone had begun to feel it, but no one knew what it meant.

Now, sitting in a tiny circle of green grass, with the whole of the world she'd known these past few weeks burned and charred around her, the fear of what she might be was palpable. It scared her so deeply she shook away any exploration of thought and instead drummed up enough courage to finally move. She'd sat in her tiny oasis of unscorched earth for so long her legs had begun to cramp and, when she moved, pain shot through them. She winced as she began to stand, swaying at first. Around her, small fires still raged and ravaged what little remained of the tiny village she'd called home the past few weeks. She was the only one left. Everyone else had been taken.

She'd been so afraid, frozen by terror and something more, so that she'd done nothing to stop any of it. Even though she couldn't recall a single memory about herself, it still seemed wrong that she'd been unable to act and that she'd simply stood by. Not knowing who she was took nothing away from being certain she was not the kind of person who behaved that way. And yet, she had.

"What happened?" Rogan screamed as she came running towards her. Her face was stained with ash and tears and her brown eyes were wild. "Goddammit, what happened?" The story of horror and heartache was written not just across her face but across every movement she made. The woman with no memory, the one who had been Kale once upon a time but who had crossed the ocean of space and time to become no one, wondered if she'd ever loved or been loved so much that the losing could destroy her like that. Her unspoken question wound its way around her heart and looked through her vast depths before rising to the surface unanswered.

"What happened?" Rogan begged, but now she wasn't asking Kale; she was asking the part of herself she believed had failed to protect her friends, family, and their home. Shaking, shocked, she was finally brought to her knees by that, the truth that she could blame the strange woman in their midst all she wanted, she could even blame forces unseen, but she was the leader and protector of this place and any failure landed squarely on her shoulders, whether she could carry the weight or not.

"I don't know," Kale finally answered, unable to meet Rogan's pleading gaze and she realized she was speaking mostly to herself. She was baffled by her own failure, shocked by her own inability to be brave, stand up or fight. In the face of that awful force that had leveled Iri with violence and fire, she could not seem to reconcile her own inaction. "I don't know," she said again, but what she meant was *I don't know who I am.*

Up until then, she'd been relieved without the story of her past, even though she wasn't sure why. Now, she began to understand there was a price for that feeling of being untethered, for not being tied to something she'd maybe wanted to escape. She was also unbound from the truth of herself and now she realized that meant she was something more than she could understand. *If she didn't remember her past, how would she ever know what she was capable of?*

How would she know if she was worthy of living amongst the kind of people who had taken her in? She couldn't help it, she began to wonder for the first time since feeling like she'd escaped her past, if to move on and build a life she might need to know where she'd come from, as well as what and who she'd been.

The woman who was once Kale, but who was no one now, finally met Rogan's gaze. The heartbreak there, the terror, it was more than she could bear and she quickly looked away. A momentary certainty rose within her before it fell away and faded, and yet for the first time since waking on the beach, she'd glimpsed a true sense of who she was meant to be. Then, just as quickly, it was gone. She was thrust back into having disappointed Rogan and the people of Iri by failing to stand up to a kind of evil she'd once known all too well.

"I don't know," she said once more, but this time she meant something else yet again. *I don't know how but I'll make this right somehow.*

TEN

IT HAD BEEN a week since the bonfire and Medea had managed to avoid Derin despite his repeated attempts to speak to her alone. They'd filled their days with family, fun, and rest. Throughout it all, she managed to make sure she wasn't alone long enough to find herself in Derin's company.

Alex had taken her and Corin on a day trip to see the site where he and Derin were building their home. At first, she'd been relieved to be away from him for the day but when they'd arrived at the beginnings of the simple, elegant home next to the ocean, settled into its surroundings as if it had been born of the very earth and rock below their feet, the feeling that settled over her was so much worse than having to face him. Even though the house was far from done, she could feel him in the gentle sweep of imagination that carried the ceilings high toward the heavens. Even in its raw construction, there was a kind of certainty in what it would become that made her long for the kind of life that could unfold inside its walls.

It was foolish she knew, but she was afraid because she was lonely and lost, because she wasn't quite sure what the right answer was anymore, and because in her uncertainty she didn't trust herself. When they'd arrived home late that night, she hurried to bed to hide from her heart and those in the world who could hear it whispering the truth.

She wasn't ready. She was sure of it.

Now, Medea sat on the beach tracing shapes in the sand aimlessly while more than one truth battled within her for a voice. She felt foolish for having come on the journey to Samnar, but she'd been certain there was a purpose to it. She felt drawn, pulled by some unknown force that she had believed was Kale. She hoped the magic of the Founders was capable of one last miracle, and she truly believed she'd be coming here to witness it. It sounded crazy now but she'd been sure something was coming and even more certain that it was about Kale.

"Can I join you?" Derin's voice startled Medea out of her musings. For a moment, she simply closed her eyes and took a deep breath to steady herself.

"I was actually just about to head back to the cabin," she said as she stood, gesturing toward the small log cabin she was sharing with Jaren and Corin while they were here. The main house, which was the original home that the Founders had built and still shared, was now surrounded by other homes and buildings where their children lived and one day their growing families would too. It was a village that offered them each their own space and homes, yet kept them near enough to one another to embrace their interdependence and desire to be close. In the aftermath of Caine's rule, even though they'd tried, Alex and Derin had never quite fallen into the same sense of longing to be close to everyone.

They told themselves it was because they couldn't trust their mother. By serving Caine for so long and by allowing Kale to sacrifice herself, Cyan had unraveled it all so that none remained. Yet, neither brother was willing to face the truth—if they released their anger towards Cyan, it left only space to be angry with their own failures. Hadn't Alex failed to act when the moment arrived? Hadn't Derin served Caine, loyally, faithfully like a fool? Hadn't they both been handed a chance at redemption while they struggled to offer it to their mother? With time laid out in front of them as far as they could see, it was tempting not to rush back to forgiving her or to facing their own demons.

Threads left loose were being pulled and cinched back together around them, whether they knew it or not. Around all of them. It would be the time sooner than any of them could believe to face both the past and the possibility of a future far different than any of them had imagined. No game was too small or insignificant for the forces that governed the universe, for it was all connected to that one great big story, forever told, over and over again.

"I'll walk you back," Derin offered. With a sigh, Medea nodded and began to make her way home. There was electricity between them, a force that could both repel and draw in. It wrapped itself around them so that the world got dim, and they became hyper aware of each other as if nothing else existed. They walked in silence for most of the way. Every time Derin went to speak not a single word would come out, and he realized he was afraid. Would he lose, for the second time in his life, the woman he loved because he wasn't strong enough?

"Medea, I..." he began but she quickly interrupted him.

"The house you and Alex are building seems like it will be amazing." The words hurried out of her, desperate to stop the coming of a truth she was not ready to hear or face. It was easy to reach for that memory of the home she'd so easily pictured Derin in. So much of it had spoken to his hopeful heart, that vast expanse that surprised her every time she realized it had room for so much. It was a mistake, mentioning the house she'd had moments of dreaming herself into in some make-believe future, because she was admitting to herself she wanted something she was also fighting against.

"That's what you want to talk about? Now? With me?" He was both accusatory and deflated. He didn't want to be alone in his longing for what was between them to come to life.

"What would *you* like to talk about?" she asked, anger already rising to protect her heart. She regretted it the moment the question was out and yet a part of her wanted to hear his answer and know what he would say.

"It's time for us to move on," he said and when fear raced through her she realized it was because she thought he meant for them to move on from each other, and the possibility of this being over was even scarier than it not being over. "I loved her. I always will. It's true." It stung a little, hearing him say it, and then she felt ashamed for being jealous of her dead best friend.

"That's why it's wrong, Derin. I'm sorry," she said as she climbed the steps to the cabin and opened the door. She didn't understand how to want something so badly and also want with equal measure and intensity its opposite.

"Medea, please, talk to me." He climbed the stairs and took a few hesitant steps towards her before he stopped, understanding there was an exact way to navigate this conversation. Until he understood or saw the path ahead, he needed to be careful, even delicate with his words and her worried heart.

"I can't." She kept her back to him, shoulders slumped under the heavy weight of loyalty and loss. The two were so fully tied together, Kale's being gone and Medea's fear of moving on, that it was hard to see where the story of one ended and the other began inside her own. She owned a fear of leaving in the past any of the people she felt like she'd failed all those years ago.

Derin closed the space between them, slowly, and paused. He felt a river of fear sweeping through him and begging him to take a few calm and steady breaths to slow its current so he could find his voice and say what he needed to.

"Medea, I know you're scared. I am too. And I know you don't want to betray her." He caught himself, realizing he'd need to speak her name if either of them was going to make this work. "Kale. I know you don't want to betray Kale. Neither do I." He gulped a big mouthful of air and then continued. "But the thing is," he paused one last time before he hurried on, "the thing is, we owe her our happiness. We owe her our best lives. Anything less than that means she died for nothing. Means she gave up her life for nothing. And I can't live with that anymore."

He stepped closer and then gently turned her around, leaving just a breath of air between them. When she wouldn't raise her eyes to meet his, he dropped to his knees in front of her and looked up into hers. Her breath caught in her throat, and she could feel that swelling of both fear and its opposite in her chest.

"I know it's not what we planned when we finally realized we'd have to move on with our lives and leave her behind, but it's what happened. Haven't we lost enough?" He reached out to her before thinking better of it, letting his hand fall back to his side.

"Derin," she whispered not knowing what more to say in a moment that felt like it was tearing her in two. How many times had she felt like that in search of her happiness in the world after Caine? When would she admit it was unfair or at least time to lay down a burden carried for far too long already?

"I love you," he whispered in reply, pleading with both his words and his whole heart for her to hear him. Really hear him.

It was the tenderness wrapped in truth that finally broke through. Yes, she loved him. She had for a long time now. She'd held on to the pain of all she'd lost not simply because it felt deserved, with her being here while so many people she'd loved were gone, but also because it was safer than stepping into what was under it all. What had grown and flourished out of sight while she hadn't been paying attention. Could she do it? Could she take the one thing that had taken Kale from her?

"Medea," he said, his voice a little louder, a little more certain.

"I don't know what to say." There was a deep ache within her but for the first time she considered it was more about what she could lose than what she already had.

"Tell me the truth, please." His crystal blue eyes, deep and mysterious, bored into hers as they begged not to be wounded yet again.

Kale, what should I do?

She thought of Ryan, now five years gone, who she always assumed she'd have a long and happy life with once they'd defeated Caine. She thought of Joah, who felt sometimes like he was a missing piece of herself meant to make up a greater whole. She thought of Kale, who had died to save them all and surrendered to destiny over and over again, trusting that it would carry her to where she was meant to be. *And where was she now?* Medea thought bitterly, though the answer that came surprised her. *She's okay. Kale is okay. And she's okay with you finally moving on.* She saw it then. That she couldn't always control the world around her, but she could choose who to be when she stepped into either the chaos or the calm. She could be brave. She could be forgiving. Even of herself, and, yes, of Derin, too. It was time.

Tears began to form and then tumble from Medea's eyes. Through that mist of hope and heartache, she met Derin's again. "I love you," she whispered, "I do." She took a deep breath, then another while he kneeled in front of her, frozen to the spot with shock. "We can try." She gave him a gentle smile, encouraging, loving, and sweet.

It wasn't until she laughed, just one happy bark at how shocked he was, that he was snapped out of it. He stood, slowly, afraid of undoing it somehow, afraid she'd change her mind or tell him she was joking but she just kept smiling. When he was standing, he bent his face to hers and kissed her so gently it made her ache. The fear rose up again. That familiar pattern of believing she was betraying her friend and her past love but this time the wave of it crashed and then washed away before she could panic or pull away.

There was both an urgency and relief in their kiss. A kind of losing of themselves in what had waited so long to be set free and a sense that hadn't it always been meant to lead here. They'd allowed things to go this way once before but it had felt different, that coming together. It had felt stolen and even a little bit wrong. They'd given in to the desire that had built up between them, but as soon as it was over, Medea had panicked and vowed never to make another mistake like that again. It had broken both their hearts when she'd left

Samnar the next day with promises to never return and yet she'd been certain it was the right thing to do.

This time felt like coming home. Now all Medea could think between the moments of losing herself utterly to Derin was that it had been foolish to think she shouldn't have followed her heart. Wasting any of her life or what her heart told her was right was the betrayal, not this, not letting love have a chance to soften the world with its power and grace.

Derin ran his hands along her arms and up and down her back, both urgent and yet certain of every movement, and the way her body lit up with his touch made her wonder how she could have waited so long to surrender to this truth. He moved kisses down her neck and traced them along her collarbones, and when he found her mouth again, she kissed him back greedily. Her hands wove their way into his hair and down his lean arms and when they found his hips she paused for only a moment before grabbing the bottom of his shirt and pulling it up and over his head. His eyes met hers and he smiled. Before he kissed her again, he thought to himself no one had ever looked more beautiful and nothing had ever felt so right.

They would spend hours tangled together. Both in passion and later in sleep, as if in either state they did not want to return to being apart again. Derin hadn't known there were so many ways you could speak a person's name until he'd heard her make a whole language out of his that night. As they drifted off to sleep, spent and blissful and satisfied, he brushed away the nagging feeling that there was something other than joy hunting him down.

ELEVEN

JOAH WAS SEATED on the back deck of the home he shared with his two siblings, Arin and Kedall, and one of the other children of the Founders, Milar. After years together as prisoners, Kedall and Milar had learned to live their lives as a pair, a unit; and even though they were five years into their freedom, they had not spent a single day or night apart in all that time. It had only been natural when the three siblings finally built a home of their own that Milar join them. They had easily become a unit, the four of them, and living together was both comfortable and joyful.

Joah wasn't sure where any of them were now but he welcomed the privacy to brood. There was a confusing mix of feelings storming around inside him and he wanted time to sort it all out. He ran his fingers through his messy mane of snow-white hair and then reached for the guitar leaned up against his chair and began to play. Random notes met for the first time, incomplete melodies bumped up against one another, some chords rushing to be first, and others hoping to be left behind. He had a gift for spontaneity—in life and in much of everything he did. But there were moments, not many, but some, when he wished he was different, and he longed for a path other than the one he was on. The song that soared into the night around him spoke of that and so many other things.

"It's beautiful," Arin said quietly as she sat down next to him. She'd been listening from the doorway, captivated by his gift to make so much gentle beauty out of nothing. In it, she could hear his happiness and his heartache. She knew if he wanted to talk about what was bothering him he would and so she sat there quietly, charmed and carried away by the music, her own longings with lives of their own because of it and brought to life by the magic he was weaving around them. She didn't notice when the tears began to fall. The night hid them well but Joah knew her well enough to sense the change in his sister. After a few moments, he stopped playing and allowed the silence speak for him, and for her.

Her cherry eyes were dark in the cover of night and her dark red hair was almost black, yet she was strikingly beautiful, even in sadness. They were so different and yet in so many ways they were similar. It was unmistakable, that they were siblings, even here in the dark, and there was an ease, a closeness, between them that was palpable. Arin smiled at her brother and then reached out and took his hand. It was a simple gesture, but it offered him everything he needed. She understood what he was feeling even if it wasn't her own. They were close enough that they could feel the other's sorrows and joys—emotions they had shared for so long that it took more effort not to be connected like this.

It wasn't that Joah wasn't happy for Medea. He'd wanted this for her, at times more than she'd wanted it for herself. She deserved to be happy. To have someone love her so fully and completely that she was the center of that person's universe. Though Medea and Joah's hearts had made a home for one another in this life, as a couple, they were still somehow just not meant to be. They'd both known it and had talked about in a way that affirmed their easy intimacy and deep connection and allowed them to forge a stronger bond because of it. A beautiful friendship was born out of it all and sustained them both in many ways. Yet, that sense of their souls having known each other for more than a single lifetime could confuse both of them. Now was one of those times. When Joah was so happy for Medea and yet he was still left with the melancholy sense that something had been lost— something he was absolutely willing to forfeit for her—yet here he was, indulging the ache of it just the same. He could be both, of course: Happy for her, happy for a love finally fulfilled, and yet sad for what wouldn't and couldn't be, in some ways because of it.

Overhead the night sky told stories much the same, of complexity and simplicity and how both could weave such lovely tales together. The siblings sat below it in companionable silence. The sounds of night and the ocean nearby were the only soundtrack that endured. Arin understood her brother's longing but in so many ways it was different than her own. She hadn't yet found someone to grab hold of or to set free. She'd had moments, a sense of possibility, but nothing ever materialized because she always managed to go unseen.

It had always been like that.

Growing up, she'd been in love with Alex. He'd been their leader and she, like all the children of the Founders, had looked up to him in a way that left them awed. She admired his determination and strength and had been charmed by his good looks so that he was a natural first place for her heart to land. Yet, he only ever saw her as a child. After they'd come home to Samnar, it became apparent rather quickly that they weren't an ideal pair and she'd been mostly amused with the dissolution of her first crush. Now, she was twenty-six and, as were the other children of the Founders, beginning to feel that pull towards finding love and a way to settle down.

She was joyful, pleasant, kind, intelligent, and intuitive and yet she was either met with a kind of indifference, as if none of that came across, or her place as one of the Founders' children became a kind of fascination. When so many people still thought of them as god-like, it was no wonder that the reverence got in the way.

There'd been one true connection. It had begun on a long ago night. More than once in the five years since, there'd been flashes of recognition for what might be, but she was still waiting for a sign that he was ready to move on or forward and that she might be the one to do it with.

It was baffling really. She was sure enough of herself to know she would find her way and the right person to walk her path with, yet there was a kind of loneliness in it, too. There were many relationships around her that were examples of true and lasting love and it sometimes left her feeling sorrowful that she hadn't found it yet. What she saw in those relationships, those of their parents, and the ones that had materialized around them since, both in friendship and in love, was a kind of rightness and righteousness in choosing to step into connection with the person you were meant for. Arin was okay with not wasting a moment on anything less. Her time would come and so would the right person.

"Will you be okay, brother?" she asked mostly to break the spell her thoughts had cast over her like a heavy mist.

"Will *you*?" was his answer. It was a kind of game they played. They knew each other so well that they asked a question they already knew the answer to. It was a different kind of saying *I love you.*

With nothing left to be said, Joah let go of her hand and began to play again. His heartache and happiness had a voice, a language as he played. It was haunting and beautiful, and more than one person on Samnar would fall asleep listening to the utter beauty of it and feeling something deep and aching answer from within.

TWELVE

FIRTH OPENED HER eyes and cringed. Her head was pounding and it screamed at her to abandon the harsh brightness of the world. She squeezed her eyes shut, both against the throbbing and against the new reality she would have to face when she opened them again.

Their captors had marched them for hours without relenting or pausing. She'd tried a number of times to question them but had been hit or knocked down in reply. Her lip had been split open as a reward for one question and she'd scraped both knees and sprained her ankle as the result of another. She finally opted to stay quiet and tried to puzzle through where they were being led and why. As the sun passed its high point in the sky, they met with another group like theirs, organized soldiers leading wide-eyed captives, some injured, all terrified. They were stopped for at least half an hour while the guards refueled and yet they were left to suffer in the sun, exhausted and dehydrated.

Firth managed to make her way over to a cluster of prisoners from the other group and found out they were raided two days ago and had been traveling since. Their village had also been burned to the ground and most of their people had been taken prisoner. A few died trying to fight back and protect themselves or each other. Just like her, they had no idea what was going on, where they were being led, or why.

As she made her way back to her friends, Firth let her mind wander to Rogan and whether she was okay. She had both a longing for Rogan to be chasing them down and a hope that she was far away and out of danger. They'd been together three years. It hadn't always been easy but Firth had known who she was in the grand scheme of things because of who she was with Rogan. They'd been friends since finding each other in those first days after the breaking and years later had struggled to realize the obvious change in their relationship. Struggled, too, to notice the shifting into deep love that meant they were going to build the kind of life together they'd both forgotten to dream about while in the daily fight to build their tiny town of Iri; a thriving community that not long ago, she thought could survive anything. She wasn't so sure now. The deep and aching feeling of defeat was palpable and every time she tried to reassure her people, her family, her friends, that they would get out of this and return home, not even she believed it. It scared her. What was unfolding now, and what was coming.

Late that afternoon, they reached the bowl of the valley that sheltered they city of Dempsey. When Firth saw the size and scope of both the city and what surrounded it, she realized they'd been foolish not to try and know who and what was around them in the world. The people of Iri thought that they could protect themselves that way, by staying separate from any other kind of humans around them. They thought they could stay out of sight, of both the beauty and the horrors that inevitably rose up around humanity. The question that plagued her now was unbearable. *Could evil, the kind that was secretly flourishing here, survive outside of places where it went unchecked and unchallenged?* Firth suspected it could not. If that were true, their hiding from it had only given it permission to grow and thrive. She worried that meant they were somewhat responsible for where they found themselves now.

Firth limped with the help of whoever could manage to hold her up. Even despite their own exhaustion, her friends and family took turns helping her walk. When they reached the outside of the towering city wall, a fortress built to both contain and keep out, she knew the minute the person in charge of their plight arrived: That kind of power had an energy all its own and even if you hadn't come across it before, it was a thing recognizable; a memory rising from the deep recesses of the human heart and mind. The part that remembered the kind of rulers who thrived on destruction and the destitution of their fellow humans.

Bex was tall, pale skinned, and average looking. She had dark eyes sunken into a scowl that had been settled onto her face so long it had become permanent. Even when she smiled, which was now, that angry downturn of forehead and brows remained. She scanned the newest additions to her collection, which is how she liked to think of all the lesser humans she captured and used, and she felt that sense of dark glee rising inside her. A wave that sometimes would not crash. Not many things gave her as much pleasure as tearing others down to their lowest point. It made her feel big, and powerful, and certain of her place in the world. It was a shallow kind of living and a tenuous power, but she had neither the insight nor intellect to glimpse that truth. Nor could she see that because she'd built her empire on the backs of others, she'd actually not risen at all.

She stood at the end of a long line of rulers, the kind who were so convinced of their own greatness they never noticed that the only ones who agreed with them were also fools. They built their kingdoms on quicksand and yet were always shocked when they were inevitably swallowed up to be replaced by things that could last. While they ruled, they destroyed everything they could and, somehow, people followed and delighted in turning away from themselves and their own hearts. Human history seemed undeterred from choosing these kinds of people to rule, conquer, and destroy. Not one generation yet had learned to turn their backs on them entirely and choose a different way.

Bex loved the first meeting when she could look down on what she now owned. People just at the very beginning of a kind of brokenness she would usher them towards so that they would obey and serve without a fight. She loved looking for the ones who met her gaze with determination and defiance so that she knew which ones would present the most fun in breaking. Her men were skilled in tearing people down through pain and fear, but she still enjoyed taking on the most challenging ones herself.

Firth couldn't have known this when she met Bex's gaze and surprised herself with feeling hate for the first time in her many gentle years upon this broken Earth. She couldn't have known how powerfully and fully that emotion crossed the space between them: Two women, so very different and yet as all people, so very much the same—united for a moment in the darkness they indulged.

For Bex it was undisputable, she'd found her next plaything and she would find ways to wound and torture the woman who refused to drop her gaze until she was just a shadow of herself, no matter how long it took. For Firth that darkness poked and prodded at the light deep down inside of her and even though it seemed foolish, hope rose inside her and curled up warmly in her chest to wait. *We will get out of here somehow*, it whispered to her in the darkness of that space, and she believed it.

Bex didn't matter. The monsters never do. Who we become to fight them however is a different story. It's the rising that defines us. In that moment, Firth realized she would fight, and rise, no matter what it took. No matter what it cost her. No matter who she had to become to do it. That's when she finally looked away.

THIRTEEN

ALEX TOOK A deep breath and then dove under the surface of the morning waves and swam as hard and fast as he could. Down, down, until the ocean stopped trying to press him back up into the confusion of the world above. Things made sense down here.

He watched as a large silver fish darted past, and smaller fish of every color wove in and out of a forest of coral reef below, and he marveled at how the sun painted patterns on the sandy ocean floor. It was simple in all its complexity. More than that, it was safe. Even with predators weaving their way through the dark of deeper waters, tempted to venture into the shallows for a chance at an easy meal, there was a sense of safety in the certainty of it all.

He let go, allowing the pressure of the deep cradle him and wondering if the temptation to stay here was strong enough for him to fight the instinct to pop back up to the surface and breathe. He knew it wasn't and yet facing his life again and all that had arrived in the past couple days was a powerful enough deterrent to let him linger until he couldn't hold his breath another moment. Still, he fought the urge to panic and instead kicked once, twice, and waited while his long muscular body slid back towards the surface and all the struggles that waited for him above.

He'd been gone not even a day when he'd begun to hear his parents calling him home. Something big was happening. But what could be worse or even more important than what he was hiding from; and what he was hiding from them all. 'This is the beginning of a different kind of life. Trust it. Trust your heart.' Even down here in the deep she haunted him, like she had for five long years. Except now she wasn't a ghost. Somehow, by some strange magic, and yet he doubted it would remain a mystery for long, Kale had crossed the universe and woken in another life, safe, and yet out of reach.

He'd dreamt of her again last night, saw her wandering through the dark. Chasing monsters. Unwilling to consider she shouldn't be because there were people in danger, lives at risk, and even though she was ill-equipped, she was determined to make things right. *How? How was any of it possible?*

Alex burst up into the air and gulped down huge breaths. His body sang as it found its fuel again. For a few moments, he simply let the ocean toss him gently about. His vision cleared and his heart began to calm. He saw the figure standing on the beach and sighed. He wouldn't be allowed to hide out after all.

He hadn't meant to leave. He'd meant to tell his brother that the woman he'd loved and lost was in fact not lost at all. There was a voice inside him, way down deep, that had begged him to keep the information to himself, to not give it away. Yet, that voice had no real power in the end and so he'd gone looking for Derin.

Alex had watched his brother and Medea as they finally stepped into a truth together that they'd been fighting for far too long. He couldn't believe what he was seeing. After so long, after so much struggle and denial, they'd made it. Now fate had come looking to knock them down. Alex had been frozen to the spot in shock. He'd wondered if he should stop them before it was too late. He wondered if the irony was in the truth that he was keeping or the truth that had drawn them together, finally. Then, Derin disappeared into the small cabin with Medea and Alex's heart dropped into his stomach. There'd been a confusing cacophony of emotions inside him: Relief, fear, worry, joy, and even rage. His brother had moved on and found love again. Finally got what he deserved.

Alex wasn't sure what the right choice was. He'd considered rushing to the cabin to bang on the door. He'd thought about finding his father to ask him what he should do. He'd thought about simply keeping the secret for himself and just setting his brother free. What he wasn't yet willing to face was the other truth that went with that last choice. Below his heartache for his brother and what all this would do to Derin, there was another truth swimming about. One that he wasn't quite ready to admit to himself.

In the end, he'd opted for space and time and left their little community in the quiet of a cloudy night to make his way back to the home he and Derin were building for themselves. He knew he'd face his brother eventually, but he kept shoving that truth aside as he laid down bricks and mud and sweated in the midday sun. At some point, his parents had begun to call out to him to come home but he'd swatted their pleas aside over and over again. Now, he knew for sure that whatever it was must be important because they'd sent someone to bring him home.

Alex sighed and then began to swim towards the beach. His long arms cutting through the water effortlessly. His oxygen starved muscles sore but savoring the exercise. His sanctuary below the waves already long forgotten as he prepared to face what new game fate would make of them all. He couldn't quite wrap his head around it. It had taken so much struggle to get to where they were, and now this. *What could they even do, now that he knew Kale was alive on Earth anyway?* She was out of reach except, of course, through this tenuous thread that connected them while he dreamed. His heart ached when he thought about it but he wasn't entirely sure why. He hurried away the thought beginning to rise and focused on getting to shore.

When his feet touched the sandy bottom, he stood up and let the ocean pull and pull against his body, trying to call him back. He fought it, but not as hard as he could have, and eventually he walked up onto the beach and dropped down to the sand next to Joah.

"Come here often?" Joah asked with a casual air. Alex felt a laugh escape him before he could help himself. He felt gratitude wash through him that it was Joah who'd been sent to hunt him down.

They sat in silence for a long while, surrounded by the symphony of the birds flitting in and out of that universe of trees behind them, blending with the gentle sigh of the ocean as it mated with the shore. There was an understanding between them that they were in a time soon to be extinct, a time before another shift in their lives that neither man wanted to succumb to just yet. They'd been through it too many times not to recognize it when it came upon them again. The world was about to shift underfoot, and nothing would ever be the same.

"If we leave soon we'll make it back before dark," Joah finally offered Alex.

Alex dug his hands into the sand as if trying to grab hold of something solid to keep him from having to leave the sanctuary this place offered him, even if it was fleeting. He looked over and met Joah's gaze and saw there both a question and a deep longing to know the answer.

"I don't know what's up," Alex said and paused to take a deep breath. "But there is something I'll have to tell everyone once we're there."

"Why do I feel like we are once again trapped with the whole world getting ready to drop out from underneath us?" Joah asked, feeling the pull of days long past, days barely remembered as a child, when they'd lost everything. Woken to a morning where their parents were sound asleep and unable to wake and four of their number had gone missing. Woken to discover they now lived in a world where the Darkness that had until then been a kind of fairytale had finally found them and brought with it Randall Caine; and they were many years from being old enough or strong enough to face either. They hadn't known then they had fourteen long years of torment and fear ahead of them, nor that there would follow years after their triumph where they'd still feel shackled to the choices that they'd made, and the roads not taken.

Alex took a deep breath in and then cast his ice blue eyes back out over the turquoise expanse that reached to the horizon. *So much beauty*, he thought to himself, *it is possible, even if it doesn't feel like it's mine.* Another deep breath and then he gave Joah what he knew he would have to give the others once they returned.

"Kale is alive." He whispered it, almost inaudibly, but Joah heard him just the same. Even though it was madness, he had no doubt Alex had handed him the truth. Still, as it sunk in, as the possibilities chased away the impossible, he began to understand just how wonderful and awful this truth would be, for all of them.

"No," he whispered, thinking first of Medea and all that she would lose and gain once she found out. "No," he repeated, horrified and afraid.

"I know," Alex said in reply. Not sure exactly what his friend was seeing but understanding just the same. It had taken them five long years to rebuild after that day on the mountain shelf when Kale had given her life for Derin, for all of them. It had taken so much struggle and heartache to come back from letting her go and accepting that none of them could have saved her. Now, she was alive and by some dark and unknown game of fate she'd been cast across the vast reach of time and space and landed back where all of their stories had begun, on Earth. It wasn't knowing that she was there that might destroy them all, it was that they wouldn't be able to leave it alone. They wouldn't be able to leave *her* alone. Earth was doomed. It had lost its fight with the Darkness and was awaiting its final sentence, or so they thought. Leaving her there was a death sentence.

That's when Alex got it—why his parents had been calling him home all day, why there'd been a dark cloud of destiny and responsibility and fear hanging over him. He'd thought he was keeping her secret and safe and all to himself, but they already knew.

"We've got to go." Alex stood up and started to march off to where he'd left his things, but Joah took a few more moments to settle into his shock. *This couldn't be happening. Not now. Not after Medea had finally found happiness and peace. Not after they'd all finally begun to rebuild their lives, and their hearts, and their destinies, so that they could move on.* He knew that's how it all worked. Fate played games with the lives of whoever it wanted to. It tortured and mocked and could bring you to your knees when only a moment before you'd been sure of yourself and standing tall.

Joah rose and hurried to follow his friend. He wasn't sure how things were going to unfold but he wasn't one to hide from any kind of fight. It didn't matter what was coming for them, he would face it as he always had, head on. He needed to get back to his family, his friends, Medea. All that mattered now was standing with them against whatever force was barreling towards them, destruction in mind.

FOURTEEN

AND SO IT WAS that not long after they'd gathered on the anniversary of the end of Caine and the Darkness on Alpha Iridium, the same group of survivors gathered once again. This time not to talk about battles fought and won but battles that were unfolding around them. Firelight danced in their eyes, some knowing and some soon to be, and the golden glow illuminated the dark and secret thing that was hurtling towards them all.

"What are we going to do?" Corin was the first to step in with what they were all trying to figure out. His blue eyes were dark violet in the firelight. As always, they looked for what others did not always want to see, the practical path ahead.

"We bring her home." It was Derin. He stood up and looked around at his friends and his family and the last eyes he met, even though he was afraid, were Medea's. He could see both the heartbreak and the hope that he believed were mirrored in his own, but she nodded once, sadly, before looking away from him.

"How in the hell do we do that?" Corin asked, but in his mind a different question rose. *How in the hell do we avoid it?* His friends, these people who had become his family, would absolutely find a way to accomplish it, even though it seemed like an impossible task. Worse, they would die trying if they had to.

His exasperation was met with silence.

"Dad?" Derin asked, trepidation carrying his voice quietly to his father. That single word was filled with so much hope and longing that Dellerim was overwhelmed for a moment. Could it be that simple? Bringing her home.

"I have to tell you a story," Dellerim whispered. The sound so quiet it was like a sigh on the evening breeze, but the fear that carried it into the night was unmistakable. There was a deep pause where no one moved or drew a breath. He reached for Cyan's hand and interlaced his fingers with hers and then one at a time he looked at his sons. First Derin and then Alex, where his gaze lingered. They were so much alike, tied together in a way that both broke his heart and made him proud. He didn't want what he was about to tell them to change anything; but that wasn't his to decide. "It's time you all knew the truth."

No one said a word. Dellerim finally looked away from Alex to meet the eyes of the other Founders. First Joah and Arin's parents. Arianna, bright and bubbly and beautiful. Her cherry hair and eyes both radiant, even in the dark, and set against her tanned skin which glowed in the firelight. Next to her was her partner Joachim, who like his oldest son was capable of both immense humor and intense seriousness. His emerald eyes were the same sparkling shade as Joah's and he wore his snow white hair long and tied back at the nape of his neck. Arianna and Joachim were leaning into one another without even noticing, which was the way they'd been since time began for them. Casual and effortless, as if being in the world was a kind of afterthought—it's why they fit together so well.

Next, he looked to Kiernan and Kendra, huddled close, leaning into one another like two exotic birds. Peaceful and yet poised, able to take flight at any moment. Kiernan's silver eyes took in everything. He was smart and discerning and of all of them Dellerim suspected he would be the least surprised about what he was about to hear. His curly silver hair almost twinkled as the light shifted and danced around them and it cast shadows across his dark skin in beautiful patterns. Kendra was a stunning contrast next to him. Honey colored eyes that were kind, and compassionate, and told the story of a heart that was meant for the wild, that had space also for everyone and everything. Her jet-black hair carved a dark river down her back that Kiernan wove one of his hands through, a nervous and unconscious habit.

They were his first family: The Founders. Them and Cyan. It was here that he would have to confess his betrayal of their deepest trust, whether he wanted to or not.

On a night long ago, the Founders had gone to sleep to try and stop the coming of the Dark. It was a decision born of bravery but also folly. They could never have imagined that trying to stop fate from finding its way into the waking world would cause so much damage. There'd been a kind of calling in the air that had begged them to try. Later, they would wonder if it hadn't been the Darkness itself, but the truth was much simpler than that. Forces they'd already defied more than once had come looking for them once again. There was a balance meant to be kept, and this time they would not be allowed to succeed or escape. They were caught in their dreaming like prey in a web, unable to wake or communicate with the outside world—a price paid for believing they had more power than the forces that ruled the universe.

They'd been aware of each other while in that strange sleep that lasted fourteen years, aware also that Caine had somehow managed to capture three of their children as well as Cyan. There they remained. Trapped, powerless, tortured by their fear for those left to struggle and fight and somehow survive the waking world after the coming of Caine. With only glimpses of the outside world, moments laid one over the other obscured the passage of time and yet it felt like an eternity, trapped in that darkness waiting to watch their destiny, and that of those they loved unfold.

Dellerim couldn't believe how much he'd lost with one simple mistake. One arrogant choice had ruined everything. He believed he was strong enough to beat the Darkness back and was certain he could outsmart Fate in doing so. Instead, he had to watch as the life he built was stolen from him and he could blame no one but himself. Day by day. Moment by moment. Breath by breath. One son raised by a monster, the other forced to become an adult far before his time, and the love of his life a prisoner, forced to become a version of herself she'd never fully recover from being.

There seemed to be no way out and nothing that any of them could do. Arianna, Kendra, Kiernan, Joachim, and Dellerim were trapped and at the mercy of whoever had built their strange prison. No matter what they tried, no matter what magic they worked or what strength they reached for, their prison held, until that final night when the Darkness began to falter and crack and the Light began to shine through.

They'd felt it the moment it happened. The outcome of the battle between light and dark shifted their way. They were finally able to see the outside world, able to watch it all unfold even as they remained helpless. They saw that final day of Caine's rule and the final fight when Kale faced him and in some ways herself. Dellerim hadn't known there could be a torture worse than the fourteen years he'd already endured, but then he watched as one son fell and the other was forced to witness it, helpless, and he knew deep down inside some of all this was his fault. In that last moment, when their prison had begun to shatter, he'd made the choice that would change the course of his life, both for all that was to come and for much of what had already been.

He hadn't entirely known what he was doing, but there was a kind of memory that rose from deep within. With it, came a rising certainty that he could intervene. Anguish mixed with fury awoke in him an ancient power from an unknown source and he'd scooped Kale up hoping to save her life. Only for some reason still out of sight, he hadn't been able to keep her on Alpha Iridium, and so he'd carried her to the only place the universe would let him, the place where she'd been born. He still wasn't sure how he'd done it. Dellerim thought at the time, foolishly, that he'd be able to save her and bring her back, but it hadn't been possible. Kale had ended up on Earth, and he'd ended up with a secret he'd kept until tonight.

"I've tried to bring her home. I can't get to her." It was barely a whisper. Dellerim's ice blue eyes dropped to the ground and he savored one last moment before he faced his biggest mistake.

Silence followed: one deep and dark, poised to unravel them all.

"Did you know?" Derin stared at his mother with both a mixture of disgust and fury. He wasn't sure why but it seemed to matter. This would be one betrayal too many and just after he'd begun to trust her again.

Cyan shook her head and took a moment to look both her sons in the eye before scanning their whole group. "No," she whispered, and then louder, "no, I didn't know." Then so quietly the crackling of the fire swallowed every word, "I'm so, so sorry."

"This is all my fault. Only me. I'm sorry." It was strange, Dellerim realized, to be the villain and yet have no one be willing to see or admit it.

The silence that followed was vast and deep and threatened to consume some of what this family of survivors had built.

"What are we going to do?" Jaren asked, intentionally breaking the spell. "We can't just leave her there." He looked around hoping he wasn't the only one sure of this singular fact. He met Corin's gaze and then Medea's and could feel in different ways what all this meant to them. When his eyes connected with Arin's, he paused there and in that safe space of their friendship realized he'd been holding his breath. She smiled and nodded, and he felt his whole being relax into breathing and arrive in the moment again.

"No, we're going to go get her. If you put her there, then there has to be a way for us to bring her back." Derin stood again and stepped into the circle, taking charge. He hadn't considered what bringing her back to Alpha Iridium would mean—that he'd have to make a choice and once again he'd have to lose something. All he could think about was that he could undo the fact that she'd given her life for his. He could make things right. It never occurred to him that things not being what you wanted them to be, didn't actually make them wrong.

Medea listened in stunned silence. None of it seemed real. Her best friend, her sister, was alive, stranded on Earth both near and somehow very far from them all. They had a chance to save her and bring her back somehow. Kale could have another shot at happiness, and Medea would get her closest friend back. It didn't matter that in returning Medea would lose the one thing her heart had finally opened up to. They were all still making sacrifices—to rebuild, to fight for justice, to create a better world. *Hadn't the biggest of all sacrifices already been made anyway?* If Kale could sacrifice her life, like so many had on that final dark night, then Medea could certainly sacrifice a little joy and happiness.

She understood now why she'd felt pulled. Kale had been calling out to her, or some kind of destiny had. Either way, she could finally make things right and give up a fraction of what her friend had given up to set the world on its feet again. She felt a sharp pain shoot through her and settle in her chest, and all she could think was that she would suffer a thousand times that pain if it meant Kale could come back to them all.

Fingers interlaced with hers, and she looked down and then up into Joah's worried gaze. He hadn't stopped watching her since Dellerim began his tale. He watched her wander from hope to heartbreak, grief to shame: a synopsis in some ways of the five years since the downfall of Caine. During that time, their friendship had blossomed into something both new and remembered and he'd gotten to know her better than most. He understood that she was a fierce friend, loving and devoted. When it came to Kale, however, beyond the sisterhood, there was a kind of reverence that lived in the space between them that made it possible for Medea to sacrifice so much of herself when it was needed. For a long time, it had been in pursuit Kale's destiny, that relentless drive towards destroying Caine. In the past five years, it had been a stubborn unwillingness to move on. Medea had spent all that time honoring her friend's heart and legacy, even when it meant ignoring her own. Now, when she'd finally stepped out of Kale's shadow to find her own life in the light, it seemed it wasn't quite meant to be. Joah thought she deserved better. He thought they all did. He would never quite understand this whole idea of destiny and some grand force in the universe playing with all of their lives.

"You okay?" he asked her quietly, his emerald eyes radiating concern. A lock of white hair spilled down and covered one of his eyes, and before replying, she reached up and swept it aside. It was such a casual gesture in the face of so much upheaval that the contrast stopped his breath for a moment.

"We're going to get her back. Kale is coming home, Joah. We can do this. I know it." Her voice sounded small and desperate and yet she needed to cling to the possibility of it all, needed to believe that if they could set this right the world would make sense in a way it hadn't for a very long time.

"Okay, Medea, I know. I know." He pressed his forehead into hers and just breathed. As always when they were near like this, they found a kind of synchronicity that drew a veil between them and the outside world. The group around them had dissolved into conversations in small clusters and no one seemed to have any answers or even an idea of the way forward. Medea and Joah stayed like that, quiet, separate from the world, lost in a kind of communion they could only find together.

Derin felt it happen—the moment she stepped away from him and out of reach. He'd spent so much time like that when it came to Medea that it was a feeling too familiar to miss. He couldn't blame her and still it hurt. She was Kale's again, and Joah's. If he was being honest, he wasn't sure how he felt about it or if he could even begin to promise her what she deserved.

Alone, unsure, and confused, Derin left his friends and family seated around the fire and wandered away. He needed time to figure out what he wanted and also who he wanted to be. In a world that had often given him very little choice, it seemed now he had a big one to make. Kale was alive. How many times had he dreamed about this day? How many times had he hoped and wished their story could've ended differently? Yet, he'd only just figured out how to move on. How to begin again? Last night, with Medea, he'd felt happy and sure and hopeful. Now, it was all gone again.

He wasn't sure where he was going but all he could think about was putting space between himself and everyone else. As the group broke up with no resolution or plan laid out in front of them, no one chose to chase Derin down. He wasn't sure whether he was grateful or disappointed.

FIFTEEN

CYAN FOUND ALEX at the end of the long wooden dock that stretched out into the ocean. She could still remember being perched in that same spot, watching her young sons as they leapt into the sea with joyful shouts and screams. As with all memories of that long ago time when she'd believed life would always be simple and easy, it came with a kind of ache that left her breathless. She'd been foolish enough then to believe their happiness would last forever. She would never make that mistake again. When she repaired her relationship with her sons, and she would somehow before all this was done, she would never again waste a moment on anything but delighting in what they had, however brief or fleeting.

Alex was dangling his feet into the warm evening sea. His shoulders slumped against the backdrop of ocean and night sky. Waves painted with silver white from the moon above rose and fell softly in the midnight breeze. Without a word, she sat down beside him and mimicked his easy seat even though she knew, like her, he was unsettled and even a little bit afraid. The silence stretched out around them for what seemed like an eternity before she chose to break it.

"I saw your face. Tonight. When we told everyone Kale was alive." She waited for him to meet her gaze. "You already knew." She stared at his beautiful face, amazed that, even in the challenges of their relationship, she could see him this way, could marvel at how something so beautiful and pure could have come from her. It never stopped amazing her, how grown up he was, that she could have a son who was almost thirty. She'd missed almost half of his life yet he'd still become the most remarkable man, even if how it had come about wasn't what she'd dreamed for him. He had moments, of course, like the one they were in, when he indulged this kind of childishness that amused her despite herself. She often wondered if it wasn't so that he could reach for a thing that should've been but wasn't. He'd lost his childhood becoming a leader and caretaker for the other children. They never spoke about it, but it was always there. He avoided all conversations about that time of his life and yet as his mother, with her blood and magic running through him, she knew.

Alex sighed, a sound he realized he'd been making frequently of late. "I've been dreaming of her. I've known for a little while." He hadn't realized it until he said it aloud how badly he'd still wanted to keep it from the one person who would know what it meant.

"I see." Cyan let the gravity of this new revelation sink in. She wasn't sure how much more she could take. She'd thought change was approaching, that she was on the verge of getting her sons back. Yes, there was a lot of healing and work to do still but something had shifted and she was sure they were finally going to make their way back to her. It had just been another cruel trick of fate. She thought they were coming back together, but it was only to make it harder when they were taken away because that's what this was she realized. Derin would find a way to Kale and Alex would never let him go alone, and not just because of his brother, she realized with a growing sense of dread.

"Did you know?" Alex asked her and then couldn't help himself when he added softly, "don't lie to me."

"I didn't." Cyan took a deep breath and tried to press away the shock and betrayal that rose up when she thought of Dellerim keeping this secret from her for so long. "I thought she was gone, just like you did. I've mourned her every day. Along with the part I played." She wondered, as she said it, if the price would now be both her sons.

"He's only just found happiness and now it's about to be torn away from him again." He couldn't keep the anger out of his voice. The thought of Derin losing what little joy he had found again so quickly broke his heart. There was something else lingering just below the surface of that truth—that for a few days Kale had belonged only to him. This secret that the world was indeed miraculous and amazing and that anything was possible. It had all gotten dulled and dirtied now that the truth belonged to everyone.

"I'm not even sure we'll be able to do anything for her," Cyan said, ashamed that she was unable to hide the hope she felt when she said it.

"Don't be a fool, Mother," he snapped, regretting it immediately. Cyan flinched but he went on, committed in anger and resentment to share some of the burden he was carrying with her. "If Dad put her there then he can surely bring her back. He has to. Derin will never let it go. Not now." Alex couldn't help it, he was furious, and though he couldn't quite understand where some of it was coming from, he needed somewhere to put it just the same, as always it felt easiest to put it on her.

"And what about you, Alex? What does this all mean for you?" She felt so very far away from him, farther than she'd ever been from her oldest son. Her first hope for a future that had never come. He'd been robbed; first of his childhood but since then of so much more. It didn't matter that she saw him making choices that kept him isolated and steeped in old anger. It mattered that the beginning of that story was him being left to care for the other children of the Founders and then leading the fight to Caine, which he still believed had defeated him. It mattered that all that had unfolded because of her choice. She shared it with the other Founders, with her partner Dellerim, but she was his mother. She should have protected him. Every time she felt that truth, it shot a breathtaking pain through her whole body.

"What I need and want has always managed to come last. Why stop now?" Alex spat the words out bitterly. They punctuated the silence so that it almost rang. On its heels came absolute quiet, interrupted only by the whisper of sea lapping at the dock beneath them. Eventually, he stood and glanced down at Cyan, giving her a sad smile. In that moment, it was the only apology he could offer. He shook his head and turned to walk away.

It hit him—that change itself could also be a chameleon. It could come slowly, so slowly you barely noticed it until something drastic was altered. It could also sweep you up in a fast and violent current of transformation so that you could barely catch your breath. It had felt so slow—the journey back from what happened on Caine's last day and what they'd learned about their mother while he ruled. Forgiveness had unfurled and unfolded between them almost imperceptibly, a flower blooming but watched in real time. He barely even noticed it, and yet it had almost fully come into being. Too long had he hesitated to reach for what they both needed even when he'd felt the beginnings of being ready to. He'd resisted because whether he knew it consciously or not, his own forgiveness would need to follow in the wake of hers and he was not ready for that just yet. Now this. This upheaval of the fragile peace they'd begun to build and settle into.

"Let's hope a new day will offer new perspective," he said, more to himself than to her. He began to walk down the dock towards the shore. "Goodnight, Mom," he threw over his shoulder, a wary afterthought. Anyone who knew him well would hear the heartache beneath the casualness. The moonlight carried him back along the dock so that she was able to watch him the whole way. Her heart ached and she fought the urge to burst into sobs even as she longed to let some of her anguish out into the night. No, she'd hold onto it a little longer. In some ways, it was all she had left of the perfect life they'd built and lived before the night they'd tried to stop Caine's coming to Alpha Iridium.

She threw her thoughts towards the mystery of Kale and how Dellerim had managed to save her, to set her free from Alpha Iridium, to have kept her from death and the mystery that awaited all of us on the other side of it. How he'd done it took her breath away. What it would cost them terrified her. Now Kale unknowingly held a kind of power that could tear her family to shreds, and Cyan wasn't sure how she felt about it or how she could possibly stop it all from ending in disaster. *Why now, after so many years, had this ghost from their past decided to haunt them again? Why had Dellerim chosen now to reveal what he'd done and what he knew?*

She'd loved Kale and felt a kind of kinship with her. In all the years she'd spent trapped as Caine's prisoner, she'd only ever been able to reach Kale. Over the years, she watched and admired her strength, determination, and perseverance, even as the world and all the losses she suffered tried to tear her down. Cyan had marveled at how a young woman, not fully herself, had managed to live up to the kind of story that was foretold in an ancient Prophecy most of them hadn't believed in. As she watched her grow from a feisty child to an impassioned and driven leader, Cyan had never doubted that Kale was a force to be reckoned with. She imagined when she truly found her whole self Kale would be a formidable woman, one she'd be proud to call friend, or yes, even daughter. Now it felt precarious, what Kale being alive could do to them all, what it meant. Cyan couldn't help herself; for a moment, she wished they'd never found out.

Her head was spinning. She felt like she was drowning in all the questions and uncertainty. She felt like that monster of truth that was barreling towards them was even bigger and wilder and more dangerous than she could imagine. She couldn't see it, couldn't understand what was coming at them, or why. But hadn't she known, felt, something big and awful was headed their way?

She looked up. With the moon nearing full, there weren't as many stars in the sky as on those dark nights she loved so much, but it still took her breath away. It reminded her things weren't always what they seemed on the surface, that sometimes you needed to get much closer to really understand what you were looking at. Yet, it was okay to sit back, far away and out of reach, and admire the beauty in that sight, too.

As always, when she sat like this under the night sky, she searched the heavens for Earth. *Which star, which sparkling light,* she wondered, *meant to be extinct, belonged to the place she'd come from so many years ago?* That very one that had also birthed Kale and now had managed to call her home.

With that thought in mind, she got up and wandered away from the ocean and her troubled thoughts, and decided it was time to face Dellerim.

She found him where she expected to, seated in a wooden chair on the balcony off their large bedroom. She sat down quietly beside him and took one of his hands in hers and she could feel the relief sweep through him with her gentle offering when he relaxed beside her. She let the silence wrap itself around them both and breathed deep, savoring the calm before she had to break it.

"How could you?" she finally asked him, though she wasn't sure if she was asking why he'd done what he had, or why he'd kept it from her.

"I don't know." He shrugged and the invisible weight of shame and worry that he was carrying on his shoulders made it a slow and heavy gesture. "I just," he paused, reaching for the right words, "Derin was so broken, and she'd saved him, us, and it was the only thing I could do in that moment after fourteen years of being helpless." He stepped back into the quiet with her, and they stayed that way while the minutes wandered past. "I didn't know I couldn't keep her here. Keep her now." He went on. "I didn't know when I began it that fate would only let me put her in one time, in one place. And I didn't know it would all come back to find us like this." But he had known, deep down, just like any of them would have. *Weren't they here because of fate's unfolding and because the powers in the universe allowed it to be so?* Yet, there was a price to be paid for balance and for taking what you weren't meant to.

She didn't need to look at him to know that tears were sliding down his cheeks, silver in the moonlight. She could feel his sorrow and his regret as if they were ocean waves crashing up against her.

"You chose not to tell me. Any of it." She couldn't look at him. She was too afraid of what he was going to tell her and too afraid of what she might see in his eyes.

"It's just...I meant to. Then when you got back and we were together again after so long, I just wanted to savor the peace and quiet of it all. It was so hard, with the boys, how angry and hurt they both were," he paused when he felt her stiffen beside him, a silent acknowledgement that she was the cause, but then he pushed on, "and then I wasn't sure we would tell them and I didn't want you to have to keep this big a secret from them because..." he paused again and realized truth could be such a big and powerful thing. Even in silence, it could be heard, echoing, echoing.

"Because they'd never forgive me," she whispered it both to him and to the night, ashamed because it was true. She'd worn out their trust with all the truths revealed about how she'd helped Caine during his rule. It still didn't matter that she'd done it to protect them because she'd also done it selfishly. She chose her own singular family over countless others, over the people of Alpha Iridium as a whole. People had suffered and been hurt because of her and that's what they couldn't forget no matter how hard they tried. "Come here," she whispered, and Dellerim dropped to his knees in front of her and met her gaze. "We will survive this. It's okay. I forgive you. I know you kept your secret to protect me. Just maybe, not again, okay? I couldn't bear it."

He nodded and then dropped his eyes from hers and buried his head in her shoulder. How could he tell her, about that other glimpse he'd had while spiriting Kale away? That momentary vision of another time and another place that had shaken him to his core. *It's not true,* he told himself as he wrapped his secret up safe and sound and buried it away.

She took his face in her hands and looked deep into his iridescent blue eyes again and grabbed hold of that one and only truth that had mattered for all the years they'd spent together. "I love you, always," she offered him, and without hesitation he quickly and honestly offered it back.

Whether they knew it or not, the universe watched, and listened, and believed them. That didn't mean it would alter its plans.

SIXTEEN

KALE

I DON'T KNOW what startled me, but waking came fast. One minute I was in that dark abyss colored by dreams; the next I was wide awake. It was the same dream again and again. Maybe because I had so few memories outside of the past weeks that my mind reached for this kind of absurdity. In the dream, there is a faraway place, seemingly untouched by the chaos and heartache that surrounds us here on Earth. It feels familiar yet I have no way of even knowing what that means. There is a great big darkness inside of me where the truth must be hiding but I can't seem to shine a light into it. For the first time, I am grateful for that dark mystery because getting lost inside it meant I wasn't dreaming about fire, and screaming, and everyone and everything I'd ever known disappearing while I sat helpless and too afraid to act.

For a moment more, as that dream world pulls at me, I can't quite remember where I am in the here and now. Or maybe it's that I can't remember what the here and now actually are. Then I let it go.

I sit up, shake myself awake, and look around. Stepping into the inevitable remembering of how terrible the past couple days have been, there is a deep ache inside me. It feels like hunger but I know that's a lie. This feeling never fades. It is a longing to be whole again, to find out what and who I am. It is a longing also, I suspect, to have the world around me make sense again. I say 'again' but the truth is I have nothing before a day a few weeks ago when I washed up on the beach and Rogan found me. Nothing except dark, and fear, and waves and stars. And cold, both inside and out. That single memory is so powerful I shiver and then focus my eyes to look around, trying to escape it.

The small fire we'd built last night, now smoldering, is offering tiny wisps of smoke into the morning air as Rogan adds fuel to it. She has a haunted look about her and there's no way for me to be able to tell which part of the last forty-eight hours weighs heaviest. I'm quiet as I sit up. I don't want to disturb her or remind her that I'm here. There is a kind of safety in not being seen or known that I can't quite describe, yet I realize it has been a habit, the hiding in plain sight, that I've indulged a lot over the few weeks since I've joined her small community.

Not knowing what to do or say, I simply watch as she builds up the fire. She is strong and elegant all at once, even this morning, wrapped in sorrow and fear and the heaviness of the task we face which isn't yet entirely clear. We've been two days tracking the party that took our village hostage. Two days keeping pace with monsters dressed up as men with motives we can't even begin to imagine or understand.

"I wasn't sure how long you'd sleep," Rogan says without looking at me. "I got up and found us some food. There's some fruit here and I found a nest I was able to raid for eggs. We'll not go hungry at least."

"Rogan," I offer into the space between us, a plea, and yet I don't know for what.

"I knew something awful was coming. I knew it the moment..." she stops herself but it's too late. I know what she means. She means the moment she found me. Somehow for her, maybe for all of them, I'm the beginning of all this. But that's crazy isn't it?

They welcomed me in and offered me shelter and a home amongst their people. They were kind, accepting, loving even. They were also fascinated with the mystery I presented, and I could tell that each of them puzzled away at it in different ways. I'd been with them three weeks and they hadn't given me a name. Of course, I hadn't chosen one either. What does that say about me?

"I'm sorry," Rogan says, finally meeting my gaze. "You don't deserve that. It's just, everything is gone, and somewhere buried in the ashes is the place it all began and it feels somehow like that was weeks ago." She shrugs and shakes her head, helpless. *Is it true*, I wonder, *did I somehow do this to them?*

I nod as I look down at the plate she's placed in front of me, a large grey-green stone, and I slowly begin to eat, savoring each bite as if it might be my last. The flavors burst and dance in my mouth. I feel starved of this kind of indulgence, of being able to pause and savor, like there is nothing beyond the experience of the moment. I can tell Rogan is watching me but I don't care. There is so very little of me to be had. Every new memory and moment I can hold onto feels precious even the ones laid over horror and pain.

I toss a handful of berries into my mouth and the juice erupts when I bite down. It is somehow tart and sweet and my whole mouth is alive with the warm syrupy liquid the burst berries set free. I realize I've gotten lost in memorizing the texture and the taste, lost in trying to make my life feel big by adding memory upon memory to a place currently void and empty. *I can't help myself*, I sigh. *It's delight mixed with resignation*, as I open my eyes.

"What now?" I ask Rogan. There is a kind of desire within me to take charge and lead us towards whatever end is heading our way. Yet, I know it's not my place even as I wonder where this desire comes from and if it's a clue as to who I was, once upon a time.

"We aren't far behind them. They're moving with a lot of people, I fear a lot of them prisoners, but it's slowed them down. We'll catch them today. That I can promise you." She is determined and fierce, and though I know we are up against something big and scary, I can see that she will be a force worth fearing in her quest to save her friends and family. To save Firth.

"And then?" I can't help it, the more she speaks the more I feel safe and certain about the world in front of us, and I want her to tell me everything.

"And then, based on what we find, we figure out how to get our people back." The fire in her eyes burns brighter, and I believe her. Somehow, some way, we will make everything right again. I will get a chance to set things right.

I can see when her mind goes to Firth. There is a kind of ease that creeps into her body and softens her, giving away that she's thinking of her partner. I've been told they've been together for a few years and there are definitely moments when you can see that familiarity between them; that sense of a well-worn path walked together that has made them comfortable as a pair. Yet, there are times when they seem youthful and indulgent also, as if they've only just met and are completely wrapped up in all that comes with new love. Every time I watch them together, I expect to feel something but there is just a hole where whatever it is once lived. It's big enough that I know what fits there matters, but all it feels like is an absence of something.

"Just you and I?" I ask it as if I don't already know the answer. Even with her certainty and mine, it's hard to imagine how we are going to beat an army back to save our people.

"That's all we've got I'm afraid." She offers me a rueful smile.

Again, I nod and then I close my eyes and, in that darkness, watch the memory of our home burning. I watch the chaos and the horror rise up inside me and I face it, not because I am brave, but because I deserve to watch what I sat by and allowed.

Of course, there is still the mystery of why I went unseen, curled up in what felt like a tiny shelter though I know that wasn't the case. The world burned and the men looked for prisoners and whatever else they could smash and destroy, and no one saw me, cowering there in the shade. I hadn't been able to feel the heat or even smell the smoke, though I knew that they were both pressing in around that tiny, safe space. I remember feeling like I'd been wrapped up, cradled, and yet I couldn't understand what that meant, only that in some ways I was safe. The terror had been an ocean I could drown in, so that I was pinned to the spot, and every time I thought of leaping up to help or fight it pressed me down and held me in place. There was a kind of energy that set me rocking, as if I was both trying to remain and trying to fight myself free, and I struggle to understand, even in the not knowing of who I am, how I stayed safe while everything around me burned.

It is a deep well that holds my shame, and I'm not sure it'll ever be empty again.

We haven't talked about it yet—the unspoken thing from the raid—why I was the only one who'd made it out unscathed and free. I suspect Rogan doesn't want to know. In some ways, neither do I because I'm afraid the truth, however strange and bizarre, is a thing that will keep me separate.

There is a deep and aching longing inside me to belong, to be part of this family, this community that has taken me in so lovingly. I want to be wanted and needed and even relied on. I want this to be home. Of course, 'this' no longer exists. It was burned to the ground while I cowered in the shadows and did nothing. *How could they ever accept me now?*

"We should pack up and start our day," Rogan has been watching me. I can feel it when she tries to look into me to grab hold of some idea of who I am and where I'm from. "We want to catch up to them as soon as we can. The more time we have to form a plan, the better."

I nod and begin to stand, wiping dried leaves and dirt off my pants. My movements are slow and sluggish. It feels almost as if my body isn't my own. There is the heaviness of the fear and worry, too—the pressure of not knowing what we are going to face when we find our people. It doesn't feel comfortable, being so afraid, and yet I can't remember if it's something that suits me or not: only that big, black emptiness remains where there would be any story of the life I had before finding my way here. I wonder if I'll ever get it back. I wonder what kind of past is so unbearable my own mind keeps it from me. Most of all I wonder if I'm better off with that fortress built up around any idea of who or what I am and why.

SEVENTEEN

ALEX WOKE WITH a start. The dream tossed him into the waking world so violently he sat up and gasped for breath. He'd only meant to close his eyes for a few minutes, but somehow that other place, the one with that other heartbeat quietly connected to his, had pulled him deep into sleep. Now, the waking was just as shocking as the dreaming had been.

He was drenched, soaked through with worry, panic, and adrenaline. He shook himself to try and break free of what he'd seen in the dream but it wasn't going to let him go. Kale was with another woman, one he was sure he'd seen before.

They'd made camp maybe half a day's walk from some kind of city. He'd seen large stone walls surrounding the outer city limit and around them fields being farmed by gaunt and worn out people chained together. He'd watched as scores of captives were led inside the city walls, wide-eyed and terrified. The men and women guarding them struck out at them often, knocking women, men, and even children to the ground in a kind of vicious triumph that made him gag. It sickened him, watching the tormentors as they took a kind of delight in whipping and punishing their captives. As he hurried away from the horrors that reminded him too much of the days of Caine but were somehow even worse, he glimpsed Kale and the woman where they'd made camp not far from the city's outer limits. He still couldn't believe it was her and that he'd found her. His awareness dropped down in front of her and across the smoldering fire his eyes had met hers.

"Did you see her?" Alex jumped when his brother spoke. Instantly feeling that deep sense of panic as if he'd been caught doing something wrong, his heart raced; in that quiet galloping, it whispered to him that he had. He pressed aside that truth and composed himself as best he could.

"What do you mean?" Alex stammered, a wave of shame washing through him.

"Don't patronize me," Derin said, unsure at first of what he was feeling.

Alex looked up and into his brother's eyes, a mirror image of his own, and nodded slowly. He couldn't manage to find his voice. Derin winced, the pain just beginning to surface, but sharp and jagged already. He wasn't sure what stung more, that his brother had been dreaming of Kale or that he hadn't told him.

"How did you know?" Alex felt both relieved and terrified to be free of the truth that had been burning a hole inside of him. He wasn't yet sure what was happening or why but the most important person in his life was his brother. There was nothing he wouldn't sacrifice for his brother's happiness, even a secret longing of his heart. It struck him then that he'd been allowing himself to get caught up with the dreaming of something he would never actually allow. Maybe that's why he'd held on to the secret for so long because now he'd have to give up on the fantasy that came with it. He'd never take anything from Derin, not after his brother had already lost so much, and even if it meant Alex had to sacrifice his own happiness and fulfillment.

"Dad has kept this secret so long. I couldn't stop wondering why now. Why tell us now when nothing has changed?" Derin tried to keep the hurt out of his voice, this deep wounding that his recent realization had left him with.

Alex answered his brother with silence, wide-eyed and filled with regret. In five years, they'd shared everything with not a secret kept between them. Five years during which they'd become so close that their pain and joy, sorrow and happiness, had intertwined so that they'd become united in all things. Yet, Alex had forgotten that nothing was permanent or guaranteed, and he'd risked too much in keeping this secret. He hadn't meant to put something in danger that mattered more to him than anything, but here they were. With that realization he made a vow, that he'd do everything he could to set things right and help his brother finally find the happiness he deserved no matter what it looked like or where it was meant to lead them.

"Except something has changed." Derin's voice was clipped when he interrupted his brother's thoughts, betraying a deep emotion being held at bay. "And there's only one reason he'd bring this up now. To protect one of us. If keeping the secret protected me, then revealing it had to protect you." Bitterness swelled up in Derin so violently he dropped to the ground, carried there on unsteady legs, and buried his head in his hands. "On top of everything else, he chose you over me."

Alex climbed out of bed and knelt before his brother.

"Derin, that's not what's happening here." He met his brother's intense gaze when he looked up, a mirror for his own, and pleaded silently that he would not lose the only thing that truly mattered to him on this world. He hadn't really thought it through, what it would cost him to keep something like this from his brother, but he could fix it.

"Why would you keep this from me?" Derin pleaded, realizing more than anything else he was hurt by his brother's choice.

What could Alex tell Derin to satisfy him? How could he both protect him and yet give him the power to make his own choice? Beyond that, how could Alex finally do what he hadn't been able to on that last night of Caine's and stand up to fight?

It had haunted him for a long time. If he was being honest, it still did, but he'd learned to build a life around what he thought was the disgrace of being unable to act all those years ago. He'd watched his brother fall and hadn't been strong enough to intervene. When Kale had shown up to fight, he'd been helpless, no stronger than a small child, so that she'd had to carry the weight of all their destinies all on her own. He couldn't escape the certainty that he'd been meant to lead and fight and yet it hadn't unfolded that way. *Unless. Unless...* whispered a quiet voice inside him, but he was not ready to hear it just yet.

Alex shook himself out of his reverie. "I thought I could protect you. Protect all of us." It was some of the truth, but not all. "And Dad didn't choose me, he chose us. He didn't want there to be a secret between us. I should have been the one to make that choice. I'm sorry I waited so long to tell you. I just wasn't sure what to do." He stopped here knowing there was more to say and yet not able to form any of the words to say it with.

Derin nodded thoughtfully. The gesture, an exclamation point on what had been said, let the brothers slip into a comfortable silence together. In it, they wandered a little further away from each other: Derin towards that pull of his heart, once again in two very different directions, and Alex towards a story not meant for him just yet.

"Why you? Why now?" Derin finally asked, afraid of the answer even as he pressed the questions towards his brother. The first thing that had come to mind when he'd realized Alex was dreaming of her and not him was just that, *why not me?* Was it because he'd moved on or was it something more, and which of those he'd wondered, upset him most?

"Does it matter?" Alex replied, not wanting to wonder about the answer himself. "We found her." He didn't know how to face what he couldn't understand or the confusing mix of emotions that surfaced in the moments after he woke from dreaming of her. It was true he wanted to keep her to himself, even though it had felt like a small betrayal, but there was something more. Because he couldn't quite grab hold of it, he wasn't ready to share.

"Alex, talk to me. What's really going on?" Derin felt like his head was spinning. Everything that had seemed certain and safe, the solid ground that he thought he'd finally found, was threatening to fall from underfoot. It left him feeling disoriented in a way that was unsettling. He would not let his relationship to his brother fall into that void. What they had needed to remain certain.

"It's just I keep wondering, aren't we ever going to escape that night and the choices we did and didn't make?" Alex looked away from his brother. He'd handed over the truth and yet it wasn't entirely the answer to his brother's question. How could he answer when he hadn't fully admitted to himself how he was feeling or what was going on.

"That's not how lives are built, are they? I'm not sure we can be whole if we tear ourselves away from who we were Alex." The irony wasn't lost on Derin, that he could live fourteen years of his life as something he wasn't meant to be, that he could spend the better part of the last five years fighting to let go of the past and live in the moment, and now he was lecturing his brother as if he was fully living the wisdom he was offering up.

"And what will you do once you've brought her back? Now that you have Medea, will you be able to choose?" Alex asked the question not because his heart longed to know but because he truly cared what happened to Derin. He would give anything for his brother's happiness, including his own. Neither of them had had the life they deserved, and they could not know whether either of them would have it yet, but the brothers knew they wouldn't leave the other behind on the path to finding happiness and fulfillment, no matter what it cost them.

"I honestly don't know." Derin let out a tired and sorry laugh. "It took every ounce of strength I had to move on and now I find out maybe I shouldn't have."

Alex felt like his breath had been pulled out of his chest and he sucked in air greedily, filling his lungs and then holding them that way. It felt like it did diving deep under the surface of the crystal blue waters that surrounded their home, and he felt that same sense of peace, calm, and rightness about the world as he did when he was down there.

"It will be okay," Alex said after letting his breath out. "You just need to trust your heart." Like his brother, Alex seemed to be giving out advice he wasn't quite equipped for or ready to follow himself.

"I'll lose one of them." Derin smiled sadly at his brother, tears threatening to fall. "And it's no comfort at all, you know."

"What?" Alex asked but he already knew the answer or his heart did at least. The brothers were too connected for him not to feel it there.

"That not many of us are lucky enough to have the choice in the first place." Derin shrugged and allowed himself a small ironic smile before his face fell again.

Alex knew his brother was right. It didn't dull the pain that shot through him, however, when he realized that unlike his brother, it felt like he had no choice at all.

"So, it's decided then. We figure this out. And if we have to, we go get her and we bring her home." Alex let this certainty settle between them. They'd been worrying about an end without having yet begun. It was time, to make the first move towards that unknown end, to take some ownership of how it unfolded and of what became their destiny, together or apart.

"And you know how to do that?" Derin asked, both uncertain and hopeful.

"No, but Dad does." Alex let that truth sink in. "He brought Mom here. He saved Kale and took her to Earth. This is much the same, isn't it?" He believed it, had to, if not for his own sake then for all of theirs. It was time for a story unfinished, one that had been winding its way through a kind of unresolved middle for far too long, to finally find its way towards its end, and in that ending offer each of them a way to begin.

"Only one way to find out," Derin said. The brothers nodded their mutual understanding. It was time to face their parents without everyone else around.

EIGHTEEN

CORIN, MEDEA, AND JAREN sat on the beach side by side, staring out at the vast expanse of blue painted with gold. This was a place you could not escape the ocean, they each realized, and so here, in the home the Founders had made, they often got as close to it as they could. A kind of surrender to destiny, they were beginning to realize, might make sense in every aspect of their lives.

"So, Kale," Corin offered it gently, aware that Kale being alive impacted them all differently. Kale had been his sister in many ways and having her in his life had inspired him to become the strongest, surest version of himself. Losing her had been devastating but it had also broken him in a different way than it had his two best friends; and maybe because of how they broke, he'd held himself together whether he'd wanted to or not.

For Medea, who had finally surrendered to how she felt about Derin, and for Jaren, who had only ever kept his heart for Kale, there was a deeper truth coming to life with all that they'd been told; and for each of them a deeper struggle prevailed. *How had they not known, not sensed, that the woman they'd loved had been alive all this time?* They couldn't know she was just a shell of herself with no memory of any of them or the lives she'd lived, one on Earth and one on Alpha Iridium. They couldn't know that for five long years she'd been nowhere and no one, trapped in a kind of timeless dark, until that day she'd woken on a beach where Rogan found her. They could not know either that she didn't miss them or long to be returned to her life because any knowing inside her was a gaping hole. She had only the dark and violent rocking of the sea that woke her from the longest dream she'd ever had, and then that short and simple life on Earth with Rogan, Firth, and the people of Iri. Kale had lost so much and yet in this new injustice she'd lost almost nothing at all because none of what was missing could be recalled.

Her friends knew none of this—only that it seemed no matter how far Kale was from where they were, she was closer somehow than she'd been since she'd died on that mountain shelf facing Caine and the Darkness. They could feel the possibility of having her come home and the temptation was one they would risk everything for.

"We go get her, right?" Jaren paused to look at each of them for a moment. His grey eyes were uncharacteristically uncertain beneath a furrowed brow.

"I don't know why I always have to be this guy," Corin offered with a soft and exasperated laugh despite the seriousness of the situation. "But how in the hell are we going to cross the universe, find her, rescue her, and then make our way home?" He could feel annoyance rising and some of it escaped with his words.

"Corin," Medea began, but he interrupted her.

"No, no. Don't tell me I'm crazy. Don't tell me some bullshit about things being meant to work out and destiny and all that. I get it. I do. It feels like we lost something that night that we've never been able to get back, until now. It's not just *her*, it's what she means to us and to the possibility of what the whole damn thing was about in the first place." Corin paused and took a deep breath. "But it doesn't mean it's possible. It doesn't mean we're all going to come through this okay. Don't you get it? There isn't a happy ending because there is no end. This isn't a fairytale. This is our lives." His breath was quick and shallow, and every few caught in his throat. A torrent of emotions swirled within him and he struggled to make sense of it.

"You just want us to leave her there?" Medea asked, upset with him but also upset by how the truth had insinuated itself into their discussion in a way that she didn't like or want.

"Goddammit. Why am I the only one who ever looks at the whole damn picture?" Corin ran his fingers through his dirty blond hair, both exasperated and filled with resentment. Each and every time they faced something insurmountable, he had to be the anchor that tied them to common sense. He was sick of it. It was unfair. Just once he'd love to dream, and hope, and believe the impossible was actually possible and yet always, always, he had to have the level head while everyone else got lost in possibilities and daydreams.

He thought they were done with all that after five long years rebuilding their lives and of cutting away the magic and fairytales that tempted them to get lost in stories instead of settling into truth. They'd fought so hard to be okay with the way the world had turned out and now, once again, the magic and mystery were hunting them down and everything they'd built would never seem enough again.

What was he holding onto anyway? He'd spent so much time taking care of Jaren and Medea; he hadn't even moved on at all. In five years, not much had changed for Corin. He'd helped to rebuild Braedon Ridge and begin to return it to its splendor. They rebuilt trade among the villages and communities on Berdune. They'd begun to form a viable government, implemented elections, rebuilt homes, and helped their society begin to thrive. When he stepped into the quiet and comfort of their home, *he* was much the same. Alone. Lonely. Waiting for what, he didn't know.

That was the truth underneath it all, wasn't it? He hadn't actually rebuilt anything for himself because he'd had so little to lose in the first place. If he was being honest, he hadn't had much of a life before he and Jaren met Kale and Medea. Even during their time fighting Caine and his army, Corin never had much outside of those deep and lasting friendships he'd had with the three people he'd shared a life and home with. Caine had been gone five years and Corin hadn't been on a single date, hadn't made any new friends, hadn't fallen in love or sought out his destiny. He'd simply coasted, telling himself what mattered was taking care of his friends, helping both Medea and Jaren pick up the shattered pieces of their hearts and lives. Jaren had become a leader in many ways and Corin had opted to follow and have his impact that way, in a kind of service that was born of believing he was never enough and not going to be more.

He was scared, he realized, not that they would fail, wouldn't rescue Kale, but that they would, because it was another thing they'd need to be afraid of losing, again. Another thing that mattered too much not to thrust your whole heart into. He didn't want Medea to lose what she'd finally found. He didn't want Jaren to have to accept again that he wouldn't be Kale's first choice. He didn't want to be reminded he was a secondary player in his own life. He wanted to go on the way he had been now for so long he couldn't see past it—head down, heart locked up safe, no big dreams to be dreamt or to be denied either way.

"Corin," Jaren said softly, pulling him away from the uncomfortable turn his thoughts had taken. "I know you always end up being the one keeping us tethered to reality. I know it feels like you have to be the bad guy or the parent. And I'm sorry. Because of you, we've paused when we needed to and been patient. We've thought twice about rash decisions and rushing into situations. You've saved our lives more than once. But this is different. Let go of the big picture, the uncertainty, the questions. All that matters is this: Can you live with yourself if we just leave her there?"

There was a long pause. All of them quiet, not because they didn't know the answer but because they all realized in that moment how astounding it was they were even able to ask it.

"No," Corin shook his head, "I can't. None of us can." He closed his eyes and looked into that darkness behind his lids for some kind of certainty about what was coming that could comfort him. When he found nothing there, he opened his eyes again and took a moment to meet both Medea and Jaren's gaze. "So, what now?"

"We find Dellerim and Cyan and we find out if any of this is actually possible." Jaren looked to each of them for a moment before he stood, sending sparkling remnants of shells and other things tumbling from his clothes.

"You two go ahead. I'll be right behind you," Medea said with a sad smile.

"Hey, in all this, we've forgotten about you." Jaren felt a little ashamed of himself. It was an old habit quickly revived, forgetting everything for Kale. It made him wonder, ever so briefly, how far they'd actually traveled from who they'd been five years ago.

"Not now, Jaren. Please. I'm not ready to even think about it all. No matter what happens, I lose. If I have to choose, I choose Kale. That's all that matters right now." Again she settled into the miracle of knowing her best friend was alive and fought the sinking into sorrow when she thought of what she might lose because of it. She even fought the urge to believe she deserved all this somehow, that she should never have allowed her heart to lead her where her mind instinctively knew she was not meant to go. There would be time for all that. Now, she simply wanted to be alone.

Jaren and Corin both nodded. After they each took a turn to squeeze her hand, they left her and went looking for Cyan and Dellerim and the possibility of having the missing member of their family brought home from a faraway place.

It was only once they'd left and Medea was on her own that she collapsed and allowed the full weight of what was happening to press her down onto the ground, practically suffocating her. She tried to hold her anguish at bay, but it began to escape her in sobs, wracking her whole body violently. *Why did it feel so familiar, the heartache, the sense that she was alone in something that not even the people closest to her could join her in?* She'd lost so much. They all had. Now, dangled in front of them, was another thing that mattered so much that losing it could truly destroy them. *How safe and certain could it even be—trying to pull Kale back from some far off world that might be teetering on the brink of its own ending? Even if it was possible for them to get there, what if they couldn't get back? What if they couldn't save Kale? What if...?* Medea stopped herself.

Instead, she surrendered to the anguish and heartache sweeping through her and simply began to let it all out. She wept for Ryan, once the love her life. She wept for her parents, and for Kale's, for all the people of Berdune who had been swallowed by the Darkness and the madman who had come on its heels to rule them. She wept for Derin and for Joah, the two men she loved most in the world. She wept for Corin and for Jaren, and for herself most of all, for the adventurous wild woman inside her that hadn't survived that last night of Caine's either. For just a moment, with a single beat of her heart sounding in the deep aching sadness that had swallowed it, she wondered if her heartache wouldn't be a little softer if they didn't get Kale back.

She sat for a moment in that indulgence, the most human moment she'd had in a long while. It stilled her and she took a look at herself. It was not even a little bit possible for her to really hope that Kale would be lost, but there'd been a kind of gentle healing in acknowledging her life would be a little easier if things hadn't turned out this way.

We're coming for you Kale, she promised, certain the message would be heard, and she let that certainty calm her breathing and her heart. *I don't know how. But we're coming. We're going to find a way to bring you home where you belong.*

She couldn't know, none of them could, that the unfolding of this story had been set in motion in a time not far from the one they were living in now. They were all still players in that great game of fate, in that unfolding of the dance between dark and light, in the great big eternity of time and space. There was both a greater purpose to it all and a simpler story than they could ever understand but as they marched towards what was already determined, they could not know how very far it would take them from their lives and, in some ways, from themselves as they were now.

NINETEEN

WHEN ALEX AND DERIN found their parents, they were seated side by side on the beach, seemingly at peace, as if it was an ordinary day and not one in which something monumental had been revealed. Slowly, with trepidation, Dellerim and Cyan rose and stood united as their sons approached. The sun was beginning to set to the west and the sky was painted pink and gold. The cherry-grey of the few clouds dotted across that vast expanse above them was both ominous and breathtaking. The brothers looked so alike at times that it was shocking, and in their anger, hurt, and fear they were twin-like. Ice-blue eyes blazing and yet crinkled at the corners with suspicion. Alex's ice blue hair radiant next to Derin's blue-black. Cyan wanted to be afraid of them but in that moment all she could think was how much she loved them. Even in their indignation and rage, they made her proud with how strong they were, and how they stood together against the world; even if sometimes that put her, and yes, now Dellerim, on the other side.

Before either of them could say anything, Dellerim spoke. "I can't bring her back. It's forbidden," which was only some of the truth.

"You've left her there for five years!" Derin shouted as he shoved his father. The shock of it sent Dellerim tumbling back while Cyan cried out, horrified. Derin went on, unable to quell his anger. "On a planet on the verge of its own destruction with a species hell bent on hurrying towards it! Worse than that, you let me believe she was gone, that she'd died, that my life is the price she paid." Derin's voice broke and he took a few deep and ragged breaths. "Do you have any idea how heavy a weight that's been?"

"Derin, I'm so sorry." Dellerim stepped towards his son and then paused. He could feel that vast expanse between them, far bigger than what it appeared to be, and he realized now was not the time to try and bridge that gap. He was only now beginning to see how far a reach the impact of his actions could have.

"It's not enough, 'sorry'. Bring her back!" Derin tried to shout but all the anger had gone out of him and all he could do was plead. He felt helpless and desperate for a chance he wasn't sure he would be given or that he even deserved.

"I can't. It doesn't work that way. We are governed..." Dellerim held his palms open to his son, as if offering him the truth, but it would neither be accepted nor heard.

"You have all broken the rules. So many times. Any time it served you." A wave of rage swept through Derin again, calmed only by the sea of fear it was carried upon. It wasn't just that they might not be able to get to her, it was that he was now also responsible for the life she lived on Earth if they couldn't. He went on. "And now, for me, for her, who saved us all, it's not enough?" Derin couldn't even be shocked by his own fury he was so wrapped up in its unfolding. He couldn't control his words or his anger as they escaped him.

"Derin, please," Cyan interjected but it only seemed to make him angrier.

"I can't believe you. Either of you!" he screamed, but just as quickly as it came the anger crashed and fell away. What remained was the confusion and heartache of a person with too many choices and yet also too few. He had only just found love again, only just had it settle into his life so that he could believe he was finally going to be able to move on. Now not only did it feel like it was being torn away from him, but he was afraid there was nothing beneath the chaos or after the storm.

Derin couldn't help it. A violent rising of rage, hate, and misery began to bubble up and out of him. He needed to throw it at someone before he realized it was actually directed inward at himself. He wasn't ready to face it. It was so much easier to be angry with his father for this new revelation, at his mother for the part she'd played. *But hadn't he spent fourteen years as Caine's son? Most of that time a willing accomplice if not participant in the horrors he'd inflicted on the people of Berdune?* Derin had finally come to question Caine, and, yes, he'd finally fought back, but that was just a breath compared to the long years he'd spent serving Randall Caine, his adoptive father. He'd been a leader in his army. Even if he hadn't seen any action, he'd inspired others to fight, to join them, to enslave and torture and even kill in Caine's name. *Was it possible all these years spent struggling to forgive his mother were actually about his own betrayals and transgressions? Was he the monster after all? Or was his most secret worry coming to life—that he would lose everything because he deserved to?*

He looked at his mother, and what he saw was all the hate he'd secreted away for the person he'd been but still wasn't ready to face. Before he could stop himself, he began to speak, "You did this. I hate..." but he never got the chance to finish.

He thought he heard his father scream the word 'no' as a violent explosion tore out from where they stood and radiated outward, causing a torrent of waves to rise up and hurry towards deeper waters while trees trembled and even fell along the beach. The blast tore down the sand to where Medea and Joah had been standing watching the argument unfold. A moment later, it buckled tree after tree beside where they'd been. In the other direction, Jaren and Corin emerged from the woods only a few moments before, oblivious to what was happening; yet as the blast reached them, only an empty patch of sand remained where they'd been. Beside that place, the trees shook and poured leaves down like giant emerald flakes of snow.

For a few moments, everything went dark and then all Derin could hear was a ringing in his ears. His head pounded, his body ached, and he realized he'd been brought to the ground. He opened his eyes slowly, afraid for some reason of what he'd see. There was the beach and the ocean and there, a few feet away, unconscious but seemingly okay, was Alex. He crawled over to his brother, surprised by how awful he felt, and gently shook him, quietly calling out his name until Alex groaned then fluttered his eyes open, confused.

"What did you do?" Alex asked, slowly sitting up. He had the strange sense that he'd lost something big in the moments that were missing in darkness. He couldn't calm his mind or focus his attention well enough to figure out what had happened but he felt it just the same, this sense that something very large had fallen away and a path ahead had also been cleared somehow.

"I have no clue," Derin said, sitting up beside his brother and wiping sand off his hands. "My head is pounding. That was some blast. You okay?"

"Fine, I think." Alex patted down his legs and arms as if looking for a sign that something was wrong but that came from the scene around him; when he finally looked up and began to take in their surroundings, panic rose in his chest and he stumbled to his feet. "Where are we? Where are Mom and Dad?"

Derin began to look around frantically but realized there was more wrong than simply their missing parents. The sun was high in the sky above them so either they'd lost a night or something else was going on. Though they were on a beach, he quickly realized this one was different than the one on which he'd argued with his parents, what felt like just a few moments ago. Slowly, realization dawned and he met his brother's gaze, as shocked as his own. They were thinking the same thing, though Derin was the one who voiced it.

"Earth," he whispered, and he knew it was true. But what did it mean?

The universe sighed. Unheard and unseen. Finally, the beginning of what it truly wanted. It was now just a matter of time.

TWENTY

THEY CAME RUNNING from all directions—the four remaining Founders—Arianna, Joachim, Kendra, and Kiernan as well as most of their children. They leapt over trees capsized by the violent explosion and ducked under low hanging branches with a speed and agility that was otherworldly, but when they stepped onto the beach each and every one of them froze. There was an echo of power and purpose still hanging in the air. It was palpable, a kind of solid thing, so that the air felt both thick and difficult to move through. It was a feeling that most of them carried a memory of, either deep down inside and out of reach, or hidden for fear of recognizing what might be coming on its heels.

The ocean beside them raged even as it began to settle and slow. Salt spray leapt into the air but couldn't seem to penetrate whatever still hung and lingered along the beach so that no matter how close they came to the water's edge, the panicked group remained dry. There was a low hum, deep and pulsing, almost alive, and all the hairs along their arms and necks stood up on end, answering some unseen call to rise.

Arin, tall and beautiful, her eyes ablaze, was the first to break the strange kind of silence that had settled over the world around them. Her dark red hair framed her narrow heart-shaped face and in the last light of day, her olive skin glowed, singing a rare kind of song with the sunset that made her both radiant and ageless. She was imposing, often looking like a warrior woman ready for battle, even when the world offered her peace. In this moment, however, her fear made her shrink a little, so that her parents had a glimpse of her as a child in that innocence.

"Something awful has happened here," she whispered, and then again loud enough for all of them to hear. She looked first one way and then the next but the beach was empty. There was a kind of shimmering here and there, a memory of something. When she squinted, it was if she was seeing beyond the world around her; though she couldn't begin to imagine what that meant. It kept gnawing at her as she worried about what had happened on the beach not long before they'd been summoned by the explosion—pulled by a sense that something big and awful was careening towards them. Shaken to her core, there was a familiarity about it all and she didn't like the feeling of being thrust back towards the days when they'd had so little control, or so they'd thought, over destiny unfolding around them.

Kendra's honey-colored eyes widened in shock, as she saw what Arin was looking at. "They're gone," she said with disbelief. "They're just gone." She'd lived lifetimes, journeyed across the vast dark of space to find their home, fallen in love and built a family that mattered to her more than anything, seen the rise and fall of Caine, and woken to find that a Darkness unlike anything she could have imagined had finally left them in its wake. Yet, she hadn't been prepared for any of what the last few days had held, for the discovery that Kale was alive, for the revelation Dellerim was more powerful than any of them could have imagined, and prepared least of all for the certainty that somehow, by some power, at least two of their number were gone. She'd always assumed they had eternity to live out their stories, together, no matter how fraught with struggle they were at times. Even in the days of Caine, she had a certainty within that they would survive.

"What do you mean?" Arin asked, but she was already beginning to understand what she was, or rather wasn't, seeing. "Mom," she said, fear lining her voice, and Arianna moved closer to her daughter unsure what more she could do. Their eyes met, mirrors for each other both in color and in fear. More was coming, they knew it, but what could it be?

"Dellerim and Cyan. I can't," Kendra paused, reaching for the right words to describe what tied the Founders together and how deeply they were connected, "I can't hear them anymore." It wasn't nearly enough to describe what they shared but those gathered on the beach understood. "They're just gone," she added, and a sorrow swept through her so swift and deep that for a moment she thought she might drown in it. She knew that the remaining Founders were with her in that awful current. In some ways, they shared everything.

They'd been bonded together since being born into existence. Even Cyan who'd been born on Earth years before had been tied to them since their beginning. Since then, they had endured so much. All of it while being deeply connected and aware of each other, except for those fourteen years during Caine's rule where they hadn't truly been able to hear or reach Cyan. It had almost killed Dellerim, not knowing what was happening to her, not having her heart in constant conversation with his own. The four other Founders had been terrified he wouldn't survive losing her or that he would go mad with fear and worry. Only his desire to one day escape and the hope that not all had been lost had sustained him in his helplessness, had sustained them all. Together, they'd carried the weight of Dellerim's loss, so heavy on top of their combined suffering and fear for the children, left to fend for themselves or imprisoned, and with them helpless to intervene.

Over the countless years they'd spent as a family, a unit, connected so fully that at times they could not separate themselves from each other, they never imagined it wouldn't always be them united against the world, destiny, or the powers that governed the universe and that continued to play with their stories. Yet now, here they were.

"My god, what happened here?" Arianna said, shaking her head, shocked and disbelieving.

The group began to look around, taking in who was with them and who wasn't as the last of the day fully faded around them and the sky began to truly darken. Arin squeezed her eyes shut and tried to block out the truth. She covered her face with her hands and, for a few moments, hid in that refuge before she let her hands fall down and away and turned her eyes up to the heavens, a place where long ago she and all the Founders' children learned to find answers.

It began when they were children, before the coming of Caine and the Darkness that led him to their tiny world. It was so long ago Arin didn't have a memory of the first years she was able to do it. It was just always there: A language written in the night sky that spoke of tomorrows and what they brought, or rather what they might offer up if the right circumstances unfolded. It wasn't something they could always trust and yet they grew to understand that defying the stars was a dangerous thing to do, with consequences sometimes far outweighing the risk. The stars had dictated many if not most of their choices and over time they became afraid to disobey them at all.

When Caine had mysteriously arrived on Alpha Iridium, causing most people to believe he'd come to fulfill an ancient Prophecy that would bring them peace and prosperity, most of the Founders children were under ten years old. Only Alex was older, and even he, at eleven, didn't have the maturity or ability to do anything but follow what the stars told them. They grew up like that, parented by glimpses of the future, one they could scarcely see a way out of or around. Alex became their leader, growing up quickly to do so, but they'd all surrendered to the comfort offered up by trusting their destinies had been written in the heavens, even if it meant letting a monster ravage the people of Berdune until the stars told them they could act. It was something that haunted them still.

After they'd watched the people of Berdune rise up and fight back, the Founders' children had realized that true power came from choosing your own path. It hadn't been an easy thing to overcome—the realization that maybe they could have acted sooner and that their weakness wasn't in being powerless against fate but in being unwilling to stand up and fight for their own destiny. In the end, most of them had surrendered to forgiving themselves and each other. Too much had been lost already and some burdens were meant to be left behind. In that first year of healing, letting go, and moving on, something both wonderful and sad happened to the children of the Founders. They stopped being able to read the stars. It was like a great big blanket was thrown over the heavens—clear and yet able to mute that language they'd grown up understanding. It was both a deep and aching loss and the fullest, most freeing relief.

So, when Arin looked up and the first stars in the new night sky told her both what had happened and what would come to pass, she gasped, and then dropped her gaze and buried her head in her hands once more. She knew then there was no freedom from the story that ruled all of time and space. Light and Dark would always dance and duel and they would always be caught in whatever followed.

"Mom," she moaned, "Dad," she croaked out next and then opened her eyes as her parents, Arianna and Joachim, drew up beside her. She looked a lot like a perfect mix of them both even though she had her mother's coloring. Her father, with his wild mane of white hair and emerald eyes, looked so much like Joah that looking at him now shot a pain through her chest that almost buckled her knees. Because he looked so much like her brother, she looked at him when she spoke. "Joah's gone. I'm not sure he's coming back." Joachim wrapped his arms around his daughter, as she buried her head in his chest and wept.

Above them, the sky darkened. Stars leapt into the heavens first one by one but then hurrying, as if they were trying to catch up with each other. In that dance, possibilities unfolded about what was to come. They winked and twinkled to life. As if filling the sky with stories of what was ahead, was all that they'd been waiting for, night after night. On all of Alpha Iridium, only the five Founders' children standing on that eerie beach beside an ocean now gone quiet, could read anything in them. Arin, Kedall, Milar, Beran and Arwyn were once again united in a way they'd often hoped to forget was even possible.

As Arin looked up again searching for answers and holding on to her hope, she realized the irony of looking to the stars for the future. Each and every one of them was a story from the past. Light traveling millions and billions of years to reach them so that many of the stars and any of the people on them would be long ago departed and forgotten. Yet here they were, above her, caught, in this moment. If only it too wasn't fleeting.

How this had happened none of them knew? Some strange and frightening power had been unleashed on that beach. That, they could feel for sure. The Founders felt in it a kind of familiarity that tugged at memories long ago left on other worlds. There were forces at work here beyond their understanding. It felt like both the beginning and end of something they were yet to comprehend even as they reached into their memories for some glimpse of it.

"We'll find him," Joachim said, looking deep into his daughter's eyes. His son was a man now but Joachim felt as if he'd been transported back to when Joah was just a child. Fear swept through him at the thought he was powerless to protect him from whatever had happened on the beach, just like he'd been powerless all those years ago.

"Them you mean," Arin corrected him, staying pressed safely into his side. "Joah's not the only one who's gone."

The group looked around again and took in who was with them as they took in who was not. Here they were again, pawns in a game they did not understand. There was no way to know what it all meant and no way to see what it was they should do just yet. Could they trust what was unfolding above them in that dark blanket painted with twinkling bodies? Were they indeed powerless to do anything but wait and watch? And was that other world, forever and inextricably linked with their own through dreams and destiny, really where the rest of this story would unfold?

TWENTY-ONE

EARTH. DERIN STILL couldn't believe it.

It meant he was close to Kale, if not in time, in space. Yet his first thought went not to her but to Medea and how he'd missed his chance to make things right with her. He'd been so caught up in the past coming alive he'd lost hold of the present. Derin hadn't grasped how strongly he was still tied to Kale until met with the possibility of seeing her again; something he realized he'd always believed might happen. It was a tenuous thread but still it had been woven quietly, secretly, into the fabric of his being, so much so that for a little while he'd lost sight of everything else because of it. Too quickly he'd forgotten the life he'd finally begun to build and the heart he'd finally found a home for. Instead he leapt back into the past and towards his first love without hesitation. Yet now, with a deep and aching sorrow, it hit him, the full weight of what her being alive meant. Suddenly, he couldn't breathe, his chest tight with heartache and regret. In this time, in this life, he would have to choose: his first love or his last. There would be no in-between.

When he saved Kale, when he took her away from this dying world and brought her home, all three of them would have to face something they hadn't in a long time. They'd been stuck, Medea and Derin, in looking back, in watching the past, because that's where Kale was. It was the only place she lived anymore, or so they'd thought. Even in moving on, in surrendering to the love that had been born between them, they'd made so much of it about what they owed her, about what she would want for both of them. They never quite managed to let her go. Now, she was back. In fact, she was never really gone, and there was nothing left for them to do but fight for what might lay ahead of them all.

Derin found himself wishing Medea was here, wishing he could let her know what he was thinking, what he was afraid of, what worried him in all this.

That's when he heard someone call out his name and he turned around to meet the second biggest shock of the day. He saw Medea and Joah hurrying, a little dazed, down the beach towards him and Alex. He was too stunned to react.

They were here. On Earth. Somehow his father, who he was certain had orchestrated their journey, must have sent them as well. Derin was so stunned that he couldn't think, couldn't grab hold of a single thought or catch his breath as his heart rate picked up speed.

Before he could even reach for something to say, he heard another voice behind him. As he turned, he saw Corin and Jaren stepping out of the forest and onto the beach. They looked shaken but relieved. Derin wondered if they had any clue where they were or what was going on.

"Thank the stars!" Corin said as he smiled and hurried towards them, Jaren at his side. "We weren't sure we were going to find anyone here." His normally neat blond hair was disheveled and it made him look more boyish than usual.

"Wherever here is," Jaren added with a rueful smile as the six friends hugged and greeted each other with relief. There was a missing piece to the truth of the moment. It was a thing that raced below the surface, waiting for a chance to rise and break free. They could all feel it swirling just beneath their feet, a truth waiting to capture them from below.

"Here is Earth, if I'm not mistaken," Joah offered and was met with both shock and silence from Medea, Corin, and Jaren. It wasn't that they didn't believe him; it was that they could feel it was true. Hadn't they known since they'd discovered Kale was alive that this moment would come? Hadn't they felt that familiar sense they were caught in a larger story unfolding around them that they could no more fight than escape? Now here they were, as near to her as if the past five years had never happened.

"Looks like it," Alex replied. He looked to Medea, Jaren, and Corin one at a time to make sure they understood he was certain.

"Earth when," Medea asked, shaking her head in bewilderment, trying to reconcile in her mind the shock of being all the way across the universe on a world that until recently they all believed had probably been destroyed.

"I don't know," Derin said, trying to catch her eye but she refused to look his way. There was a chasm between them now, a vast expanse that it would only be possible to bridge with a lot of work and willingness. Derin was overcome with sadness for how quickly things could be undone, even those it took years to build. Relentless and determined, Medea would keep their hearts from interfering with the only task that mattered anymore, finding Kale, and Derin's fear of choosing, of facing his destiny, would not only allow her to do it, but would risk everything in the process.

"Earth whenever Kale found her way here," Alex said thoughtfully. "Or, I guess when my Dad put her here. I don't know when it is, some far off future I suspect, but she's here. I'm sure of it." Alex closed his eyes and reached for that memory of her, the remnants of a dream that lingered and would not let him go. He could feel her, this kind of echo of the woman they were all hoping to bring home. The longer they were tied together by that tenuous thread the louder and surer that echo became. Alex wondered what it would feel like to be near her, finally, after glimpsing her only in dreams.

"How is any of this even possible?" Corin asked, still struggling to step out of his shock and into the present.

He was met with silence, one filled with more questions than answers. None of them doubted that Alex was right even though it seemed unbelievable. Hadn't they all seen and lived stranger and more impossible things than this? What was one more? This was what they'd wanted, a chance to find the missing piece of their hearts and lives so they could carry her home, safe and whole, to where they believed she belonged.

Joah watched Derin, wondering what it must feel like to be caught in the middle of two great destinies, knowing each path meant you'd lose something you could never get back. Corin and Jaren exchanged a worried look then quickly looked to Medea who was staring blankly ahead, unseeing, as she leaned in to Joah's side. Derin did his best to avoid watching them, amazed by the pain it shot through his chest when he did. He knew he had no right to be jealous but it was there just the same. It wasn't fair, he realized, to remain caught in between the two women he loved, unsure which way to turn. They deserved more than his confusion and fear of making the wrong choice and yet the way forward remained obscured. *You probably don't deserve either of them,* a quiet voice inside him whispered and he couldn't help himself, he began to believe it.

Alex watched the horizon to the west, thoughtful and quiet. Waiting, for what he did not know. When he caught sight of a tiny tendril of smoke curling up towards the heavens, he knew what was next.

"There," Alex pointed to the smoke carving a path up towards the white clouds that dotted the late day sky, "we go that way."

The group turned their gaze westward and watched what seemed like an omen: Darkness rising into the brightness of day.

"How do you know?" Medea asked, finally fighting her way out of that tiny place deep within she'd retreated into. It was a place too small to hold all of her and so in hiding there she could hide from herself. It wasn't something she was proud of, wasn't something she liked to admit, but the past few years had made her insecure, had pressed her to become uncertain of her place in the world and within herself. Once impulsive and unafraid, she was just a shadow of the woman she'd been when they'd lost Kale.

She met Alex's gaze and was struck by how like Derin's it was, even as it was entirely unique. A wave of envy washed through her. She felt a deep longing for what the brothers shared but then quickly realized that if Alex was right they would soon find Kale and Medea would miraculously have her best friend back. Every cell in her body was aching for it to be true—for the person who knew her best in the world to really be alive and just a short journey away from where they stood now.

"I don't know," Alex replied, half a lie and half the truth. He could feel her—a magnet of some kind—calling him to close the space between them. It was the same pull that had somehow opened up their connection while dreaming, he was sure of it. Yet, he realized that maybe the reason she'd reached out to him was less about them being connected and more because Derin had pulled away from her when he'd begun to move on. If that were true, then Alex was simply a substitute and a stand-in for his younger brother until Derin made his choice. Alex realized he wasn't entirely sure how he felt about that. Inside rose a kind of reminder that in the five years since Alpha Iridium had known peace, unlike his brother, he hadn't actually bothered to live much of a life. At least Derin had tried to move on, tried to honor what they'd lost by building something that mattered. Maybe the reason Alex was a place holder was because he hadn't chosen a place of his own.

Looking around at the others, his friends and family, he realized none of them had really done a great job of moving on or rebuilding either. *Why was that*, he wondered. *Why had they all got stuck?* Yes, they'd lost Kale, but they'd won the war and, given enough time, lives were meant to be lost. That's how every story ends, eventually. That's what makes life precious, makes lives worth living and fighting for, that their beauty is tied inextricably to their fragility, and to the fact that they are fleeting. How was it that none of them had stepped fully out of that last night of Caine's rule? As if they'd been tethered to the young woman who had sacrificed her life for them, as if even across the vast stretch of time and space that had separated them they'd been waiting for this, a chance to set it all right? Then, maybe they could move on.

"We follow that smoke. We find Kale. Then, we go home. It doesn't need to be any more complicated than that," Derin said, sounding so much more certain than he felt.

No one asked how they'd get home. No one asked what the others thought they might find on this Earth. They would know soon enough what they were in for. They turned away from the ocean, something that felt both symbolic and ominous, and began to walk, towards what end they did not know.

They felt strong and certain as they journeyed towards a moment that felt like it was five years in the making. They couldn't know it had been in the making much, much longer than that—both from some far off place in the past, and a not too distant moment in the future. Time was like that, both mysterious and strange. They were marching towards a moment that would set in motion the very thing that gave birth to them all, in a place not far from where they'd landed on that lonely beach, on an Earth that was just a shadow of what it had once been. As they made their way towards their long-lost friend, the forces that balanced and governed the universe delighted a little bit.

TWENTY-TWO

KALE

AFTER BREAKFAST, as we packed up our meager things and prepared to chase down our friends and family, my mind wanders back to that first day I'd arrived. Rogan had helped me back to their village and taken me into her home without hesitation. She got me dry clothes, water, and hot coffee. Despite a desire to figure out who I was, she restrained herself from questioning me. Firth told me later it was because she'd felt sorry for me and wanted to give me space and time to heal and find my voice. I knew it was more than that. She could tell I was broken in ways that made me fragile and she knew pressing me for answers would shatter me into a million pieces, no closer to any kind of truth or revelation. For days, she gave me space and time until protecting her family became more important than protecting me; she had to ask, to know who I was and where I was from.

I remember wishing I could tell her, not for myself but to ease her heart and mind. By then, they'd all been so kind to me, so welcoming, that I had already begun to feel like I found a kind of home with them. But there was something else, something darker and more sinister as well. I'd begun to wonder at the purpose for a person losing all of themselves. What awful thing had I done or survived to leave me without any inkling of who I was and where I'd come from? Even in the moments when I got lost in happiness or joy, or belonging, there would be a tiny voice inside whispering that my coming here would ruin everything.

The longer I stayed, and the happier I became, the more certain I was that I didn't belong. I'd packed up a small bag—

a few things that hopefully wouldn't account for stealing and added a small amount of food as well. I'd planned to leave that morning. The morning it had all gone wrong. When it had first begun, I'd honestly thought it was about me. That I'd done it. That I'd finally brought some kind of awful destiny down on the people who'd taken me in. It was only in the madness that followed that I realized something very calculated and terrible was unfolding and below the dark, blank expanse of my memory an echo rung once and then faded. There was some kind of memory there. I was sure of it and yet nothing since has stirred any kind of recollection or familiarity.

It had happened only one other time. A kind of tingle that danced along my skin and told me my body remembered something even if I could not. It was in that first week living with Firth and Rogan. I'd walked into the kitchen to catch them in the simple beauty of an intimate moment. Firth was washing the dishes and didn't notice she'd gotten bubbles on her cheek somehow. Rogan gently scooped them up and off and for a moment watched the swirling of rainbows settled on her fingertips before closing her eyes and blowing them away.

"What did you wish for?" Firth had asked her, the sweetest of smiles on her face.

"What more do I need?" Rogan had answered lovingly, stepping towards her and pressing her lips softly onto her partner's.

I'd felt it then—a kind of ache and longing that felt both familiar and out of reach. For a moment, it was so strong it almost buckled my knees. I was tempted to feel foolish for spying but their love seemed so pure and perfect it felt kind of like a gift. Still, I turned away from them and hurried outside, feeling almost like I needed to catch my breath. After that, I avoided seeing them in loving and intimate moments. The pain was too confusing and I had no way of knowing why or how it related to who I was or who I'd been. Three weeks I'd lived with them and yet they'd built a home up and around me and welcomed me in so quickly that it felt like so much more. I can't help thinking about how quickly it had all been burned to the ground. Now here we are, chasing awful men with weapons, trained in ways we could never understand, and I can't help feeling like all of this could have been avoided somehow.

We walk less than half an hour when they capture us—three soldiers, imposing and yet gleeful when they realize they have the two of us to themselves. The way they look at us chills me and my tiny breakfast sours in my stomach. All I can feel is helpless and terrified and, not for the first time, I wonder if the woman I'd been before I'd lost my memory was scared all the time, too, and powerless. Who was she and why can't I get to her? Even more than that, if I knew who and what she was, would I even want to?

Two of the men grab Rogan. Though she's kicking and screaming, they easily pin her down, tearing at her clothes and hitting her. One punch lands sharply in her side and she goes quiet for a moment. It all happens so fast I don't even have a chance to move before the other man rushes me, wrapping a hand around my throat and tossing me to the ground. My head smacks the hard earth and, for a moment, the world dips and dances out of sight and I wonder if it might be safer there in the dark before I realize that I'd rather fight back. Rogan is shouting again and thrashing, trying to keep them from hurting her. I can't help myself, I rise and rush at one of her attackers and launch myself onto his back, biting into his neck while scratching at any bare skin I can reach. Behind me, my attacker grabs a handful of my hair and lifts me up and into the air and I meet Rogan's wild gaze before I'm tossed to the ground again. This time, the world goes dark; for how long, I do not know. It feels safe and familiar—a place without a name, where light and dark have mated to make nothing. I drift and float along; when I feel the waking world begin to pull at me, I struggle against it and what I'll find once I'm there again.

When I first open my eyes, I forget where I am. When I realize I can't remember anything, not who I am, not any of my story, I begin to panic and then realize *that* knowing has been gone for weeks now. I take a deep and steadying breath. My body begins to complain in all the places I've been bruised and ravaged and I wince and squeeze my eyes shut tight again.

"It's okay," a quiet voice soothes, "we've taken care of them." Slowly, I open my eyes again only to see a pair of the strangest, lightest blue eyes I've ever seen staring back at me. There's something vaguely familiar about them but I can't fathom what. They're set into the most beautiful face, with rose-colored lips, and a mane of ice blue hair that hangs down over his forehead. The colors are striking, too vibrant to be real, and I am captivated. "Derin, she's awake," he calls out to someone unseen, and then to me, "do you think you can sit up?"

I must be dreaming because as I sit up I see another guy with emerald eyes and a mane of white hair that stands out starkly from his light brown skin. He's far too young to have hair that color and yet here he is. Their colors are so vibrant they can't possibly be real, and I shake my head trying to shake off the absurdity of the moment as I open my mouth to speak and then freeze. There's another guy staring at me, maybe around the same age as these two, and I know he's related to my rescuer because they look so alike it's eerie; the only difference being that the second guy has dark blue hair, almost black really.

It feels like something big is happening. Around me, it seems like the sun has brightened and like the air has gotten clear. I feel a current running around the space between us all in a way that tells me something strange and wonderful is about to happen but I can't fathom what it could be. They all seem frozen, unable to move or do anything else, as if the next thing that happens is really important and yet none of them wants to step into that moment.

"Rogan?" I ask, fear squeezing my throat tight as I remember how we all got here.

"I'm okay. I'm right here," she says, as I get to my feet. I walk over to her on unsteady legs and she gets up to wrap me in a hug. "I'm okay," she repeats, I suspect more for herself than for me. "We got lucky these guys showed up," she says it with a mix of wonder and relief. I can't help looking to the three incapacitated men who are now tied together against a large tree. I shudder at the thought of what they'd almost done to us.

"Are you okay?" The second brother with the blue-black hair has finally found his voice as he walks over to me and stops so near I'm tempted to take a step back, but I don't. He lifts a hand to my face, fingers graze my cheek, and I'm wrapped up in curiosity for the way he's looking at me. "I can't believe we found you, after all this time."

"Found me?" The question is a whisper on my lips as I look first from him, to Rogan, and then to the brother with the ice-blue hair to match his eyes. "Found me," I repeat, confused, and I feel the fingers drop away from my skin leaving just the memory of intimacy there.

"Kale!" a voice shouts. A moment later, a woman and two men come running out of the forest, panting and out of breath. "Oh my god, Kale, I can't believe it." She moves towards me quickly but the white-haired guy stops her with a shout.

"Medea, no!" She stops and looks from me to him and then back again, staring deep into my eyes, looking for what I do not know.

"Kale?" she asks desperately, her voice small, and again steps towards me.

"I'm sorry," I say, stepping back to keep the space between us, "I don't know who that is."

It's not a memory really that rises in me, just a kind of longing to be known and wanted that badly. When I see her face drop in disappointment, something inside me breaks. Whoever Kale was, she's lucky to have been loved and longed for that much. Even then, with that envy boring a hole deep inside me, I wonder if I'm not better off than she, though I'm not sure why the thought passes through my mind.

"No," she says, shaking her head, "No. I know you, Kale."

"I'm sorry," I repeat, shaking my head helplessly, meeting her devastated gaze.

Tears well up in her eyes but she doesn't relent. "Stop it! Just stop," she pleads. "We grew up together. Lived together. Became ourselves together, because of each other. We're family. You, me, Corin, and Jaren." The two men who came out of the woods with her step towards us and offer pained smiles but stay silent. "You don't have to be afraid. We've come to take you home."

I take a few more steps back and away from her, from all of them. I look back at the dark-haired brother and wait, for what I do not know.

"Kale," he begins, but I interrupt him.

"I am home." It's the first time that I realize it's true. Home has become this place, even though I have no memory of it from before a few weeks ago. Home has become the village of people who have adopted me. Rogan and Firth and the rest of them. Home has become a certainty I belong, not without my brokenness but despite it.

That's when it begins, in that moment of realization, the bubbling up of anger at the injustice of where we are and why. A community willing to take me in, a stranger. A community of people simply trying to survive, to care for each other and move through a broken world with love and kindness and compassion. I don't know who destroyed our village and took our people and I don't know why, but somehow I'll make this right. I didn't act in the moment and I'm not sure if I could have done anything to stop them but I'm going to act now.

I have no clue who I was before three weeks ago but I do know who I'm becoming because it's who I choose to be. I'm not going to be afraid anymore. I'm going to fight and somehow I'm going to stop whatever awfulness and evil is going on and the people who are perpetrating it.

No one speaks around me. There is a kind of pregnant pause in the air so that I wonder if each of the others must feel that something big is coming. I feel it. And for the first time since finding myself awake washed up on a beach in the sunshine with an empty mind and memory, I feel hope. Hope that it's possible to build the world you want even if it means you have to fight your way from nothing, towards that peace.

TWENTY-THREE

THEY WERE GATHERED a couple of hours away from where they left the three unconscious men tied to a tree. It didn't quite feel safe but putting some more distance between themselves and Dempsey felt safer at least, for now. Until they had a plan and knew what was next, it didn't make sense to go much farther than they had. They'd journeyed in silence, each aware there would be a time for questions and answers. Now, here they were seated in a circle in the late day sun waiting for the beginnings of a truth not many of them could fathom.

It was Medea who began the story. Her voice was quiet and sad and yet carried with it the weight of truth and certainty. "We've come from a world far, far away. Connected to Earth because, well, this is where we began, where their parents began anyway." She nodded at Derin and Alex and then Joah, who gave her a smile and a reassuring nod. "There, you and I were best friends. Sisters. We grew up in the time of Caine, which means, well, I guess it doesn't really matter anymore." Her voice trailed off and she made no attempt to keep going.

"We lived together. The four of us," Jaren offered standing up and sitting down again only when he was next to Medea so that he could settle in close to her for support, both hers and his own. "And you, you led a group of rebels to overthrow an evil man and the empire he'd built. You stopped him. We all helped. Then you gave your life," it was here he was interrupted.

"For me. You gave your life for me even though I didn't deserve it." Derin said. "That was five years ago. We thought you were gone. Dead. But now we find out that you're here and so we came to get you." Derin wasn't sure how such a big and sweeping story could be told in so few words.

"Kale," it was Medea again.

"Don't call me that." She stood and looked around at the group of strangers and then her only friend, Rogan. "I'm going to take a walk. I won't go far." Before any of them could answer or protest, she turned and wandered off towards the sound of the ocean crashing against the shore. She didn't stop walking until she stepped out of the trees onto the sand and was greeted with the warm salt air. It filled her lungs and her heart with a sense of peace and calm that she hadn't realized she'd been longing for since their village had been burned to the ground.

She sat there for a long while all on her own, trying to make sense of the absurdity of what they'd told her and trying to make sense also of what she was feeling deep down inside. It was a strange kind of being pulled, magnetic and powerful, towards the truth they were handing her even though it didn't seem possible or real.

When Derin approached and sat down beside her, she shifted uncomfortably but didn't make a sound. She wouldn't even know how to begin. She had so many questions and yet she wasn't ready to face the answers to any of them.

"Are you okay?" He reached out for her hand and then paused, pulling back and away from her. It wasn't that he didn't want to touch her, to hold her hand, to wrap his arms around her and hold on tight and this time not let her go, except that was a story that had been finished long ago and was most likely not to be theirs anymore. *Hadn't the universe already told him that?*

"I don't know," she answered simply. "I don't know what I am."

"You're Kale," he answered as if there was nothing more certain in the world. It was the depth of feeling he offered it with that made her catch her breath while her heart, a thing suddenly with wings, fluttered in her chest. He looked over to her and realized she was his Kale. In fact, she hadn't changed at all since he'd last seen her, and a trickle of worry wound its way through him before he chased it away. Her skin was golden, sun-kissed, smooth, and flawless. The light settled on her face now so that she was radiant, and her brown eyes had that ruby glow that was so unique to her. Her long brown hair, sometimes red in the places the sun lit it up, hung over her shoulders in waves and curls and once in awhile she tossed it one way or the other unconsciously. She was both plain and beautiful and Derin couldn't believe he was here, with her, finally.

"I'm sorry, but I'm not Kale. I don't remember her at all." She felt bad not being able to give him what he wanted but also relieved, though she wasn't quite sure why. For so many weeks living with Rogan and Firth, getting to know the people of their beautiful community of Iri, she'd glimpsed and witnessed what love could build among friends and lovers.

Hadn't she longed for her own story like that? Hadn't she wondered what it would be like to have someone, anyone, love her so much she became the sun, a kind of center to their journey through life? Now maybe here it was and she was suddenly more afraid of it than of anything else.

"It's okay. I do. We all do. What do you want to know?" He gave her an encouraging smile and waited. In the silence, he realized how little he knew about her, how little of her life he'd shared with her. She'd joined the ranks of Caine's army to destroy him from the inside and so when Derin had known her much of what he saw had been a lie. Even though he'd seen through her act, he'd still only known her a mere number of weeks in the grand scheme of her life. He knew nothing of her heart, of her likes and dislikes. He'd known only the version of her that was driving towards that final end, set on destroying Caine, unknowingly meant to destroy a kind of Darkness not meant for Alpha Iridium or any of them. *How could you love someone so much when you hadn't known them in any real sense*, Derin wondered and then an even darker thought prevailed. *What if loving her had been a kind of momentary endeavor and it had always been meant to end?*

Derin shook away the awful thoughts even though he knew in some ways they could free him from the struggle that faced him now. He didn't want to be free. He wanted to be here, with her, now. *Wouldn't he rather have a tough choice than no choice at all?* Before he could spend any more time with his thoughts, she interrupted them with a question of her own.

"You said I gave my life for you. Were we..." she couldn't quite finish her question because she wasn't even sure what she was asking.

"It's complicated. But I guess underneath it all, we were kind of in love." Derin found himself smiling, genuinely, for the first time. It was comfortable here beside her, talking about something that he'd thought was gone. Wasn't she the only one who could understand what they'd lost?

"Kind of?" she asked, a little caught up in the same kind of feeling he was, her mouth sneaking up at the corners into an easy smile for just a moment before she chased it away.

"Like I said, it's complicated." Derin couldn't help himself, he laughed, drawn fondly back to the image of Kale and how stubborn she'd been when it had come to so many things. "You'd never have admitted it, but I believed it. I knew how you felt."

"And you loved me?" It was both genuine curiosity and that deepest of human longings to be loved and seen. She couldn't help it, for the briefest of moments she wanted to be Kale.

"I did. Very much so. I still do, Kale." He hadn't meant to say it and a sliver of regret followed the truth. He did want her to remember, wanted her to tell him that she still loved him, too. Under that was the truth, that he would lose Medea if he grabbed hold of this story from the past. He wasn't at all certain if that's what he wanted now that it was in front of him.

"There's nothing left of her. Of me. It's all darkness and silence inside," she said it without feeling. Simple truth, but she noticed a bit of resentment rising up in her as well. She hadn't built much of a life on Earth yet but it still felt unfair for these strangers to show up and insinuate whatever they had to offer her was better than what she had here. They kept assuming that she was theirs and that she belonged where they said she did, that her story now wasn't nearly as important as the story they'd kept for her, even though it sounded to her like it was meant to be done.

She suspected this was a group not entirely sure of themselves, whether they saw it or not. They'd told her a story about a girl who was certain of her purpose and destiny; yet when she'd chosen her end, they refused to believe it's what she meant. They'd crossed the sea of stars, space, and time to find her and take away the final choice she'd made. They didn't see it, not yet, but she did.

"Then we'll figure it out. We'll find you again. We'll help you remember and find your way back." Derin's words were hurried and fierce, but she wasn't fooled; there was something missing and unsaid. She wasn't ready to trust any of it just yet.

"What if," she paused, knowing her words would wound him, "what if I don't want to be found?" He looked from the ocean to her and she turned to meet his gaze. Those beautiful crystal blue eyes wounded and afraid, so vulnerable and open. She could see why anyone would fall into those depths and never come out again.

"I refuse to believe that." Derin shook her truth away frantically. They hadn't come all this way for nothing, even if she didn't see it yet.

"Then why else am I here?" she asked him. It was a simple question. Yet, it felt like the answer would be a bit more complicated. She realized she wasn't sure she wanted to know it. Not now, maybe not ever.

"I don't know," he replied truthfully, "but the thing is, now so are we, and we can all go home, together."

She didn't answer him. There were too many thoughts churning in her mind, too many unbelievable truths fighting to be heard, and none of them had a home inside her, inside that vast expanse of darkness where her past was hidden. She tore her eyes away from his and looked back out to the waves rolling in from some far off place. Every wave was different—born once and then once it crashed, forever gone. She had a feeling lives weren't quite like that and so maybe it was possible, maybe she'd had another life on a far away world where she'd been a hero for a little while.

"We should get back to the group," she said beginning to stand and wiping sand from her hands. "The longer we take the longer my friends and family remain prisoners."

"We're your friends and family, too, Kale," Derin implored her with his steady gaze to really hear and believe him.

"In another time and place, you mean." She smiled at him sadly. She could feel a deep sense of loss brewing inside her even though she had no memory of what she'd even had. It was an unsettling feeling to be shown the things that had been stolen from your mind, heart, and memory with no real sense they'd ever really been yours. "You coming?"

"I'll catch up with you," Derin said and let her turn and walk away from him without another word. He watched the waves and let their crashing carry him back to another shore, millions of light-years away. He found the day in his memory of when he'd first met Kale, when he'd felt that shift of destiny that had signaled his life would never be the same, even if he didn't entirely realize it. In that reaching back, a terrifying thought took hold: What if, no matter how much he loved her, no matter how much they wanted her back, she didn't belong to them anymore?

TWENTY-FOUR

MEDEA FOUND ROGAN amongst the trees. It was a new sanctuary for Rogan but there was something about both the familiarity and the constant churning of the ocean that she was trying to escape. She needed to feel grounded. She needed to feel a little more certain of herself, a little more like the world she'd built these last few years wasn't falling to pieces around and underneath her. She knew she was being foolish and that she only had time to be brave and to act. The arrival of the strangers, supposedly from another world, was a little too much to process just a couple days after her whole world had been burned to the ground and everyone she loved had been captured.

Medea sat down on the large fallen tree next to her and they simply sat there, quietly listening to the sounds of the forest around them. Golden sunlight filtered down through the radiant treetops above and lit up pollen and insects in the air around them so that they glowed. She let herself get lost in awe, in the magic that danced around them, in the fact that she was even here on a world that for her had lived only in legends and stories.

"What's she like?" Medea asked finally, both afraid of the answer and dying to know, craving some glimpse into the person her best friend had become.

"She's gentle, I guess, and kind, easy to get along with. She's likeable and when she wants to be, even funny and charming. She's captivating in a simple and yet spectacular way, even though I couldn't really tell you why. Maybe it's the great big mystery of her and that no matter how much you're seeing you know it's just a tiny fraction of a whole." There was more than that but Rogan struggled to put it all into words. How could she express that there was a kind vastness to the woman who knew and remembered nothing about herself, that there was always an air of magic around her that made you wonder what she'd once been and what kind of epic story she'd forgotten? It's why none of what she'd learned surprised her, even though it was fantastical. It would have been more surprising if she'd turned out to be just another lost, lonely soul among many.

Medea wiped at the tears that tumbled down her cheeks. She couldn't believe how much it hurt, hearing about a version of her friend that was at once familiar and strange.

She thought back to the moment earlier when the world had fallen out from under her yet again. First that awful scream and a sense in her heart she knew it was Kale. They all had somehow. Joah, Derin, and Alex had taken off at an otherworldly pace and, no matter how hard or fast they pushed their bodies, she, Corin, and Jaren hadn't been able to keep up with them. She'd been terrified, thinking something awful was happening while they ran to catch up. When they broke through the trees, there was Kale and it had been like everything she'd hoped for the past few years was finally coming true. Only Kale was actually just a shadow of herself, kind of like an echo with no real substance or form.

Kale was really gone. Seeing her standing there, not herself, had shocked Medea to her core.

"Tell me about Earth, about what it's like here, about your life." Medea couldn't help herself. After learning Kale had a life here long ago, after finding out the Founders were real and had begun their lives on this world before it had taken its last steps up to the brink of its destruction, she'd always wondered what Earth had been like. Now, here she was, and it was so very different than she'd expected.

Rogan realized she never thought about Earth before the era they were living in now. Nor did their community ever bother reminiscing about it. It was like they had let go of the way things were because that awful time had led them here. And, here was about surviving and about moving on from what they'd been, moving on from the true horrors they'd almost brought about in that last moment of destruction. But she reached back for it now and asked herself if she could hand it over honestly, and lovingly as well.

They'd almost destroyed themselves. Slowly, ravaged the Earth with greed, with unrelenting self-serving consumption, with an unfounded belief that resources were limitless and everything in the realm of creation had been made for them to use, take, and keep. They took it all and the world heated, raged, and tried to fight and fend them off with storms, fires, and violent shaking. Yet, they remained, a plague unlike any the Earth had ever seen. When they'd finally taken everything and run all their resources dry, they had to build a machine to remake the world into something that could still sustain them. The day the machine, a clean infinite power source went online, began like any other and yet there was a current running round and round the world that spoke of endings. It whispered that this day would be unlike any other that had come before.

None of them could have known that their destiny had been decided long ago. They'd been tested by the higher powers in the universe to see if they were worthy. They were not; and not just because of what they'd done to the planet but more so because of what they'd become—a species with no soul, capable of cruelty and violence unlike anything the Earth had seen or known. Obsessed with the story of their own greatness, they moved farther and farther away from any true sense of it. Hateful, foolish, determined in their singular stories and conquests, uninterested in caring for each other, convinced that that kind of compassion cost them something, their sentence came calling for them. The day that had already been written in the stars finally arrived. The machine failed. Their greatness and superiority was an illusion finally revealed. Earth, sky, and sea all began to tear apart; as the atmosphere poured out into space, the Earth was crushed by the pressure careening in on them all. Cities toppled and burned. Oceans swelled and buried the coasts. Almost everyone perished. Even in its destruction, the Earth rejoiced with their leaving.

Then, just as quickly as the devastation began, it was as if someone hit pause. It was like a big breath in, the very way a new life was meant to begin, and suddenly some of the destruction unraveled and undid itself. The Earth settled back into place and its deepest wounds were healed. Nothing humanity had built or destroyed for their own purposes remained. The Earth had been remade as if they'd never been there so that it was whole, beautiful, and thriving again in ways it hadn't for a very long time.

Rogan hadn't seen all that. It had been like a dream, an awful, terrifying dream and yet one that had set them free. When she'd woken, just a child, everything had been different. The cities were gone. The Earth had been wiped clean. A kind of peace remained in the aftermath that even as children they understood was a sad legacy to what they'd once been as a people; that the Earth and the life upon it should be so much better off without any trace of them. Only a few thousand humans remained to rebuild and start over and all of them children, scattered across the globe in tiny numbers. They'd foraged and eaten what they could and over those first months and years slowly found more people with whom they could build a home.

"That was a long time ago now. More than twenty years. Some days, it feels like forever. Some days, it feels like another life, one not possible as the beginning of the one we're living now." Rogan couldn't believe how much sorrow settled into the space inside her.

Medea was trying to digest it all and to wrap her head around a world that like her own had survived the possibility of plummeting over a precipice into complete annihilation. Something felt a little different about the story of Earth in contrast to the story of her own world. She knew that the Founders had been brought to Alpha Iridium long ago because Earth had lost a fight with the Darkness. In that failure, it was doomed to be destroyed by the billions of greedy, all-consuming humans swarming across its surface like a disease. Yet, it hadn't been. Medea wondered what intervention could have saved them when they'd been so unworthy.

"What was it, you think?" Medea asked quietly, hoping for her answer here, now. "That pause that changed it all?" She knew she was hoping for magic, for something beautiful. She knew also that wasn't always the way of things. Reality was ugly and at times senseless, sorry, and sad. *Hadn't she lived through enough to know all that and more?*

"We'll never know," Rogan answered. "I've never bothered worrying or wondering about it honestly. Sometimes you simply need to take the chances that you're given and not hold on to the why or the how." She offered Medea a small smile but neither of them believed it was real.

"Yeah," Medea said sadly, "yeah, I guess you're right." She pushed away a truth that threatened to rise, one she still wasn't ready for yet.

They let the silence wrap itself around them and in it the forest began to speak loudly again as if giving them an excuse to pause and move on. Birds chirped and sang, and the wind tossed leaves around, creating a kind of gentle symphony. To that soundtrack, Medea wondered if they'd ever be free of destiny, if there were any choices left or if it had all been decided already.

"We should get back," Rogan said with an air of finality. The time for wandering through the past was done. They had enough to face in the here and now. "I'd like to check on..." Rogan paused rolling the name around in her mind before speaking it aloud, "Kale. It's been a wild few days, and I'm sure they've been hard on her. I want to make sure she's okay."

"Right, yes, of course." Medea nodded once but hesitated a moment more, holding on for just another breath to the peace of being with Rogan and a story that wasn't hers.

Eventually, they stood and without another word started to make their way back towards where they'd left the group. It was time to leave the past where it was and face both the present and the future.

TWENTY-FIVE

THAT NIGHT THEY slept under a radiant blanket of stars. It had been a strange night and not one of them tried to breech the deep and heavy silence that had settled over them all. For Kale and Rogan, their friends and family were suffering in unknown ways at the hands of people they couldn't even begin to understand. Over and over again, their thoughts were drawn towards imagining what they didn't want to and to the inevitable possibility of how they were going to save them. Corin, Jaren, and Medea swung like pendulums between elation for having found their friend, the missing piece of their little family, and absolute shock she wasn't even a shadow of the person they'd once known and loved. One moment, Joah was caught up in worry for his friend, Medea, who it seemed would have her heart broken in more ways than one, and the next he was consumed with the dilemma of how they were actually going to get home when they finally convinced Kale to come with them. Derin found himself watching either Kale or Medea. Miserable and sick, afraid to let his heart make a choice yet in that cowardice, he realized that's exactly what he was doing. Alex found himself lost in thoughts of battles still to be fought and hopefully won, if he ever got a chance to redeem himself by rising up to fight, either for what he wanted or for those who could not do so for themselves. More than once, he'd caught Kale's eyes over the fire they'd built and each time a shock of recognition and longing ran through him, though he didn't entirely understand either.

Kale couldn't help herself; she dove over and over again into the darkness that was inside of her, looking for any kind of memory or confirmation that the Alpha Iridians were her friends and family or that she belonged with them. She caught Jaren or Corin's eyes a number of times and there was a kind of comfort and ease there that surprised her. *Was it memory?* She wondered to herself, but not once did her body or mind give her a clue as to whether she really knew them or not. She watched Joah and Medea, tied together by an invisible thread so that they seemed like they belonged together in a way she'd never quite seen before. It opened up inside her a deep sense of longing that for the first time reached back and through the darkness of her memory. She knew for certain there was something hidden there but still she could not fathom what.

Derin had told her they'd been in love, and from the little she'd gathered about him it wasn't hard to see why someone would get lost in that deep well of troubled gentleness and compassion. Yet, he hadn't been entirely honest had he? She could see by the way he tried not to watch Medea and Joah, by the way he burned with a kind of simple jealousy when he did look their way, and by the sad longing in his eyes that followed Medea everywhere, that there was a kind of love there that wasn't meant to just be thrown away. It was a kind of power she did not want—the ability to decide the fate of anyone other than herself. Even that singular task seemed daunting without a sense of who she was or what she was meant for herself. She couldn't even begin to grasp the irony that once she'd been born to decide the fate of a whole planet, and now she didn't really even want a glimmer of that kind of power over her very own destiny.

As she watched them all, unnoticed in her observation, or so she thought, she realized there was a kind of strength in moving on that none of them had quite stepped fully into yet. How deeply had they all been wounded by Caine and the world he'd pressed down upon them, if the only one who'd been able to really move on was her, and only because she'd found herself on another world, in another time, unable to remember anything?

It was strange, to watch these pieces of her past and yet have no real connection to any of them. It was strange, but also a little sad. People and histories so much a part of her and yet when they'd been erased she'd had no sense that they were gone. Until now, until they'd found their way to her in the hope of bringing her home. This was a story she was still uncertain she'd let them write for her because it felt very, very wrong.

The silence had become another member of their group, so much so that when they finally realized it would not share the spotlight with anyone they begin to stand and gather up their things. One by one, they went off to their makeshift beds without more than a word or two, and each of them stumbled into sleep quickly. It had been a long and exhausting day for all of them. It felt like everything that could and should be said and done before another dawn arrived had been. What more was there to do but rest, so that they could face what the new day would bring?

When Kale woke in the middle of the night from some kind of awful dream, she saw that the fire had dropped down to a smoldering pile of ash. The clearing they'd settled in was lit only by the dim sliver of moon above. She sat up and paused, taking in the silhouettes of everyone in their group.

The steady rise and fall of chests and makeshift blankets cast over them like nets told her she was the only one awake. She savored the chance to be free of them all, for even just a little while.

What could she make of all she'd been told? Of being a leader and a fighter, of beating back a kind of mystical Darkness that crossed the universe devouring worlds, of love and loss, of friendship and family? None of it really belonged to her anymore. The young woman they spoke of was gone. Even if she could believe she'd been her, she was still only a shell of the woman they kept claiming belonged with them.

Kale rose, as quietly as she could, and wandered off into the woods. She wasn't going far, just back to that place where the sea met the sand so she could breathe deep and find some calm. Even asleep, their presence was oppressive; that sense of having so many people need you to be someone you simply could not be.

She sat down on the sand as soon as she reached the beach and looked out over that vast expanse where the ocean met the sky. It was dark enough that they looked almost the same. The ocean painted with just a hint of moonlight, a living mirror for the dark world above sprinkled with stars, galaxies, and stories long ago told and ended.

What could it all mean? She wondered. *That the great big mystery of creation had a purpose and a plan, that they were all simply playing out a story that had been written eons ago, that you could be something special and amazing on one world and then on another be almost nothing at all? How could she make sense of any of it when none of it stirred even the remotest of familiarity within? It was true, every once in awhile, she had a feeling deep down but nothing like a memory, nothing that confirmed for her they were telling her the truth. They kept calling her Kale and she'd begun even to answer to it, but how could she really believe any of it was real?*

When Alex sat down beside her, she wasn't really surprised. There was something about him that made her believe he had something for her, some offering, some kind of truth that only he would know. Yet just like the rest of them, he felt far away and out of reach.

He had a magnetic pull she found hard to ignore. She was drawn to both how he seemed out of place, even amongst his friends, and how he simply seemed a little different than they did, though she couldn't quite figure out how. He wasn't thirty yet but he seemed old in the way he carried a sense of sorrow and wisdom; and also the weight of the world. He seemed full in the same way she felt empty, as if it was something given instead of chosen. Though she didn't understand it, she felt comfortable with him in a way she didn't with any of the others.

"You didn't know me like the others did?" She felt ridiculous asking it, but also realized that in the asking she was admitting she believed everything they'd told her.

"No, I didn't," he said, almost sadly. He realized in that moment he would be the most equipped to accept her like this because there was nothing of her in the past that he could reach for or expect her to be again.

"And yet, here you are." It was both a question and a challenge, but he noticed only the first.

"It's complicated," he offered with a shrug. He had so much to offer her and yet could not find the words for any of it.

"Yeah, that seems to be the way of all of this." She smiled and turned her gaze to meet his. When she met those eyes, almost silver in the moonlight, she had a flash, a quick and fleeting memory. Not from out of the darkness that was everything before Rogan had found her, but from after. Something deep within her chest rose and fell and in that crashing, her breath stopped in a pause that spoke of things eternal. For just a moment, she had the urge to lean in towards him, to get closer.

Alex felt it, too, that pull towards her that he hadn't been able to admit to himself meant he was betraying the most important person in his life. When the possibility of actually taking something from his brother hit him, even when his heart longed for it to be his, Alex shook himself out of his longing and tore his eyes from hers, ashamed.

"Must be frustrating," he said to cover the awful feeling rising inside him. "Hearing so much about yourself and none of it matches what's in your mind or your memory."

"It's strange. Sure. And I guess a little sad. You keep calling me by her name, but the truth is I'm not her. I don't remember any of it. And who are we if not the result of everything we've done and built and dreamed and survived?" They sounded true but as her words settled into the narrow space between them, she noticed they didn't feel entirely true either. Was that all she was? A collection of the experiences and choices she'd made over the past few weeks; the ones she could remember. Wasn't there something beneath all that? A certainty, a sense of being, something that could not be obscured by the black nothing that served as her memory?

"I mean sure, there's that. Who we are because of what we've been through in our lives. But it's not all we are. There is a part of each and every one of us that exists before the layers and lessons and living gets poured on. It's the same part of us that remains when we step out of our lives into whatever comes next. That, that part of you," he turned towards her again, waiting until she looked away from the sea, so dark, and met his gaze, "that hasn't changed. That's the part of you we recognize." He shrugged trying to minimize the weight of what he'd just offered her.

"Oh, yeah?" She turned away from him again and sought refuge in the rolling thunder of the sea.

It was a lovely idea, Kale thought to herself, and she couldn't help wondering what kind of world had given birth to so many people able to get lost so willingly in magic and dreams. People would just cross the ocean of time and space to rescue a friend, a loved one. Or so they claimed. It was absolutely absurd. Yet she hadn't really doubted them for a moment. That, to her, was the most amazing part of it all.

"How well do we know each other?" she asked, looking back to him, captivated and afraid, though she didn't know why. She'd heard so many parts of her story and yet still there were so many pieces that were unknown. So many holes in the timeline of the life they kept telling her she'd lived.

"I was there when you died. I watched, helpless, useless," he punctuated that last word with bitterness and disgust, "while you saved us all and then gave your life for my brother's while I could do nothing." Alex paused but she didn't interrupt the silence. Instead, she waited until he went on. "You told me that night that it was the beginning of a different kind of life. You told me to trust my heart, but it turned out to be a lie."

He told her then about what had followed that last night of darkness and then because he wanted to sit with her here as long as he could, and because she made it easy, he told her everything. He spoke about waking on the morning after their parents had gone to sleep to stop the Darkness from coming while instead they'd locked themselves in a dreamless sleep. He told her about being just a child and having to become a man to take care of the other children of the Founders, and how, in leading them, he carried the weight of every choice, right and wrong they'd ever made. He told her about losing his mother and then finding her again only to press all his own self-loathing, misery, and sense of failure onto her instead of facing it himself. He spoke about how he'd had moments over the years of hating her, Kale, because her last choice had left them all to pay a kind of price they'd never imagined possible; and of course her last words to him had been a lie.

"Finally," she laughed softly, and Alex thought the melodic sound, added to that of the waves and the gentle salt breeze, was beautiful there in the dark. Captivated, his heart tried to coax him into believing betrayal wasn't the worst thing you could do. She went on before he could indulge his dark thoughts any further, but the feeling they'd drummed up within him lingered. "Someone has something not so flattering to say about Kale. Except..." she paused and he couldn't help himself.

"What?" he asked, intrigued.

"Well, what did you do with what she gave you?" she asked him, a gentle prod towards a truth he'd worked hard over the past five years not to think about.

"Well, I...I mean," he stumbled over his words, exasperated, and let the silence answer for him. The truth was he'd done nothing with what she'd given him except wait. He waited for destiny to draw him one way or another and when nothing came, he'd settled into the monotony and disappointment without a fight or a struggle.

She nodded, thoughtful, but remained quiet for a moment or two. "Is there something more?" she asked him and surprised herself by hoping that there was. Hoping this beautiful stranger, so wounded, so open, had something for her she hadn't quite figured out was missing yet.

Alex thought of all the times he'd woken from dreams of this place, dreams that had shown him she was still alive. The dreams had shown him that he could finally have a chance to make life right, not just for her but for his brother, and for everyone else he'd failed by being unable to fight back when that final fight had come calling.

What could he tell her?

"I dreamed of you. It started not long ago. I saw you here. With Rogan. I realized it wasn't just a dream. That we hadn't lost you after all and that if I was seeing you, there must also be a way for me to find you and bring you home." It was as much as he was willing to hand either of them in that moment, there by the sea.

"For your brother," she said slowly and yet she knew it wasn't entirely the truth because she could feel it, a living thing in the subtle space between them, even though she couldn't quite understand what it was.

"Because it's where you belong," he answered. A part of the truth. "With us," he added, when inside he could hear it, finally, that *with me* is what he wanted to believe.

She nodded, searching his eyes for the rest of the story but deciding not to ask. The day had been full enough of truth and she wasn't sure she could take any more, even here in the dark of night. She didn't want to know any more. She didn't want to be a player in some cosmic game that meant she had no power or say in her life because some higher power in the universe decided for her what was next.

"You make it sound like we are just characters in some story written by Fate and Time." She took a deep breath, really letting the thought sink in. "Are we?" she asked him, wondering which would be easier, having no control or having all of it.

Alex laughed before he could stop himself, a quick bark that betrayed the absurdity of it all. It was both heartbreaking and astounding to think that they might not have control over their lives. Yet, hadn't he seen it, lived it? Didn't he know? How many years had the stars foretold the story that unfolded in front of them? How many years had they surrendered their power to that certainty? Could fate be more an agent of their unwillingness to decide than a true master itself and if so, didn't that mean that all the regrets were their own? He just wasn't sure anymore. He sat quietly for a moment before he answered. Savoring the closeness to her even though he knew it was wrong.

"I don't know if I believe that," he said unconvincingly.

"I'm not sure we need to believe for something to be true," she said sadly, as she began to stand. She reached down and offered him her hand. When he took it, she felt a jolt of something inside her that recognized him. Her eyes widened as they met his. She quickly dropped his hand, leaving him to stumble back to the ground before finally getting up on his own.

"I'm exhausted," she said as she backed away from him. Her only willingness to acknowledge what had just happened. He nodded as he brushed the sand off his hands, like her, ignoring the moment that had passed between them.

"Let's try to get some rest then shall we?" he asked, as he met her eyes one last time. Something in her chest fluttered and she felt her cheeks get hot. She was relieved he wouldn't be able to notice it in the dark. She was confused. How could she have loved one brother and yet here and now with no memory of any of it have a sense there was something also with the other? She pulled her eyes away before she turned and for the briefest of moments, wished none of them had come.

He followed her through the trees and back towards their camp, all the while fighting the urge to reach out to her, to grab hold and not let go. It was as if here in the dark something else had found him, the idea that what his heart wanted might be possible, even if he hadn't bothered to truly face it just yet.

When they got to the clearing, it was exactly how they'd left it, with everyone asleep, their gentle breath and snores adding to the soft cacophony of sounds that spoke of night and people lost in deeply dreaming. When he lay down, Alex closed his eyes and moved through everything he was feeling. It was a jumbled-up mess inside him and yet deep down some thoughts were very clear. The most important person in his life was Derin. More than a brother, Derin was his best friend, his soulmate. There was nothing he wouldn't do for him, but someone else had begun to take up space inside his heart and had been there far longer than he'd realized. As that knowing rose and bloomed inside him, he took a few deep and steadying breaths. It wasn't an impossible situation because he would actually never reach for what he wanted, not when it meant he'd have to take it from his brother, no matter how badly he wanted it for himself.

The truth of his heart was finally fully awake inside him. He faced it because it would have to be put to rest. Set aside to fulfill a task that mattered more than anything else: making things right. He owed that much to Derin, and to himself.

On the other side of the smoldering fire, Kale did much the same. She wondered about what she owed people; those who'd taken her in, and those who told stories of having lived most of their lives with her. Nowhere in any of it did she glimpse a path she chose for herself. Neither could she see a path where that other Kale did the same. Both their stories it seemed were to be authored by fate with no sense of their own choices carving the way ahead. She didn't see how she could fight it. Not yet. Because if she were being honest, she didn't quite know what she wanted.

Sleep would come for them both, eventually, and so would dreams of other worlds and other times.

TWENTY-SIX

THE NEXT MORNING they broke into two groups and headed off in opposite directions. They were in search of allies and answers and it made sense to cover the most ground possible by splitting into two parties. They agreed to meet at a midway point between their two destinations wanting to make sure they were a safe distance from Dempsey the next time they made camp.

The heavy silence that had consumed them the night before was now a willing indulgence as four of them hurried towards the rising sun and four of them hurried away from it. Rogan led Joah, Alex, and Derin towards the trail they'd been following in search of their captured people. She pushed them as fast as she could go, hurrying towards her friends and family and the love of her life. Even if what they found horrified her, it would be better than all the awful things her imagination kept dreaming up. She needed to see Firth and know she was okay. She needed to know the people who had shared a life with her as far back as she could remember had survived the raid on Iri.

It had been difficult for Rogan to explain to the others why the people of Iri had kept to themselves and they'd actively avoided interacting with people other than their own. It lived in a kind of collective memory that, as a species, the only thing they did united was charge towards destruction, so they remained steeped in their isolation, a small and simple community, with small and simple lives. It seemed that not only was someone else choosing another path, they'd also been gathering enough info and intelligence to launch an attack that captured almost everyone and destroyed their whole village in a single morning.

When the foursome reached the borderlands of the big city that called itself Dempsey, Derin could feel the heaviness in the air and the sense that this was a place where hope had been lost. Hadn't he helped build a place like this once? He felt a familiar ribbon of shame weave its way through him but shook the feeling off before he could indulge it too long.

The foursome kept to the forest that surrounded a large swath of land that had been cleared for farming. In the fields, they saw people chained and bound. They were gaunt and sagging, as if they carried both the weight of heartache and their broken worlds upon their shoulders.

Rogan couldn't breathe. She didn't recognize any of her family in the crowd of prisoners, but knowing they might be subject to a similar fate broke her heart. The injustice of it set alight a kind of rage in her chest that she didn't know it was possible to sustain inside such a small space. It burned almost painfully and stung her eyes; she couldn't imagine not making the responsible parties pay.

"Was this what it was like on your world?" She'd stopped walking and couldn't help herself. She needed somewhere to press all the pain and anger.

"It wasn't exactly like this, no, but it was some of the worst that people are capable of." It was Alex who replied, softly, a gentle offering of truth.

"And you," she looked at Derin, horrified, angry, "you helped chain people up and rip families apart?" The accusation hung in the air between them. It was hard to reconcile this gentle person in front of her with what she knew had been done, but wasn't that the way of evil, hiding so beautifully in plain sight? Coaxing people across a moral line millimeter by millimeter until they were miles from where they ever thought they would be. No matter how slowly they arrived or how good their hearts were underneath it all, evil was evil, and it was no less destructive or wrong just because good people were the perpetrators of it.

"It's not that simple," Joah said, trying to break the tension in the air around them with his conviction.

"No, she's right." Derin shook his head, resigned, and dropped his gaze to the ground. He'd thought about it so many times and relived moments where he could have gone another way or chosen a different path. Maybe fought back. But he always landed in the same place and the path ahead would need to be both honest and forgiving if he was truly going to move on. "Yes, I helped. First, I believed what Caine said he would do. Then, when I realized it was a lie, it was just easier for me to stay wrapped up tight inside it and hide. To believe in the prophecy that he would be our salvation despite what I was seeing. It took me a long time, not just to face the truth but to stand up and fight it. Some would say it was too late. I'm one of them. But I can't change any of that. And every single day I have to live with what I did in servitude, and what I didn't do by standing by."

Derin could only shake his head. In that moment, he had a strange and profound realization about how much like his mother he actually was. Neither of them had set out to do harm and yet their circumstances had made space for them to do so. There had always been a choice and yet both of them had chosen wrong, sometimes over and over again. He'd asked the world to forgive him, he'd worked to forgive himself, and yet he expected her to pay the price that he could not—to go unforgiven, to remain bound by every mistake and wrong. It had been unfair, he realized, to expect so much from her and not to offer the same compassion he'd been given, by everyone, including the people his very way of life had taken something from. They'd all been quiet so long it seemed their conversation was done, but Derin had one last thing to offer.

"That's the thing, isn't it? We are both the people we've become and the collection of all the people we've been. So yeah, Rogan, in some ways that awful young man, the one who was a coward and pretended not to see what was right in front him, is still inside me. I look at him when I need to be reminded of what I'll never become again." He breathed deep and dropped his eyes to the ground again. He wiped at the tears tumbling quietly down his cheeks, and a longing for his mother swept through him so fiercely it took his breath away.

"I'm sorry," Rogan said, caught in the dissatisfaction of making him suffer. She'd thought it would make her feel better, facing something in him like she would be facing in the awful people of Dempsey. A river of worry wound its way through her. What if, like him, they were ordinary people led astray? How would she fight and destroy them if they turned out simply to be fools; too weak to fight the evil that flowed through them like it flowed through every human since the beginning of time? An opposite to the light they were born from, a delicate balance within, that not a single generation yet had managed to maintain.

"No, it's okay. It's good. Some reminders, no matter how painful, are worth keeping near." Derin wiped at the last of the tears and turned back towards her. "We are going to get your family back. We won't go home until it's done."

She nodded, letting a newfound peace land between them. She turned and began toward Dempsey again. "Then let's figure out what we're up against here, shall we?"

They stuck to the cover of trees as they wound their way towards the main city. When they rounded the final curve, they all stopped short. There, in the bowl of the valley, was a city surrounded by a large, towering stone wall. Outside of it, small houses dotted the fields and surrounding area but the bulk of the buildings were inside. It was a fortress, one that offered not a single sign of weakness at first glance.

The four of them were quiet, a mixture of shock and worry settling in.

"We don't have time to indulge in being afraid," Derin finally said. "We need to find out exactly where and how they're keeping their prisoners and then we need to get back to the others as fast as we can."

"Slaves," Rogan whispered, then louder so everyone could hear, "let's not fool ourselves about what's going on here. Even after everything, after a second chance, we've found a way to be the worst of ourselves again." She fell against the tree next to her and let her head hang. How quickly it seemed they'd forgotten. That was the problem with second chances. Sometimes they allowed people to pretend they were better than they had actually been, when really they were the same. It was just the circumstances that had changed.

They let Rogan sit with her devastation for a little while. Some things needed to be felt. They did not touch her or even reach towards her, but there was more than one way to hold someone. In that quiet, Joah, Alex, and Derin all had time to face just how close they'd come to having no second chance at all and to acknowledge how precious the one they were living in actually was.

TWENTY-SEVEN

"WELL, THAT DIDN'T go exactly as planned." It was Medea, uncharacteristically serious and discouraged in the face of what seemed like an overwhelming failure.

Medea, Corin, Jaren, and Kale had hurried away from the town that called itself Ariabore. A mixture of anger, disgust and hopelessness propelling the disappointed foursome to put space between themselves and what they'd witnessed in that place. They were gathered on the dirt road they'd first glimpsed the town from. To one side of the road, fields rolled towards Ariabore, while to the other the sea stretched out towards the horizon, ever vigilant and all knowing. The road here was edged with boulders on either side and somehow, in silent consent, they'd stopped in this spot and sat in a kind of shocked silence before Medea broke it.

When Medea, Corin, and Jaren had rushed to rescue Rogan and Kale the day before, they'd noticed the town. It was perched upon a cliff overlooking the sea, overlooking also the land around them, wary and watchful. The city was near enough to Dempsey that the inhabitants would have to know something about their neighbors to the south. Though it was possible that like Rogan's people, they were hiding here with no desire to connect with any of what remained of humanity, no matter how close in proximity. Yet what they'd come across in Ariabore was a kind of evil that was insidious and lurking, and an hour after they'd left that place their shock had still not worn off.

Corin spoke next.

"It could have gone worse," Corin took the positive side for once, but he looked worried and shaken up. "I guess," he added, his blue eyes betraying some of what they were all feeling.

Jaren and Kale looked at each other then quickly away. She was still struggling with a mixture of anger and outrage and she hadn't figured out where to direct it after letting it loose on the leaders of Ariabore, who had ultimately turned them away.

"We aren't going to make it back before dark," Medea said, resigned. "I say we camp near here." She could feel the weight of their meeting in a way she hadn't realized when they'd first left the city. It was hard not to indulge in hopelessness after what they'd heard and seen.

"We'll find another way," Jaren said but he didn't sound certain and their group remained unconvinced.

Earlier, when they arrived at the city by the sea, the foursome took a few moments to come up with a plan. They'd found another gated city in Ariabore, one trying to keep the world at bay; or perhaps they were trying to keep something in. Either way, it didn't set their minds at ease that this didn't feel like a place that would welcome strangers, friendly or not. In some ways, it reminded them of Braedon Ridge with that towering military compound and castle at its edge where Caine ruled. This was a city under some kind of siege but they'd need time to figure out from what.

It became apparent soon after they'd been let in the front gates that in some ways this was a town hiding itself away with the hope of going unnoticed. There was nothing about it that was extravagant or indulgent. It was a town built on necessity. Yet, it was also a wealthy place. Even in its desire to be modest, there was a kind of comfort and ease that came from being without struggle. From what they could see, no one in Ariabore had gone hungry a day in their lives. People walked through the streets casually, strolling as if they didn't have a care in the world, and it was only the strange sight of their visitors that startled them enough to interrupt the flow. The houses and other buildings that lined the main streets were well cared for and painted an array of colors that spoke of people with both the time and the ease to indulge their creativity.

Beneath the surface of ease though, there was a dull sense of suspicion. They could see it in the way people glanced at them then quickly looked away. They could feel it in how shadows passed hurriedly by upper windows, first there then quickly disappearing if one of them looked up, so that there was a sense of being watched with trepidation. Even the men who had greeted them at the gate were friendly enough, but there was a sense this city knew to be careful who and how it trusted.

The guard, who led them to the main hall at the center of town, left them there alone and avoided eye contact on his way out, saying nothing. After some time, they'd been joined by Sumira and Sheeran, a brother and sister who together ruled this tiny democracy. Sheeran was tall and dark, with caramel skin, grey eyes and soot black hair. He looked like a large cat brought to life, stalking towards them, a jaguar or something more dangerous. Sumira was almost like an echo of him. Smaller, with lighter skin and eyes, and light brown hair that tumbled down her back towards her waist. Like him, she was elegant when she moved towards them but there was an air of ease about her that was both gentle and imposing. Unlike her brother, she wasn't threatening, and they found themselves looking to her more often than him as she seemed worth trusting in a way her brother did not.

What they'd learned in Ariabore had both infuriated and terrified them and more than once they'd been tempted to tell the siblings where their choices would lead them. They'd gone looking for help, searching for allies who could either provide information or support as they tried to rescue Rogan's people from the mysterious force that had captured them, but all they'd gotten was an affirmation they were on their own. It was a heartbreaking day that had left them despondent and yet not surprised that the people of Earth had failed a chance at moving from darkness into the light.

When Sheeran admitted they already knew their neighbors in the city of Dempsey employed slavery to sustain themselves and build the power and reach of their empire, it had been shocking. He told them they'd reached an agreement with Dempsey and that they wouldn't challenge how the Dempsians lived; as a result, the people of Ariabore would be left alone and safe from suffering the same fate as other towns and villages they raided and destroyed. Neither Sheeran nor Sumira bothered to tell the foursome that they had tried more than once to rally their people towards change but the majority were afraid of risking their own peace and tranquility for people they didn't even know. It had been one of the great battles the siblings had fought, first together and then against one another, as Sheeran chose to keep the peace and Sumira had wanted to keep fighting and to make their people understand their selfish choice would cost them all one day.

It had been Kale who'd raged at the siblings. Exasperated. Disgusted. Disbelieving. For the first time since they'd made their way to Earth and found her again, she was truly recognizable as the person they'd shared a life with. She accused the siblings of being worse than the Dempsians, of being keepers of evil simply by standing by and doing nothing. She told them they could not pretend to be better simply because they weren't willing participants.

"Indifference and inaction are two of the greatest crimes you can commit!" she'd shouted at them, not even sure where the words or the anger had flowed from and yet certain both were entirely her own. "You are both monsters," she said to them finally in a quiet voice that carried so much authority it was eerie. "Don't try to tell yourselves anything else." She turned away from them and did not looked back.

It was Corin who offered them the last bit of judgment and truth before the three of them followed Kale out of the building and into the sunlight. "You aren't safe. They will come for you eventually and you'll have no way of stopping them. You'll end like everyone else. Trust me. But unlike the others, you'll deserve it." He'd met Sumira's intense gaze for a moment; when she didn't look away, something rose up in him akin to hope before he swatted it away angrily and then turned to follow his friends away from that rotten place.

They'd made their way out of the town the same way they'd been led in, though now in a kind of heartbroken shock. For the first time, they were united again in something. Even Kale, unable to remember who she was, felt connected to them. She felt a kind of understanding for the world and the people they'd fought to save on the other side of the universe.

"This is what it was like? On Berdune. For you all?" Kale stepped into the heavy quiet that had settled over them.

"Not like this, exactly. But it was a picture of what a world can become when we trust one man with everyone's destiny and stand by while evil, big or small, marches on unchecked." Jaren offered the words not just to the Kale in front him but to the one who was gone, the one who had spoken words almost exactly the same as she built their ranks of rebels and allies to rally against the man who had almost destroyed them all. He went on, "So many of our people simply believed what they were told despite what was obvious. What was right in front of them. Then, when it got bad, it was easier to submit, to hide, to try and go unnoticed rather than to stand up and fight and risk their security or their lives."

"Then, you stopped him. Caine. How exactly?" Kale surprised herself by realizing she was hungry for details from that other life. Famished and longing to fill herself up on stories of a girl who was a hero and the people who remembered her best. Hungry also for hope that what they were facing wasn't insurmountable, that they had faced something like it before and were therefore able to face and fight something so much like it again.

"Well, I guess we convinced the people to rise up and fight. That's what beat the Darkness back at the end of it all. And you. You giving your life fulfilled a kind of requirement. You paid a price the universe demanded for us to get a second chance." It was Corin who offered her this piece of the story. "We're not sure if you ever really had a choice. If any of us did. We will probably never know. But who can know everything anyway." He shrugged as he said it, but she could feel in the space between them it wasn't entirely what he meant.

"It's just so strange," Kale said, shaking her head, "to think so much magic and mystery are real and most of us just don't know it. None of it feels possible and yet at the same time it does. Like every unbelievable thing you tell me sinks and settles into me in a way that makes perfect sense." It was like that first morning when Rogan had offered her coffee. That warm, rich, bitter brew that she could feel spreading out into her whole being to soothe and warm her. She'd had no memory and yet the taste was familiar. It was somehow something she knew. An experience of comfort, of being cradled and carried in familiarity offered her the smallest hope she was something beyond her momentary self.

"You don't remember anything?" Jaren asked.

Kale shook her head sadly, wishing she could offer them something more, some bigger piece of herself that would satisfy their longing to get their friend back. Yet, becoming their Kale again would mean that she wasn't herself anymore, wouldn't it?

"What was life like, for us?" she asked, not just for herself, but for them. So they told her about their home and the woods that surrounded it, about the sanctuary the forest and river provided them for so many years, together. They told her about the rebel alliance, the one she'd created and led. They told her about the Mission, and all the people who went there for food and assistance and that they'd helped in various ways. They told her about the beauty and the ugliness, about struggle and triumph, about love, family, and friendship. They told her about the longest, darkest night Berdune and Alpha Iridium had ever seen and how they'd all beat the Darkness back together because they'd finally figured out how to bring to life that long sought dream of rising up as a people. There was a lot they didn't tell her, she could feel it, the missing pieces of her life and theirs, and she accepted the story they handed her so lovingly, knowing that all stories are but a fragment of the truth.

"It sounds like quite the story," a voice startled them out of their collective reverie.

Jaren instinctively stepped in front of Kale while Medea and Corin stepped closer to them both. For a moment, it felt like they were back in the story they'd just told. Instinctively united against any threat.

"Sumira," Corin said, surprised, and yet not, "what are you doing here?" He felt something in his chest expand and open wide and it took him a couple breaths to come back to himself entirely.

"The thing is," she said, stepping towards them, "not everyone feels the way my brother does. He means well, he's trying to protect our people, to keep us all safe and secure. And yet some of us feel..." she paused here, searching for words that struggled to come because in some ways they felt like a betrayal.

"Feel what?" Corin prompted, unconsciously stepping towards her.

"That condoning the evil the Dempsians live and die by will catch up with us one day. No, it's more than that, we believe what you do, that condoning evil, standing by while it lives and thrives, is tantamount to participating in it." She paused here and took a couple deep breaths. "I don't know what's next. I don't know how many of my people will rise up and fight when the time comes. But I'll stand with you. I'll help you bring your friends and family home safe." Her gentle grey eyes flashed with power so that, for the first time, they realized who was the true force in the sister-brother duo that ruled Ariabore.

"So, what now, then?" Corin asked, feeling elated that she'd joined them and unsure what to make of the unfamiliar set of emotions swirling inside him.

"I'll gather some people. As many as I can." Sumira stood taller when she spoke of action. "We'll join you outside Dempsey as soon as we can. Two days at most, I would say. We will do whatever we can to help." She met Corin's eyes as she nodded and was surprised to feel a kind of heat settle in her chest and her cheeks.

There was a question hanging in the air but none of them gave voice to it. How could something so little, like what she'd offered, feel like both too much and not enough? There were no guarantees that any of it would make a difference. And, wasn't the real question, why hadn't more been done already? Sumira would deal with facing that question soon but in the moment she was captivated by something other than that. Caught up in this sense something big was unfolding, a kind of rushing torrent picked her up and was carrying her downstream. It felt momentous, what was and wasn't happening, and she knew it was related to their arrival and the strangeness of the story she'd overheard.

"Can I ask you something before I leave?" Sumira looked directly at Kale and waited for her silent nod before she went on. "That story you were telling when I arrived..." she let her words trail off because she simply wasn't sure what to say.

Her grey eyes met each of theirs, a gentle challenge, before they settled once again on Kale: A leader acknowledging a leader, even though neither woman truly knew that's what they were.

"Like all stories, it's a little bit true and a little bit not," Kale offered sadly. The moments came like waves but rarely, and, this was one of them, when she desired to be the young woman from the story rather than herself. It wasn't necessarily that she wanted to be her, *their Kale*, it was the love, belonging, and sense of purpose and destiny that called to her. It was being wanted so very badly, in so many different ways. Even momentarily, it was quite the weight, and she found herself grateful when the moment washed back and away from her. She took a deep and steadying breath.

"You're trying to tell me you're from another world?" Sumira was astounded, not by the strangeness of it but by the fact she really believed what she'd heard.

"And possibly another time, if we're being technical," Medea said with a smile.

"Medea really?" Jaren rolled his eyes but he was smiling. Relief was already settling around them. Knowing that Sumira would help and bring others with her to do the same had released some of the tension and lifted much of the heaviness that they'd carried. They could feel it, this sense settle around them that they were both fighting together and once again fighting against an evil that needed to be stopped. One they could face and overcome, like they had before, only this time they would do everything they could to make sure they all came out of it on the other side unharmed.

"I can't believe it," Sumira said, shaking her head in amazement. But, she did.

"And yet something inside you knows we're telling you the truth." Corin met her eyes and again they lingered in that gaze. Corin felt a rising of something deep within but knocked it away as he dropped his eyes confused and a little unsettled. He felt foolish for indulging a feeling so bright and unfamiliar when so much was uncertain around them.

"Yes," she said simply, turning to face the rest of the group. She was a little unsettled herself and not entirely sure why. "I was here when the Earth was torn to shreds. I was young, not even seven years old, but I'll never forget it. I still see it in my dreams sometimes." It was true. She'd woken from those nightmares soaked in sweat, a scream stuck in her throat, her muscles tense and rigid.

"I feel it so fully it is like it happened only yesterday," she continued. "Then some kind of power stopped it, all before it was too late. And when the world came back together again, it was different. Changed. There were so few of us left and we had to start over. Rebuild. The Earth had wiped any trace of us away, a beautiful clean slate, except for the very few of us who had managed to survive. Who knows why? Even in the wreckage it felt like a gift. Like we'd been given something we hadn't quite earned."

She paused here, seeing a time long ago and feeling long ago things, and then she went on. "So yeah, I believe in magic. I believe the world, all of the universe really, is far more complex and mysterious than we believe it to be. But I also believe that we have power and dominion over our own destinies. Which means yes, I agree with you, we are responsible for no longer standing by while evil is done. Even if facing it feels daunting or impossible."

Sumira took the time to meet each one of their gazes, as the friends searched for any sign they were being fooled or misled. She settled her beautiful grey eyes on Corin last and felt a deep yearning for him to believe she was with them, though she couldn't fathom why it mattered so much. Maybe it was that in him, even the little he'd offered, she'd glimpsed that sense of righteousness she'd longed to see in both herself and her brother, though they'd yet to step into it.

"Thank you," Corin offered, hoping to break the strange spell she cast over him when she stared like that. "We'll need all the help we can get." When he finished, he tore his eyes away from hers, a way to escape, and avoided looking at Medea and Jaren who were both watching him with raised eyebrows.

"You can count on me," Sumira said, looking to each of them before she settled her gaze on Corin one final time. When she spoke again, her voice was soft and imploring. "I won't come alone. I'll bring help. I promise."

Sumira left them shortly after that. They believed she meant to return as promised but they also knew not all things went as planned. Corin watched her go, a strange mix of emotions stirred up inside him. When she looked back, he smiled, delighted, and so did she before she turned and disappeared into the dark. He wanted to believe she'd come to their aid, that they could count on her, that they weren't in yet another fight alone. Of course, there was more to it than that. He just wasn't ready to see it yet.

Sumira had managed her shock well, but she had no clue what to make of the story she'd overheard about them fighting a kind of powerful Darkness that had threatened their lives and their planet. Had she not been witness to a miracle herself when the Earth had been saved she may not have believed it at all. But their story carried with it that ring of truth, and she trusted them for some reason. More than that, she wanted to believe it was possible that the intriguing group of strangers had traveled all this way to save them, to keep the story of humanity from becoming just an encore of ones already ushered offstage.

Her people had been peaceful for so long. Maybe that's why it was so easy to stay that way, even at the expense of others. It was such a safe and comfortable thing and the awfulness of Dempsey was so far away and out of sight. Yet, their peace had come at a price and was soiled and ill earned. Could it even be peace if it came at the expense of others? Sumira had argued with her brother many times about turning on the Dempsians, about fighting back against an evil that would inevitably devour them all. Had they learned nothing from the past? Had the fate of Earth taught them so little about indifference that they still couldn't remember action and impact were everything? But conflicted as he was, his people had spoken; he was not the kind of leader who would take them to war against their will. As Sumira made her way back towards her home, she hoped this biggest step away from him wouldn't divide them permanently.

When she'd been gone only a minute or two, it was Jaren who spoke first. "Think we can trust her?" He looked around at his friends. They'd been here before: them against the world wondering if it would remain that way or if help would arrive; they were willing to fight until the end, together, whether the help came or not.

"Do we have a choice?" Medea asked, shaking her head.

"Feels like we've had to ask that question way too many times. Anyone else sick of it?" Corin asked a little more sarcastically than he'd intended to. He was shaken up and more off balance than he'd realized and the daunting task ahead, even knowing help would come, felt too familiar.

"It doesn't matter if we have a choice. There's only one way ahead." Kale took a look at each of them and then went on. "Come on. We should make camp and get some rest so we can make an early start in the morning."

They left the path just far enough to remain hidden if anyone came that way along the road and made their camp there. They chose not to build a fire for fear of being seen and instead settled into the oncoming darkness together. It felt strange, the four of them together without anyone else around. Gathered in the dark, voices low as they planned and then abandoning that, remembered. It felt like they were back home and like nothing had changed from that time more than five years ago. But, they couldn't be farther from there in time or space. All of them had been changed, transformed really, from who they'd been in those days. That foursome of long ago would hardly recognize the older more worn and jaded versions of themselves sitting here in the dark.

They talked for hours, while above them the stars told stories of eons past. Yet, they danced around the big and awful truth that could wait until another day to be faced fully. What would happen when it was time to go home? Would Kale go with them to where they believed she belonged?

TWENTY-EIGHT

IN THE DREAM, she was falling, tumbling end over end towards the ground at an unstoppable speed. She went looking for fear, reached deep into herself, but it wasn't there. Instead, for the first time, she felt certain of herself.

The air rushing past her began to slow and then it stopped completely, and she found herself afloat, suspended in a sea of sky above a great big black abyss below. She could feel it, both the possibility of finding herself and losing herself here as well. *I'm ready*, she realized, but it was more than that, *I'm willing and I'm okay with it.*

She saw the woman as if she appeared out of nowhere but somehow understood she'd always been there. There was a sense of familiarity, of deep knowing that rose up within her so forcefully she caught her breath. They'd met before. Of that, Kale was certain.

"We've been waiting for you, Kale," Cyan said, her kind brown eyes imploring. Her dark hair spread out around her like an aura.

"I don't know what you mean," Kale answered confused. *We've done this before,* she thought.

"Yes, in some ways, we have," Cyan answered as if hearing her thoughts. "It is time to step out of the dark. To allow yourself to become. Not the story of what you were but the truth of who you are now. It's ok," Cyan reached out but stayed where she was, "you are strong enough for it all. For both the light and the dark. Come home to yourself. It's time."

"I don't understand. Who are you?" Kale asked, trying to shake away the sense something big was rising inside her, but before Cyan could answer gravity wrapped itself around Kale again and she began once more to fall, spilling over herself as she drew closer and closer to the ground. Her wild mane of curls obscured anything she might glimpse above or below as the wind whipped it about.

When she connected with the earth, a painless and yet violent thud, the dream changed. She was catapulted towards that moment when she'd found herself standing on the mountain shelf above the darkness. Medea and Corin and Jaren were there. Wounded and disheveled but okay. Derin was on the ground, lying in a swollen pool of blood, his face pale and lifeless. She saw Joah standing with Arin, who she could tell was his sister just by looks despite their vast differences. There, beside them, was Alex, looking broken and ruined while, near him, Cyan stood, beautiful and regal, even in her misery and heartache.

None of them were moving. It was as if someone had hit pause and she found herself in some moment that would stretch on and on to eternity with nothing but her changing. She walked over to Derin and knelt down next to his body. The feeling was unfamiliar and strange and yet sorrow shot through her—a river of heartache that seemed to have no beginning or end. When she touched him, he was cold and lifeless and she drew her hand back, shocked and a little ashamed though she wasn't sure why.

"I love you. I always will." Her own voice floated through the darkness towards her but she couldn't quite fathom what it meant or why it was chasing her down.

She stood and looked around at her friends, the people she'd supposedly called family, trying to find inside herself what she must have felt for them, if they loved her enough to cross the universe, to come all this way to get her back, and to also stay bound to a night five years ago when they'd lost her so that none of them had fully moved on.

But wait, that was waking, and this was somewhere else. She looked around again. When she met Alex's eyes, she felt a jolt and then blinked, thrown off balance, confused.

"Kale," he said, his voice hopeful, "is that you?" He looked both desperate and certain. She didn't want any of what he sent across the space between them. It was too much, being wanted and needed that badly, being tied to some great big story she couldn't remember.

"No, it's not real," she said, stepping back and away. She repeated it over and over again, shaking her head, not wanting to be here or see any of it anymore. She didn't want to be Kale and to be responsible for so much pain and heartache and for living up to a destiny already fulfilled.

Alex reached towards her but he was frozen to the spot, unable to move towards her or act. It was terrifying how familiar it felt, that helplessness. "Stop, Kale, please," he was shouting now, "the edge!" He tried one last time but she wasn't listening; when she went over and into the dark, the shock of it threw him into the waking world so violently he sat up and almost choked on his breath.

It was still night. The others were sound asleep and not one of them stirred when he stood and walked off into the woods on shaky legs. He was running away, he knew, from the truth, from himself. He was also running towards something too; he just wasn't quite sure what it was. Destiny was still a quiet voice, but sooner or later he'd have to listen; and do the only thing destiny would accept in the end, surrender.

TWENTY-NINE

DERIN WOKE JUST BEFORE dawn. He noticed right away that Alex was gone which didn't surprise him. His brother could be a troubled sleeper and would often walk to keep from being caught by bad dreams or memories. Derin knew he'd be close by or returning soon and didn't even bother to worry, despite the fact they were in a strange place on a new world.

Rogan was still asleep and engulfed in what seemed like deep stillness and peace. He knew that could be an illusion and hoped her dreams were free of the awfulness that would assault her again once she awoke.

When he saw Joah stoking the fire, he took a deep breath and then got up to join him. He'd known this moment would have to come, but he'd carried with him a secret hope it was avoidable.

They'd forged a tenuous friendship over the years, one that often revolved around Medea. There was love between the men, sure, but because they stood on either side of her, it had been challenging at times to truly be comfortable together. Joah would always put Medea and her heart before almost everything else. In his relationship with her, he was both overprotective and fiercely loyal. For a long time, Derin had seen him as an adversary until he realized that Joah could be an ally. Yet, there was still a sense that Derin stood on the other side of a great divide, with Medea and Joah forever united—sometimes against him—on the other side of that vast expanse.

Derin couldn't help it; whenever Joah was around, he was always acutely aware of his own inadequacy, both to be enough for Medea and to measure up to the love that she and Joah shared. His inability to either capture her heart or keep it safe had always been a point of contention between the two men, even as they worked to forge a friendship that had a solid foundation. In moments like these, Derin couldn't help but be aware of how very complicated their friendship could be.

"Couldn't sleep," Derin said lamely, surprising himself by being nervous.

"Small talk huh? That's the way you wanna play this?" Joah's words were clipped and Derin realized they'd have to get right down to what needed to be said. He thought back to those first years he'd lived on Samnar, having returned to life with his family and struggling to find peace within and outside of himself. So much had been challenging and yet so much had not. Before he'd fallen in love with Medea, he and Joah had formed a friendship that was easy and comfortable, which was common for anyone Joah let his guard down with. He had a way about him, like his father, that felt like it made space for you to be yourself, unapologetically. He loved to joke and laugh, made everything seem like it was nothing to worry about, and couldn't help but make even the dullest of tasks or undertakings fun with his quick wit, constant joking and playful manner.

It had been Joah's relationship with Medea, that deep love and intimacy, that had begun to point Derin towards the truth of his own heart when he'd started to feel those first stirrings of envy that crept towards subtle jealousy. He'd expected Joah to be his rival, and though the shift in his feelings had challenged and changed their friendship, which Derin had always regretted, Joah had also shown him what true love could be. How it could demand you sacrifice so much of yourself for what the other person needed. Derin knew, even now, Joah was a better man than him and he wondered if he could take his example to make the right choice in this moment.

"Joah," Derin took a deep breath, "you have to understand, I didn't mean for any of this to happen, not like this." He could hear it in his own voice, a longing for this man he admired so much to know he was trying to be better, and stronger.

"You know, you and I have had our moments," Joah paused. More than once he'd been faced with a moment like this in his relationship with Medea and Derin, where he could step in or get out of the way, and he was never fully certain of which was best for them or himself. He went on, "All of them come down to you not believing in yourself or in her. Don't you think it's time to be brave, finally?"

"Goddammit Joah, you've always got to be so righteous." Derin couldn't help it, every time Joah did what he could not, put Medea first, that seed of jealousy for what Joah and Medea shared began to grow and bloom. "I'm not trying to hurt her. I don't want to hurt either of them. I just don't know what to do." He looked at his friend, who was sometimes his foe, and hoped he would hear him, would know he was pleading for help and for understanding.

"Derin, I can't absolve you of responsibility just because I love her. Or you." When their eyes met here, Derin felt a wave of love and sorrow sweep through him. Joah felt it, too. This was a story with more than one sad ending, and it wasn't up to either of them to try and control it all. It was time for him, like Joah, to be honest.

"I can't imagine what you're going through," Joah's voice had softened, "how hard all of this must be, and yet while you take your time to figure out what you want, people are being hurt. Medea's heart is the one that's breaking. I'm not going to tell you it's okay, that's for sure." Joah's emerald eyes blazed in the dark, lit by the firelight and a passion he rarely showed, and betraying a power he often hid.

"What am I supposed to do?" Even as Derin asked it, he wondered if deep down inside he didn't already know. "Kale... we just found her again. She's been through so much. Now you want me to just leave her behind?" He was exasperated and annoyed.

"I hate to break it to you, my friend, but you're not that special. None of us are. Both of them can survive just fine without you, can do even better than that actually. Trust me. What they need and deserve is your honesty. And your courage." Joah felt that familiar ache deep inside. Even though he knew what was right, it was never easy stepping out of the way.

For a moment, Derin let it sink in. He had been thinking about it all wrong. He wasn't the center, not for either them. He could be strong enough to step into the center with the woman he loved, but he had to earn that right and to deserve it. It wasn't enough for him to be unsure and remain undecided.

"Thanks," Derin finally said, and when Joah's eyebrows went up in a question, he answered him, "for being honest with me. I needed it."

"You know, sometimes I don't think you deserve her. But it's what she wants whether or not she knows it, and I believe it is what's meant to be, so I keep fighting for you. Don't make me regret it." Joah paused and looked up to the last stars lingering in a lightening sky. "And if you are going to choose Kale, be fair, do it soon." The words landed between them with a sense of power and finality. After a moment of silence where Joah kept his eyes turned upwards, Derin turned away from him and wandered off into the woods to find his brother. It had been enough for one night. There was nothing left to be said and nothing left to be done but be courageous. He hoped he finally had it in him.

THIRTY

THE DREAM WOKE HER just before dawn and her fear of landing back in it had her rising in search of the waves and the salt air instead. She strolled with easy steps, the kind with no purpose except to carry you to more comfortable places than the one you were already in.

When she arrived at the cliffs that met the ocean far below, for a moment she was drawn back and into the dream, but she shook it off quickly. Here, there was light. A golden thread painted on the horizon that brightened with every breath she took. The sky was a soft pink where the day was beginning out over the sea and above her the last couple stars leapt out of the night to hide behind that dark blue blanket of sky.

It was beautiful, she realized, and it took her breath away. The miracle was placed out before her, the one she was beginning to understand she was a part of. Not what she'd been told about rebels, reincarnation, space and time travel, battles fought and won, no, it was the simple act of being that took her breath away. *I am here*, she thought to herself, *even without a true sense of who I am or why, I am here and I matter.*

"You scared me," Medea said as she stepped next to Kale and looked out over the great big curve of a world not really theirs to know. "When I woke up, you were gone." Medea took a deep breath in and a slow, steady exhale. "You scared me."

Kale was quiet. It was hard to wrap her head around owing these strangers anything and yet it was a force, their wanting and needing from her, like gravity. So powerful in its pull, any time they were near, she could feel it. What could she even offer them when there was nothing inside of her to give? How could she make them understand the person they loved and needed was gone and she was simply trying to find a way to live with who she was, the woman who was born only just a few weeks ago, on a beach, in the sun?

"I'm sorry," Kale finally offered, but she meant it more about not being who they needed her to be than anything else.

"We're the ones who should be sorry." Medea smiled, laughing at herself a little and Kale couldn't help herself, she smiled, too. "It's just, we came all this way, not even on purpose really, and we just expected everything to be the same. We expected that because we didn't really manage to move on, you wouldn't have either. That you'd be waiting for us to rescue you. But, of course, some things never change." Medea shrugged but her eyes carried the same smile that found her lips. It was a moment of feeling like Kale, *her Kale*, was really near.

"What do you mean?" Kale asked, curious.

"You were the independent one. Fearless. You didn't really need any of us. I mean you did, and we were your family. Yet, deep down, we all knew you'd undertake your biggest adventures and struggles alone. You were always okay with that. It was us who could never let go. Even when you were alive." Medea paused here, shocked by her own admission. "I mean before," she corrected herself. She met her friend's gaze and offered an apologetic smile before she went on. "Sometimes, I could see it pressing in too tight, the world taking and taking, grasping at you and holding on. I should have known you'd cross the whole universe to escape it." Medea let out a quick laugh, acknowledging both the truth and her heartache.

"I'm so sorry," Kale said, aware she was apologizing for things she could not remember.

"Don't be. You were," Medea paused here, needing to correct herself again, "are, you are my sister, you always will be. We don't love each other for some ideal, some perfect picture of what we should be like. We love each other for the messy, honest truth. For the good stuff, but the bad stuff, too. For the great big whole of what we are, and what we aren't."

Medea's thoughts traveled back to Alpha Iridium, to awful days when Caine had ruled but that had not seemed so awful when they were wrapped up in their own little world: Making breakfast in the kitchen of the home they shared, drinking hot coffee, sometimes with a small spoonful of sugar and cream. They were luxuries, not ones everyone could afford, and yet what they did for the people of Berdune, and who Kale was in the community, afforded them some things, once in awhile at least—an oven-baked dessert after dinner, a loaf of soft buttery bread, fresh squeezed orange juice—all rare things in Caine's Berdune and yet all had at times found their way into the home in the woods that Medea, Corin, Jaren, and Kale had shared. They'd built an oasis, their foursome, and they'd believed neither time nor fate would find them there. Hadn't they learned once that you could not hide from those things? Medea promised herself she would never make that mistake again.

"Did I appreciate you as much as I should have?" Kale asked playfully, drawing Medea back from her memories. There was a warmth in her voice that spoke of sisterhood, that hinted at the deep well of love that could flow between two women. It startled Medea a little until she realized it was less a thing being offered and more a thing being perceived. This woman, who looked like Kale, who was her in every way except memory, wasn't even aware it was something that had belonged to them, and she couldn't know that not long ago it was something they'd indulged fiercely and with their whole damn hearts.

"Hardly!" Medea answered and they laughed, united, for a moment or two at least until a contemplative silence enveloped them and both felt tempted to wander away from each other and into it. Kale couldn't help but be curious about what it had been like to have a friend, a relationship, so intimate and honest with another woman. All she knew was what she had with Rogan and the other women of Iri. Between their fascination and curiosity for her and Rogan's subtle mistrust, she was far from being comfortable with anyone as much as she felt here with Medea; even if they were strangers in some ways.

"And what would I have to say about you and Derin?" Kale finally asked. For a long while, Medea sat there quietly beside her best friend, who wasn't really that anymore and maybe wouldn't be again, and wondered, for the first time, what it all meant now that Kale was alive and they'd found her, even if she didn't remember any of it.

Medea hadn't really faced what she was going to lose until now, hadn't been willing to let in the truth or the pain that came at its heels. Yet here, with Kale, that shadow of herself and all she'd been, Medea finally looked at what she'd not wanted to face and let the magnitude of it barrel into her. She took in half a breath, a sob really, and then covered her mouth with her hand. When Kale wrapped her arms around her, she finally let go and wept into her dead friend's embrace. She wept for Derin and what they'd finally found and now lost, or so it seemed. She wept for Corin and Jaren, just as stuck as she was in so many ways. She wept for her parents, for all of their parents lost in one way or another to

Caine's wrath and evil. She wept for herself, so broken, wounded, and afraid to live a great big life because the thought of losing it scared her so much. And, she wept for Kale, who never got to live the life she should have, who had given everything for a better world and then never gotten to see it, who had somehow survived her self-sacrifice only to wake on another world, on the other side of the universe, with not a single memory to help guide her back to the people and the place that loved her. She wept and wept until there wasn't a tear left in her to be shed.

They stayed like that until Medea's body stopped shaking and she was able to pull back and away from Kale and take a few deep and steadying breaths.

"I know so little about her...your Kale, but I think she'd want you to be happy." It was true, of course. Hadn't they told her enough about Kale, her old self, to make it clear? She'd been willing to sacrifice everything including her own life. *Except,* she wondered, *hadn't destiny played a part in all that*? What might their Kale have chosen five years ago on another world, on a dark night, if it had been her own choice? What might she choose now if everything she wanted could be hers; and did she even know what any of that was?

"She would, yeah," Medea interrupted her thoughts. "But it's not just up to us. You have no idea how long it took him to begin to get over you and to forgive himself for living when you didn't." It was so strange to be talking about it, talking about Derin, when Kale wasn't really here to have a say. Yet, even here in the dark, he was there between them. If Kale did get her memory back, if she did find her way back to herself, she might feel differently but all she could offer was what she knew of herself now. It was hard to picture standing between this amazing woman in front of her and what her heart deserved.

Medea felt much the same. Derin had been a love, however brief, that had seemed to anchor Kale to the world in a way she'd never seen before. Who was she to step into that path and demand her heart come first? Who was she to expect he'd want her when Kale had finally come back to him? Medea couldn't even be angry because she was so damn happy her friend was alive. If giving up the love she'd finally found brought Kale back to them, she'd give it up a thousand times even if it broke her.

The full truth went unsaid between them, yet it was so big it had a voice of its own. It didn't matter what they wanted or what they tried to build. They were expecting Kale to be someone she was not. They were expecting her to remember a life that may not be hers anymore to lay claim to. They were reaching for something that was already past and so it was not meant to have a present moment *anything* anymore. Their Kale was gone. Maybe she hadn't been meant to live past that last day of Caine's. Maybe the only way she could have a life beyond it was to forget everything, and all of them. Medea hadn't seen it before. She'd thought they were going to rescue Kale but maybe what would save her was not having to remember what she'd been, what she'd both survived and then finally lost on that last dark night on a mountain's edge on Berdune.

Could she accept it? Could she let her friend go, finally, and find a way forward that left her both in the past and in this new life she'd begun to build on a world stuck in some kind of limbo?

"I guess it's hard for me to understand because I don't remember what it all felt like." Kale smiled sadly and Medea's heart squeezed tight and ached. She wanted to be angry, to rage and lash out at the world. It all seemed so unfair. Yet from the right perspective, they were also so very fortunate. They'd had each other, and Corin and Jaren, too. They'd stepped into the ever-flowing current of destiny and found themselves and their way in the world. When it had all come crashing down at least, she'd had people around her to pick her up. Now, here was Kale, alive, a second chance at a life and happiness and maybe even love, if only Medea could take her turn being selfless and step out of the way. Could she let her heart lead her away from love towards her friend to make space for Derin and Kale to come back together again? To answer that call of their hearts that had been silenced unfairly once before?

It was hard to sort it all out. Her mind had an answer and her heart had two more. In the confusion of it all, Medea did the only thing she could think of, she gave Kale the advice she needed herself.

"Our memories aren't just written in our minds, Kale. They're written in our hearts and on our souls as well. Remember that when you go looking for yourself. For your past. For any of us and for what the road ahead looks like." She shook her head and smiled but it was a sad and sorry thing, and it didn't reach her eyes.

They looked back out over the ocean, a silent agreement they'd talked enough for one morning. The sun had risen fully and hung over the ocean like a ripe piece of fruit ready to drop from a tree. The waves rolled in from somewhere past the horizon, reminding them that some beginnings, just like endings, were meant to remain out of sight.

THIRTY-ONE

WHEN FIRTH OPENED her eyes it was too bright beautiful sunlight and at first she thought she was back in her bed, waking up next to Rogan, in a place and time where the whole world made sense again. It only took a second for her aching, wounded body to wrench her back into the present moment and then she squeezed her eyes shut tight trying to close out the awfulness waiting to greet her with the new day. Along with a large group of others her people had been herded into a big enclosure and then within that a smaller pen in a long line of them just south of the city. The first few pens they passed were filled with people. Gaunt, haunted, broken looking and unable to meet their eyes when they peered in through narrow gated doors as they passed. In their own cell stone walls, no roofs for protection and barred windows left them open to the elements and captured them inside a kind of oppressive hopelessness they could all feel. There was a kind of exhaustion that came with both the fear and the anticipation that they were being made to endure as the day carried on and they had no idea what was ahead of them. She suspected that feeling was at the root of why they were being detained and yet not told what was coming next;

nor what their fate would be. It was a calculated part of how everything had unfolded so far, and would unfold still, and she hoped she would be able to see past the theatrics of it all in order to make smart decisions in the coming hours, maybe more.

They'd not been fed. Not been given anything to drink. Not offered information or a safe and warm place to rest. They'd been left to roast in the bitter, angry sun while they found no shelter from their fear or from the truth of where they found themselves.

Firth moved amongst her people and the others they were penned in with and offered reassurance and a calming presence even though she wasn't actually feeling either deeper than her surface. She was by no means a leader, that had always been Rogan's role, but she stepped into it now out of necessity. She didn't want to be in charge, she didn't want to be here at all, but it seemed essential, this kind of uniting, even despite where they were and what they were facing. Maybe even more so because of it. It felt like a kind of remembering she could neither understand nor explain. Maybe in the same way humanity found ways to become monstrous it found ways to unite and rise. The only comfort she could find was in telling herself that together they were strong enough to survive this, whatever this was, and in keeping everyone tied to the feeble hope that there was a recognizable life on the other side of it all. If she kept at it long enough maybe it would become real, hope, even here in this place.

She sat down near one of the gates, her back to the monster of a city that loomed behind them, ever threatening, and watched. She was looking for something. That much she knew. But for what exactly she couldn't quite tell.

It was hard to believe that just a few days ago she'd been home. Safe and happy. Had she appreciated it? Had she reveled in how precious it was? Had she steeped in and savored every moment in a silent acknowledgement they would all pass, gone forever, never to be reclaimed. She thought she had and yet she wasn't quite convinced, sitting here, in the sweltering day, a prisoner to people so foreign to her that the concept of capturing and using people like this was nothing she'd ever even imagined was possible outside the dark and sinister story that was humanity's history.

She'd been so young when the world had broken that she mostly had no memory of it. Even the day that everything had changed was not a conscious memory. When the world had danced with complete annihilation and then had somehow waltzed back and away from the brink. It was a memory that lived in her like it lived in everyone who had survived. It had become a part of them, whether they realized it or not. It was a sleeping dragon, ready in their minds, and hearts, and bodies to awaken at any time. What kind of damage could a thing hidden for so long inflict, she wondered, and suspected that in the city of Dempsey there was an answer to be found.

The oldest of them had been twelve the day the Earth had broken. No one older had survived. When she thought about it, she suspected there was a wisdom to that, almost as if the universe understood that after a certain age, humans could and would not change. But she shook that foolish thought away every time it rose. Nothing was predetermined, she reminded herself, and no one was moving them around like pieces on a chessboard.

Even the younger kids, like her and Rogan, had had to grow up fast and take responsibility for so much. Looking back now all she could do was marvel that they'd been able to survive and eventually rebuild. Except while they'd been building a small and simple community others had built this, a city that prospered off of the backs of others in ways that disgusted her and made her sick.

They'd been fools, she realized, to think they could live isolated instead of trying to both know and understand what other threads of humanity had survived. They'd thought by staying away from other humans they were protecting themselves, but really they'd set themselves up to not know what was coming. To not know what was going on. How many prisoners had built this awful place, she wondered, and how many lives had been ruined or lost while her people had wandered blissfully unaware through their lives just a few days walk away? She felt ashamed, and sorry, and knew that yes, anger would come eventually too, but in the moment all she could feel was disappointment that humanity hadn't really traveled all that far from where it had been before the end of the world as they knew it.

Firth was drawn away from her dark thoughts and back to the moment by the unsettling sense that she was being observed. A kind of panic rose up in her until she realized that about twenty feet away, curled up together in a corner, were two young children, so striking in their beauty it made her heart ache. They huddled together, for safety or for comfort, or both, she couldn't know, but she wanted immediately to reach out to them. As they whispered and eyed her a pang of longing swept fiercely through her before she could hurry it away. There was enough to be heartbroken about without old stories and yearnings trying to make their way to the surface to be felt again.

The children were filthy and disheveled and though like many in their cell they seemed anxious they didn't look scared or even entirely lost. Firth was immediately drawn to them. She glanced around, looking for who they belonged with, but no one seemed interested in them. She gave them an encouraging smile and when they both intensely met her gaze she felt emboldened to get up and casually wander their way. Their whispering intensified but Firth wasn't deterred. She sat down beside them and at first the trio ignored one another, silent and seemingly aloof. Firth felt like it mattered, this beginning. Like something big was happening though she couldn't fathom what it was.

It struck her then, the full force of where she was and what it might mean. She'd not considered the possibility of remaining in this place. Of suffering whatever fate their captors had planned for them. What if she never saw Rogan again? What if her life was no longer her own? The swelling in her chest, this space expanding to hold so much sorrow and fear, was unbearable. She breathed deep and halting breaths, a woman about to drown in dread and gasping for the only thing that might prolong her life. *What would never be*, she wondered, *now that I am here*, and with that thought came another, *what other lives of mine have never had a chance to be already?*

She tried not to get caught up in an overwhelming sense of loss for all the lives that would never come to pass, even as they seemed in this moment to be so near and also so very loud. She squeezed her eyes tightly shut but couldn't block out any of what was rising in her. She would never be the woman who grew up in a world that hadn't almost been destroyed. She would never be a woman with parents, who hovered around her life to watch her become all that they'd dreamed. She would never be the woman who had children birthed into the world of her own body like she'd always longed for; until of course she'd discovered as a teen it wasn't her destiny. It wasn't in her nature to wish for another life or a better partner than Rogan, but still there was a version of her that would never be because of who she was. In this quiet moment it felt closer than ever. The story of the lives unlived and not to be.

She was silent for a long while and the children let her wallow until she finally opened her eyes and began to speak. Chasing the sorrow away with the sound of her own hopeful voice. She told the children about Rogan, and their life. About her own forgotten childhood, the pieces of it she could remember anyway. She wasn't sure why it all poured out the way it did but a little while later, sitting in silence, she felt better for it. She offered them every piece of herself that felt worthy and all the ones that did not. When she had nothing left the silence danced around them all again, but it was comfortable and it cradled each of them in a kind of safety, for a little while at least.

Eventually the children began to speak. They were so much alike that it was hard to tell them apart but it turned out Bella was eight and Andre was nine and they'd grown up in a village that they made to sound like an idyllic and happy place where other children and families lived and thrived. Their father had died a few years before from a mysterious illness and by how they spoke it sounded like their mother, trying to protect them, had been killed in the raid they were captured in, though they weren't quite able or willing to admit it just yet. Firth was hopeful they were wrong and that she'd be able to find their mother for them. She decided to stay with them awhile but silently promised herself, and them, she'd do everything she could to locate their mother and try to make things right.

She refused to believe it was hopeless. That any of it was. But when Egan grabbed her, lifting her off the ground like she weighed no more than the children, a ribbon of fear wove its way around her heart and squeezed tight enough that its beating momentarily stopped. She hadn't considered the worst was yet to come, but she did now, and her heart began to race. She was no match for his strength even as she kicked and flailed, connecting with him over and over again and once even scratching his face.

None of it fazed him.

He'd been watching her as she moved amongst the prisoners offering solace and strength. She was a fighter, that much he could tell, and she had the spirit of a survivor. He'd seen so many like her over the past few years. Strong, willful, determined, and unafraid. They all broke. Crumbled under the weight of torment, torture and hopelessness. He was certain Firth would be the same.

She swung and connected with his jaw coaxing a wild and menacing smile out of him. Fear coursed through her body in a way that threatened to paralyze her, but she fought it like she fought him, with every part of her being. More powerful than the fear was the rage, that these people should take and harm and pay no price for any of it. Her fury made him jealous Bex would be the one break her, because he knew it would be fun.

THIRTY-TWO

WHEN CYAN OPENED her eyes, she thought at first she must be dreaming of a day long, long ago when she'd first had the inkling her life would be more than that of an artist, and a widow, living on the Atlantic Ocean by herself, dreaming of that first moment when she'd found herself afloat amongst the ocean of space, with Polaris Mu, the giant star behind her while Alpha Iridium and its four siblings roamed around it. It was where she'd first met Dellerim. Floating there, convinced it was a strange and wondrous dream, yet it was actually just the beginning of the one that would become her life. She hadn't known then that that solar system would become her home. That she'd build a great, big, beautiful life there. That she'd forget Earth in a way, over the millennia that she'd revel in love and happiness and joy, even as she looked to the stars and wondered which of them carried with it the long ago story of her past.

It had begun in dreams, ones she'd woken from with a sense that she'd left something big and important behind. They'd called to her day and night and she'd painted their mysteries and the beginning of a life she'd found while sleeping while every night she dove deeper and deeper into falling in love again.

She hadn't known then that the five perfect beings she met while dreaming carried with them a bigger destiny than she could ever have imagined. That they would leave Earth and make their way across that vast and somewhat infinite expanse of time and space to start a new life and a new kind of hope for humanity. Led by a timeless being who called himself Froste. He loved and cared for them in a way that was both astounding and heartbreaking; and carried with it a kind of familiarity that would haunt her for years to come. Haunt her until a moment yet to come but nearing so very quickly.

She'd lived in that time of humanity that had yet to admit it would be the author of its own destruction. A time when they still took and took from the Earth without any sense of balance or consequence. They swarmed across the planet like a plague, convinced of their own superiority and entitlement to it all, completely unable to care for the very world, life forms and ecosystems that sustained them. Their arrogance and ignorance led them towards a false sense of immortality and self-certainty so that even as the planet began to fight back and fail they could not fathom they were living in the very beginnings of their own great demise.

Her father had been a man of science. Determined to find ways to save humanity but even he in all his genius thought the answer would be found in better, more perfect humans when in fact it had been far more simple and astounding than that.

They'd lost their sense of awe, both for their own tiny place in the great big whole of creation, and for the world around them and how they were connected to it. Without that sense of connection, of both belonging to something and having that thing belong to you, they were powerless in the story of their own destiny and that ancient Darkness that balanced out the universe easily devoured any hope they had of surviving when it came calling.

The Founders, Arianna, Joachim, Kiernan, Kendra, Dellerim, and Cyan, had left long before that time. The final hope of a species who really didn't deserve another chance on any world, including their own. Yet, it had been granted and given. So it was that the Founders began a long and happy life on Alpha Iridium. For countless years, they went unseen by the Darkness, until they decided to play God by birthing people and a civilization into being to keep them company. In that single selfish act, they became like their predecessors, truly human, and so it was that the Darkness found them.

They'd been given so much power and too often they'd used it poorly. Too often they'd disobeyed. Stepped out of the boundaries of time and space and taken what shouldn't have been theirs. Cyan was afraid. What price would they pay for this last great taking? For sending six of their number across that dark and eerie sea of space to Earth to save another who really wasn't meant to be anymore.

It had only been a moment since she'd woken and yet all this had tumbled through her mind and more. When she first woke with that same scene of stars and eternity, adrift in the dark, she'd thought she was dreaming of then; that first night she'd met Dellerim and in meeting him met the beginning of her destiny. For a moment, she grabbed hold of it and held on tight because the present she realized, was pulling at her violently, and she wasn't quite ready to face it.

Dellerim was there with her. Looking worried and resigned. Though he hadn't changed or aged much since that first night she'd met him, there was a weariness about him now that startled her into the present moment and anchored her there.

"My love," she began, but didn't know what she was meant to ask to try and figure out why they were here. "Do you know..." she tried again but couldn't go on. Something inside, some deep intuition, told her she didn't want to know what he'd done.

"I am so very sorry," was all he could offer. Simple words and yet they were big and heavy. They terrified her. She realized that that long ago moment when her destiny had begun to unfold had not just landed her here, in this moment, but was also leading her toward an unknown end and yet already decided. Somewhere she wasn't sure she was ready to arrive.

She drew close to him and wrapped her arms around him tightly. They floated that way. Suspended in a kind of limbo. Neither in the waking world nor in the dreaming world either. *What did you do*, she wanted to ask him, but she wasn't ready for the answer just yet.

THIRTY-THREE

IN THE CENTER of their camp, they'd built a large bonfire, which lent sparks of light to the night sky as the curling, dancing flames seemed to reach for the stars. There was a kind of heaviness in the air and also a kind of anticipation that none of them were able to put a voice to and so they sat in the quiet serenade of crackling logs and wind gently nudging leaves far above, and once in a while the sound of a wolf howling in the vast dark of the wilderness around them.

They'd come back together in the late afternoon and by some silent agreement hadn't yet shared what they'd learned on their prospective missions. Despite a sense of urgency about rescuing Rogan's people there was a strange sense of knowing on top of it that they were in a time they would never regain. The last of a kind of peace they'd experience before whatever was coming for them arrived. It was strange to think they'd all been here in a way before. With that monster of destiny barreling towards them and on the other side of their fight with it was a life completely different than the one they were in now.

Only Kale's story was different and far stranger than the rest and yet she couldn't remember any of it. How many times could a life be remade, be put back together? Too many was a possibility it seemed for this last time she'd come back without the entirety of herself. They'd told her she'd first been born on Earth and then reborn on Alpha Iridium the night Caine had arrived, when she'd entered their world at the age of five. She'd been born again, fourteen years later, fallen from heaven that final night as well. And what of this third and final rebirth, back where she'd begun long, long ago when the people of Earth still hadn't been sentenced for no longer being worthy of a place in the story of the universe.

More than one of their party thought about the strangeness of it all. About how it seemed absurd they'd travelled all this way from a place that had finally found peace to fight in another battle against a kind of darkness that had always been eating away at humanity.

It was Rogan who finally broke the silence. She needed to know they were working towards having a plan. She told Medea, Kale, Corin and Jaren about the city penned in by stone and wood while they kept slaves in communal cells inside a huge enclosure just outside the gates. They'd watched as some of them were led in chains to and from various places, no doubt to fulfill jobs to help the city flourish while they were being stripped of their dignity.

It had sickened her. She couldn't understand any circumstance where it would be okay to treat another person that way. Like their life mattered less than your own. She thought of her friends and her family living out their days like that. Separated. Kept like animals. Their own needs and wants left unmet. She couldn't understand the kind of people who would be okay with treating another human being that way. It just made no sense. Everyone could have what they needed if they simply worked and contributed. What kind of people built empires on the backs of others while doing nothing themselves? It terrified her that they'd lived so near to this monstrosity of a society with no inkling or sense that these horrors were going on while they'd moved blissfully through their lives. How long had other people suffered, been separated from their families and loved ones, been forced to work and serve while being treated like property? *How long have we been a small part of the problem,* she wondered, *by not taking a look at the world around us and what it contained?* A current of shame wound its way through her so that she kept those final thoughts to herself.

"We didn't act for a long time," it was Alex, "we obeyed the stars. This gift we had of seeing the future unfold. Of knowing what was coming and how." He looked around at his friends and then settled his gaze lastly on Kale, holding it there as long as he dared before looking back to Rogan. "It's taken me a long time to forgive myself for waiting so long to act, stars or not." Gratitude swept through Rogan before she dropped her gaze.

"Destiny is funny that way," Kale said almost sadly and yet her words carried a kind of power that had them all waiting, poised for what would come next. "Not one of us can escape. Not it. Not what it asks us to become. Or what it takes from us in the asking."

The fire leapt, a huge pop issued sparks into the night sky, and with that interruption they were set free from wondering what she'd meant as she went on to tell Rogan, Alex, Derin and Joah what they'd found in a town pretending it wasn't party to slavery. Alex watched, captivated, as she tried to contain the anger simmering under the surface. It carried her friends back to a time when she'd raged at Caine and his armies and it made her seem almost like the young woman they'd known on Alpha Iridium. In that retelling her true fury for the injustice of it bubbled up and out, finding a life in the world that brought Derin back to knowing her as a soldier in training. She'd seemed so fearless then but really she'd simply been so angry that she'd had no choice but to follow that deep and aching instinct to stand up and fight.

In watching her, angry and wounded at the thought of so much cruelty, Alex realized he was seeing her like that for the first time. Unlike most of the others, he didn't have a story of her that went back before that night on the mountain shelf when she'd healed his wounds and told him life would be different. He'd built a version of her in his mind in the five years since she'd died that had been based on other people's stories, and memories. All the good parts gathered up to keep alive someone who was gone. He could see it now in their faces. They were still only looking at fragments of her. The ones that drummed up memories of a warrior, a beloved friend, and a savior. But the truth was she was more than that. Or had been before every piece of her had been stripped away. Maybe she'd left those pieces of herself scattered across the dark of time and space Alex thought. Breadcrumbs that would lead her back to them all eventually. Or maybe she'd left them behind to finally be free. To have a life separate from the story destiny had demanded she write with her life and death.

What he realized then was that maybe it wasn't fair to ask her to come back. To return to a place where she would have to contend with this great big idea of who she'd been rather than getting to be herself as she was now. Didn't he know what that was like? Didn't they all in a way?

When Kale finished raging, no one spoke. The group was quiet, thoughtful, and unsure what to make of it all; both what they'd heard and seeing Kale so much like herself again, even if it was an illusion and not the truth. Her cheeks were red and her heart was racing, and her deep brown eyes wavered between furious and heartbroken.

Derin couldn't help it—she was breathtaking in a way that carried him back to that version of himself who'd first stepped out of the shadows and into the light because she'd invited him to do so. It had been that first waking of his heart, that first glimpse of what love could be that had tempted him to question himself and consequently Caine. In loving her, that fierce and passionate young woman, he'd finally stepped away from the path that led into darkness and he'd found his way to his true self. He'd never had the chance to sit with it all after they'd beat the Darkness back. There'd been room to mourn her loss and to hope what he believed they'd had was real, but he'd never had the chance to figure out what a life with her could be. Now here she was and instead of it all seeming clear it was just more confusion and uncertainty.

He looked from her to Medea, then back again. The story of his past and what he thought had been the story of his future. He realized he was bound in both directions and sooner or later he'd have to let go of one of them or all of it would come tumbling down. A broken ruined mess.

Beside his brother, Alex felt a deep stab in his chest that for a moment startled him into thinking something was wrong. When he stood he avoided meeting anyone's eyes and simply excused himself. He didn't know what he was feeling but he knew he wanted to be alone. To be away from this group that so intimately knew him and always left him feeling tied to a past he was forever trying to escape.

Alex's leaving punctuated the fact they had yet to make a plan and so instead of getting caught up in the injustice of it all they began to put together some idea of what they would do next. They'd wait for Sumira and whatever people she could manage to convince to join her and then they would set the slaves free. They didn't discuss what would come next. Neither the consequences of upsetting a powerful city nor where they would run or how they would rebuild. There would be time enough for that in the light of day. Instead they settled in to a comfortable and companionable silence.

Jaren, Corin, and Medea met each other's eyes and in that silent connection knew exactly what the other was thinking. This was like a time they'd already survived, and now here they were again. Somewhere in the not-so-distant future and yet moving through what felt like the past. Getting ready to lash out at a kind of monster that had no real place in the world. Except if that were true why did the monsters seem to keep showing up. History was littered with them. Both here on Earth and of course where they'd come from. What did it mean? And what did it say about humanity?

Sitting there, minds wandering back to a past intent on living again, each of them faced it in a different way, and yet the sentiment was the same. If humanity kept making monsters maybe they were a part of the very fabric of their being. If that were true how would they ever escape this story that came upon them repeatedly; of greed and oppression, prejudice and injustice, of hatred and ultimately self-destruction. There was of course no way of knowing what it all meant and where it was all going to end. What plan the higher powers in the universe had for any of them, or why. They'd learned long ago that those stories would play out with or without their intervention and so sometimes all you could do was tend to your little corner of the world with love and kindness and compassion, and hope that enough other people were doing the same.

Even though Kale was just on the other side of the fire, she might as well have been a million miles away. They could feel that missing piece of their foursome in moments like this so poignantly. Moments that carried them back to a time when they'd been united. When they'd been a family and looked out for each other and taken care of each other. Survived because of one another. They'd come a long way from those days and from how it felt to be a unit and yet each of them held on to that tiny thread of hope that Kale would find her way back to them all in the end.

THIRTY-FOUR

KALE

I KNOW IT SOUNDS strange, but yesterday was the first day I felt this sense of another me under the darkness that holds all my memories and history at bay. Standing in that great hall listening to those people justify standing by while people are gathered up to serve and slave away for that rotten city. I didn't know I had rage or anger in me like that. It came from so deep that it felt like pulling something heavy and large free from the sea. There was a kind suction, a pulling back, a resistance. Like I was pulling something loose that wanted to be kept in place. But there was nothing beyond the anger. When I tried to pull it aside to see past it, there was still nothing there. Yet it felt like both something new and something old, remembered even, that felt both exhilarating and familiar.

I've watched them now for days. The one's who crossed the universe for me. Sort of like the way Rogan's always watched me. I get it now. I know that they have answers and yet not enough of me is left from that young woman they knew to even want to dig into it all. There's too much in the present moment to face. How can I go looking for the complicated life and death of a girl who lived two lives - and yet neither fully from what I can tell – when the world seems to be falling apart in the here and now.

They remind me of planets. They have a sort of rhythm that carries them round and round each other in familiar ways. Whether they know it or not they are deeply connected. Always aware of each other whether it's conscious or not. When I'm deeply in the noticing of this dance, I feel awkward and heavy, acutely aware that I don't have the grace or what it takes to move with them in that way. I am a stone at the bottom of a pond, and they are the fish swimming elegantly round and round. I will never be like them. I will always be anchored while they're not. It surprises me how much the knowing of this hurts. It opens up a deep ache within that makes me wince and want to get away from them.

I wonder what it was like for Kale. Being so very different than the people around her. Even though she was unaware, deep down she must have known. Must have felt a sense that there was some fundamental difference between her and her friends, and all the people she shared her life with in one way or another. What must it have been like for her, surrounded and yet so alone? Living her life as a fragmented piece of a greater whole. I guess in this I feel deeply connected to her; in the sense of being in the midst of people and yet being so damn isolated still. Like her I was something so much more, and now I'm just a fraction of that, and yet I'm not sure I want to know where the rest of me has gone if I'm being honest.

There's anger here now, too. What right do any of them have to ask me to be her again? To ask me to step back into a life that tore me to pieces and that I left willingly? Can they really believe I'd want to go back? To live in the shadow of a life that was lived so single-mindedly and that ended in much the same way? I'm not sure they really knew her, not entirely, because the young woman they keep describing to me was okay with leaving when she did. Unless maybe, that love between her and Derin really was big enough to be worth sacrificing her life for. It's hard to know.

I watch Derin so much. This great love that I was supposed to have found so briefly. I can see he's afraid. Some of it is me, sure, but some of it has to do with Medea too. How many years have they waited to finally be together, and now this, me. I don't want to be a wall between them. I want them both to be happy.

With Jaren and Corin, it's the same. It surprises me how much it makes me sad that they've not built much of a life since that darkest day they are always talking about. There is a kind of ease with Corin that tells me our relationship was simple and yet still deep and loving. He's honestly the easiest of all of them to be around. Jaren's a little bit more complicated, as I suspect our story was as well. He seems both certain of himself and kind of lost and I wonder if he isn't waiting for the world to tell him what's next rather than chasing down what he really wants. There is a kind of longing in him that feels both familiar and frightening and more than once I've had the desire to tell him everything will be okay even though I'm not sure why.

Joah and Rogan have hit it off. It delights me to see her with something to distract her from the torment of waiting to act. To give her mind a break from picturing all the possibilities of what will happen to our friends and family while we're sitting here forming a plan and waiting for Sumira. I feel like ever since Rogan found me cowering in that last patch of green grass things have changed. Even though I decided to run away it had started to feel like I'd belonged. Like I was part of something bigger than myself. Like I mattered in a way that if I were missing it would alter the very fabric of what had been left behind. But all that has changed. She's not been the same with me since that day. Whatever I'd built has been swept away in that current of my inaction and all that remains is this deep well of shame. When I watch her with Joah and see the anxiety in her face fall away and that weight on her shoulders ease a little, I feel a deep sense of gratitude for his easy manner and gracious heart. I suspect he is often underestimated and taken as merely a joker when really he is deeply empathetic, kind, and thoughtful. I wonder how often he plays into the misperception of who he really is because it's safest or maybe just easiest to keep people at a distance.

Alex sits down beside me and I shrink for a moment before I catch myself. I don't like the effect he has on me. I feel exposed when he's near and when our eyes meet, which is too often, I feel disarmed. Like he knows something about me that I don't yet know about myself. Which of course he does, they all do, and yet it feels different with him. I always know when he's near, always know when he's watching or looking at me. It's unsettling and strange and yet also wakes up in me a deep sense of curiosity. In some ways, I am only three weeks old and this is the first time I've come across this sense of awareness about another person. He says we didn't know each other on Alpha Iridium, it was just a few moments on that last night, and yet it feels like it's more than that. I keep wondering if it's simply that I did the one thing he spent a lifetime expecting himself to do, stop the one they called Caine and set free the new world. But what should it matter, here I am with no memory, no sense of myself at all, and he's got everything else he wanted, his family reunited and peace on their planet.

"Kale," he says it quietly but it still stings. How've they accepted it so quickly while I can barely bring myself to acknowledge it. "I guess I should have asked, is it okay if we, if I, call you that?"

I have this desire to rage at him, to scream and shout, to beg him to stop pressing down on me the expectation of being someone I'm not, but I know that to them I'm her and it's not their fault. "It's fine," I say lamely. "Thanks, for asking I mean."

"Of course," he says and then steps back into that deep and brooding silence he seems so adept at weaving and all I can do is sit here and wait. The silence stretches on so long I begin to believe he's not going to say anything more, but it's comfortable enough that I settle into it.

"We'll have to go home soon," he finally says. "I don't know how I know it, but I do. You'll have to decide what you want to do." He pauses here and again the silence stretches on so long I'm not sure if he's done or not. "It's okay you know, to stay here." He says it so sadly I'm not sure if I can believe him, "You don't actually owe us anything."

I don't say a word but I catch myself smiling a little. It's a sad and sorry thing. A reminder that I have nothing much here and nothing much to go back to either. Honestly, I'm not sure I belong anywhere, and I don't know what to do.

He speaks like he can read my mind.

"I know you probably don't know what to do," he begins, his voice a clear but quiet whisper. I lean a little closer despite being able to hear him already. After a deep breath he goes on, "but I got some good advice once and I think it applies here."

"Oh yeah," I say, both curious and a little caught up in this moment that feels a bit like it's somehow outside of time. Like we're stealing something that's not really ours and yet I cannot fathom what that could be.

"You don't need your memories back." He's so desperate for me to feel okay with what I choose that I want to believe every word he says. "Whether you stay here or come with us there will be a home made for you. So, trust yourself. Trust your heart."

I want to laugh and cry at the same time but instead I just sit there mute and nod. Of course Kale would know what to do. But even as I think that I can't help but wonder if she would take her own advice.

After a long silence that feels both comfortable and companionable he shifts awkwardly and then he goes on. "I should go," he says, and I see him nod in the direction of his brother, deep in conversation with Jaren and Corin. "He deserves the world you know. Though he hasn't quite realized it yet. He's too busy still paying the price for who he was all those years ago."

"Sounds to me like you all are." The words are out before I can stop myself and after a long pause, he shrugs.

The conversation has led me back to that deep sense of loneliness and melancholy that's been hunting me down all day. I'm barely a whole person which makes me wonder, how could I ever manage to be enough for someone who deserves the world. And do I even want that responsibility? Would anyone? Maybe I should talk to Derin. Find a way to figure out if my heart remembers anything and if not set him free.

Alex stands and meeting my eyes sends that jolt of recognition through me. He leaves without a word. Like he knows I'll struggle to find any and I don't want to hear anymore. How am I ever going to figure out what I want and who I am in time to give them an honest answer? What if they go home and then I suddenly remember being her and wish I'd gone with them? Watching the fire I can't help reaching back for Alex's advice. 'Trust your heart,' he'd said, but I'm not sure mine remembers enough to know what to do either.

THIRTY-FIVE

WHEN MEDEA WOKE, it was to this sense of deep and aching sorrow. Her body was sore and tired and her heart was heavy. She felt instantly that pull to fall back into sleeping even before she remembered what day or time she was waking to. She'd been dreaming of a day long ago, on a night when her world had changed. She couldn't help herself, she closed her eyes again, longing to get lost in the memory of it and not face the coming day.

It had been at one of their yearly reunions. She, Corin, and Jaren had journeyed to Samnar just like they had on previous years to spend that difficult and yet celebratory time with some of the only people on Alpha Iridium who knew both what they'd lost and what they'd truly won. This year was slightly different as Derin was sailing back with them. He'd been on Samnar as a kind of emissary. Strengthening that tenuous thread of love, and peace, and goodwill that had formed between the Founders and the people of Berdune.

He'd traveled many times to their continent and visited every single town and village across it. Meeting leaders and ordinary people alike. On these trips, he had flashes of Kale. The way she'd walked amongst the people, at times revered, and he wondered what that must have been like for her. To live a life so loved and yet held up so high in regard you were actually often out of reach of true connection and intimacy. He, of course, didn't inspire that kind of reaction with the people now, nor did he want to. He simply wanted to make sure that he continued to be an active participant in rebuilding Berdune and wiping clean any remnants of Caine's rule. In some secret way, it was also his penance. Facing the very people he'd once worked to oppress and enslave.

Always, he'd feel satisfied with that deep wounding of himself. He deserved it, didn't he. After so many people had suffered and lost their lives and he'd lived a life of privilege even if he'd been a kind of prisoner in it. Derin had tried to talk to his brother about it so many times but who could understand what it was like. People wanted to focus on the fact he'd chosen the right side when it counted. They reminded him Caine had raised him as his own and how could he know his father was a monster with so many years inside that poisonous and toxic world that Caine had built around them. But he had known, his heart had anyway. In the dark of night it whispered to him that he was on the wrong side of history, only he hadn't listened.

Derin had never been able to accept how others gave him a pass because he'd been so young when Caine had found him. Because of that he kept the truth of how he felt to himself. The certainty he'd deserved to die on that mountain shelf for the role he'd played in Caine's rule. The struggle he had in forgiving himself because the person who'd deserved to live had given her life for his. The fear that he would never live up to that gift or deserve it. He'd never told anyone that. Until Medea. Until a friendship that felt safe and certain in a way that allowed him to open up.

Maybe it had been years of being Kale's best friend that had prepared her, but Medea understood that things weren't as simple as they appeared. She knew what it was like not to challenge someone's way of looking at themselves. Not to challenge how they believed they were one thing while those who loved them could see they were so much more. Medea understood that loving someone meant allowing them the space to walk their own path. More often than not they'd find their way to the truth in their own time. It was a gentler way of coaxing them out of and then away from the stories they'd long told themselves, true or not. Like Kale and the way she'd never really believed she was worthy of a life outside of her mission to stop Caine.

With Derin, it was his inability to forgive. He struggled to offer it to himself. He couldn't figure out how to offer it to his mother. Resentful, angry, and stuck he suffered and still, even that pain, he felt he deserved. Yet he'd found a kind of sanctuary with Medea. Like him she felt a sense of having lost Kale because of her own shortcomings. Like she could have prevented Kale's death if only she'd been stronger, or faster, or surer of herself. Even though in some ways she blamed Derin for her best friend being gone, there was still a deep sense of understanding that showed up between them. It was during that last visit where their bond had truly deepened and something else, unseen until they were both its victims, began to take root under the surface of their friendship.

He'd been meant to leave Berdune a month before. Then his trip was delayed not once but twice and then it simply made sense for him to travel with Jaren, Corin and Medea for the yearly celebration. It was during that last month that things had really changed. There'd grown a sense of intimacy between them. Medea hadn't seen the signs until it was too late. She'd gotten so lost in him being the guy that Kale had loved, allowing it to make her feel closer to her lost friend, she didn't notice something was coming to life inside her that she may never be able to escape.

Derin, too, had fooled himself into thinking it was entirely about Kale. About spending time with the person she'd been closest to. He'd begun to forget tiny details about her. Her voice. Her hands. What that space looked like between her ear and the nape of her neck. He'd had so little of her to begin with, and he didn't want to lose any of what remained. Didn't want to let her go like that; to have her fall away and out of sight in tiny little pieces. One minute there, one minute gone. Yet that's how she was slipping away from him and so he reached for the one thing he thought might save her, completely unaware that he'd lose his heart in the midst of it all.

They'd spent all that time together, seemingly lost in the past, and yet their hearts, unseen, were secretly plotting the future. Medea had realized it first. Had been at some menial task humming and daydreaming when she'd finally snapped back to the moment, as if she'd caught herself from the outside looking in. At first, she'd been too shocked to feel anything else. She'd said it over and over again, 'I'm in love with Derin,' but every time was just as unbelievable as the last. It both exhilarated and terrified her but after letting it settle she realized it would have to be put aside. She wasn't ready to feel that way again and certainly not with the only man her best friend had ever loved. What would it say about her as a friend if she finally moved on, with Derin?

The rest of their time on Berdune Medea became distant. She was friendly and kind as always but never let him get close and refused to open up or engage in conversation. It baffled Derin, the change in her, but he wasn't sure how to approach it because she wasn't exactly doing anything differently. She was simply colder, a little aloof and out of reach, and had lost her easy way with him.

It was a confusing time for Medea. In some moments she wanted to indulge in the being in love. It wasn't just that it felt like a kind of coming home for her heart that she hadn't noticed she was missing in all her grief and mourning. It was that it made her feel closer to Kale, loving the same man she had, and so in secret she delighted in it. Maybe that's what led to that first big mistake.

They'd been back on Samnar for the reunion. She spent days with Joah wandering through the woods, chasing new trails and looking for new beaches to test the waters in. Joah had spotted the secret truth of her heart the moment she'd arrived. It had surprised him that he'd felt wounded, hurt and a little jealous at first but all that had wandered off and left him with a deep sense of happiness that his best friend and the person he loved most in the world might actually find her happiness after all. But he'd quickly realized she wouldn't allow it to happen because she believed it would be a kind of betrayal she'd never survive. So, she spent those first days avoiding Derin and hiding out in the safe and loving space that Joah and her had found together over the years.

It was on the anniversary that everything unraveled and all her plans to keep her heart to herself would be forgotten. Arin and Joah had been brewing a kind of berry wine with their father over the past year and it came out that evening and everyone began to sample it. As they sat around the fire telling the story of that last night of Kale's life, the story took a different turn. They spoke of all the beauty and joy that had drawn them towards those final endings and that had carried the rest of them past them. When the story was done, the fire burning bright and tall, music began to play in the trees, a favorite trick of Kendra's, and they all began to dance and sway and laugh.

Standing with his brother and a few others, Derin caught sight of Medea out of the corner of his eye and his breath caught in his throat. She was dazzling. Laughing and happy and there was a kind of aura around her that was so vibrant and alive it felt magnetic in a way that drew him towards her and away from his companions without even excusing himself. When he reached the group she was standing with, she finally noticed him. She turned her radiance towards him, smiling, and again it took his breath away.

"Hey," was all she managed to say before he placed his hand on her cheek, bent down, and pressed his lips fully onto hers. It was firm and yet cautious. Curious even about whether it would be returned. But she answered almost immediately. Tilting her head and leaning up and towards him their lips began to move, and she opened hers slightly, and stole some of his breath before the kiss deepened and intensified. Her hand went to the back of his neck and she tugged him closer as his tongue pressed into her mouth, so soft and sweet. There was passion even in their gentle hesitancy and the whole world evaporated out of sight around them so that there was no sense of time or of needing to break away from one another; yet eventually they did. Everyone had moved away from them and was either dancing or talking in small groups, leaving the pair alone. There was an unspoken knowing of how hard it must be for them to finally step into what everyone else could see was happening.

Derin had paused, pulled back from her ever so slightly, and pressing his forehead to hers breathed deep. His heart was racing, his head was spinning, and he couldn't believe that he felt this way, and with who he was feeling it. He finally slid his lips down to her ear and whispered, "Let's get out of here," and she'd simply nodded because she wasn't sure she'd be able to find her voice again. When they'd gotten back to Derin's house, the one he shared with his brother, they'd undressed each other slowly in the dark. Like the big and scary truth of what was happening might go unseen this way, at least for now. It seemed things might stay that way, slow and careful, and yet when they came together after they'd undressed a slow and smoldering passion ignited and they were lost to it immediately. That's how they'd made love that first time during a night that seemed endless. A kind of gift they couldn't even have known they needed.

That's what Medea had been dreaming of. That night and then the first moments of waking when she'd been so swept up and overwhelmed with a kind of gentle wave of bliss she'd thought it might shatter her into a million pieces. But then the morning sun had lit up more than just what they'd found together the night before. It lit up the truth that she was happier than she'd ever been. So was he. But if she was this happy with Derin it meant her life was better off now that Kale was dead.

It slammed into her so violently she shot up and out of bed. The bubble of warmth and certainty she'd only moments before been suspended in burst. She felt awful. Ashamed and disgusted with herself. She was certain if Kale could see her she'd feel betrayed. It was unbearable and not only did she pull away she threw awful, hateful words at Derin when he tried to reach out to her.

He'd known of course what she was doing. Who had shown up in that room with them and torn their short lived happiness to shreds. It had felt so real and certain and yet it turned out to be no more substantial than ashes scattered on a breeze. Could he blame her? Could he blame either of them? Kale or Medea.

The ache that followed almost knocked him down it was so painful and yet in its own way it was comforting as well. He knew this kind of suffering. Too often he'd sat in the certainty that he deserved it. That he was paying for past mistakes. That's why he didn't go after her. Because she deserved better and he deserved the pain.

She'd left later that day. Saying goodbye to no one. Joah was the one who took her home. It almost destroyed Derin, the thought of her with him. Joah able to give Medea something he couldn't. Something he would never be able to. It was unbearable, knowing his love was a thing that could only take. First Kale and then Medea. Neither one of them seemed better off for loving him, or for having him try and hand them his heart. Derin didn't know what it meant but he thought he might be done with love for awhile.

Medea had hurried home and tried to rebuild that careful façade of being strong and sure of herself. No one mentioned Derin or the scene at the party. She didn't want to talk about it. That's how things remained. She'd vowed never to return to Samnar so she wouldn't be tempted to betray her friend again and despite his broken heart Derin tried to respect her choice. He knew what it was like to owe the dead. Those were debts that weighed heavy and cost the living dearly.

That's what Medea woke with at sunrise. A confusing taste of a past that looked very different now that Kale was alive. She'd had that same sense she'd had on the last morning she'd spent with Derin all those years ago. At first there been a perfect kind of bliss. A sense she was waking into something wonderful, and special, and divine until reality slammed into her and she felt thrown off balance and heartbroken all at once.

What did it all mean or matter now that she was here? Now that Kale was alive. Now that Derin would try and help Kale find a way back to him and what they had. She hadn't known her heart was whole enough again to get broken but here she was. That familiar ache starting deep inside her and threatening to spill out into the space around her until she might drown in it.

She wanted to reach for this sense that life was unfair. To indulge in wallowing in it even. But a reminder of where they were and why hurried all that away and Medea began to rise. She was strong enough to face this too. She allowed herself a last few moments of longing for another life, an easier one, before she reminded herself even in all they'd suffered, how much more did they have to be grateful for, and so who was she to want to change a thing.

THIRTY-SIX

DERIN AND ALEX woke that morning at the same moment and instantly found each other's eyes across the smoldering fire. Without a word they rose and walked off into the dawn to find some privacy. They walked for ten minutes before their pace slowed and they found somewhere to stop that was both comfortable and undeniably isolated. They never considered they wouldn't be able to find their way back to camp. There was something inside both of them that always seemed to remember the way home. It was a thing that had been tested many times and would be yet again before their story was done.

There was silence between them at first. An acknowledgment that once they said what they had to aloud none of it could be taken back. No matter how many times you dreamed of the truth, or saw some destiny hurrying towards you on an ocean breeze, carried your way from the horizon, it didn't change the fact that nothing was quite real until it was given a voice in the waking world. With that in mind they savored their last moments free of a devastating truth they'd only just learned.

It had begun of course as most dreams do. Nonsense mingled with truth. Then something had changed as their father drew them first together and then towards where he and Cyan were being held. Suddenly, as the nonsense slipped and tumbled out of reach, the brothers found themselves adrift in the ocean of space with the background of Polaris Mu the giant star and the five planets that circled around it; their own home Alpha Iridium among them.

They had embraced. It was an easy sort of the thing, that first coming together as a foursome, even though not long ago there'd been so many moments of tension and misunderstanding between them. Then they'd naturally broken off into pairs and when Derin wrapped his arms around his mother he had a flash of the very beginning of their story together and his anger towards her no longer had a place inside him. She'd been his first home. When he had a glimpse of the love, and care, and fullness to which she'd given her heart and being for him, he couldn't even fathom holding on to his anger and hurt a moment longer.

"I'm so sorry," Derin whispered in her ear, and he knew the words were not enough even as he knew she'd understand and accept them. "It's okay," he went on, "all of it. You did what you had to, did your best with what you were given. I can see it now. I'm so sorry it took me so long. I forgive you." There was a kind of keening that started in Derin's throat but he swallowed the sound before it could be born into the world. "Can you forgive me?"

"There is nothing to forgive," she offered him, the words rising in his mind though she hadn't spoken them aloud.

Cyan felt the heavy weight that had anchored her in place for so long begin to shift and then fall away so that she felt a kind of buoyant joy she hadn't known in a very long time. She hadn't realized she'd been afraid this moment would never come until it was upon her and a sob rose up and broke in her chest so that she couldn't calm the heaving. It was an ocean of feeling not to be denied. Derin held her. Sorry for the role he'd played in her anguish. Sorry that it had taken him so long to get here. It all seemed so foolish now. Holding on so tightly to something that gave them nothing. He saw it then, that this was a mirror for his own story, one he wasn't ready to finish yet. *One day I'll forgive myself as easily as she's forgiven me,* he thought, *but not today.*

They stayed that way, mother and son, savoring what would be the last of their peace, until Derin looked up and around and then gasped audibly. The stars were speaking again, in riddles and that roundabout way so that so much of what they said was unclear. Still, he was surrounded by glimpses of a future he was both unready for and one he did not want to step into.

"Alex," he said, with just a hint of panic in his voice, and as he looked over to his brother he could see that their father, Dellerim, was speaking hurriedly. Handing something over that could not wait. Derin left them to finish. He knew in that moment what the stars had just shown him was true even though he couldn't fathom what it all meant. Somehow this would be the last time they were like this, all four of them; safe, somewhat happy, and together. He left his brother to those final words with their father and he took that time to tell his mother that he loved her and that everything would be okay. He could see the question in her eyes and he was sorry he couldn't tell her everything he'd seen. Maybe she knew some of it, her heart aware of what was speeding towards her, towards all of them, faster than they could avoid or stop. It was almost time to pay the price for choices and mistakes that had already been made; some so long ago it seemed as if they should have escaped the consequences by now.

"They're back," was all Derin said when Alex met his eyes and that was all it took for Alex to look up and around and see what Derin had already had time to accept. Their freedom from being tortured by glimpses of the future, gifted in riddles often unclear, was over.

That was all it took to move Alex into his mother's arms for the first time in five long years. Cyan couldn't even breathe she was so overwhelmed by the absolute joy of it all, and yet below the surface of that bliss was a tiny voice, whispering, whispering to pay attention. Something was unfolding that was yet out of sight and if she wasn't careful it would sweep her away before she even realized that the ground underfoot was unsteady and crumbling beneath her.

"Dad," Derin said as the two men hugged fiercely. They were mirrors for one another in the same way Derin and Alex were. So many features and details could have been copied from one to the next so that you could've argued it was the same person captured at different moments in time. "What's coming for us?" Derin finally asked when they broke apart.

When Dellerim finally answered he seemed sad and worn out. "We don't have time now for all of it. I've told your brother what I can." He shook his head, a mixture of frustration and sadness overtaking him before he went on. "I wouldn't change a damn thing. Not any of it. Except maybe, well some of what's coming won't be easy."

"What is it?" Derin asked, afraid and not even trying to hide it.

"You have a day at the most and then you'll all need to come home. This doorway I've opened won't hold much longer than that. Remember that nothing really ends. All of it, all of us, interconnected in astounding ways. Threads in a tapestry with no beginning or end. In that infinite story we will find each other again." Dellerim paused here and breathed deep, once, twice, then closed his eyes.

"What do you see?" Cyan begged, looking from her oldest son to her youngest. "In the stars. Please, tell me." She was terrified but not of the truth. Of not knowing. Of feeling this sense something once again was coming for her, for all of them, and she didn't know what it was or how to stop it.

"She'll sacrifice herself again, Kale, to save us all. And all this will have been for nothing." Derin's voice was emotionless. It was too much. Too much to bear and too much to fathom. How could it all be for nothing and what did it mean they would not see their parents again?

"No. It can't be." Dellerim shook his head in disbelief. The pain that swept through him was unbearable. He'd given up so much. Everything. If it was for nothing, then he was a fool and the universe had indeed tricked him. He didn't want to believe it.

"What else?" Cyan went on desperately, "If we know, maybe we can stop it."

The brothers could not answer. It was too big and too awful to put into words. It was their father who saved them. By handing over some if not all of the truth. There in the black of space, with all of time and history laid out around them in stars and galaxies, it was hard to imagine that their tiny lives could play both such a big and insignificant role all at once.

"It doesn't matter now. We won't surrender our destinies to the stars. Not this time," Dellerim said it so seriously that his words carried a kind of weight that would cement this moment into his sons' memories forever. "Nothing is written until it is past, remember that for me."

It was strange to think of how it all worked out, Alex thought to himself as the waking world began to reach for him. He didn't want to think about any of what he'd seen or what his father had told him. He wanted to stay here. To take a few more hours to make up for time lost and time that would never be again. He struggled and fought to remain with them, but the dream continued to disintegrate.

"Less than a day," Dellerim said again, then, "I love you both, so much. I couldn't be prouder of who you've become." He could feel the ache in his heart so fiercely he thought it might crack his chest wide open. He had so much he wanted to tell them but he was out of time, and how much even would be enough with the people you loved.

"I love you," Cyan echoed. She reached for them with her heart one last time. Nothing could change or fade what she felt for them. They knew that now without question.

"It's too soon." Derin shook his head, panicked and afraid. "And it's too much." But they couldn't hear him any longer. The scene had already begun to fade. The brothers reached for their parents, desperate to grab hold of something no longer theirs, but the dream disintegrated around them and the waking world grabbed hold and wouldn't let go.

Some endings were harder to survive than others and this one left them both feeling shocked and numb. It was a feeling that had followed them into the waking world and down the path into the woods where they now sat in silence trying to make sense of it all. It was so very tempting to heed the stars but that would be foolish. At the same it could be foolish not to. To risk anything when they'd already been warned what might be coming. Yet who but them had any right to author their own destiny? That would have to be their choice heading into this final fight or they'd have to admit that once again Kale would sacrifice herself to save them all and they wouldn't have it, not again. Not here, not now.

"What are we going to do?" Derin finally asked, unable to keep all of the heartache and worry out of his voice.

"We aren't going to settle for some bullshit story about how this is all going to go down that's for sure," Alex replied, a little more vehemently than he'd intended. He was scared, he realized, more so than he'd ever been before, and there was only one way he knew how to face it, with determination and certainty, so that's what he would do.

"What did dad tell you back there?" Derin finally asked, even though he was terrified of the answer.

"He told me not to be afraid. And that no matter how we think it might end, to trust ourselves and our strength." Alex paused and closed his eyes, picturing his father as he'd been in that dream. Then gave his brother the rest of what his father had told him even though he didn't entirely understand it all himself. When he was done he opened his eyes and saw that like him Derin had tears drying on his cheeks.

"Will we see them again?" Derin asked, so quietly Alex almost didn't hear.

What could he tell him but the truth, not the one written in the stars which spoke of two lives, those of their parents, finally torn apart, forced to spend what remained of this eternity without each other, though how that might look was beyond them both. What Alex told him was what he believed, that they would not return to a way of life where the stars or the universe took charge and they were simply actors in that great big play called Light and Dark. He fought the temptation to dive into anguish and give up hope and told his brother what he too needed to believe, that they would fight, never stop until they'd won, just as they always had.

Alex wasn't sure how the next twenty-four hours were going to unfold but knowing that fate was again playing games with them drew him back to that day so long ago when Caine had been delivered to their tiny world by a force none of them could understand. His life, and the life of every single Alpha Iridian had been changed forever. He'd been so young and yet destiny had demanded that he become the closest thing to an adult he possibly could. From that day onward everything had been different. He'd let go of his hopes and his dreams, of all of his childish longings, and he'd stepped into the role of being a leader. What still haunted him was that even as a leader he'd ceded the true power to the stars and how they spoke of certainties and of never being disobeyed. Well, not this time. Stars or not Alex was grabbing hold of his own destiny and he would not make the same mistakes he'd made long ago, nor the ones he'd made five years ago when he'd watched his brother die and stood helplessly by while Kale did the same.

Alex couldn't help himself, he took refuge somewhere far away, indulging in something he never did. He wondered what it was like, an idyllic life. A life where you did ordinary things and followed routines. A life where maybe you didn't have to wonder what great big awful turn of events was headed your way next. A life where you could get caught up with the mundane, with every day foolish thoughts and ideas. A life where you could have a family and settle down, and dream of things like kids, and family adventures, and time spent wrapped up in joy and love and companionship. In all of those longings one thing was the same. Kale. Even in a make-believe future he couldn't escape her or how his heart longed for what he knew could never be. The ache that drove its way through his center was so violent it tossed him out of his daydream and back into the world, where he belonged. He laughed to himself at the absurdity of it all and then he met his brother's gaze, foolishly hoping Derin wouldn't know that he was hiding something.

"What was that?" Derin asked him, though deep down, where he kept secrets from himself as so many of us do, he already knew.

"Just got lost for a moment there." Alex dropped his eyes from his brother's and Derin came over and put a hand on his shoulder, squeezing once, before letting go.

"Alex, I know." It was all he needed to say. It was enough in a moment that was already filled with too much grief. The brothers came together in a fierce hug. One that began mourning what was yet to be lost. Derin hadn't seen it until the moment a look of longing so deep and aching had passed across his brother's face. He understood Alex was missing something he could finally glimpse the possibility of, but something was in the way. That's when it hit him. When all the pieces finally came falling into place. The dreams, the looks filled with longing, the shame, the way Alex watched her when he thought no one was looking. His brother was in love with Kale. Not the Kale from the past, but the one who was alive and well now, if not a fragile echo of her former self. Derin wasn't sure how he'd missed it, but it didn't matter. What mattered was how he felt about it and what that meant for them both.

"I'm so sorry," Alex began but Derin interrupted him before the wave of shame could fully rise from deep within.

"Listen to me, there will be no apologies. This is us," Derin said as they pulled back and out of their embrace. With a pained look Alex shook his head helplessly. "We will figure all this out Alex."

Derin expected to feel something different, or maybe more. Shocked or appalled, hurt or angry. But it seemed after so many years of using his feelings to stay stuck or hurting, after so much time using what he felt as an excuse, it just didn't seem to make sense anymore. Who knew what time would truly allow them to have and keep? Who knew what still was to be lost or left behind? He just wasn't willing to lose anything else if he didn't have to. Not this time.

"So what do we do now, Derin?" It was the obvious question, and there between them sat the obvious answer as well.

"We're going to change what has been foretold. We will save Kale and our parents and then we will write our own stories. Brothers first and always." It was a fierce and beautiful truth that Derin offered, but it also wasn't everything. Despite the strength of love and friendship they shared things weren't as simple as they seemed. There was still so much they could not control, and neither of them was entirely certain of what his heart was capable of. In that they were much the same.

They let the silence stretch itself out around them, both a comfort and a place where they could stay hidden from moving forwards just yet. Eventually their conversation wandered slowly back towards what was next and how they would make sure they got home with everyone intact, including Kale. They didn't talk about the most obvious thing, which was what would happen with Derin, Medea and Kale. For now that story went untold. When they began to walk back to the camp the sun was well up into the sky and they felt like they had a plan. Only Alex felt that nagging sense that he should feel guilty for what he'd kept to himself. This inkling he had that maybe not all of them were meant for the obvious paths ahead of them and how they would face those unknown roads when they came.

THIRTY-SEVEN

THEY'D DECIDED TO split up the chores that morning as they packed up their camp and got ready to make their way to the borderlands of Dempsey. Sumira had arrived with the new day and along with her a group of around thirty people willing to join their fight and help them free the slaves from Rogan's village. Coming from a town of more than three hundred people it was a disappointing number but they came with weapons and supplies so at least the group could finish forming a plan now that they had some resources.

It was simple. They would travel to Dempsey and act during the cover of night; as close to dawn as possible without actually risking the danger of a lightening sky. They were hoping that the guards on duty during the night would be a little less vigilant nearing the end of their shifts and they would be easier to get past and outsmart. They'd need luck. But they'd had plenty of experience with having none and still here they were. They simply had to believe things would go their way if that were the case too.

Jaren and Kale had just finished their task when the comfortable silence that enveloped them drew Kale out of herself and into conversation.

"This feels a bit familiar," she said, and Jaren's head snapped up and towards her almost right away. "Don't get excited," she added quickly, though not quick enough to avoid having tempted him into thinking she may have remembered something. "I just meant, I don't know, there's a kind of comfort and ease here that makes it obvious to me we knew each other fairly well." She saw the disappointment settle over his handsome face but then he laughed and so did she, and the easiness was back just as quickly as it had gone. "Sorry," she added when they'd both stopped.

"It's okay," Jaren said with a smile. "It's all so strange isn't it. I mean, well, all of it." He shrugged, unable even to find the words to pass along what and how he was feeling in being here with her, after so long thinking she was gone.

"What were we to each other?" she asked him, "I mean apart from being family. It's something more isn't it?"

Jaren was quiet for a long time. He wasn't sure if he could tell her the truth because he'd never actually spoken it aloud. Even in the pause there was an ease between them that swept him up and carried him along that current of uncertainty towards the truth. He realized that maybe now, with her unable to really remember or to even fully be Kale, he could tell her; all of it.

"I fell in love with you the very first time we met. You were brave and passionate and determined, and I didn't know it was possible, to not just hope for a better world but believe in it. Believe that I could be a part of bringing it into being." He paused here, surprised at his own willingness to finally begin setting it all free. Then he went on.

He told her about the years he'd spent at a distance because he loved her so much and yet he'd been too afraid to act. Or he'd been waiting for the time to be right. He knew she'd never consider finding her own joy or happiness until all Alpha Iridians had the same choice. They'd lived as best friends, even a kind of sibling, though Jaren had never been able to think of it that way because of how he'd felt; yet he'd never once told her and she'd never known. Until that last day of her life when she'd figured it out. When she'd known because of what she was and what she could do.

The strange thing had been what came after her death. When he'd expected to be heartbroken and devastated that she was gone, and he had been, except, it wasn't the same as losing the love of his life, even though he didn't know what that felt like either. There'd been a distinct sort of waking up in his grief that never having confided in her, never having been brave enough to share his heart and find his way into loving her as a partner, kept some of the possibility of grief at bay. Or maybe the truth was, if he was facing it now, that he'd never really loved her the way he thought he did. Because loving her from afar wasn't a whole kind of loving after all.

"So the thing is," Jaren said to her now, quietly, offering up the truth to them both in the gentlest way he could, "there was a difference, between being in love with the idea of you, this radiant force in the world, and being in love with you in the most human way, that flawed and imperfect and frustrating girl who was one of my best friends." Kale smiled sadly at him and he returned the gesture before he went on. "I guess I'm telling you this because I want you to know, that what we want for that girl we all loved, the one who is somewhere there inside you even if she is taking a rest from the harshness of the world, doesn't matter as much as what you want for yourself. You don't need to be her, the great, big idea of Kale who saved us all, you just need to be yourself, and if that means coming with us, back to Alpha Iridium, then we will make a home for you there just as you as are. We won't ask you to be anything you're not."

Tears had formed in the corners of her eyes and were threatening to fall. Even though deep down inside her there was an instinct to hide them away, she let them spill and tumble to find their own way in the world. To let them tell the story of a sorrow so deep it had buried itself well out of sight where the world would never find it.

"You know," she finally said, "I have moments where I wish I could be her again. Not just for me but for all of you as well. But mostly the thought of it just scares me." She was quiet so long he wasn't sure she was going to finish and yet he let the silence sit between them, comfortable and companionable, and waited. It felt like she was near, Kale, his Kale, and he didn't want to interrupt the closeness by demanding the moment be something more than it could be. Finally, she spoke again but what she offered needed nothing but a nod as their eyes met. "She has quite the story to live up to, doesn't she?"

He wanted to say more. To tell her about Kale and everything she'd been and meant but he realized it wasn't really fair. What if this was her life, what if she never remembered any of it. How much more could they press upon her the story of a person who'd already been gone five years and might never return. Maybe it was time to let her go. To let the memory of her live in the past forever meant to be left behind. To let this Kale have the life she chose, without needing her to be anything more than the story she decided to write for herself.

In the years since she'd left them, hadn't he wondered more than once how much of Kale's life had really been her own? So much had been handed over in pursuit of her mission to stop Caine. So much of it had been authored by destiny. So much of it also had been written in the stars. Yes, in the end, and maybe always, she'd surrendered and become what the universe had demanded but had they ever considered none of it was what she wanted. Maybe there was something to her turning up on a planet far away, in another time, without any memory of any of it. Maybe she'd finally chosen her freedom. Maybe she'd finally taken a step away from what was foretold and towards an idea of a whole life all her own; and yet, she'd still landed here. On an Earth in the midst of finding its way back from the brink of destruction. In that lonely journey humanity had returned itself to the awful thing it had become more than once before. In waking here Kale had put herself once again in the path of a kind of rising darkness. The Kale he'd known would have landed exactly here, or somewhere like it. To stop a kind of evil she knew all too well—that of indifference to the suffering of others in pursuit of power, an evil that had deep roots in every human heart, whether it blossomed or not.

Could it be there was a purpose to where and when she'd woken for another chance at life—one of her very own unconscious making? Or maybe, Jaren wondered to himself, it was much more simple than that. Maybe we were all meant to live a certain kind of life and fulfill a certain kind of destiny. Maybe more than once. If that were the case, was it possibly time to let her be. To leave her to become what she chose as she fulfilled her destiny, even if that meant starting with a blank slate, something each of them had craved in their own way. It was time to make space for where they were by letting go of where they'd been. Jaren realized it wasn't just Kale who deserved it. They all did.

"I guess," Jaren finally said, "she does have quite the story to live up to. But all that matters is what you want. None of us are the same as we were back then. God, none of us are the same as we were just a week ago. Why should any of us have to be anything but who and what we are, here and now." He smiled. It was joyful at first but after only a moment sadness pulled the corners of his mouth down to settle into a frown. "Even if you don't remember, any of it, I hope you'll set yourself free. I hope you'll build your own life and reach for a present kind of happiness that is honest and real and that's spacious enough for you to find your whole self within."

The tears tumbled quicker now but she ignored them. They were a kind of offering meant for the new life she was building even if she didn't entirely realize it. Their Kale had mattered, she'd changed the course of a planet and its people, and yet her life had been lacking. It hadn't had space for anything but a destiny she'd not entirely chosen for herself. It was time to let go. For all of them to begin moving on. Jaren's advice wasn't just for her. It was indeed for all of them.

"I think I might be ready for that," she finally said, "what about you?" Their eyes met and she saw through the haze of tears and sorrow that he understood. That like her he was ready. That maybe all this was actually about all of them finally being ready to begin a new story. No matter how far it led them from the one they'd expected to live.

A moment of knowing passed between them. It offered them each a kind of peace that was born for the very first time in each of them. They could not know it was their last chance to be together like that. But they'd made the most of it; and wasn't that all we could ask of any moment of our lives.

THIRTY-EIGHT

BENEATH A BLANKET of stars and night sky, with the ocean coming and going just a few feet from where she was seated, Arin waited. She was early of course. But the past few days had been a struggle and because she knew tomorrow's dawn would lead them to this spot she could not stay away another moment. Her parents had already checked in on her once, as had her younger brother, Kedall, along with the other children of the Founders at one moment or another. They'd brought her food and water, sometimes offering it with conversation, sometimes joining her in silence. They knew what was foretold. Like her they could see what the stars said was looming and they understood her sense of urgency for it to begin to arrive. The stars weren't always right and in the present at least she could try to fight them.

The story above her had changed yet again. She wasn't sure why, but it didn't matter. She was done being a pawn in a game she'd never wanted to play. She refused to believe that what the stars foretold would come to pass. Or that with these new revelations Joah would fall and that Derin would not come home to them. She refused to accept that they didn't have a say. It was just unfathomable that they were still losing anything to the games of fate and the powers that ruled the universe. But they weren't children anymore and the time for allowing anything other than their own determination to lay out the path ahead just wasn't good enough. She would not surrender ever again to a story of destiny written by anyone but herself.

When her father sat down on the cool sand next to her, she allowed him to pull her close so that for a few moments she could get lost in that sense of being sheltered and safe. A feeling she never tired of, even at her age. Joachim's long white hair was messy and wild which she knew was a sign he was troubled; something he rarely was and even more rarely showed. His emerald green eyes, usually bright and mischievous, were dull and worried. As he pulled her a little closer she realized he was here for his own comfort as much as hers, and a wave of love and appreciation swept through her almost violently. Like his son, he was softer and sweeter than he appeared and she realized how deeply he would be wounded, if Joah did indeed die as a result of some strange fate he suffered on a planet far away.

"How are you holding up?" he asked her without pulling away. Breaking them both free of their worried thoughts.

"I'm going crazy honestly," she sighed, frustrated by how helpless she felt. She wasn't sure what more she could say. She'd never been this far away from her brother. Not since they were kids. Sure, there'd been all that time he'd spent on Berdune keeping Medea company, but Arin had often joined them.

She had fallen into synch with their little family so easily it had been hard to come home when it was time. Corin, Jaren, Medea, Joah, and Arin would spend their days in a mix of work, play or service to the community. They'd travel to other regions of Berdune on business, sometimes overnight, but would always return to the familiarity and comfort of the home they shared, nestled in the woods outside of Braedon Ridge. They'd take days off at the beach, or early morning walks to marvel at the sunrise. They'd spend time at the Mission preparing and serving food to those who still needed support or were simply in need of those most basic of human necessities, connection and community.

They would have family dinners a few times a week and even Jet, Archer, and James would make regular appearances, at times with girlfriends or with other friends or family. Sometimes Corin's mother Sarah would join them, and would cook the most amazing family feasts. Arin loved that it was such an ordinary life even though it was hard for her and Joah to hide within it. With their bold features and height, there was no mistaking that they were children of the Founders and that still inspired a kind of awe in most people. Any time they were around the siblings couldn't help but remind people that the world, the universe, could be mystical and because of that they often drew attention.

Arin loved those long visits away from her home and the cloud that hung over everything. They'd worked hard to move on but there would always be the remnants of a single truth, that the Founders had willingly made the mistake that left their children to raise themselves on their own. She, like most of the children of the Founders had let it all go but the past had an echo. That story would forever be behind them, unchanging, reaching for the present no matter how gently. Their lives on Samnar were beautiful and amazing in so many ways but a break from those quiet and yet effective chains of the past felt welcome.

She'd become good friends with Medea, Jaren, and Corin, each in different, surprising and wonderful ways. There'd even been a moment where she thought maybe something more might arrive, but as always she went unseen and her heart went unanswered, and it was so expected it didn't even really hurt all that much. In each of their inability to move on or open themselves up to love, she glimpsed a kind of stuckness that she dreamed of escaping one day. A hope she carried for each of them. Especially her brother, who was the most loving, compassionate soul she knew even while he indulged in hiding it.

Watching him and Medea in those months was a doorway to all the kinds of love that were possible. She didn't always understand it. How Joah and Medea could love each other so much, how they could have a relationship that spoke of other lives and other times, and yet not step fully into it in this life. How they could have a sense of the great big story of their love and still accept that in this time there was a kind of pause, a deep breath, that led their hearts away from each other in one sense. Of course she hadn't felt anything near that profound and she often wondered if she had maybe it would all make a little more sense to her.

"You know everything is going to be okay right?" Joachim interrupted his daughter's thoughts as he finally pulled away from her enough to meet her eyes. She looked so much like her brother in the dimming light, even with her cherry hair and eyes, that Joachim felt his breath catch in his throat. He wasn't one for worrying. It just wasn't in his nature. But like all the Founders he had felt something coming. Something out of their control and unrelenting. Something that would alter the path ahead in ways they had not yet imagined possible. He would give anything, even his own life, to make sure his children weren't the victims of this next great turn of fate.

"I can't accept he won't come home," she said and then added with more conviction, "I refuse to believe anything but the fact that he will fight his way back here with the rest of them." Her voice sounded certain and calm. She was more like her father than either of them gave her credit for.

"Joah," was all he could say before his voice caught in his throat betraying the deep worry that had settled in his chest. After a slow breath he went on, "if there's one thing I've learned in my lifetimes on this world it's that nothing is certain, and that it is always worth it to hope."

She leaned into him again and let her thoughts drift across the vast expanse of the universe until they settled on a world far away. The pair would stay like that for a long while. Until the moon had risen and all of the stars came out to whisper about truths and possibilities. Arin didn't look up. She was done listening. Done wanting to know. They would make their own fate. She refused to believe anything else while she kept her gaze fixed on the dark of the horizon and the inky waves that wandered their way from somewhere out of sight.

A universe away her brother sat beside the woman he loved, his best friend, and thought about home. Wondered about his siblings, and their parents, and what they all might be making of this. Did they even know where he'd gone and why? The stars on Earth were quiet and Joah didn't know that the stars of Alpha Iridium had much to say about what was coming for him. Like his father, and now his sister, he would want nothing to do with them. He didn't want to be tied to possibilities, good or bad, because he loved to be present, fully engaged in what was unfolding in the moment. Of all of those who had survived the days of Caine he was least attached to his life remaining unchanged. Maybe it was that he'd so quickly found Medea and then soon after they'd realized their story wasn't meant to be. For him the worst thing had already happened, had passed him by, and so in some ways he'd been set free. He could have an easy life, indulge in friends and family, and take care of the people he loved while he figured out what particular destiny he'd like to claim for his own. Now here he was on Earth, about to embark on an insane rescue mission, and he couldn't help wondering if he'd indeed escaped the past like he'd convinced himself he had.

"What are you thinking about?" Medea asked him and he couldn't help it, he laughed out loud. Instead of answering he pulled her close and they stayed like that, quiet, comfortable, and for the moment safe. Hidden from the world by a friendship and love that was like a shield.

They didn't say another word. The silence was comfortable and comforting. In their closeness and ease was an intimacy that had almost always been between them. They could both feel the longing for it to have been more. For their story to be something easier and simpler than it was. That quiet secret was always there between them. Yet neither one of them was unsure of the path they were walking together in this life, even if it was hard for others to grasp.

It was a gift. Knowing that love could be so much more than the few narrow definitions it was often given. There's was something wide and deep and ever flowing. That eternity had always been between them. Within that sense that their story was so very long was the freedom to accept what it was in something as small and yet infinitely vast as the moment they were in.

They stayed that way, in the quiet, companionable and safe. They didn't talk about what might be coming. They didn't talk about Derin or Kale. Every conversation was a path away from where they were, and so they remained, and all that could be shared was done so without speaking.

Around them, birds danced and sang amongst the trees. A symphony that was each and every moment unique and yet familiar. The sun was sinking behind the canopy to the west letting them know time was running out. Not far from them a city built upon the worst of what people could be was waiting to be stopped. Nearer still was the group planning to undertake that task. Still they savored their last moments of peace before they rose, linked hands, and wandered back to where their friends had set up camp.

THIRTY- NINE

ALONE, IN THE DARK, Firth curled in on herself and tried to stop the violent shaking that wracked her body. She'd not known you could suffer in ways so deeply beyond the physical pain and torture she'd endured but she was certain that the violent spasms that tore through her now were to try and shake off the truth of what Bex had done to her.

Her lip was bleeding; painfully split open in two places. Her left cheek was swollen and bruised, and throbbed painfully, while her left eye, almost swollen shut, had stopped seeing clearly halfway through the beating she'd suffered. She'd seen a blurry second Bex swinging at her over and over until she'd finally passed out. Her head was pounding. Her ribs ached in a way that terrified her and the spot on her arm where she'd been burned was searing hot and sore. Yet none of it compared with what she felt beneath all that. With the shame, or the terror, or the deep and hollow certainty she would never be the same.

She'd fought Egan the whole way into the city and it had shocked her that he hadn't struck out in response. He'd taken every blow and scratch almost as if in some demented way he got something out of them. His eyes wild, his lips set in a vicious sneer. When she fought harder, he only laughed. Delighted. That's when her fear had fully intensified.

She'd felt exposed as he carried her through Dempsey. Her thin shirt and underwear, her favorite way to fall asleep, betraying her need to feel covered and safe. She wanted armor. She wanted these people to stop glancing through her as if she wasn't even there. She could not fathom the kind of place that had normalized dehumanization and violence like this even though she knew now such places did exist.

When they got deep into the city, Egan carried her towards a large building that sat at the centre of an empty square. They stopped at the entrance so he could talk to the guards and then they carried on. It was as if she wasn't even there and her fear was devoured by a new sense of fury at the injustice of it all and the nerve of these people to be so captivated with the illusion of their own superiority and others' lack of worth.

Ten minutes later she was sitting with her back leaned up against a concrete wall, alone, in a cell somewhere in the basement, waiting. She understood it was a kind of game. That her terror was meant to intensify while time slid by and she had no hope of escape. She also understood it was working and so she fought to hold on to her anger even as it cooled and disappeared out of reach. She missed Rogan. Missed her home. Missed the peace of her life and the person she'd been within it all. Astoundingly, only a few short days before.

She slept in fits. Stumbling in and out of strange and sometimes terrifying dreams only to wake to the one she was living in. For hours they left her in isolation. Frightened, exhausted and unsure what time of day it was or what was coming, she struggled to remain calm. She paced the room when she was awake. Her tired, shaky legs carrying her through a marathon of worry and uncertainty. She rested curled up in the corner, hopeful she would not be caught unaware while sleeping.

When the door finally opened, Bex walked in. Slow. Predatory. Firth's anger flashed again and before she could stop herself she met those dark, sinister eyes; her own defiant and furious. There was the logical part of her that knew it was safer to be small and scared but her heart raged at the injustice of it all and that's what rose to the surface when Bex drew near. She knew what Bex wanted but she couldn't imagine how she would hand it over. She was so angry. Disgusted. She wanted to strangle the woman and no matter how meek Firth made herself huddled against the wall, there was no mistaking the look in her eyes. Bex had seen it many times before and had never failed to snuff it out. Firth stood, shaky and afraid despite her fury. She didn't know what was coming but she would face it and fight back if she could.

"I want you to know this stops when you give up. When you submit. When you become fully, wholly mine, which you are already, you just don't know it yet." Bex's voice was filled with dark glee and malice as she snarled the words out.

"When you know it, you go back to your cage and your little family, and I move on."

Firth lunged at her but Bex was ready and the first punch landed with so much force Firth thought she might pass out. She sucked in a deep breath, panicked, eyes wide and did the only thing she could think of, she lunged at her again. Bex knocked her down so many times Firth lost count. She taunted and tortured her with words. She told her unspeakable things. Things she'd done, things she would do to Firth if she wanted to, things she could make her watch if she so desired; all in the name of delighting in torture, brutality and domination. When Firth finally stopped rising on her own Bex would help her up. She was wild with cruelty and violence and it became so bad that Firth finally stilled, broken and giving up. Hopeful only that surrender would hurry along the end. She thought again of Rogan and wondered where she was. Wondered if she would see her again. Touch her again. Know the gentle embrace of love, and ease, and companionship. She would never again take any of it for granted and all she could hope as she reached with her heart and let go of the world, was that she would get the chance.

There was a moment of calm and quiet. Firth began to pass out as she drifted further away from the waking world and she welcomed the escape. Then searing hot pain, excruciating, startling her awake. She cried out, shocked and terrified, then she began to shake.

"Feels kinda like you're mine now," Bex taunted. "But just to be sure I'll see you tomorrow my love." She pressed her thumb into the brand she'd burned into Firth's right forearm, causing her to cry out again before she started to whimper. Bex hadn't enjoyed toying with someone this much in a long time. She was almost disappointed the fight had gone out of Firth so quickly.

"I don't know how or why, but you'll regret this," Firth's voice was quiet but clear, and though her heart wanted so badly to believe it she still began to weep. First softly then the tears became a torrent as her body surrendered to that shaking that stayed with her and did not relent.

Bex considered for a moment keeping her for another night but then immediately changed her mind. She'd be more fun after a couple night's rest. She summoned Egan and sent Firth with him back to the gathering grounds just outside the city wall where almost all the slaves slept. As Egan carried Firth out of the city he thought to himself that they always broke sooner than you'd expect.

Back in the enclosure, her people had been checking on her since her return, but Firth didn't want any of them near. She couldn't speak, couldn't answer their questions, couldn't pull herself away from what she'd been through in that room with Bex. She shook and whimpered, struggling to keep her breath from coming in panicked gasps and she only stilled and calmed when the orphaned pair rejoined her. They were the only ones she'd let touch her and so Bella settled Firth's head gently in her lap and Andre curled his tiny frame inside hers and they fell asleep like that, there in the dark. United in their suffering and pain but also in something so much more powerful than that.

FORTY

ROGAN, THE ALPHA IRIDIANS, Sumira and her people, and Kale camped that night under the stars. Just a breath away from the beauty and horror of Dempsey. A reminder that duality was often the truth of all things and that they could contain the entire story of the universe in their becoming. The awful could still contain beauty, poised to emerge when things seemed the bleakest. The most beautiful could still be hiding within their radiant depths some kind of terrible secret, someday meant to step out of the light into shadow once again.

Most of them had expected silence. As if what they were facing had struck them dumb. Instead Rogan began telling stories. She spoke first of the beginning. Of being lost in the dark all alone, her very first memory, and of how that first dawn could not have come quick enough. How in that day that felt like the very first, because in some ways it was, she'd met Firth, also alone in the woods. She spoke no more of those long ago days and how they'd found their way. Even in listening to her offer the few tiny pieces she was willing to share they could tell there was a kind of necessary guardedness about what those first days and months of survival had been like. But she did tell them about her home.

About a place, now gone, that had sheltered and kept both her and her heart safe. She told them about falling in love. About a friendship that had become so much more than that. She told them about destiny, and second chances, and about a world that maybe wasn't supposed to have one, and yet it did, and here they were. While she spoke the universe listened, and it remembered why this world had ventured back from the brink so many times, including this last one.

When she finished, there were a few moments of silence and then someone else began to speak. One by one they shared while the night wandered past. It was as if they knew they wouldn't be able to sleep, and so instead they kept each other company. There in the dark, together. United. A symbol of what humanity could be at its best.

They told stories of every kind, though Rogan's was the only one that spoke of love. As Kale listened she wondered what it could mean, this thing that bound the whole of time and space together, how could it not now wander into this moment, how could it not have found its way into their lives for the past five years. But of course it had. She just didn't see it. It was there in the story about how Jaren and Corin were rebuilding Berdune. It was there in the story of how Medea and Joah had once travelled north to marvel at islands they were the first to discover. It was there in the story of how Derin and Alex were building a home for themselves to be free of their past and start fresh. It was there in how she listened to them all, looking for herself in the missing pieces of what they shared.

When the envy hit, Kale wasn't quite ready for it. Every story told of belonging and there was nowhere that she seemed to fit. Not in the stories Rogan shared of Earth and not in the stories the others shared about Alpha Iridium. It didn't matter that they were simply trying to protect her from being forced to face someone she might never be again. All she heard was that she didn't belong. She stood, abruptly, her agitation getting the best of her, and she excused herself to go check the perimeter. It was a sad and sorry excuse and yet they gave it to her, letting her wander off into the darkness alone.

An hour later, when she hadn't returned a few of them ventured off into the night to find her. She hadn't gone far, just far enough to be free of their stories, and their hope, and their certainty that they belonged. It was Medea who found her there in the deep dark of the woods, a lone traveler stranded in unfamiliar heartache and uncertainty. She was seated on the ground leaning up against a wise old oak that had most certainly survived the almost ending of the world.

At first, Medea simply stood, waiting, for what she did not know. Then finally, she sat down and leaned back, taking in that dark and luminous story of sky and stars unfolding above them.

"Hard to believe one of them might be home," Medea said with a sigh, referencing a game she knew Cyan used to play, first on her own and then with her sons when they were young. Derin had told her that story not long ago while he was reaching for a life long gone, just like it seemed the rest of them were now. Like Kale he didn't remember that life. He'd been too young. *How many of us reach for stories of ourselves that are no longer true*, Medea wondered, and the truth of it slammed into her so forcefully that for a moment she could not breathe.

Kale had left the silence to settle between them, unsure how to reply, and so with a new kind of knowing just beginning to flow through her Medea spoke again. "You know, I still remember when we first met." Kale could sense her friend smile into the night before she went on. "It doesn't matter now, I guess. It's just, I thought you should know, it was one of the best days of my life. Doesn't matter if you remember it or not. Doesn't matter if you ever do again, what's behind us is unchangeable." Medea couldn't believe how much it hurt. Both the thought she might never get her friend back and the realization it was time to accept her as she was.

"I can't be what you need me to be," Kale said sadly. "There's nothing left of her inside me. I can't find it, not a single moment. All there is…" she paused here, surprised by the sob that caught in her throat.

"You know, I think it's time we set you free of all that." Medea turned towards her friend and smiled again. "I love you. We love you, and we want you to come home. But you don't have to be anything more than what or who you are. You are enough, exactly as you are, for all of us."

They sat in silence for a long while. As if this wasn't a night on the verge of a fight they weren't sure they could win. As if there was all the time in the world to find their way forward. As if it were an ordinary night, and they were two best friends sitting under the stars, marveling at the miracle of the universe, unaware it could also be an awful, hideous place if you let it be. In that silence Medea found her way fully back to her friend, memory or not.

"Kale," she whispered into the night and though her friend said nothing she knew she was waiting for her to go on. They could both sense the truth hunting them down. "You don't need to be afraid. Not of who she was, not of being her again. Because the thing is whether you remember or not, you are her. She was brave and unrelenting when she believed in something. She didn't entirely know who she was but she knew fighting for others, for what was right and good, would lead her closer to the truth. Her truth. And she was always willing to sacrifice herself for the greater good." She paused here, letting the silence speak for her friend who she realized was right beside her, with her, memory or not. "Don't you see, the memories don't matter," Medea finally went on, "it's deeper than that. You are her. You always will be, no matter which path you choose."

Kale struggled to hold the tears at bay. There was both relief and heartache. It was the beginning of coming home to herself, whether she remembered anything or not. She could finally admit it was too big and too scary to live up to the story of the Kale they'd come looking for, and what she'd done and accomplished and sacrificed in another life, on a planet far from this one. There was something else, and though it felt tempting to keep it to herself, she gave it a voice in the world.

"If I stay here, your life, it'll be easier. You can finally be free of her, of me, between you and Derin." Kale felt another rising wave of sadness as she spoke. It wasn't what she was giving up that made her heart ache it was that she had no memory of so many things that had meant so much, that had mattered so deeply. She began to long for the life she could not remember. For the love of her friends and yes even Derin. No, they weren't hers anymore, none of it was, but she wanted a sense of herself to come back to her. She wanted to be whole again. Finally.

"I'm not interested in easier," Medea said without a hint of uncertainty. "I want you to be happy and find your way home." Their eyes met and Kale couldn't help reaching up to wipe the tears that had been threatening to fall. "Besides, it's not that simple. Nothing ever is. Make your choice. It'll be alright no matter what."

They came together in a hug, wrapping their arms around each other fiercely. In that silence and safety the friends found each other again. Even when so much was different, so much was also still the same. Without her memories Kale could still surrender to the deep sense of trust and belonging that lived here, with Medea. It was both familiar and strange, the kind of love she felt now, and she settled into it and let it fill her up with a kind of joy she'd not yet known.

It was Derin who found them. He'd stepped through the trees and heard those final gifts between two old and dear friends and his heart felt like it might burst with the beauty of it: that these two women could be so loving and compassionate and strong, that they could also be willing to lose more on top of what they'd already sacrificed simply because it meant the other would be okay. He saw it then, how much he loved them both. He could feel the great big whole of it pushing at the confines of his heart to get out; to find more space in the world. He realized that maybe it was not up to him to decide: that he could lay down his needs and desires and just be what they needed him to be. Standing there, looking at the two of them, he wasn't quite ready to admit what it was he wanted, though deep down he finally knew whether or not he was meant to reach for the past or step towards the future.

There was a long drawn out silence where the trio let this single moment light up a great big truth that was chasing them down. There would be no easy way forward. Someone would lose something. But would any of them lose everything was the real question and as time ran out and choices were made, Derin couldn't help wondering what their lives would look like on the other side of this next day.

FORTY-ONE

CYAN SQUEEZED HER eyes shut, trying to close them and herself to the truth that was hurtling towards her. She could feel it and yet she wasn't ready to accept what it was. When she finally opened her eyes, she looked deep into Dellerim's, willing him to convince her that their love could wind its way around eternity and persist.

"It's almost time," Dellerim said sadly. "I can get you all home, but I can't go with you this time."

Cyan said nothing. She was too shocked and overwhelmed to know what it was she could offer him that would press this moment back into a place that made sense. So she waited and she let him go on, and she listened as he told her, finally, the whole truth of what he'd done and given to keep them all together the way he thought they were meant to be.

It had begun of course that first night long ago when they'd dreamed a civilization into existence on Alpha Iridium to cure their loneliness. That single act carried them into the path of that ancient half of what balanced the universe and so the Darkness began to hunt them down.

"It was in that very first dream, the one where we brought people to Alpha Iridium, that I first glimpsed the very fabric of the universe, and how I might be able to pull at it here and there, if I ever needed to." Dellerim paused here and took a deep breath, "So I knew, you see, when we slipped into that dream to try and stop Caine's coming, I knew we could change destiny, but I also knew there would be a price. I should never have convinced us all to intervene. I thought I was strong enough to protect us." He couldn't look at her. It was too hard to see past his own shame and he was too afraid he'd see a mirror for it in her eyes.

But there was more, and he forced himself to go on. It was on that final night of Caine's rule that he began to see through the veil of darkness back into the real world. He'd finally been able to find his sons and to learn that Cyan was okay, that his partner for so many eons had not been swept into a current of darkness and oblivion somewhere out of reach. He'd still been helpless but there were whisperings of his power, a kind of quiet memory, and in his fury and desperation, he'd glimpsed how fully he could harness it. When Caine was destroyed and Kale had given her life he'd somehow broken free from his prison and it was almost as if he'd become someone or something else as he scooped her up and put her in the only place he could, back where she'd begun, on Earth, though in a far different time, one that was still to come.

Dellerim hadn't thought much about it but time and its complexities had always played a big part in his life. He'd been born on a world running out of it, then lived on a world that hadn't been found by it yet. He'd spent fourteen years trapped outside of it and then the last five trying to make every moment count. You could lay it out, end to end, a single moment before and after the next, and yet in truth Dellerim had learned time was much different than that. He'd discovered that moments were mostly laid on top of one another, so that what has come before, might also come again. It meant he hadn't just interrupted a single story when he took Kale to Earth, the force and the power of disobeying the universe had cracked all of time wide open for just a moment, which was in some ways all moments, and in that eternity he paused the destruction of the Earth. Needing somewhere safe to put her, in his desperation, he pulled and cinched the decimated planet back together again. It had been an astounding feat of will and strength and there would be a price to pay for wielding it without permission.

"The cost," was all Cyan could say, horrified but also heartbroken because she knew the price would be too high for her to survive.

"I didn't know when I began it what it would take or what it would cost. At first I didn't want our son to live with a broken heart, and I didn't want the one person who acted to save us to bear the weight of it all. Once it had begun, the power, I couldn't resist it." He'd been waiting for this moment to tell her the truth, to confess all he'd done and given while he'd hidden it from her. Now that it was here, the heartache threatened to overwhelm him and he took a few deep and steadying breaths.

"What did it cost you, us?" she asked him, terrified. She felt already a kind of quaking deep within as if her body already knew what was coming.

"Service," he said simply. No other words would come.

"For how long?" He met her with only silence. "Tell me!" She begged.

"There will be other times" was all he could offer her in place of the full truth. But she understood. He had given everything, every moment he had left.

She cried out. Anguish mixed with an emotion she couldn't even recognize or process. For a few moments she curled in on herself and tried to catch her breath as the truth tried to crush her from the inside out. It was too much. Their lives, so wonderful, and rich, and miraculous, should still have been too small and insignificant to catch the attention of the universe like this. Of course, they'd been too small, until they'd been too big. How could both be true, she wondered to herself, before drawing herself back and into the present moment. Time was running out. She could not waste any of it.

She wrapped her arms around him and allowed herself to get lost in that embrace. Tears, wrapped in the silence of solemnity, wandered down her cheeks and found their way onto his shoulder, both comforting and heartbreaking. It hadn't really seemed real to him, Dellerim realized, until he'd offered the truth to Cyan, finally. Now here they were and the pain of it was almost unbearable. But the universe had given him time, to love, to laugh, to fill a lifetime with joy and memories. He'd had so much more than the average person already. Did it matter if he'd first been promised eternity? This was still more than he could have ever dreamed of. There were always all those other possibilities. Other lives, other dreams, other times. No, their love story wouldn't end like this. He'd find her again, no matter what it took. That much he was sure of even as his heart broke.

FORTY-TWO

KALE WOKE WITH a start and instinctively reached for the dream and that sense of comfort and warmth it had wrapped around her. Was it a memory trying to break through, that feeling of always being trapped in a struggle of some kind, or was it simply the new day and what lay ahead calling to her?

She'd been standing by the sea and though it could have been anywhere she knew it was one of Earth's oceans that kept reaching for her feet every time it crawled up the sand in front of her. Hesitant and yet beautifully relentless.

"It's just a dream." She'd realized and sighed, staring out at the stunning expanse of ocean and sky painted with pastels.

"Just a dream," he answered, as if she'd asked a question. She turned towards him standing there beside her and smiled, a gentle offering. When their eyes met Alex felt a pull deep inside him that threatened to stop the beating of his heart. He dropped his gaze to her lips and when she leaned slightly towards him he closed the small space between them. He brought his lips to hers and pressed them there gently. It wasn't electric exactly. It felt safe and certain and his heart relaxed a little for the first time in so long he did not at first recognize the feeling. *It's just a dream*, a voice inside him whispered, but he wasn't sure if it was to discourage him or to give him freedom. He didn't care, he couldn't stop himself, he deepened the kiss, moving his lips over hers as she opened her mouth just enough to press her tongue to his. Even in the urgency of it there was softness and a kind of ease that eventually pried them apart, so gently. Kale's heart was racing, and her face felt hot, and she wasn't sure if they'd been lost like this together for a few moments or much, much longer than that.

"I'm sorry," Alex said, "it's just, I wanted to know what it was like, before we go back, before it's too late. Once we're home, everything will be different. I just wanted to know what it was like before all that."

She smiled at him sadly and then looked back out towards the horizon where the waves must have been born before they began their journey her way. "I'm not coming back with you. I don't belong there anymore." It was nice to be certain even if there was a whispering inside that she didn't want to put a universe of space between her and Alex.

"And you belong here?" Alex said, panic rising inside him. It wasn't possible. He refused to believe it. He could live with having her near while she chose a life with his brother. He could suffer, alone, so that together Derin and Kale could both have a life full of joy, but if she chose to stay on Earth he knew it would be unbearable. *And if your brother chooses to stay with her*, a dark voice wondered within him, *it would be even worse.*

"The universe put me here didn't it," she said with conviction, but she wasn't actually sure if it was what she believed.

"That's not exactly what happened." He was exasperated and terrified.

"Alex, listen to me." For a moment, he delighted in the sound of his name on her lips, but she went on. "None of it matters. Where we've been, where I began, where I'm supposed to be." She took a slow breath and shook her head. "I am here. This is the life I know and though I have this deep sense of belonging and yes, even love when I'm around all of you, it's not my life anymore. I'm glad that I got to know Kale the way you did, even just a little bit, but I want to move on. I don't want to live some other person's life, even if it was this great big epic story. I want one of my own."

That's when it hit him. They hadn't really stopped to think about what it would be like, her coming home without ever remembering. None of them had wondered if some shadows were too big to live in. They hadn't even asked her what she wanted. They kept assuming they knew best because she couldn't remember but they hadn't stopped to consider if maybe even without knowing her past she still knew her own heart in the present. They were all hoping she'd come back to Alpha Iridium, except who among us can return to who we were, memory or not.

"Then you'll have it," he finally said. "A great big, epic story of your own. Or an ordinary life filled with love and happiness. Or anything else you reach for." He shrugged and was surprised at how heavy he felt. There was a kind of incomprehensible sorrow dragging him down. Could it be this, losing someone he barely knew, and what it would cost them all when they went home without her, his brother included. Or maybe it was what they'd seen in the stars. This looming awfulness that meant everything they'd done was for nothing. They'd stop it of course. They were done listening, done being told how their destinies were going to be laid out in front of them. Stars or not, they were taking charge.

"We should go," Kale said, almost matching the sad and sorry tone in his voice, "the waking world is calling and we have one last thing to do before you go home."

He nodded and took her hand in his own and squeezed it as she smiled up at him. He drew it up and turned her palm to the sky before bending to place a single kiss there. Her hand tingled where his lips had touched it. When she woke a few moments later the sensation was still there and she closed her palm around the offering and held on tight. A few moments later she sat up and let the dream fall away. It was time to face the day, first rescuing her friends and then letting go of the last strands tethering her to another life. She wasn't sure how she felt about any of it but it didn't matter, she would have to face it all anyway.

She climbed out of her bedroll in the dark and greeted the others as she rose. She quickly sought out Derin because it was time to face the one thing still hanging over her and over them both. They wandered away from the camp together, through the dark, just far enough to have some privacy. She'd leaned up against a tree as he stood there watching her, waiting. He didn't want to admit it but he'd been a coward. He'd come all this way to find her and yet hadn't bothered to face the truth. He loved her, he always would, but things weren't that simple. They never were.

"I'm not coming back with you." She stated it simply and all he could do at first was stare.

"Kale, I'm so sorry. It's my fault you're even here. If I hadn't been such a fool, a coward, you never would have had to give your life for mine in the first place." How long had he wished for this moment? To face what he'd allowed and what he'd been. To reach out to her not for forgiveness but simply to take ownership of the part he'd played in her final day. To admit how his failures had led them to the tragic end to their story.

She stepped over to him and took his hands in hers and smiled. She wanted to set him free. To have him let go of where they'd been and all they'd suffered so that he could move on. She felt a little like she was betraying Kale, the one who had loved him so deeply, but she was gone and there was no way to know what she'd want. Instead she considered her own heart and longing and what she also knew he deserved. With that in mind she offered him the truth.

"It's not your fault. Don't take away from her the biggest choice she ever made. She gave her life so you could have one. It's time for you to finally and fully move on. Find some peace and happiness. Build the life you were meant to, Derin." She realized then that that was it. That she was not a victim. She wasn't sure by what strange fate she'd arrived on Earth but she could choose her life here, with or without her memories. There was nothing to be afraid of anymore.

"I don't want it to be over." He began, and in so many ways he meant it. But Kale, his Kale, was really gone. So also was the time and place where they were meant to be together. The truth was staggering and yet it had been with him for a long time. He was finally ready to admit it. There was another truth alive in his heart now and if he were being honest there was a kind of pull towards that other beating that he did not want to resist.

"But..." he paused, not sure if he could move forward with the truth aloud. He felt a deep sense of sadness and loss sweep through him even as he knew he was finally fully stepping towards the story he was meant to, one that had been waiting long enough to unfold.

"It's okay, Derin. The thing is, I belong here now and you both belong together. I'm happy for you. Truly." She smiled but it was a thing not quite whole. Yes, she was happy for him, but she did also feel that sense of loss and longing that flavored the moment with sorrow.

He knew it was coming and yet it shot a pain through his chest that was almost unbearable. He took a few deep and steadying breaths and tried to speak, "if only," he began but it was all that he could manage before words failed him and he couldn't go on.

"Ah," she sighed, a small and gentle sound, "the universe is not so simple. Don't we all know that?" When she spoke next, she sounded just like her old self and it stunned him a little bit. "In another life, in some other dream, maybe." She'd meant it as a kind of offering to the possibility of what might have been but could not be. Even though she wasn't quite sure where it had come from it also felt like something more. Something big and important and familiar. There was a kind of tearing that went through her, violently. She cried out and fell to her knees, grabbing at her head with both hands. She squeezed her eyes shut as flashes and images raced through her mind, a film of some other life on fast forward, and then just as quickly as it had assaulted her, it was gone.

Derin was kneeling beside her when she opened her eyes and slowly straightened up. He looked terrified and shaken but she offered him a weak smile.

"I'm okay. Just a sharp pain. It's gone now." With his help, she stood and wiped at the dirt and leaves on her pants while he held on to her shaking body. "I'll be fine. We should get back to the camp. It's time." She met his eyes and he nodded as he slowly took her arm.

They walked back towards the others but Derin held on to her the whole way. She seemed off balance and a little uncertain of every single step. He wasn't sure what had happened but he knew one thing for certain, nothing was random in a universe that seemed to delight in design and destiny.

FORTY-THREE

KALE TRIED TO ignore her headache as they crept towards the prisoner enclosures just outside of Dempsey's towering city walls but it was difficult. Her head was pounding and every once in awhile iridescent spots would jump out of the darkness to startle her, throwing her off balance. She knew they weren't a threat and yet she was on edge. For the first time since waking up without a memory a few weeks ago, she was feeling a strange kind of pull she hadn't felt or experienced before.

Derin walked up beside her and whispered, "you okay?" and at first she could only nod in response, not quite sure what else she could say. She was deeply unsettled and couldn't seem to get a sense of having her feet under her. There was no time to think about what it all meant. They'd come for a reason and she was going to see it through no matter what.

"I'm okay," she nodded again, once to confirm and then once towards Medea just up in front of them. "We don't know what's coming, don't wait."

"Thank you," he said, meaning so much more than he could ever truly express. He met her eyes and they shared a last moment of knowing between two people who had once been meant for forever, only had never gotten it.

He hurried ahead and pulled Medea aside. "I need to talk to you." His voice was filled with pleading, but she shook off his arm and kept moving. "Medea, please," and this time the tone in his voice, so desperate, so full of longing, stopped her. She turned to face him letting the others in their group move around them like a river traveling around a large rock in its center.

"What?" She wanted to be angry, but she was too tired, and hurt, and afraid for there to be any space for anything more inside her. He knew he'd caused a lot of it, her pain, and even if he couldn't make it right, he had to tell her how he felt. His inability to know himself had drawn a deep wound across her heart, but he didn't want to live in the past anymore and he finally knew who he was. He wanted to be here, with her, in the moment. As honest and open as he'd ever been.

Before she turned away, he started speaking. Instead of telling her some great big story with all the right words to charm her into believing him, he told her the simple truth. He'd been unsure, not of his love for Medea, but of how to hold onto it at the same time as he held his love for Kale now that she was alive again. He was afraid of who it meant he was if he left Kale behind after everything she'd already lost and given. Admitting the story of their love hadn't been about eternity but something else entirely was just another thing from the past that was fading out of sight and he was just so tired of losing things. He told her he'd been afraid, that if he let go of who he was when he loved the girl who'd given her life for his, that he hadn't been worth her sacrifice in the first place.

"So you see, I couldn't face you, not while it was all just so mixed up inside me. I didn't want you think I'd given up on us while I was just trying to figure it all out." Derin paused and took a deep breath. His heart was racing at the thought of losing her and knowing it would be his own fault entirely. "I'm so sorry I let you believe my heart belongs to anyone but you now. I'm sure I don't deserve forgiveness or a second chance but I'm asking for them. Life's too damn short and fragile to waste on anything but this, us." When he paused his breath felt ragged and his chest was tight. He knew he was out of time. "I love you Medea. I'm so sorry I've hurt you. Can you forgive me?"

She wanted to turn away, to stew in her hurt and anger, to make him suffer and wait. Except she knew what he said was true. At any moment everything you loved could be torn away and so there was only this, the present, and what you did with it. She tried to let everything go except the one thing that mattered, but everything was happening so fast.

"I don't know," she began, and his heart dropped. Before she could go on one of Sumira's men came out of the dark and called to them to hurry. It was time.

"Medea please," he said, panicked, wanting desperately to know what was next even though he knew he had no right to demand it.

"We're out of time," she said sadly, turning away from him to hurry down the road disappearing into the darkness, and in his heart all he could do was hope that wasn't the whole truth of things. He wasn't sure how he could go on without her and so he prayed as he hurried to catch up with her that he wouldn't have to find out.

FORTY-FOUR

THEY KNEW EXACTLY where they were going as they made their way through the dark. Their small group ready to face an army in order to do what was right. They hoped it wouldn't come to that. That destiny, and time, and luck would all be on their side. But whatever it did come to they would face it, united.

Sumira and Corin had led a group of scouts the day before and they'd figured out that inside the gathering grounds there were fifteen small enclosures spread out along one side of the city where the prisoners slept and lived when they weren't being forced to work and serve. As they'd walked back to the camp, it had been comforting for them both to talk and share, to break the silence of shock and sadness with hope. They could relate to one another easily. Growing up in vastly different worlds and yet faced with the same questions. When did enough become too much? When did the line get crossed so that you could no longer stand by and allow awful things to transpire? How could you find a way to forgive yourself when you realized all your justifications for waiting so long were simply about your own comfort and fear?

It wasn't easy for Sumira to admit she'd been complacent—a coward even. But it also mattered that she was facing it all now. That she spoke aloud her own culpability in what was happening in Dempsey. She'd discovered change cannot occur in the world if it does not first happen within and she wanted to be different and to be better. So she began with Corin, by admitting what she was and what she'd allowed, and by begging whoever might be listening, be it god, or the universe, or some other force, to forgive her. Somewhere in the aftermath of her revelations she hoped that she could begin to forgive herself.

Corin told her about his own journey on Alpha Iridium and she still marveled at the fact that he was actually telling her the truth. It all seemed so impossible and yet anyone who'd survived the breaking of Earth knew amazing and unbelievable things were absolutely possible. He spoke about always being the voice of reason; about always being cautious and playing things safe. He told her what he'd never told the others, that he wasn't certain without them he would have done anything at all about Caine, would have been entirely complicit in the horror that was Caine's rule even if he wasn't a willing participant.

"I don't believe that for a second," she'd said, pausing and taking hold of his arm. He felt a jolt where she touched him—a shock of electricity and something more. It was like remembering something so long forgotten it no longer had a name or a form. Still, it pulled at him in a way he'd never felt before. He met her gaze, intense and serious, looking for some sense she'd felt it too, whatever it was. She must have, he was sure of it, but instead of saying anything she hurried on, "you don't see yourself the way... the way your friends clearly see you. I hope one day you'll know yourself as you are and not as the story of all you haven't done."

How could she know him so intensely already, he wondered, and looked deep into her eyes in search of his answer. Startled by what woke up inside her she dropped his arm and quickly suggested they get back to camp, breaking the spell that had wrapped itself around them both. She didn't want to get lost in what she felt. That pull. He was going home in a few hours and they needed to focus on the mission at hand.

It had started when they'd first met. They were like magnets, drawn together, forever aware of the other when they were near. After that first shock of deep recognition, it became so strong that she always felt a little tickle at the periphery of her awareness any time he was near. Now, as they made their way in the dark towards the salvation of more than two hundred prisoners, she did her best to press it out of reach.

Corin felt the same sense of burying something that had only just found its way to the light. He was focused on the task in front of them and yet couldn't quite silence a sense he was about to lose something that he hadn't even fully found yet. There was no time left to dream or indulge possibilities. The time for action was upon them and they needed to focus on the present, not what might have been or might be yet.

When they arrived at the city of Dempsey, they split up into small groups, most tasked with freeing the people in the enclosures, while a few remaining pairs were tasked with either disarming the guards or keeping watch for trouble of any kind. They'd found three pairs of guards, two on the periphery and one further in doing rounds, and within the first few minutes of their arrival had them all bound and gagged so that they posed no threat to the work ahead of them. Dempsey's arrogance and certainty of its own indestructibility would work in their favor it seemed.

They meticulously moved from pen to pen, unlocking the gates and stepping inside to wake the prisoners within with urgent whispers. They could barely cover their anxiousness to hurry so that they could get out of there and as far away from Dempsey as possible by the time the sun rose.

Rogan was in one of the groups freeing people from enclosures and every gate she opened she looked around frantically for Firth and her friends and family. Each time she met the gaze of those hollow-eyed strangers, terrified, looking gaunt and broken, almost unwilling to hope their freedom was so close, she felt disappointment layered on top of the triumph. Most of the prisoners hesitated, groggy and confused but also afraid to believe their prayers had been answered. Afraid also of the kind of punishment and torture they knew would meet them if they were caught. They'd seen what disobedience earned you in this place and it was terrifying.

Each time that they emptied two of the tiny prisons, they began to lead the people out, heading towards a rendezvous point where they intended to meet in twelve hours, giving each group a chance to take a different route and putting none of the others at risk. They'd decided in advance that Sumira's people would lead them to safety since none of the Alpha Iridians expected to be around that long. None but Kale of course; but most of them did not know that yet.

It seemed so long ago now, the realization she had no intention of going with them and then confessing it aloud to Alex and then later Derin. It had freed her somehow, given her a chance finally to breathe deep. She hadn't realized how oppressive it had been, their unrelenting expectation that she willingly go back to another life, and her own trepidation about being an old version of herself that she might not be able to live up to. But she realized she could face it if she had to, all of what she'd been, and still find a way to choose a new life for herself. Every cell they opened, every scared and haunted look that met hers reminded her how precious it was to even have a choice.

Just off to her left, Rogan was just about to break the locks on the tenth pen when somewhere overhead an alarm sounded and men began to shout down from the top of the city walls. It was an awful wail, that siren that announced they were there, and Rogan felt panic shoot through her. She still hadn't rescued her family yet. What if they weren't here, she wondered for the first time, what if she couldn't find them and this had all been for nothing? She threw the gates open and ran inside and finally, finally found familiar faces amongst the prisoners. Two more gates flew open, Corin and Jaren at one and Kale and Medea at the other, and they rushed inside, waking the prisoners, ignoring the fact that they were out of time. Hadn't they all learned time was not a thing always to be obeyed.

As Rogan rushed from person to person looking for Firth, shouting at each of them to tell her where her partner was, she could hear behind her when their enemies arrived in greater numbers. When she turned towards the entrance of the enclosure she was in she saw Sumira swinging her axe at two vicious looking men. Terrified and nearing hopeless, Rogan grabbed the large blade she'd been carrying and ran to Sumira's side, joining her in the fight. She called over her shoulder as she ran, "as soon as you have a chance you run for it. Get to the trees if you can. Don't stop for anything." Then she threw herself at one of the men and cut him down with a single stroke.

In all her life, she'd killed only what she needed to survive. Food and sustenance but never anything like this. She stood frozen to the spot, shocked at the pool of blood that flowed towards her feet, until one of Sumira's men showed up, hurrying her out of her trance, and she was able to send her people with him with assurances everything would be okay. She spotted Kale and Alex fending off a pair of scary looking soldiers as Jaren worked to open one of the last enclosures behind them. Further down she saw Medea and Corin fighting a beast of a man while Joah opened the enclosure behind where they fought. It seemed foolish now. Impossible. More men were coming. The alarm was still sounding and there would be no way they'd all escape without being captured or killed. Still, all she could think about was finding Firth, of seeing her again before all this fell apart or went the way she thought it would.

Sumira finished off the second man and seemed unfazed by the necessity of violence. When Rogan caught the hint of anguish that flitted across Sumira's face, she realized that none of them would go unchanged by this night, even those of them who would be able to hide it well. Sumira turned in time to see Corin take a spear to his left shoulder and she screamed and ran at the man who'd stabbed him. Corin fell a moment after his attacker and Sumira was kneeling next to him after cutting down her opponent with a single stroke.

"Don't move," she begged him, "just stay still." Terror swept through her as the reality of what was unfolding slammed into her. She couldn't lose what she hadn't had a chance to hold onto yet, it just wasn't fair.

"You're beautiful," he said, smiling up at her. "I should have told you sooner," he added, trying to make a joke of the moment. When a single, sorry laugh made him wince and he slumped against her, going quiet, all she could do was hold him tighter.

"Corin," she looked around frantically, "damn it, I don't know what to do. I'm sorry."

She watched as a group of slaves fleeing into the night were being cut down one after another. Not far from her she saw that Jaren had just been captured and that Joah had been badly injured and lay on the ground bleeding from a large wound across his upper chest. His breath was shallow and uneven and Medea held onto him, speaking frantically into his ear, trying her best not to cry as she rocked him. Alex and Kale were the only ones left fighting. Alex kept swinging his axe at a large soldier who never tired of coming at him. Not far from them Kale defended herself from two men with clubs while she moved as if she'd fought a hundred times before even though that didn't make any sense.

"Help them," Corin pleaded, and Sumira looked at him and nodded before she took off towards the fight. She got to Alex first and between the two of them dancing and pivoting side-to-side, they were able to knock down the soldier. She held the large knife to his throat and drew a line that heaved an arc of red into the dying night.

Kale couldn't believe how quickly and fluidly she was moving. It was like her body remembered something she did not. She knocked the first man down by sweeping his legs out from under him and swung her club into his chest connecting with his sternum so that she heard a great big crack that stole all of his breath. As she turned the second soldier was so close that she could see his bright blue eyes, even in the dark, and when she met them she realized he was just an ordinary person.

She'd told herself they were monsters. That they were capable of great acts of evil because they were just that, evil, and yet looking into this stranger's eyes, all she saw was his humanity. Both the possibility of bringing awfulness and cruelty into the world, and also yes, of giving birth to hope, compassion and beauty. *How different is he than me*, she wondered, and in that pause he got the best of her. His club connected with her head and sent her sprawling. The world dimmed and then brightened and then disappeared as Kale slipped away into a darkness that was both familiar and for most, deeply feared.

Not far from her, Rogan reached her arms through the barred window of that last cell and held on to Firth. The wall between them an expanse far too big and solid for either of them to bridge. Yet they'd found each other hadn't they. Rogan had come for her, as Firth knew she would. As the night began to fade around them and the sky began to lighten there seemed to be no hope of them finding their happy ending, but they held on anyway.

Part Three

Awake

FORTY-FIVE

KALE

THERE IS ONLY the darkness. And a sense of coming home.

I can feel all of time and space around me, spreading out towards the far away shores of eternity while also drawing in close. I am a part of it all, vast and reaching, and yet still so very small.

I see my beginning through that infinite sea of stars and galaxies, and I finally understand.

I remember my very first becoming, long ago on an Earth with a way of life now extinct. I remember also, waking as a child in the woods near Braedon Ridge on Alpha Iridium. Once, that planet had begun in a dream and then somehow found its way into the waking world, like me. Something meant, and something woken, how beautifully simple it all is. Deep down there was always a memory of what I was born to do. To stop the monster, posing as a man, with Darkness spreading in his wake like a rising wave. I knew it so fully that the truth devoured almost every other part of me.

Still with me is the memory of a lonely life on the eastern shores of the Atlantic Ocean, solitary and somewhat broken. Steeped in a deep and aching dream to live an extraordinary life. I had so much hope and longing, in both lives, on both worlds, and yet neither left me feeling like I'd lived the entirety of a life.

In one life, I wished for the other, and to be whole. In one life, I gave everything I was because it's what I was meant for. When that final moment came, to step away from it all, to acknowledge both stories had wound their way towards an ending, I gave the last of what I was meant to. I thought it was all that I had left. Yet somehow after passing through the dark and deep of oblivion I found myself here, on Earth, a place still fighting its way towards the light; but aren't we all.

I stepped out of that life on Alpha Iridium what for me is only a few short weeks ago. Now, I can recall that last moment, clinging to Derin, wondering how love could be a story both achingly short and infinitely long. With that last breath, a single truth remained even when I could not. That love is the one thing that will endure. Surrounded by my friends, with Light rising all around us, I slipped out and away from the world. But instead of falling into nothingness, my life was caught and carried here by some unknown force.

For them, so much has changed in all this time and yet not enough to keep them from coming for me as soon as they knew I was here. How did I not know how much it all meant until now? How could I have been so swept up in the story I was destined for that I missed a chance to truly live a life on either world?

Both those Kales are gone now, and yet everything they gave and forfeited has brought me here to this world, this moment, and this life. All I had to do was forget everything I was so that I could remember who I am.

The dark is pulling at me again but so too is the waking world; as is the brightness of a new day. I realize I am finally free to remake myself in what follows. I can step into the void to wait or I can wake into a new life, on this distant and unfamiliar world, a universe away from everything I love.

I can be brave enough to reach for something of my own. I can find the courage to be imperfectly human. I can reach for what I'm afraid to lose, and be sure enough of myself to grab hold of what might be fleeting. I am ready for joy, and happiness, and fulfillment, within myself. Then maybe too, when I am ready, out in the world. Ah yes, I am all of myself once more, and in this wholeness I realize the only way to finally and fully live is to move on. To let go of a story that was not so long ago meant to end. To accept that I was made for a kind of destiny, but it is past, and yet somehow, I remain. I get it now. It's not about what we lose or sacrifice, it's about what we build in the aftermath. I can be brave enough for that, and I think I might be ready now.

In the last of the dark, faint and fading, while the waking world calls, I pause behind the veil of life and death, and finally I see myself. A spark. Eternal. Born to live a life and one day too to leave it. Whose end is but another beginning, and so on. Whose story is but one tiny thread in the great big tale woven of love and time and creation. It is that simple. It is that infinitely complex. It is breathtakingly beautiful, and I am ready to be swept up in it again. In that current that forever carries us home, first to ourselves and then back to that light where each of us is born.

FORTY-SIX

WHEN DAWN BROKE over Dempsey and the valley that surrounded it, no one could have foreseen what the new day would bring. The sun began at one edge of the bowl of the valley and began to stalk slowly towards the other side as Egan, shocked and furious, took in what had transpired overnight. They'd lost more than two thirds of their prisoners to this surprise raid and Bex, whenever she arrived, would be furious. He outweighed her by almost a hundred pounds but that didn't mean he was unafraid of her wrath when she was angry or disappointed. Now all he could do before she arrived was assess the damage and losses and get as much control back as possible.

The slaves they caught escaping that hadn't been killed were crowded into the holding cell they used for new arrivals. Egan had cut some of them down out of spite but also to strike fear back into the hearts and minds of the prisoners who'd thought for a moment they were entitled to escape the lives the Dempsians had shackled them to.

Egan knew the drill. Examples had to be made. The kind of power they wielded, though absolute, could not falter even just a bit or they'd lose control. Humans, like all life, were dangerous when they discovered the true power of their own resilience. They'd worked tirelessly over the years, as they'd built their empire on the backs of others, to stamp it out along with the sense of hope that seemed forever to rear its ugly head. Almost as if it was a part of the very fabric of their humanness.

The group that had come with Rogan suffered a much different fate than the other prisoners. None of them had seen a gallows before but they saw one now. That large wooden structure used to hang things from struck fear into each of them. As they were forced up the steps towards its platform there was no mistaking what awaited them. Egan's men had carried Joah towards the gallows and simply thrown him roughly down in front of it as if he didn't matter at all. As soon as he hit the ground he began to spill blood onto the green grass beneath him drawing a sob from Medea while the rest of them watched, helpless. Corin, wounded but alert, still seeping blood from his shoulder wound, was tossed to his knees next to Joah but they still guarded him closely. Up above Medea, Alex, Kale, and Sumira were placed in front of nooses hastily made, swinging in the breeze as if marking time like the second hand on a clock. Rogan, Jaren and a small group of Sumira's people were forced to their knees behind them to watch and wait their turn.

There was kind of demented theatrics to it that had been used before. They were acts of extreme evil, made more so by the delight the Dempsians were going to take in it all. They fed on fear and cruelty, Egan, his men, and their leader Bex. Even the people they governed had gained a taste for it, and they understood there was a kind of power that came from crushing others beneath the weight of it. Especially those who were committed to a different way of being. Those wrapped up in love and compassion, those who cared for one another and sacrificed where they could. The people of Dempsey weren't entirely immune to all that and yet they paired it with the control and torture of those they imprisoned and worse, they convinced themselves it didn't matter. That the people they enslaved weren't worth as much as they were and so they weren't really doing anything wrong. They couldn't see that their desire for dominance actually made them small. Rotten little remnants of what a person was meant to be and become. Out of that rot rose a greater desire to steep themselves in power and oppression. They could not know how very unoriginal they were. That humanity had told this story so many times before and never triumphantly.

Some of the people had streamed out from the city, some on their way to work or in pursuit of other early morning tasks, some simply drawn by the commotion. A crowd started to form in front of the gallows and as Egan's men put the nooses around the first foursome's necks it grew and grew. Egan looked about for Bex, wondering what had kept her from joining them. He'd sent word to her at least half an hour ago and she should have arrived already. He felt a small river of worry wind its way through him that he quickly swept aside. It was the first moment since the alarms had started to wail early that morning that he began to have an inkling that things might not go their way. But he knew that was absurd. They were all-powerful and nothing would stand in the way of who they were and what they were building.

"What do you have to say for yourselves?" Egan asked them. It was something they asked every time they carried out a death sentence and often interrupted the answers by pushing the prisoners off the ledge to drop to their demise. The swinging of that broken weight the only thing left to be said. The truth was when slaves or errant townspeople were sentenced to die the true crime was always the same, disobeying the establishment and threatening the ultimate power of rule.

It was in that heartbeat of silence Egan used for dramatic effect that Sheeran and a hundred people came swarming over the ridge, armed and wild and angry. As they spilled into the valley the crowd that had gathered to watch the strangers die for their own satisfaction and amusement began to scatter in fear. Dominating helpless people was one thing. Standing up to fight however took a kind of courage that didn't live inside of them anymore.

Egan, always ready to react and take charge, kicked Alex in the back sending him flying off the platform and towards his death. Kale screamed. Across the valley Sheeran did the same when he realized he was too late to save them and that meant most likely his sister was about to die.

While he fell, Alex's life played out before his eyes and time stumbled to a slow crawl. He saw not just what had been but what was laid out ahead; what would be again. He saw the story of himself in moments and snapshots so that he realized there was a kind of missing element to his life that truly would have made it vibrant and fulfilling. He saw that it was okay. That the universe had a grander story for all of them. Not simply in this life, but in all the lives they lived.

They were each of them a kind of chance for the universe to have a life. To play in light and dark, and the brightness and shadows that ebbed and flowed between the two. And so he knew he would be returned to where he'd begun and even in that going home have another chance, and another, and another, for as long as the universe decided play at this game of life and love and awe.

He had a moment to be relieved. To find comfort in what he hadn't known but now did. Then time ran out. The explosion hit right before Alex reached the bottom of the rope. And with it, everything went dark.

FORTY-SEVEN

DERIN WOUND HIS way through the dark corridors like a whisper caught on the wind. No one saw him or noticed he was there. He understood how these places were built. Knew how to move through them without being detected. Knew where they kept the weapons, where they ate and slept, and yes, where the monster running it all would live and sleep and dream of more horrors to inflict on the world.

When he'd come to the wing that was Bex's, he knew it right away. There was an opulence not reflected in the other parts of the large central building in Dempsey. There were guards stationed in a number of spots and he disarmed and incapacitated them easily, becoming a version of himself he hadn't had to be in a long, long time. Years of training came back to life as he moved like a shadow in the night closer to the ruler of Dempsey. He knew he would be able to get to her and end her life, putting a stop to the horrors this sad, sorry city was using to sustain itself.

The two guards outside her door had gone down easier than the rest but Derin stayed vigilant as he entered the dark of her room and crept towards her bed. Moonlight and a whisper of dawn filtered in through the windows in her large suite so that his eyes, once adjusted to the dark, had no trouble taking in the richness of how she lived even as she oppressed and ruined the lives of others. Derin felt a flash of rage so forceful that he stopped short just feet from where she slept and for a moment instead of seeing her he saw the man he'd once thought of as his father. A confusing mix of emotions fought their way to the surface but there would be no time for them tonight. He shook the memory off and stepped towards her all at once pressing a hand over her mouth and bringing the large blade to her throat.

"You make a sound and I'll end your life without even a second thought." He'd whispered the words but they were powerful and she did not doubt, even in her shock and fury, that he meant every single one.

Her eyes went wide and then narrowed and she poured out at him a kind of disgust, and hatred, and anger that were palpable. So much so it felt for a moment like she had struck out at him and connected.

"I'm not afraid of you," Derin said. "Your kind are all the same. On the inside you're small and rotten and caught up only with trying to dull that monstrous ache deep down that tells you you're worthless. The thing is, you always choose the only path ahead that confirms everything you're afraid of." Something in her eyes flashed but he could feel her straining against him a little less. "Get up," he said forcefully, "and if you make a sound I will kill you. Trust me, I missed my chance to destroy a monster like you once and I won't make the same mistake again."

Bex rose, silently, hate radiating off her in waves, and yet she seemed so shrunken that he didn't even consider it might be smart to be afraid of her, even like this. He marched her through the corridors and she urged back the few guards who came upon them, panicked, fearful Derin would end her life. The guards followed at a distance until Derin and Bex made their way outside.

It was already day. Full light had arrived along with the sense that a whole new world was opening up in front of them. When the blast hit, Derin was thrown back and through the air until he connected with the front wall of the building they'd just left. He was plunged into a kind of dark he'd known before and there was nothing he could do but surrender to it.

FORTY-EIGHT

THE GALLOWS HAD been incinerated. Every piece of it turned to dust. All that remained of the buildings that had held Dempsey's slaves was a fine grey mist slowly floating back to the earth to settle amongst the people, unconscious and unaware, that were scattered along the earth. The wall that had surrounded the city of Dempsey only moments before was now crumbled and collapsed, and in some places it had been breached entirely so that no one could call the inner city a fortress anymore.

When Kale opened her eyes, she saw a world both familiar and strange and it rattled her a little, this sense that she was waking up again for the first time in a very long while. There was a kind of stillness in the air that was eerie and it drew her back, back, to somewhere she hadn't been in a very long time though the memory wouldn't quite rise. The sky, fully bright and yet with that rosiness that comes only with morning, was dotted with a few errant clouds above her and she watched them through the dust and floating bits of debris that danced through the air. Her ears were ringing, still, so that she couldn't hear the groans or movements of those around her and yet she could sense it all as she sat up and began to look around. As she came to her hands and her knees she saw Alex lying in the dust and wreckage not far from her and she remembered watching him fall to his death, a strange swirl of emotions inside her, fighting to get out. She crawled over to him, body aching and sore, and held her breath as she looked for some sign he was okay. There was nothing and she drew in a big gasp of air and prepared herself for a truth that terrified her.

"Alex," she said, her voice sounding strange and tinny to her own ears as the ringing persisted, though softer now. She still struggled to take in the quiet and calm of the world around her, in the aftermath of whatever had happened here.

"Alex," she said again, her voice louder yet no more certain of itself and she crawled up next to him and then froze. How many times had the world taken something from her before she knew what it really was? Too many, she thought to herself, and wondered if that said more about her or simply about the way of things.

To her left, Medea had forced her way out from under a pile of wood and rock that must have been part of that awful wall that held Dempsey in, though it had not managed to do the same for its evils. Not far from her, Joah was coughing and sputtering, his red rimmed lips warning that something was very, very wrong. When Medea got to him she cradled his head in her lap and spoke softly while bending down to be as near to him as she could. They would get him home and then everything would be okay, she promised him over and over again, her voice rough and worried.

Corin and Jaren were just past them, helping Sumira to her feet. She couldn't put any pressure on one of her legs and she looked both shocked and terrified as she looked around at the destruction that seemed to have engulfed them. Corin's shoulder leaked enough blood to stain his dust covered arm red but he didn't notice it in his worry and concern for Sumira as she leaned into him.

"Alex," Kale said again, wiping dust first from his forehead and then his cheeks. It was strange to be here, leaning over him, a face so much like his brother's and yet in so many ways also distinct. She gave voice to his name one last time, afraid of the stillness it was met with and then his eyes shot open, shocked and afraid, and their blueness went wide around a tiny speck of dark. They were the same crystal clear and radiant color the ocean made when it laid itself down over ice in the arctic and though they were the same as Derin's they were vastly different in the life they'd witnessed and the dreams they looked for on the horizon.

She wrapped herself around him and helped him to a seat while he wheezed and tried to catch his breath. When he was upright she pulled back and away from him and for a moment she took in the scene around them, suddenly feeling small and afraid, though she wasn't sure of what. When she finally met his eyes she felt a jolt of recognition.

"You came back," he said, his hand reaching up to touch her cheek, "I thought... I thought you were gone." She smiled, because she thought she knew what he meant, and yet it all seemed so strange and impossible.

She felt a swelling in her chest and the sense that something long out of reach was falling in to place but instead of feeling comforted it threw her off balance and unsettled her. When she looked away Alex felt like he'd been thrown into a sea of ice cold water.

"Derin," she said, suddenly aware of where they were and what had just unfolded as dawn broke over Dempsey. "Derin!" She repeated again, this time yelling and looking up and around so that she missed both the terror and the heartache that flitted across Alex's face.

"He's not here," came a voice through the dusty air, and when Kale and Alex looked towards it they saw Cyan and Dellerim standing in front of a large spinning void. Cyan stepped towards them and spoke again, "Where did he go Alex?"

"He went for Bex. We decided, well, we decided to take matters into our own hands." They'd known, when they made the decision, that it hadn't been the only way, but it was the path they'd chosen. Too long they'd both regretted not stopping Caine. Now here was a chance to stop one of his kind, an instrument of the dark. A symbol of all that was wrong in the world and within humanity.

"What?" More than one of their group asked in that first shocked moment.

"It's just, we thought if we stopped her, we could put an end to all this." He looked around, the destruction, the wounded people starting to stir and to help each other up. It hadn't just been that. They'd decided to defy the stars. Instead of simply trying to fight what they'd been shown was coming, they'd actively tried to tell a different story. If they could change that single thing, they could also save their parents, and Kale, and stop what seemed like it was barreling towards them with no indication of slowing or passing them by.

"Oh Alex, my love, Earth and its people have struggled with this story since the beginning of time. No matter how many of its monsters you stop another is always waiting to take its place. The only answer is for good people to keep fighting back. To rise up against this drive towards greed and oppression, fear and hate, that seems to live within them, and maybe therefore within us all. I wish I could say it will one day be different, but I'm not sure that wouldn't be a lie." Cyan thought back to the world as she'd known it. Hadn't it been the same then too. Humanity had never found its way to greatness or good, not as a whole, and she couldn't be sure it was a story that would ever unfold for them.

"Mom," Alex said, wanting to tell her what he'd decided. Wanting her to know that he was sorry he'd been such a fool and that he understood it all now. Why she'd done everything, why she'd fought so hard and made so many mistakes, and yet all of them for love and so wasn't that the right reason however misguided in the end. He wanted, needed her to understand what it was he had to do, not just for himself, but because it felt right.

"Oh Alex, I'm your mother, I already know. Your war has always been inside you. I hope you'll find your peace finally, even here." She said this placing a hand over his heart and then she wrapped her arms around him and held him tightly. "I love you. I will always love you." She pulled back and away from him and their eyes met.

He nodded. Lost for words and breath. A kind of destiny unfolding around him that he'd believed they could stop. That's why they'd gone after Bex. To finally fight the story the stars held over their heads. To break the cycle of feeling like everything they went through was authored, and orchestrated, and foretold somehow. Yet here they were. Standing in the very place the stars had told them they would be.

"You have to find your brother, Alex. It's time to send everyone home." Her voice was calm but urgent and underneath both was a kind of sorrow he'd not heard before, and he understood that he wasn't going to be able to keep from losing some of what he loved. She knew it. Now so did he.

Alex stepped back from his mother and met his father's eyes over her shoulder, and they exchanged a knowing that could not have been understood by anyone else around them. An anguished look crossed each man's face and then a gentle smile as they stepped together to hug, fiercely, for the very last time. They were both ready and resigned to let the story play out the way it was meant to. A whole conversation passed in just that moment. Then Alex stepped away from his father for the very last time. There would be time for the rest, for feeling it all. Now he had to save his brother and get him home before it was too late. One last look at each of his parents then he took off towards what remained of the front gates of Dempsey and without a moment's thought Corin was fast behind him despite his injury.

In front of their only doorway home, Dellerim cried out and fell to one knee, his face working in effort as the portal he'd opened constricted and pressed down upon his back. "I can't keep it open much longer," he shouted at them, "there isn't much time left."

"I can help," Kale said, stepping towards him. "I know how to hold it open."

"It will destroy you," Dellerim said, with no hint of casualness.

"It's okay." Kale said stepping closer, a memory now of what she'd glimpsed when the world had slipped away from her and for a little while, just a moment, she'd been between lives. In that place, both infinitely bright and dark, she'd known all of what she was and what she could be. Some of it remained within her, however dull and fading, and she knew she could use the last of it to save them. She'd been shielded from time, and space, and evil, and yes even fire and now she could do this one last thing. A gift to fulfill a destiny, now long past. She understood whatever it was had almost run its course but there would be enough left for this. *And if not for this then for what* she wondered, as she stepped towards him.

"No," he said, stopping her in place and yet there was a moment where he indulged the possibility that things could end differently than he knew they would.

"Let me help you," Kale implored, and it was in this moment that Medea realized her friend had come home to herself. Standing there, no longer an empty memory but the whole damn truth. "If I hold it open, you can all go home."

Kale met Dellerim's gaze and he understood, like she did, what it meant. 'Who else had nothing to lose', is what she thought when she offered it, but all that had changed, and even though she remembered the girl who was born to give up everything, she wasn't meant for that story anymore.

"No," Cyan said, stepping between them and as she stared deep into Kale's eyes she gave her a smile born of acceptance and love, "not this time. It's my turn to be strong, and yours to live a life. The one you've been robbed of, too many times." A wave of sadness washed through Kale, for what had been lost and what would be lost still. In that moment she understood the price Dellerim and Cyan would both pay and it broke her heart even as she glimpsed the beauty in having so much to lose in the first place. "Make him happy," Cyan added quietly, "and when he forgets why he gave up so much for it, remind him for me that love is always worth it."

Kale didn't entirely understand. Still, she nodded, once, twice and then whispered, "thank you," as she wrapped her arms around Cyan to say goodbye. It was brief and yet everything that needed to be said and known lived in that moment between two women who had both given up everything more than once.

"My love," Dellerim said as Cyan stepped towards him, the tears had begun to fall as he spoke again, "please don't," he said even as he knew it was the only way.

"Hey, hey, don't cry," Cyan said but the tears streamed down her cheeks as well. Without speaking aloud she offered him the last words they would share in this life. "In another time, in another life, we will dance again together under the stars and it will feel like all of eternity is stretched out before us. Just like before. We will let love rock us to sleep at night, and hope wake us every morning. We know this story. It will be ours again." She knelt down beside him and kissed him then like she had a million times before, only this one was the last of its kind so that there was both a beginning and an end wrapped up inside it. When they broke apart, she stepped into the mouth of the portal with him and pressed all her strength towards the task of keeping it open long enough to save her family.

"We have to get Joah home now," Medea said, panicked and overwhelmed, "he doesn't have much time." She felt like her heart was being sawed into a million pieces. Derin was missing, Joah was dying in her arms, and her best friend, only just having found her way back, wasn't coming with her. She knew it just as certainly as if Kale had told her herself. She let Jaren carry Joah towards that doorway home as she stepped up to Kale and wrapped her arms around her friend. So many stories unfolded in that embrace, a truth too long kept to herself, of what it had meant to lose her friend and to try to find her own life in the aftermath of that sacrifice.

"I love you," they said together, then as they broke apart, "always." Medea met Kale's eyes and then added, "You are too good for another life like this Kale, but I hope it offers you what you've been searching for." Medea could feel the unfairness of it pressing down upon her. They'd finally come back to one another only to have to say goodbye.

"You are too good for anything less than complete and utter happiness. Don't settle Medea, please, find that great big life that's been waiting for you." They hugged again, it was brief and yet deep, a well of sisterhood and love weaving its way between and all around them before they broke apart. Then Medea stepped towards the portal and took one last look back before it swept her and Joah out of sight.

Jaren looked back at her for a moment and smiled sadly. "Jaren," she said, but she wasn't quite sure how to go on. She ran up to him and gave him a hug, holding on tight as long as she dared, before stepping back and away.

"I love you," he said, "find the happiness you deserve." Then he was gone.

For a moment, all she could do was stare at the place where they'd both been just a moment before. Two of the people she'd loved most in the world. They'd been separated by darkness and time for so long, and now only to find out their paths were always meant to diverge.

She didn't know this kind of heartache was possible and she indulged it for just a moment. Then, she looked to Dellerim and Cyan one last time before she took off running towards Dempsey and wherever Derin, Alex, and Corin were somewhere inside.

FORTY-NINE

AFTER THE BLAST knocked them down, Sheeran and his people had at first been slow to rise. There was a collective remembering of the breaking, that almost ending of the world so many years ago, that had them afraid to move. Afraid to test the possibility of the same thing happening now. But as the Earth settled and stilled underneath them they began to stir, then stand, and look around. The city and all that surrounded it in the valley below them was concealed in a cloud of dust and destruction, and though Sheeran knew his sister was in there somewhere, possibly hurt, or worse, he also instinctively understood something bigger than any one of them was unfolding and he had a part to play still.

His heart pointed him towards the ruined gates of the city and that's where he headed, first at a quick walk, then at a run, calling his people after him.

He hadn't at first wanted to face what needed to be done. To face what standing by quietly ignoring how Dempsey made its way in the world said about him. Said about any of his people who chose not to challenge him or who argued that what they'd built for themselves mattered more than risking something. That staying out of it all didn't make them complicit it just meant they were protecting their own. He'd thought of himself as a man who'd built a community of free thinkers, of people who would ask for what they needed and who he could trust to challenge him when they thought he was wrong. Yet no one had been willing to face the great big monstrosity of Dempsey or his unwillingness to stand up to it either.

Sheeran wasn't sure if he'd ever feel free of his shame, but he was done taking the easy path, and done ignoring injustice just to get by in the world. It had been a hollow kind of safety and certainty and he wouldn't do it for another moment more. He only wished it hadn't taken a group of strangers and his sister's action without him to make him see he needed to be a better man.

Up ahead, he saw Kale running through the place where the front gates had been and though he wasn't sure what was happening he felt driven to follow where she'd gone and to help in any way he could. He slowed his pace, then stopped and turned to face his people.

"Dempsey's army cannot be allowed to regroup. Stop them by whatever means you must. Half of you this way with me," he pointed towards Dempsey and whatever lay beyond its ruined walls, "and half of you that way," he said as he pointed towards the wreckage of the gallows. "Help in whatever way you can, as warriors or healers or whatever else might be asked of you. We will not go home without having had an impact here today!"

They screamed and shouted as their band of latecomers parted and streamed around the wreckage, towards what end they could not know. He led half his people through the quiet streets of Dempsey, almost a ghost town as its people hid from view, sensing their way of life would never be the same and that they might have to pay for their transgressions should they be caught or captured.

When they came across soldiers, they subdued and captured them easily. All the fight having left them as they wandered through the ruined streets in confusion; still dazed from the blast that had leveled much of their home or the shock of discovering they weren't invincible after all. The further into the city they got the more people they left behind gathering up soldiers and leading them by some silent agreement back towards where everything had seemed to begin just outside the crumbling outer walls of Dempsey. Sheeran longed to head that way as well, to see if Sumira was okay, to make sure he hadn't lost the most important person in his life, and yet something drew him further in to Dempsey and he surrendered to that insistent pull towards a moment he had long been meant for.

FIFTY

KALE FOUND ALEX and Corin kneeling in rubble and ruin and at first thought they were gathering up a pile of rags coated in dust and grime. She paused, struggling to make sense of what she was seeing and then her heart dropped and all she could think was, *not again.*

She stumbled towards them and when she got there she could see that Alex's face was streaked with tears and dust and sorrow as he cradled his brother's head in his lap. He was stunned and so forlorn that he was unable to see anything but Derin. Corin sat beside him, shocked and devastated as well. Kale refused to believe what she saw and when she reached them she knelt down slowly and drew her face level with Alex meeting his eyes, imploring him with her steady gaze to tell her what was going on.

"He won't wake up," was all that Alex could offer, but it was enough to send relief rushing through her. He was alive. She lowered herself next to Derin and paused. *We've done this before*, she thought to herself, *except you're much nearer this time and it's not me you're coming back to.*

"Derin," she said into his ear, "Derin," again, and louder. This time he moaned and his eyes fluttered for a moment before they stilled again.

She met Alex's worried gaze with one of her own and shook her head helplessly.

"What have you done." Bex's voice, angry and hateful startled them all. It wasn't a question but an accusation.

Kale stood and turned, facing her with so much certainty and strength that for a moment Bex blanched before she took a step back and away. She was covered in dust and ash and a wound in her forehead was leaking blood. She seemed otherwise unharmed.

"You won't get away with this. Nothing will change and I'll destroy every single one of you and all of those slaves before the day is done." She was seething with rage. It was unfathomable to her that she wasn't entitled to the people they'd captured and used. That she and her people weren't somehow worth more than the rest of them. She fully believed that something had been taken from her and from Dempsey. Something that belonged to them. All the simmering, festering poison from living a life built on the exploitation and ruination of others bubbled up and out of her and there in the morning light it was grotesque.

Kale could see in her a kind of darkness that had been born there. It was a kind of rot that could spread and wreck a whole civilization. Hadn't they all been told the stories time and time again. Hadn't a story like that found them on Alpha Iridium. Human history was littered with people who weren't quite whole in the way a person was meant to be. In that void there always swam a kind of wickedness capable of dreaming up horrors with which to torture the rest of world; while the weakest among them followed and obeyed and perpetuated crimes in their name.

Will we ever find our way away from this story, Kale wondered, *and we will we ever learn the responsibility we all hold in fighting this kind of darkness?* Bex could be labeled evil, sure, but if a whole society hadn't stood behind her, hadn't delighted in what they got as long as they turned their backs on how, then none of this would have happened. How long could you make excuses for a species that repeatedly surrendered to the easiest path and in doing so the worst of themselves?

There was no time to listen for an answer. Bex was running towards her, arms raised overhead with an axe that had until that moment gone unseen at her side. Kale's arms flew up in front of her and at the same moment Alex leapt between her and Bex to take the blow. She heard someone scream 'no' and saw that Bex was poised to swing the axe down at them both. In that moment, Kale realized she would once again lose something she never really had the chance to know.

Bex stopped suddenly, frozen in mid step, and her eyes went wide before a single breath dragged its way out into the world between her shocked and parted lips. She dropped first to her knees, then fell to one side, the axe falling nearby. In her back, between her shoulder blades, a single arrow stuck out awkwardly. It had pierced her heart and though she'd never used it for good or decency or love she'd needed its beating just the same.

Sheeran lowered his bow and gave them a reassuring smile and a silent nod which both Kale and Alex returned. Kale couldn't believe it. Once again, it was not her time. She shook away the shock and the beginnings of a story rising inside of her that she was still a pawn in a game she might never win.

Behind them, Derin moaned and when she and Alex turned around Corin was helping him to sit up. Kale rushed over to him and knelt down. She took his face in her hands and stared intently into his eyes, looking for an answer to what she did not know.

"I thought you were gone." She struggled not to cry.

"Kale." It was both a question and a statement of fact. "I knew you'd find your way back." He moved towards her and she leaned in towards him and when they kissed there was a kind of coming home that felt both wonderful and sad. There was no passion in it. Just a deep and aching love and longing that belonged to a different time and a different place, and to two very different people.

It was for her both barely a moment ago and an eternity since she'd left Alpha Iridium. Almost no time at all had passed since being pulled from that last breath in his arms to waking on Earth and yet also everything it had taken to cross time and space all alone made it seem like so much more than that. She smiled, happy that their story was ending a little differently than she'd thought it would and that they would both have a chance to find something more, even if the something more was meant to take them on different paths, and far away from each other.

Alex turned away from them. Shocked at how fierce the ache was in his chest. He was happy for his brother but in that moment, his heart breaking, he couldn't help feeling that deep wound too.

"We're out of time," Kale said sadly, when her and Derin broke apart. "Here and now anyway."

He nodded and smiled sadly. "In another time, in some other dream maybe." He let the words hang between them. A whole lifetime carried in that single wistful statement. What more could he say. The universe was indeed a place more mysterious and mischievous than they could ever have imagined and yet they were both willing, finally, to trust that it would lead them where they were meant to go, and towards the people they were meant to share this great big adventure of a lifetime with.

She stood and then with Corin's help brought Derin to his feet.

"Come with us," he begged. "Please." But neither of them was sure he meant it and both of them knew it was not meant to be.

"That story has already been told," she said sadly and for a moment the great big whole of it swept over her. She saw their first meeting, eyes finding each other from a distance, and that next meeting again near the sea. She saw one of the bravest men she'd known, first trapped within uncertainty, then willing to turn even against the idea of himself to do the right thing. It passed in a moment, gone in memory like it was gone in truth, but it still made her ache for how beautifully fleeting all of life could be.

"I love you," he said. "Always."

"Be happy. It's time." Tears tumbled down her cheeks carving paths through the dirt and dust. "I love you too. See, you were right." She smiled and he returned it. A simple ending to something that was so much more than that. "Now go, before it's too late."

Without another word he turned away from her. "Come on Alex, Corin," he shouted as he took off towards where he hoped his parents were waiting outside the city's walls. Alex glanced at Kale, a deep and aching hurt swelling up inside him. He wanted to reach out to her, to say something, but all he could do as their eyes met was give her a nod and a sad smile. He met Corin's eyes for a brief moment, long enough to understand, and then he turned to follow his brother, faster than he'd ever run before.

"Corin, hurry!" Kale shouted, but he walked over to her slowly and wrapped his arms around her and in that ease and gentleness Kale understood. "You're not going back." Overwhelmed, she collapsed into him and finally let the sobs overtake her. They were a mixture of heartbreak and relief, and she couldn't figure out where one ended and the other began; or where any of it belonged. All she could do was let it out, sharing herself with the world in a way she hadn't before.

Corin wiped at the tears tumbling down his cheeks as his face crumpled in anguish. They clung to each other like that. Safe somehow in a world gone mad. She could be anchored even in the wildest storms if she had the right people with her, Kale realized, and though she didn't quite understand it, she was grateful Corin had decided to stay and that she'd have something of Alpha Iridium with her here.

"They'll understand," she finally told him, a hand on his cheek as she looked deep into his eyes. Even though she knew it was true she knew also they were words that didn't have any meaning for him just yet.

He hadn't actually known until he'd seen that gateway to Alpha Iridium and realized there wasn't a life for him waiting on the other side. Sure, the people he loved were there but a purpose, a life that felt full and rich, he just didn't feel it. More than that he didn't really want to go back to the confines of his other life. He'd felt it, when five years ago the world around them had shifted into a kind of beginning. Yet it had felt to him more like the beginning of getting left behind. Five years and he wasn't sure he'd even taken a full step forward. Then they'd come to Earth, a place stuck in its own kind of limbo, and something in him had come to life. The thought of fighting for justice, of fighting to stop Dempsey and even show them how they were wrong, of maybe helping this world step back from the brink once again, well it all drew him in to a kind of possibility that he hadn't known in a long, long time.

There was also Sumira. He hadn't known her long enough to justify how he felt and yet the thought of putting a universe of space between them seemed unimaginable to him. Maybe nothing would come of it, maybe it was all just a foolish dream, and yet it felt wonderful to be caught up in it, and wonderful to be free of a version of himself he no longer wanted to be. He wasn't sure it was the right choice but life wasn't about making only the right choices, it was about being brave enough to trust your heart. For the first time in his life Corin decided to do just that.

When the friends broke apart for a moment, it seemed like neither of them knew what to do. Then, Kale remembered Rogan and Firth, the people of Iri, and of course Sumira and the rest of the group who had helped them lead a rescue mission what felt like days and days ago. She suddenly felt a sense of urgency, needing to know what had happened to them all. Needing to be sure they were all okay.

"Come on. We're not done yet," she said to Corin, and he didn't need any explanation to know they needed to get back to where the gallows had been to finish seeing through what they'd started.

As they hurried back towards whatever was waiting for them outside the ruined gates of Dempsey, the city was eerily quiet around them.

FIFTY-ONE

WHEN ALEX AND DERIN came running out of the city the gateway to Alpha Iridium was just a tiny spinning disk barely two feet across. Neither of their parents was visible and both of them blanched, feeling that deep sense of having lost something without really being ready for it to be gone. The stars had been right of course. Their parents hadn't survived this last great fight.

It took all of their strength not to surrender to the tragedy of the moment as they paused and turned towards each other. They both placed a hand on the back of the other's neck and leaned in until their foreheads were touching. Deep breaths and a moment to acknowledge what they'd just lost, then another to savor a deep love between brothers that hadn't truly had enough time. Five years they'd been the other's best and closest friend, sharing almost everything, and now this story too had found its end.

"Alex," Derin whispered and then he paused. He wanted to beg his brother to come home with him but there wasn't time to indulge a hope that would go unfulfilled and so he said the only thing that mattered. "I love you. Be happy. I'll always be there if you need me. We'll find a way."

"I love you too, Derin. Finish the house. Then fill it with love and laughter and joy. I'll be listening for it. Even all the way from here."

They wrapped their arms around each other. It was a fierce hug. An exclamation point on a relationship that had saved and sustained them both. There was nothing left to say and so it was silence that eventually broke them apart and they met each other's eyes one last time. Then Derin stepped away and moved towards the portal. He looked back once, and then with that deep and aching void inside him he crawled through the shrinking opening and was gone.

The earth rumbled beneath Alex's feet and yet the portal closed with barely a whisper, making the moment seem smaller and sadder than he ever could have believed. He fell to his knees and buried his head in his hands and he wept quietly for everything they'd lost, yet again. He wept for his mother and his father, and for the life he wouldn't have with either of them or Derin. He wept for all the cruelty that could be born into a human heart. That could build the kind of tragedies that kept demanding ordinary heroes sacrifice everything. He wept for himself. For knowing he'd chosen the right path and yet how lonely it would be without everything he'd known up until then.

When his body stopped shaking, he began to find his breath again and after wiping away the remnants of his sorrow and tears he stood, slowly, and began to look around. Seeing the world that was his now almost as if for the first time.

The people they'd freed had begun to tend to each other in whatever way they could. Some had ventured into the city and returned with water and even food. Some of Dempsey's citizens came with them ready to help, already willing to accept that things would be different and that they could be part of what changed. They were wrapping wounds, and checking injuries, and even in the ruin and chaos Alex could see the triumphant spirit of what it meant to be truly human. Sheeran's people moved about them helping out while others had gathered some of Dempsey's fallen army into an area near the ruined city wall and were guarding them there.

When Alex turned towards the city gates, he saw her. She was beautiful, regal even, standing so still, shocked and something else, though he couldn't quite tell what it was. Corin squeezed her arm and then headed towards where Sheeran was standing with Sumira, checking his sister's wounds, worried but smiling, and overwhelmed with relief. When Corin got to them, the trio wrapped their arms around each other in a big hug. The sense that there would be a time to face their mistakes opened up space for them to revel a little in the joy of the moment.

Kale made her way to Alex slowly, shaking her head in disbelief. "What have you done?" she asked him softly, unable to shake off her shock.

"You told me once to trust my heart. Well, it belongs here, now." He shrugged and smiled but the gesture didn't reach his eyes. Even within the sense that he'd made the right choice Alex understood it would be a long time before he'd be fully happy again.

"And Derin?" Kale couldn't help but ask because he was there in the space between them even if they didn't mean for him to be.

"He made it home," was all Alex could offer, fighting off the tears that wanted to surface again, and she nodded, smiling sadly. Another moment together that way and then they let the noise and chaos of the scene unfolding around them pull them even further apart as they went to help sort out what would happen next. Kale went looking for Rogan and Firth, shouting their names into the crowd, and Alex joined Corin and Sheeran as they discussed what to do with Dempsey's fallen army.

On the other side of the portal, on the shores of Samnar where the Founders lived, Derin was tossed out of that closing doorway and onto the beach he'd spent so much time on during the past five years.

He hit the ground hard and for a moment had to struggle to catch his breath. Not far from where he landed he saw the four remaining Founders, Arianna, Joachim, Kendra and Kiernan, huddled close over Joah who was ghostly pale and unconscious. Medea was kneeling near his head and speaking feverishly into his ear and Arin stood back and away from the group, crying quietly while she waited for a destiny she'd glimpsed in the heavens to either unfold itself in the moment or curl up and leave them be. When she looked up and over at Derin her eyes went wide with shock and she looked from him to her brother and back again. She pushed through the group, frantic to get to her brother's side and she knelt down and brought herself close to his ear and began to speak to him some secret truth that no one else could hear. If the stars could be wrong about so much they could be wrong about this.

"Come back to me, Joah," she said as she held back tears, "come back, to all of us." She refused to believe they could not author their own destinies. Joah could survive. Who but him was more equipped to defy the stars. To be brave enough to write his own story, in his own way, in his own time.

Derin stepped towards them but wasn't sure what he could do. Watching Medea so terrified and heartbroken tore into him in a way he hadn't experienced before and all he could hope was that Joah, his friend, his family, would find his way back to the waking world.

Joachim dipped even deeper into his son's mind and pushed with everything he had to help show him how to heal; but the wound was so very bad and Joah was so very far away already. Arianna, his mother, and Kiernan and Kendra were there too. Fighting to do something they had done only once before, help another step back from the brink of death and heal the things that had sent them there.

Not like this, was all Derin could think, *please not like this and not now. We've lost so much already.* He sank down to his knees and let his head hang as he tried to make sense of it all. That's when it hit him, not what he'd lost, but what he'd found. How full a life could one person have if there was so much to lose, and so many things even in the awful moments to be grateful for. What did it mean, that life could be so many things at once? That you could lose everything and still have a heart capable of love. That you could be wounded and broken and see the worst of the world, of people, and yet still end up someone capable of hope, and of trust, and of believing that people were worth fighting for no matter what. Derin felt a swelling in his chest that made his heart skip a beat, and then another.

"We're losing him," Arianna cried out, "please no!" She shouted, more a shriek than anything else, and in response Medea and Arin both let out a cry so strange and awful that Derin felt it tear through him like a violent storm. He was drawn back to the moment and away from his thoughts and the fear that he might lose his friend was palpable.

"Joah don't leave me," Medea begged, and from somewhere very far away, almost a beginning again, he heard her. On his other side Arin was close to him, whispering in his ear desperately. Begging him to be the maker of his own destiny. Reminding him they wrote their own stories and his was far from done.

Beside them, the ocean was as calm as if it had been painted there. Derin couldn't help it, he looked out across that vast expanse and wondered, *how will we go on?*

FIFTY-TWO

ON EARTH, in the days and weeks that followed the defeat of Dempsey and the freeing of the slaves there was a collective sigh of relief. Almost everyone could feel it, that narrow escape of some dark destiny. There were so few of them left and it felt like it mattered, that not being the same story humanity had written repeatedly until it had almost written itself into oblivion.

There was a sense once again that something big and profound had unfolded around them. If they could just hold on to the sense that they'd been a part of that becoming then maybe they could be different this time; more connected and aware, more rooted in the goodness that was born and then waited inside each of their hearts to bloom.

Whether it stayed with them or not, they could sense the fragility of it as well, of what they'd won and how tenuous a thread bound them to the story that they would successfully go on. No victory came without a cost and those of them who were ready to fight for a better world knew not to forget that.

Rogan stood in her favorite spot watching the sun inch its way above the horizon to the east. Not far from there in the village they'd begun to rebuild, the love of her life slept, forever altered, but alive and whole. Firth would carry the scars of her time in Dempsey for the rest of her life. Some would fade and some would not, but she would go on and her life would be joyful, and beautiful, and she would find peace, eventually. Sometimes in the dark of night, when a dream of her time in Dempsey chased her awake, she'd go through the list of things she was grateful for and that hopeful lullaby would eventually rock her back to sleep.

Rogan used to come to the sea for her own kind of peace, for the chance to begin the day on her own. But she'd realized after the first week back that she was waiting for the cougar to return. She had something to tell the large cat, something she'd learned while she almost lost everything that mattered.

She'd discovered humans were still indeed something to fear, for they could not help themselves in falling back into that darkness that lurked and loitered deep within them. Yes, they often fought their way into the light, but it wasn't a place they'd yet learned to remain without effort and vigilance. She wanted to tell the big cat not to trust them, to steer clear, but maybe the only ones who hadn't yet figured out the kind of awfulness and greatness humans were truly capable of, were the humans themselves. She shrugged and shook her head, *maybe the cat knows better after all*, she thought to herself, and she turned away from the waves and began to wander back home.

It had only been a few weeks since Dempsey had fallen and they'd only just begun to rebuild but she felt grateful that Kale had decided to stay with them even though she often kept herself at a distance. Rogan was even beginning to enjoy the community that was growing between her people and the people of Ariabore and she'd already begun to see how those ties could strengthen not weaken them. Corin had spent the weeks traveling between the two cities working with Sumira to arrange supplies and to help rebuild. Some of the freed slaves chose to join the town of Ariabore while others had chosen to stay with them in Iri while they rebuilt, including a pair of orphaned children Firth had met while captured. Alex had stayed in Dempsey to oversee the beginning of rebuilding with those who were permitted the chance. The worst of the army had been banished but most were being punished and now there was work to be done to carry out their sentences in the hopes of rehabilitating those men and women rather than simply giving up on them. He kept himself busy and it made her sad to see how heavily he carried the many burdens of his heart.

She understood that Alex and Kale were two broken souls in a storm yet to calm and she found herself hoping that they would find their way to each other so at least they'd have company in their sorrow. She didn't know either of them well, not yet, but she suspected it would be a long while before either's heart was ready to find its way towards another and who knew what could change or be different by then.

She sometimes worried about Kale, who seemed strong enough to endure anything and yet so fragile in the aftermath of so much loss. She kept to herself a lot but had also begun to open up and join their community in a way that warmed Rogan's heart. Still, she often saw her wandering towards the sea alone where it seemed she felt the most comfortable and at peace. Hers was a strange story. One that would be hard to believe if she hadn't witnessed so much already. Yet wasn't it also so very simple. Weren't we all just trying to find our way on these solitary journeys called lifetimes, in search of company on these lonely roads, hoping for someone to share the burdens of our hearts with for a little while?

Rogan wasn't sure where it would all end or what would become of Earth and its people. At times she settled into the moment and being present so fully the wondering didn't really matter. But there were other times, when in the dark of night she'd look to the stars and realize the universe was far more vast, complex and mysterious than a single mind could ever grasp and wouldn't it all be as it should be, whether it made sense to her or not. In those secret moments she swung between hope and fear and only would either abate when she crawled back into bed with Firth and reminded herself the present moment was full enough with everything she needed.

Kale was waiting out of sight and when Rogan finally turned towards home she emerged from the trees and sat down on the sand. She had her own spot of course, further down the coast, but this morning she'd wandered a different direction, while her mind had wandered in others, and she'd ended up here where Rogan had found her what felt like so long ago. She hadn't been back to this spot since washing up from that dream of darkness, and sea, and stars. Arriving here now she was a bit disappointed it felt like an ordinary piece of beach. So much had happened and unfolded in her life that it seemed strange there should be so little to mark it all aside from her memories. At least now she knew how very precious those were.

She hoped she was far enough away from Prophecies and Darkness to be able to step into an ordinary kind of life, something she hadn't had in a very long time. She didn't bother to wonder what it all meant or why, weren't some mysteries meant to remain that way, and if so she was happy to let this one pass unsolved. What she did know is that even if we couldn't control the universe, we could, in these humble human lives, still be our own storytellers. Kale was ready to write her own story. To make something of her life, however small, as long as it mattered and she put her whole damn heart into it, for herself first, and then for the people she chose to share it with.

She'd lived an ordinary life long ago on Earth and dreamed of adventure. She'd lived an extraordinary life on Alpha Iridium and had not dreamed anything for herself at all. Now here she was, on Earth once more, and ready to dream of living. Of being content and fulfilled and making a difference in the lives that were intertwined with her own. It was amazing. All of it. With that deep-rooted knowing, a sense of awe and her place within it swept through her, taking her breath away.

She laughed then. Overjoyed, though it was fleeting. The wind picked up the sound, so precious, and carried it away, a story to be shared with whoever might be listening for it.

Alex watched her from a distance. It was easier than getting close. He saw her sit on the sand and stare out at the sea and he followed her gaze, knowing that vast expanse could show you both its beauty and also sing you songs of eternity. Of comings and goings that never ended, only changed. All of it coaxing you to believe in things like forever and happy endings.

He was ready to begin moving on from the tragedies of his life. To begin another story for himself. But there were things he needed to do first. There was a kind of battle that still needed to be won within him. A kind of healing that needed to fully unfurl and a kind of hope that still needed to wind its way towards the light. He wasn't sure what it would look like, the path ahead, but it was finally the beginning of a different kind of life, and he was ready to trust that, and to trust his heart. Even while it took time to heal.

It's what his father had told him in that last dream. That there was time for all things. Especially when they were right. That there was a time for leaping, for stepping in, and for knowing when to wait. There was a time even for love, and for how it could make eternity out of even the smallest of moments. But he'd warned him as well. If you got greedy with it all, there was a price to be paid. Alex didn't entirely understand, couldn't know all of what it had cost his parents, but that would have to be okay. He would believe the most important things his father had told him. That not everything that was past was gone. That all of what had come before could in some ways come again. That no truth or story was final and within that possibility was the chance for us to find each other, over, and over again, in different ways, with hearts that could remember, even when we could not.

When Kale's laugh reached him, he smiled. He didn't know a single sound could bring you so much joy, or stir up so much longing. *One day*, he thought to himself, and then he turned away from the sea and the woman he loved.

Kale remained. Alone, but happy. Here and now.

On Alpha Iridium, in some ways it was much the same. There were deep wounds that would need time to heal. All of them now fully understood the simple truth that no one person or pair could have eternity. Lives were beautiful and profound because they were fragile and often short. It was in their impermanence that lived so much of their beauty.

On a mountain shelf on Berdune, overlooking Sunshine Bay where once a monster posing as a man had tumbled to his death, five friends stood near but apart. They could feel it, this pull to get lost in the past. To get stuck in a story that was both already written; and unknown by them to be told more than once. It was time to move on. To step back into that current of time so that they could finally move forward and find their way to stories of their own joy and happiness. Hadn't they all been players in someone else's tale. And weren't those people gone now, leaving them to finally write stories of their own.

It was sad and scary and there would be voids in their lives that would never be filled no matter how rich and joyful their lives became now; and yet the losing of so much made it more important that they fought for the lives they deserved. It wouldn't be easy to move on, to move forwards with so much lost, but wasn't that they way of things. Some things fell away, some got left behind, and yet we made and remade our lives despite all that with what remained, until it was our turn to step into the void.

Jaren looked at the faces of his friends one by one and took a moment to consider what they'd been through. What they'd endured together and separately. When he looked back out over the bay he took a moment to think of what had been lost, one last indulgence, one last pause for who could not stand with them anymore, and then he let the breath he'd been holding sigh out into the world. He was finally ready to move on. He looked to his left where Arin was standing tall and proud, her cherry eyes sparkling in the sun, and a thought swept through him, brief but powerful. How much could you miss in the reaching, in the chasing of something that was never meant to be yours. How much could be lost while you were holding on to something that was no longer meant for you. But of course none of that mattered because he was here, now, and he was ready to live in the moment. Finally.

He smiled. A moment of happiness. Arin looked over and smiled back at him.

Medea stood between the two men she loved most in the world and couldn't help but wonder how you could have so much and yet feel so poignantly the loss of so much more. She wasn't sure what was coming, what her life would look like, but she knew that it was miraculous, and weren't all lives that. She wasn't going to waste another moment on fear or doubt. She was ready to live and wouldn't even bother wishing she'd started sooner. The time was now. When Derin took her hand and interlaced his fingers with hers she held on tight and knew she'd never be foolish enough to let go again.

For a moment, Derin set aside his heartache and allowed himself to feel hope. He'd lost so much, so many times it seemed, and it could feel in certain moments impossible to pull apart the messy knotted threads to try to make any sense of it. He also knew sometimes all you needed was the story your heart whispered to you in the dark, messy or not, and his whispered of love and of being brave enough to risk something for it.

On the shores of Samnar, the Founders still live. For them who had been gifted lifetime after lifetime together the loss of two of their own was both a devastating shock and a heartbreaking reminder of how fragile life is. Even their lives could be caught in the current of time, and life, and death, so that what they'd thought they'd had in eternity turned out to be far, far less. Losing Cyan and Dellerim, the two people who had sat at the center of their story, their becoming, made the road ahead a little less clear and the journey down it feel a little more lonely. It made each of them face the simple truth that in the end each great journey must be undertaken alone.

They'd been born out of nothing, long ago on another world, and how very far they'd journeyed since that time. If anything had been gifted to them it was the knowledge that the universe was both dark and light, simple and complex, mysterious and also quite ordinary. The story you wrote with the part of it that you borrowed for a little while, be it one of greatness or some other thing, would be entirely your own, even if fleeting.

A borrowed spark for a finite amount of time. A drop in the ocean of eternity. A chance for the universe to play in the light and shadows of a life. One, if you were lucky, that would come around more than once.

Epilogue

One Year Later

ARIN AND JAREN MADE their way through the forest at a brisk pace and said very little along the way. It was a comfortable silence, one they'd shared many times before. Arin had spent much of the past year on Berdune, in and around Braedon Ridge mostly, helping to continue the efforts to rebuild after Caine but also to help make their world better in any and every way. A legacy of peace, love and goodwill she believed in wholeheartedly. Humanity, their humanity, was a thing woven both of the very brightest and darkest threads the universe contained and the fight to fill the world with good and right was one that had to be undertaken every single day. Both in the world and within themselves to be worthy of it.

She'd come to understand life was meant to be both good and bad. Meant actually to carry all of creation within it. A story of only half of it all is a story half lived and not at all how the universe intended for life to unfold. It was hard to grasp sometimes, to accept, and yet it was true whether they understood or not.

When they stepped through the trees, the house on the edge of the forest overlooking the sea appeared. *Of course they'd built it here*, Jaren thought to himself, before he paused to take it all in.

He couldn't help it. This idyllic little oasis on the coastal wilds of Samnar reminded him of what had been lost alongside all that had been won. So many times throughout his life he'd been reminded that no tragedy was an exclamation point. Grief and loss were stories that wove their way into the entirety of your life and those threads, sometimes bold, sometimes faint, were inescapable, nonetheless. Even more surprising was how they were woven so intricately with all of the beautiful stories that made up his life as well, so that he could not always separate the sorrow from everything else.

"Hey, you okay?" Arin asked, but it was less of a question and more just her letting him know she saw him in that moment and was here for whatever he needed from her. She came up and leaned into him and in that simple gesture he felt like he could do anything. He turned towards her and brought his lips to hers, gently, such a simple and intimate moment. One that still shocked him when he realized that what he'd needed to be happy and fulfilled had been so very close all this time and yet he'd never quite seen it because he'd been reaching for a story of what his life should have been instead of the truth.

"Jeez, get a room!" Joah called from the front porch, startling Arin and Jaren apart. She laughed out loud, delighted to see her brother and went running towards him to throw herself into his arms as he stepped off the porch and onto the sand. He lifted her easily into the air and swung her around once, twice, before setting her back down. "Well that's a greeting isn't it. You'd think I'd almost died."

"Don't even joke," Arin said seriously and shuddered at the thought of how close she'd come to losing her brother on that beach almost a year ago. They'd talked about it many times, where he'd been as he'd drifted away from them all and what had drawn him back. He wasn't actually sure what it had been. Sometimes in the dark of night, alone, he'd poke and prod at the memory of coming so close to stepping into the place after this one. He wanted to see if he could grab hold of where he'd been, and of what had set him free at the last moment, but he just wasn't sure. All he could figure was that his story wasn't done yet. Not in this place and not in this time anyway.

Jaren got to them then and the two men hugged. They shared that silent moment of knowing, that they'd come through something almost impossible together and they were bonded for life because of it, and stronger as well.

"Do you want to come meet our girl?" Joah finally asked, beaming with joy.

They nodded and followed Joah into the house, simply but beautifully decorated, and towards the large bedroom in the back. Joah knocked first and when Medea called out for them to enter he led Arin and Jaren into the room. Medea was there on the bed, sunlight streaming in the windows and the ocean behind her forever watchful and vigilant. In her arms was a tiny baby barely a few days old and she managed to tear her eyes away from her daughter long enough to give them each a loving and grateful look.

"You came," she said, and in that statement was all the love she felt for them both and all the heartache that came with knowing there were those who would never be able to step into her home or meet her daughter.

"Of course, we did," Jaren said and moved towards the bed, sitting down near Medea and the beautiful little girl. "The others will be by over the next week or so but there was no way I was waiting that long." Jaren moved aside the soft blanket wrapped around the tiny bundle and took a long, loving look at the child. He felt a deep longing swell up inside him that shocked, scared, and delighted him before he let it pass.

"Can I hold her?" he asked but Medea was already pressing the child towards him carefully and when the baby was nestled in his arms Jaren realized that all you could need or want in life to be happy could actually be quite small and simple after all. He looked up and met Arin's knowing gaze and she laughed out loud when she saw the same realization in his eyes she knew was mirrored in her own.

Derin stood in the doorway, watching unseen, marveling at how it was possible to have so much even in the wake of losing everything. He watched his friend cradle his daughter and he felt his heart swell for having a life filled with so many blessings even after being littered with so much heartache and loss. He felt grateful and happy. When the inevitable ache rose up that his parents were gone, that Corin, Kale, and his brother were somewhere far away living a life he could know almost nothing about, he let remind him how lucky he was to have had a life rich with so much love that the eventual losing of it could hurt so much.

Medea spotted him then and smiled, drawing him into the room with one long, loving look until he crawled into the bed next to her, leaning into her warmth. He didn't know you could be this happy. That you could have so much. That you could make hard choices and know that the other path might have worked out also and yet have no doubt that you wouldn't change a thing about where you were.

"I love you," she whispered into his neck. And he smiled because it was all he needed, that and the little girl in Jaren's arms.

"What will you name her?" Jaren asked, curious.

"We haven't quite decided yet," Derin said with a mischievous smile.

"Oh no, she'll have her own name, and her own destiny," Medea said, smiling. "But she'll also know where she came from. She'll know our story, and her grandparents' too. She'll know the story of two worlds, inextricably linked in the tapestry of the universe's unfolding. She'll know there is more to each of us and the world than what we can see, and we'll teach her to be awed by both the surface of things and what's beneath." She paused here, her voice caught for a moment in sadness before she went on. "And she'll know her aunt and uncles are far away on another world, building lives of their own, and that a universe of space between you and the people you love is in some ways no space at all."

The room was quiet as they all let the truth of it sweep them along for a few moments. In that current of loss and longing, they were carried very close to the pieces of themselves living lives not so far away after all.

"IT'S CALLED CHESS," Sheeran said with a smile, "just trust me, you'll like it. It's a game where pawns matter just as much as kings and queens."

"Sounds a little too real for me," Corin laughed, but he sat down across from his friend ready to learn.

They were in Ariabore's main hall where they met on a regular basis to discuss how the world was changing and how they were fighting to change it all. After Dempsey, Sheeran hadn't wanted to rule, hadn't felt quite worthy anymore, but Corin had convinced him that great leaders were made of just as much humility, humanity and errant mistakes as everyone else and admitting it made him stronger not weak and unworthy like he had first believed.

He now ruled Ariabore on his own as Sumira had stayed in Dempsey to help rebuild and to stamp out any remnants of the poison that had led them to build their city on the backs of others' labor and suffering. Every day was a challenge, but she believed in the work and despite what they once were she believed in the possibility of helping them see there were other ways to thrive. Those who'd carried out acts of violence had been tried and punished but the townspeople had been given a chance to begin again. If history was any indication it would not be so simple to heal the wounds that had been ripped open with Dempsey's rise to power but Sumira believed there was a compassionate and hopeful way forward and she was determined to be a part of forging that path.

Corin made his home in Dempsey too but he travelled between the towns and villages in their area to make sure they were forging ahead on the same path, in the same way, with the same ideals in place. He served as an ambassador to the kind of future they were trying to build and the kind of story they were trying to avoid writing again for humanity.

Sometimes, in the dark of night, lying next to Sumira, listening to her steady breaths as she dreamed of peace or love or other things, Corin would admit to himself he wasn't sure humanity would ever escape its journey towards ruin. How many times had they been given a chance to step into the light and instead chosen to cower in the shadows?

His thoughts would chill him and send him to the window to look to the stars. He knew the future could be written there but so could the past. That's where he was looking. To a life he left and a planet where the remnants of humanity had fought the Darkness in the world and in themselves and won. To the people he had fought alongside and who had taught him to believe anything was possible. Eventually his heart would slow, and his breath would quiet, and he'd step back into the story of love and hope that had kept him here on Earth.

Always, before he returned to his bed and the love of his life, he'd send a thought or a prayer up towards the sky and the pieces of his heart that were living on a world once born in a dream, and now for him out of reach. He'd wonder for a moment if they ever did the same thing from their little corner of the universe and then he'd smile and chuckle to himself because of course they did. Even from all this way he could feel that certainty reaching across the dark of space. Some things, even in the mystery of it all, were absolutely certain.

The sky was a pastel rainbow painted from the horizon to that dark of night that was fleeing across the heavens above her. The waves radiantly told the story of every single shade above them. They couldn't help themselves.

Kale stood there. Watching. Waiting.

She got up early almost every single day to greet the dawn and to begin with a kind of reverence and awe for the miracle of it all. She knew it mattered, even if every task ahead of her was mundane or ordinary, to step into it all with a sense of gratitude for how very fortunate she was to be here. To marvel at how many things had had to unfold, line up and come together to lead her to each and every moment of her life. It was a second chance she didn't want to waste and yet if she were being honest it was time then to face what she hadn't yet in the year since Dempsey fell.

She'd returned to life with Rogan, Firth and their people and they'd rebuilt their community with the help of others. They'd welcomed refugees from some of the villages that had also been burned and though some of them chose to rebuild some opted for the safety of joining bigger or more established communities like theirs or Ariabore. She had her own home and a sense that she belonged and mattered. She'd even become a kind of Aunt to Bella and Andre, the two orphaned children Firth and Rogan had adopted. She loved spending time in their home. Surrounded by laughter and lives fulfilled and the kind of spontaneous delight only children could provide. Welcomed without question into that beautiful cocoon of love and trust that Rogan and Firth had woven together to build a happy, purposeful life.

Life had become simple and joyful and quietly fulfilling, and she loved having the time and space to heal. It was a lot to come back from. Facing that she'd given up her life for Derin, and for Alpha Iridium, and yet now both things were a universe away. It was hard to sit with the knowing she'd been made for something so grand as fulfilling a prophecy and yet at times she felt so ordinary it was baffling that that other life could possibly be real. She missed her friends and she marveled at how once she'd stepped so easily away from them into oblivion and now she would never take anything for granted like that again. It was hard being so far from Medea and Jaren without a way to see or speak to them. Every day she was grateful that Corin had stayed and that he'd found a life and love here on Earth, the very place where all their stories had begun, so long ago, in different ways.

When she wanted to sit with the ache of all she'd lost she'd dream up their lives and settle into those fantasies with herself painted in. She couldn't help it. And didn't she know better than anyone else that dreams were truly possible. Sometimes it felt like the pain and the hurt mattered too, and she didn't want them to fade too much because she never wanted to forget what she'd had, once.

Lost in her daydreams, she stood there, watching as the sun, still hidden behind the waves, painted a golden sliver across the horizon. She breathed deep and let that song of sea and wind soothe her. She knew the moment he was there behind her, but she didn't stir or say anything, instead waiting for him to begin.

It had been months since she'd seen Alex last. He worked with Corin a lot. Travelling between their community of towns and villages, working hard to help Dempsey find a way forward that didn't tempt a kind of darkness back into their world.

They'd forged a friendship in those days or even hours when he did visit her but nothing more. He'd been too full of his own sorrow for all he'd lost and she'd been too full of her own for either of them to step towards each other in any other way. Yet, he was always there, in the periphery of her life. He had a kind of pull that most days made her mind wander towards wondering where he was or what he was doing.

She'd found out at dinner the night before that he was expected early the next day and for some reason she'd been thrown off balance for the rest of the night. She'd tossed and turned while sleep eluded her until she'd finally just gotten out of bed and made her way here, where she felt certain and safe, and where everything made sense.

She wasn't surprised he'd found her here. Anyone who knew her knew this was her sanctuary. Yet because she felt like something big was looming, she felt startled by his arrival just the same.

He crossed the sand and stopped beside her to stare out at the ocean and the sky lightening in gentle shades of pinks, purples and golds. There was just a sliver of space between them and yet Alex felt connected to her in the same way he did whether he was near or far from her and Iri. He wasn't sure why it had taken so long to find his way to this moment but he was here now and he was ready.

"I didn't know it at the time," he said softly, "but I fell in love with you on that mountain shelf six years ago when you told me it was the beginning of different kind of life and I believed you. For a little while at least."

He'd learned in the past year that courage was more than single acts and grand gestures. It manifested in showing up, in fighting for what you believed in, in vulnerability and honesty, and in risking something. He may not have been a hero on Alpha Iridium, but he'd raised and led the children of the Founders when he'd been a mere child too. And now, here, in this moment, he could be brave by stepping fully into the truth. He didn't need to be a hero he'd finally realized, he needed to be brave enough to live an ordinary life, full of love and honor and grace, and to stay with it all even when it got hard, or ugly, or when he was afraid.

He was ready. Of that he was certain. He hoped she was too.

Kale watched the sky as it continued to lighten and though she wanted to speak she stayed quiet, knowing he had more to say.

"Only, I didn't do any of things that I needed to for that other life to begin, instead I lost my way. But I've found it again, my way, and it leads me always to you. All of you. The first glimpse, so easy to get swept away with, sure, but also everything beneath it, the real parts and the messy parts as well." He paused for a moment, trying to gauge her silence. Trying to hear her truth as it settled in the space between them. "My life won't really feel full or whole if you're not a part of it Kale. Not on any world." He turned towards her, his breath held, more scared than he could ever remember feeling, and waited.

At first, she felt afraid. In some ways, she was still the girl who surrounded herself with a kind of armor so that she could move towards a single end without being vulnerable. Only that end had passed, and she'd survived it. In the aftermath she was finally being given the chance to decide who she wanted to be, rather than having destiny or some unseen force decide it all for her.

"Hey," she said when she finally turned towards him and met his eyes. "Do you believe in destiny?"

"Yeah, I guess." Alex said with a tentative smile, not entirely sure what she wanted him to say. "I mean after everything we've been through it would be kind of hard not to." The amusement in his voice was unmistakable.

"Right," she said a little sadly, nodding to herself before her gaze fell away from his. That's when Alex understood. That for once she wanted to be certain something was hers, not gifted or bartered by the universe. Not planned, or destined. He put a hand on her cheek and as she raised her eyes to meet his he looked deep into them and told her the truth.

"This is ours. All of it. To live and dream and decide and create. However we want. That's it. That's all." His heart swelled with that same hope he'd offered her, realizing he'd needed it for himself as well. For a moment she closed her eyes and leaned a little more firmly into his hand, the gentlest of offerings.

With that, the last of something that she'd been carrying for far too long, fell away. She wasn't ready to offer him words, but she was ready to step in. To risk something, finally. To trust her heart and to trust that it deserved this kind of loving. To give herself a chance at this kind of happiness. She opened her eyes then leaned towards him and when their lips came together a small spark shot out between them. Neither of them noticed.

Their hearts found a single rhythm, one both new and familiar, and they lost themselves in that embrace.

This was their beginning.

ACROSS THE VAST expanse of time and space wanders a widowed being who serves the greater powers in the universe. He travels from planet to planet, gathering up the remnants of species who have failed to beat the Darkness back and he offers them a second chance; something he knows so very much about. His name is Froste, though once, in another time and another place, he had a different name and lived a different kind of life. One that was both unrelentingly exceptional and blissfully ordinary. He'd had two sons and a long, long life with the woman he loved. Once upon a time they'd dreamed a whole civilization into being and in that dreaming truly found their way to wakefulness. To what it meant to honor both the miracle and preciousness of this thing called life.

All of that is gone now, along with so much more, as is the way of things, and yet he knows there will be a time when it will all come back around again. For now, he does his work, and when the universe isn't watching, he looks for her, his other half. His destiny. Somewhere in the ether she waits for him and for time to tell their story once again.

For all of them.

The universe delights. For all is as it should be, in darkness and in light.

END

ABOUT THE AUTHOR

NIKKI MARTIN is a Writer and full time Yoga Teacher living on the eastern shore of Nova Scotia. Her love of stories, both reading and creating them, started very young and with the release of her first fictional novel, *A Momentary Darkness,* in August 2018 and its follow up *The Beginning's End* in 2021 comes the realization of a lifelong dream. She has become a passionate advocate for diversity in yoga; working hard to make her classes accessible, empowering her students to look within for what they need, honoring the tradition of yoga and all it encompasses, and working in her community as a leader to make change. In her time off, you'll find her near the ocean, in the woods, or under the stars, forever listening for another story to share with the world.

www.ingramcontent.com/pod-product-compliance
Lightning Source LLC
Chambersburg PA
CBHW021244060726
47590CB00005B/1895